Praise for The B...

Seduction & Scandal

"One can become addicted to Featherstone's sexually charged romances.... Secrets, passions and conflicts abound as readers are led through a labyrinth of plot twists...and love scenes that take their breath away and leave them panting for more."
—*RT Book Reviews*, 4 1/2 stars

"*Seduction & Scandal* is the first in Featherstone's Brethren Guardians series, and the author has left little bits and pieces of information temptingly along the course of the story, leaving readers solidly in need of the next installment to find out what happens next."
—*Eye on Romance*

"Ms. Featherstone has the phenomenal ability to transport me into another time and place with each of her books... I am lying in wait for the next addition to this remarkable series."
—*Fresh Fiction*

"Taking its cue from gothic novels of old, *Seduction & Scandal* has everything I love in darker historicals.... I literally could not put this book down. A very solid 5/5 stars, and highly recommended for fans of gothic historical romances."
—*The Romanceaholic*

Pride & Passion

"Sensual and intriguing...[an] engaging and steamy yarn."
—*Publishers Weekly*

"Featherstone mixes her haunting erotic style into a tale tinged with mystery, paranormal elements and the atmosphere of the era...[she] stirs the pot, merging deep sensuality and a frightening, chilling mystery: a hunt for a madman that will have readers on the edge of their seats."
—*RT Book Reviews*, 4 stars

CHARLOTTE
FEATHERSTONE

TEMPTATION
& TWILIGHT

H
HQN™

Recycling programs
for this product may
not exist in your area.

ISBN-13: 978-0-373-77662-7

TEMPTATION & TWILIGHT

To Aly—better late than never, right? Thanks so much for coming up with the "Duke of Deliciousness." I owe you for that one! Thank you for being such a good friend.

TEMPTATION
& TWILIGHT

CHAPTER ONE

THERE WAS A SPECIAL PLACE in hell for men such as him. A small berth closest to the hellfires, one that reeked of smoke and brimstone and rotting souls, would be his home for eternity. His berth, he was quite certain, would read Blasphemer. Seducer. Whoremonger and Licentious Rogue, to name only a few. But to list all his failings and sins would require a tablet the size of which Moses used to recount the Ten Commandments.

As a man not given to excessive description, he found the above-mentioned failings communicated quite well the depth of his amoral, unfeeling soul. He was rather enamoured of that—it had taken years to cultivate a hardened shell with no humanity within.

He wondered if even now the Black Angel's minions were preparing for his reception into the underworld. How he hoped so, for he would need a merry party after the conclusion of tonight's business.

Shifting into the light cast by the gas lamp, Iain Sinclair, Marquis of Alynwick and laird to the clan Sinclair, gazed into the looking glass, only to see the devil himself staring back at him. He wondered, with a self-deprecating grin, if it wasn't a premonition of sorts. A prelude of where his eternal soul would rest if things did not go as planned tonight.

The devil, he mused, as he stared into the mirror, was a strikingly handsome fellow with long dark hair, given to curl, that had sent many a lady into swoons. Chiselled cheeks and chin, and a set of dark eyes—their colour could only be described as obsidian. Dimples in both cheeks flashed when he grinned in mockery, as he now was. His lips—oh, such decadently full lips that promised every kind of pleasure and rapture while indulging in the most wicked of sins.

The devil, Iain thought, as he motioned for his valet to pass him his tumbler of Scotch, looked remarkably like himself—a beautiful male, a dark, soulless bastard.

He was not a vain man—self-deprecating, true, but never vainglorious. The women of the ton might think him beautiful, showering him with compliments on his handsome face and muscular body. But he knew the truth: that what everyone saw on the outside was the polar opposite of what lurked inside him—a wretched ugliness that was slowly eating away any inner beauty he might have once possessed. No, his shell might be worthy, but inside he was anything but.

A sigh from the bed behind him confirmed this observation.

"You're as beautiful as Lucifer, and as wicked as the lord of the underworld could ever hope to be."

His gaze flashed back to the mirror, where the image of a woman lying naked and flushed pink amongst the white, rumpled bedsheets greeted him. His body jolted at the sight, as if he had all but forgotten the visitor. The lady—a rather loose term for the female—was not the sort he was used to cavorting with. She was too thin and slender, almost fragile. He preferred buxom. Blowsy, they used to call women such as his ideal back in the day, when a plump, luscious armful was every man's fantasy. How could he help it? He adored the female shape, with all its softness and curves. With breasts and hips, and thighs that made a man feel like a man, that cushioned and welcomed him and made him think of safe harbours and all the other melodramatic sap spouted by the poets.

Poetry be damned. The truth was Iain was a fool for a set of lovely big tits, and a nice round arse to grip in the throes of carnal pleasures. It had always been this way for him; a pair of plump breasts could keep him pleasantly occupied for hours on end, and the lady deeply satisfied. As coarse as his mouth was, it was highly skilled—and devilishly wicked, able to produce the most wondrous results while pressed against his favourite part of the female anatomy.

His gaze slipped to the lady's breasts. Rather disappointing for a man of his proclivities and appetites, but there it was. He was doing his duty, seeing to his obligations as one of the ancient Brethren Guardians.

Sighing again, she watched him, one arm tucked beneath her head, making her back arch in the belief she appeared more buxom. It was a useless endeavour. She would never possess the sort of body he liked to worship—or the one in particular he craved with every amoral fibre of his being.

Her knee rose, her delicate foot sliding along the crisp sheets. When her leg dropped to the side, so did his gaze, following the sensual action. She was well made *there*, he supposed, but already he'd tired of it. Strumpets never could hold his attention.

"Won't you come back to bed and play with me?" she said, her voice coy, yet her tone holding just a hint of cloying desperation. "I'll let you be as naughty as you desire."

"I doubt you could handle that. My sort of needs would make you swoon."

"In ecstasy, I'd wager."

"In shock."

He shared a secret grin with Sutherland, his valet. Iain supposed he should be rather mortified that his servant was here in this room of utter debauchery, witnessing such a thing while assisting him with dressing. But it was habitual for his valet, who had been with him for decades. Sutherland had witnessed one sort of debauchery and debacle after another. Besides, the lady lounging on the bed rather fancied the whole idea. She had been the one to suggest the activity, after all. She had a fantasy, she'd admitted to him, of lounging naked in his bed, watching his valet assist him with his toilette.

Iain was all for fantasies. He had a few very special and intimate ones of his own—so deeply personal that he wouldn't dare share them with anyone, except perhaps the lady who always featured in them. Those were for his own private pleasure, when he was alone and could indulge himself without interruption.

He didn't really relish this particular fantasy. However, the lady seemed to be enjoying herself, and that was the objective. He needed her cooperation.

"It really is scandalous how handsome and magnificently built you are," she murmured as she studied his body in the mirror. "The gossip spread by your past lovers certainly wasn't embellished. I think *magnificent* a rather bland word to describe you, and what you possess below the waist. Monstrously marvellous is what I call it."

"My dear, I am a Highlander. We are brawny lads built for hard work, both menial and more pleasurable tasks."

"Then put me in a carriage to Loch Lomond and gift me with an entire clan!"

She giggled, and his brow arched as he slipped his arms into the sleeves of the shirt Sutherland held out.

"Oooh." She sighed dramatically. "If only I hadn't met

Larabie first, I might now be Lady Alynwick, and what is it the Scots call the laird's wife?"

What the devil made her think she would be the one, after a long—*very long*—list of lovers? He would never marry. *Never.* And certainly, he would never think to marry someone like her. He was jaded, but he wasn't cruel. The women he cavorted with were no more interested in a lasting liaison than he was. Which made them infinitely good choices. It was a mutual, if unspoken agreement: all parties were in it for themselves. Women for pleasure and the notoriety and novelty of sharing his bed, and him for a relationship born of convenience, and to assuage his animal's needs—of which he seemed to have more than his share. Another sin, no doubt.

"Oh, come now, my love, you give the impression that you are emotionally unavailable. But I know the truth," she pressed.

"Do you? So you've realized that I am not 'unavailable,' but vacant. Completely, emotionally empty—which means, of course, that I am 'available' to no one."

"How your disdain for the world and everyone in it arouses me."

"We make a good pair, do we not? Everything we touch turns black."

Her gaze raked over him from head to foot and he felt as though he were being devoured, his statement of how he saw them completely missing its mark. "Oh, you might act that way now, Sinclair, but I assure you, when I want something enough, I get it. And I want you…very much. Available, unavailable, vacant—it matters not. I want to possess you."

He heard Sutherland's grunt, which meant he was either smothering his amusement or enjoying himself at his master's expense. Either way, Iain glared at his valet while buttoning his own shirt.

"You've already had me, luv," he murmured silkily. "Be content with that."

"Contentment eludes me. I peaked three times tonight, and already I want more. I have learned that I'm rather insatiable when it comes to your skill in the boudoir. You truly are a master of lovemaking."

No, not lovemaking, but fucking. He hadn't made love in years.

"Oh, I've already done myself in, haven't I? I married Larabie when I should have waited another month till I met you. Perhaps you'll remedy that tonight when you're duelling my husband over my honour."

Iain winked at her while Sutherland wrapped the pale green and sky-blue plaid of his Sinclair kilt around his lean waist. The lady nearly swooned at the sight, which made her forget all that nonsense about possessing him. No woman possessed him—*ever*.

"And Highland dress to fight for me, my lord? You make my head spin."

His was spinning as well, and not in a pleasurable way. Reaching for the Scotch, he drained it in one long swallow, emptying the tumbler. He motioned for Sutherland to refill it, which the faithful retainer did while Iain saw to his kilt.

If he was going to die tonight, he wanted to meet his maker in the clothes that best suited him—Highland dress. It was a bit elaborate for an old-fashioned English duel, but it fit him. He was an outlandish character, forever scandalizing the English peers with his brutish Scottish ways. He'd never fit into this world of delicate manners and anaemic pleasures. It was not his way. He was not delicate, not polite and his sexual desires were anything but staid. When he fucked, he didn't want to remember to be gentle and soft. He wanted to lose himself in the woman, be taken to a place where no god or devil dwelt—no demons, no memories, just unspeakable pleasure. During that rapture, he wanted to say the words in his own way, to lose all control and let the cultured English accent that his father had literally beat into him fall away, leaving his Highland brogue to whisper in the woman's ear. He couldn't hide his more amorous emotions behind his English accent. That accent was cool and mocking, designed to disguise what he was feeling, giving him that devil-may-care aura. When he talked thus, he sounded like his late father, a pompous prat with little concern for anyone, which strangely enough enthralled the ladies.

Hell, Iain could barely remember a time he felt that much at ease to let himself go. In the bedroom he was always calculating, every move a choreographed dance. He didn't lose himself, and most definitely had never been transported to his imaginary plane of pleasure on the wave of a fierce climax.

"Shall I wait here for your return, my love," she asked, "or will you come ravish and debauch me in Larabie's bed?"

Iain smiled at that and watched her in the mirror as he belted his kilt with the little leather strap and buckle. "A wicked creature you are. Have you no shame, Georgiana, mussing up the earl's sheets with another man's body?"

Her smile was scheming as she sat up and came to her knees, unashamed of her nudity and the fact that there was another present in the room with them to witness it.

"Very little, I'm afraid. You've stripped me of any decency I might have had."

"Indeed?" he asked before taking another drink.

Her eyes were glittering. "You've stripped me of many things with your immoral ways, my lord. I fear being bad with you is really rather addicting."

"Rather like Scotch," Sutherland grumbled as he knelt to fasten Iain's clan pin to the kilt.

"Watch it," he growled, "or I'll slam my knee into your nose."

Sutherland, immune to his moods and taciturn disposition, merely ignored the threat and squelched a grin.

"Well, my dear?" Iain inquired as he slipped his dirk into his woollen sock. "Do I pass muster?"

"Indeed you do. I see that the story one hears about a true Highlander is correct—you do wear nothing between the plaid and your flesh."

Halfway to being good and sotted, Iain turned away from the mirror and faced his paramour. Lifting the kilt, he showed her what she wanted to see. Grasping himself, he let the lady admire it.

"That part of you is magnificently made, Sinclair, even in this state."

Quirking his lips, he stroked himself once, giving the lady what she wanted, so that later, she would give him what *he* wanted—which differed vastly from what she desired. He was bedding her only to get information about a secret club she frequented—the House of Orpheus. Orpheus was an enemy of the Brethren Guardians, and had to be destroyed. Iain was playing the part of a Casanova to gain what he and the other two guardians—the Earl of Black and the Duke of Sussex—needed.

Casanova, he mused mockingly as he let his kilt fall back into place. No, he did not feel like the legendary Italian lover, but rather like a male whore—as filthy and corrupt as an East End flash boy.

When he had concocted this plan, his friend the duke

had told him that nothing good would happen out of it, but he had laughed, mocking him for the prig that Sussex was. Iain believed his soul was already gone, believed himself impervious to any more pain. But the truth was, he was not. He was drowning in sin, and any time now, he believed he'd wake up one morning only to look in the mirror and find all the sins he had committed marring his face. It would be a horrific sight, but a true reflection of what resided in his soul.

"Have you time for another round? Sex always invigorates men."

"You think me full of sap, then?" he teased, when he did not feel the least bit light and cajoling. "You *are* a biter, aren't you, sweetheart?"

Sutherland did laugh then, smothering the outburst quickly.

Her eyes narrowed. "I hope that isn't derogatory, my lord. I would hate to have to instruct my dear husband to shoot you dead."

As if Larabie, that fat, pompous bastard, could even try. "My dear, a biter is a term used to describe the most lascivious and wanton of wenches, which I am quite certain you will agree you are."

"Oh." She eyed him with a glittering glance that told him she was pretending not to know the true meaning of the word. How he loathed the game of playing innocent when she was so far from it. "Tell me, how does 'biter' play into the description of a wanton?"

She wanted to be shocked, and he was in the right frame of mind to appease her. "A biter, sweet Georgiana, means that said wanton is so eager for sexual congress that she will offer herself, bottom up, to her lover. A man calls her thus when he knows she's aching for a little slap and bite on her arse, hence the term."

"Cunny, too?"

His lips curled in distaste, but he hoped she would see it for something far more appealing. "By all means, if you wish to have your cunny bitten, I shall be happy to oblige."

Thankfully, Sutherland had departed before the conversation turned to this. Even he had some personal level of decency, and this crossed the boundary.

"How I adore it when you speak filth, Lord Alynwick."

He gave her a mocking bow. "I aim to please you, my lady."

"You do. Surely you know that."

He did. Who would ever see to his own pleasure was another matter entirely.

Now alone together, Georgiana smoothed her hand down her body, her thighs spreading in invitation as her pale hand slid between them. She was as insatiable as he was. Any man looking for a mistress would find her ravishing—would likely even empty the family coffers for her. But Iain was not looking for a mistress, and her avarice made him feel empty and cold.

"Tell me your fantasies," she whispered. "I've told you mine."

"As I've said, I have none."

"Please?" she purred.

"Shall I make one up to appease you, then?"

She pouted, and her sharp, glittering eyes told him she knew that he had one. "Someone to spank and punish you?"

He winced. "Good God, no. I'm not one for pain with pleasure." He'd had enough pain inflicted on him by both sides of his family, and while away at school.

"To be tied up, to give up all your control?"

"No."

She eyed him thoughtfully. She would never guess what the Sinful Sinclair, the Aberrant Alynwick thought of when he was alone at night in his bed, with nothing but the moon and stars to keep him company. He hardly allowed himself to think of it. Only when he was deep in his cups, and his feelings unguarded, did he allow himself to dream of his ultimate fantasy—a saint with a sinner. An angel cavorting with the devil. An innocent offering herself up to him—a sordid, sinful man who wanted to partake of her goodness, while showing her how delightful it could be to join him on the dark side of seduction. But not just any innocent. No, that would be too easy. There were numerous virgins in London. He could seduce any one of them, and live out his fantasies. No, only one innocent—in mind and soul, in deed and thought—would do for him.

And damn her, how her guileless eyes and goodness rattled him. He'd walk through the Moroccan desert for her, would bleed himself dry for one chance to taste her lips, feel her breasts in his hands, pressing against his flesh.

But good girls did not like bad boys. Good girls gave wide berth to men who indulged in the sort of behaviour that governesses warned them about and etiquette books forbade.

Ladies like her did not allow men like him to partake of their innocence, while corrupting them with sin. And the woman of his dreams was every inch a lady by birth and character, and she called to him like gin to an East End drunk.

"You are in a strange mood tonight, Sinclair," Georgiana observed. "Almost contemplative, I would say."

"Really? How droll. I suppose I should be thinking of how I might spend the next few hours lying in sin and regret before I am forced to confront my future. I might very well be dead come the morrow. A send-off worthy of the most proliferate rake should be in order."

"It should. I offered and you declined."

"Ah, yes. Well, a man needs to have his head—both of them—in the right place during these matters. Rest assured, after I have satisfied the terms of your husband's duel I shall come and release all the pent-up frustration and contemplation that is building inside me. Will that suffice?"

She flopped back onto his bed with a pout, her legs sliding evocatively against each other. "I suppose," she muttered. "But you'll think of me when you are on that field, fighting for my honour?"

"Trust me, I shall be thinking of nothing else." Christ, he needed another drink. He was getting bilious, nattering away about such tripe. All he could say was that she—and this damned duel—had better be worth it. If he didn't discover anything about Orpheus from Lady Larabie, he might just end up putting a bullet in his own chest.

"Are you afraid to meet him?"

"Larabie?" Iain snorted. "Not in the least."

"No, the Grim Reaper."

"Him? Why should I? I already know the path of my destiny."

"And have you any regrets?" she whispered, watching him with eyes that were suddenly very clear and knowing—eyes that made the hairs on his neck rise in warning.

"No, none."

"No business left unattended? Nothing left unsaid? No apologies to be made?"

"Not a one, I'm afraid," he growled as he fitted his

sporran around his waist. "I never apologize. It means I was in the wrong—and I am never that, luv."

"Such brass bollocks you possess, my lord. No atoning for your sins before you fall to the earth, never to speak again. No absolution for past transgressions."

He froze, not wanting Georgiana's words to have any sort of impact upon him, but they did, damn it. Unknowingly, the witch made an image flash in his mind, one that left him tense and uncomfortable, his mouth curling in disdain—for himself, for his foolish, hurtful past, and a damnable pride that had caused his fall.

"Ah," she whispered, and he saw cruel delight flare in her dark brown eyes. "Perhaps the Aberrant Alynwick is not so deviant, after all?"

"You goad me, and I shall exact punishment upon you after this infernal duel is complete."

"I do look forward to it."

After bowing to her, he reached for his tumbler of Scotch and headed to the door. Before leaving he turned back around. "I expect I'll find you tonight?"

"I expect you will—and most likely someone else."

Slamming the door behind him, Iain hurried down the stairs. Tossing back the remainder of the Scotch, he passed the crystal glass to his butler, who then handed him his greatcoat. Waving off the hat and walking stick, Iain left his house and hurried down the steps to his waiting carriage. Ducking his head after barking out the direction he was going, he climbed in and settled himself against the crème-velvet squabs.

Lurching forward, the carriage began its journey, the click of the horses' hooves echoing down the street. It was November, and Mayfair wasn't as busy as it was during the Season. Pity that, for he could have used the noise of life outside to keep him from reflecting on life inside the carriage.

He had thought to go to his club, have a bit of supper, a hand of cards and a few more drinks before his dawn appointment at Grantham Field. But all that had changed now. He had something he needed to do—not just out of duty, but because he felt compelled, driven, utterly consumed to see someone before the unthinkable happened tonight and he landed on the damp grass, toes cocked up, blood seeping out onto the green blades, while Lucifer's hand rose from the ground, grasped him and tugged him down to his lair below.

Yes, Iain needed to see that person and…apologize.

But how did one effectively seek mercy and forgiveness for a crime that was more than a decade old? "I'm sorry" hardly seemed enough.

By the time he reached his destination, he had practiced a dozen pretty speeches, all better than the one before. As the footman opened the carriage door, he was firmly fixed upon the one he would use, assured that, at least, the lady would give him a moment to vent his spleen and do the honourable thing.

The Sumners' majordomo took in the sight of him from head to toe before holding out his white-gloved hand for the invitation to the insipid musicale.

"I have a standing invitation," Iain muttered.

"Very good, my lord," the butler murmured. "I shall announce you."

It was rather disturbing that the old geezer knew him by sight. It was not good in this instance to be reminded that his reputation preceded him.

Clearing his throat, the retainer announced in chilling tones, "His lordship the Marquis of Alynwick and laird to the clan Sinclair."

Emerging from the shadows, Iain entered the room, aware it had gone still with shock. He stood tall and proud, wearing his Highland dress as he scanned the room for his quarry. He found her, and any thoughts of apologizing flew out of his head when he saw her arm in arm with a man. They were whispering and smiling to each other beneath a portrait of a classic nude, completely unaware of others around them.

Apologize? No. Murder, most likely. With eternal life in hell a damned surety.

Feral and enraged, and sotted from his finest Scotch, Iain prowled the room, the guests parting before him like the long grass of the African savannah does when a hungry lion presses through.

He would go for the throat—the man's first. Then he would carry off his prey and bring her to his den, where he would play with her, torment her, before finishing her off.

CHAPTER TWO

THE SUSSEX ANGEL WAS feeling far from angelic on this, the most exciting evening she had experienced in years. Such a strange notion, because she, Elizabeth York, elder and only sibling to the Duke of Sussex, was as giddy and mischievous as a schoolgirl attending her first ball.

Such a strange observance, for she was far from a young girl. In truth, she was only a few months shy of her thirtieth birthday, and most firmly on the shelf.

If her age hadn't turned her into a spinster, then her infirmity most certainly had. To put it bluntly, she was as blind as a bat. But Elizabeth didn't care—not tonight. Tonight she had the strange sense that anything was possible. She had not felt that way in a long, long time, and the sensation was a welcome one. She had never wallowed in self-pity, but would be a fool not to admit there were times when she hid her true feelings behind a shield of strength and determination—a shield that was sometimes little more than a thin veneer.

But she would not think such things now. Tonight she would let herself imagine that she could be as beautiful and desirable as any woman present.

"Ah, let us stop here."

And that lovely deep rumble was the reason for the impulsive giddiness currently ruling her. The Earl of Sheldon was escorting her about the room as if she were not an old maid, and disabled, too. It was worthy of a girlhood swoon—something the spinsterish Elizabeth would never contemplate, most especially before her peers, who, she was certain, watched her with rapacious interest as she made her way, arm in arm, around the room with the earl.

"Lovely."

"It must be a portrait, then?"

She got the impression that they had stopped their promenade for a reason. Since she couldn't smell any food or wine, she assumed it was not so that he could hand her a refreshment. The way he stood silently beside her, as if studying something, gave her pause, made her think that something must have caught his interest.

"Indeed. A rather interesting one."

His voice seemed strained, and she thought she knew the reason behind it. Swallowing hard, Elizabeth felt some of the giddiness leave her. They had only been introduced, and he had asked Sussex for permission to escort the duke's sister about the room. After Lady Lucy, her friend and companion, had most effectively catalogued the earl's every feature, Lizzy had allowed her imagination to run rampant. *Silly fool.* Men like Sheldon didn't need a blind woman hanging on their arm.

"Oh, I beg your pardon." She felt the muscles of his forearm tense under her fingertips. "I quite forgot that I am to describe the art to you. What a great clod I am."

"It is a queer concept, I grant you," she murmured, hating that she was right about Sheldon, "but it is the only way for me to see—through your eyes. My friends Lady Lucy and Lady Black have quite a skill with descriptions. I feel as though I can actually see when they describe something."

She sensed his gaze studying her profile, and fought

back a fierce blush. Women of her age did not blush, for heaven's sake!

"Well, then, let me see if I can at least meet them in skill."

Perhaps she was wrong about him, after all? Smiling, she nodded for him to proceed, while waiting to hear more of his delicious voice, and to feel again that tonight anything was possible.

"We are standing before a classic Greek portrait. Atlas, I think."

"With the world perched laboriously on his shoulders?"

"Indeed. Zeus is in the background, floating about on his cloud throne, with an ominous lightning bolt in hand."

"Oh, yes, I can see it now. Poor Atlas grimacing beneath his agonizing effort, and Zeus, the pompous God, snarling at his success."

A soft chuckle whispered between them. "Yes, that's it exactly. Oh, and did I tell you that this portrait is a classic nude? Atlas appears quite as he did upon birth."

"Scandalous!" she teased, her mood improving by the second. "Although I won't ask you for the description. But rest assured, I would not allow Lucy and Lady Black to get off so easily without parlaying the particulars." A whisper of breath, a pulse—a wave of something…

"Oh, dear, I'm afraid I've shocked you," she said.

"No… Yes…" His voice sounded strained. "Of course not." She heard the fabric of his coat move, and imagined him raising his arm to run a nervous hand through his hair.

And that moment was lost….

"Forgive me for speaking so bluntly," she exclaimed. "A terrible habit, I'm afraid. I have just recently begun reacquainting myself with Society. It's been rather more difficult than I first believed, but I had not thought my manners had deteriorated to this extent."

He laughed. A deep, full laugh that was rich and warm. "No, it is I who must beg an apology. You did shock me, Lady Elizabeth, but I must admit, it was not in a negative way."

"Oh," she murmured.

"Oh, indeed. I think you a woman who knows what you're about, and it's rather refreshing. Puts a gentleman a bit behind, in a way—we're only taught how to converse with silly young women who are searching for husbands. There is never any fun in the conversations. I usually find myself drifting off to some other time and place, I'm afraid."

"I do that frequently, too. Tell me, what place do you drift away to?"

"The Middle East. I spent most of my childhood and youth there. Egypt and Jerusalem, mostly."

"Ooh," she whispered, and heard his neck crack as he whipped his head in her direction. "How I envy you. I have long dreamed of travelling to the East. I might have gone, too, with my brother, if I had not lost my sight."

There was a period of silence—not borne of discomfort, but of thought. "If you might permit me to call on you, Lady Elizabeth, I would greatly fancy an opportunity to tell you some stories, and draw you a picture of the East through my eyes."

She did blush then, a flush she hoped wasn't discernible. While she tried to keep her composure, inside she was dancing for joy. Her emotions were suddenly volatile, something she never permitted herself. But then, she hadn't allowed herself to think of a future in a long time. "I think that would be most lovely, Lord Sheldon. I anxiously await your call."

"Will tomorrow do, or does that smack of a sort of desperation?"

"Not desperation," she said with a smile and a slight lift of her chin. "But an eagerness to share a part of the world that few see, and even fewer Englishmen get to experience."

"Indeed," he murmured, and the sound slithered down her spine, awakening something dormant deep inside. *Careful now,* she warned. It was far too soon for feelings like this. She was being fanciful, allowing herself to be swept away. She had been impulsive and fanciful before, and it had ruined her.

"Zeus appears to be frowning even more now," he murmured in a most becoming baritone rumble. "Do you think it a reflection upon our unseemly conversation, or is it the way our heads are bent together while we whisper?"

"Oh, dear, are we causing talk?"

She heard the smile in his words. "Talk of any sort is much better than the music we were forced to listen to tonight."

"Do you not like Mr. Mozart?"

He shrugged; she felt the movement. "I have spent too long in the East. I prefer, I think, or perhaps I have just grown used to, the sounds of the *doumbek* and the *darbuka*. There is a haunting sensuality about it. Even having never been there, one may close one's eyes and listen to the sounds and imagine silk veils and dancers before you. But that is a story for a visit, is it not?"

"Yes," she said, and frowned slightly when she heard how breathless her voice was. "What is it?" she asked suddenly, aware of a sensation that swept the room. "I hear rumblings."

"I fear that we were lost to all but our conversation."

The earl shifted beside her and Elizabeth sensed that he half turned away from her. "It appears as though the majordomo is preparing to announce someone."

"Really?"

"Quite a character, it seems. Decked out like a marauding Scot, actually. Has an expression that would have given Genghis Khan fits of apoplexy."

"Oh, dear," she whispered. There was only one character of the ton who fit that description, and she wanted to be far, far away from him. "Well, I think it's grown rather close in here, don't you? Perhaps we should heed Zeus's silent counsel and stroll to where a window might be cracked open, or perhaps a strategically placed terrace door?"

He was very intelligent, the earl was. He took her hand and deftly but discreetly manoeuvred her to the periphery of the room, where she could sense a door awaited their escape.

Suddenly, there was an almost violent brush of air that forced their hands apart. Then Sheldon was snatched from her side, right before she heard the thud of his body hitting something solid.

"I doona know who ye are," Alynwick growled in his unmistakable brogue, "but yer hands are no' where they belong."

The earl tried to reply, but his rasping voice alerted Elizabeth to the fact he couldn't take in air. The wave of shock from the crowd told her that the Highland beast was either choking him with his bare hands, or had thrust his arm, which she knew was as thick as a tree trunk, against poor Sheldon's windpipe.

"Stop this at once," she demanded in a hiss. "You're making a scene."

She could feel when those dark eyes landed on her.

"*I'm* making a scene?" he retorted as if accusing *her* of making tongues wag.

Prickles of awareness raced down her spine, and Elizabeth knew the cause stemmed from the fact that every guest of the Sumners had their eyes fixed firmly on her and the mad marquis. "I insist you stop this *now,* Alynwick. Everyone will talk."

"Doona worry, lass, we'll give them somethin' tae talk about, because yer leavin' with me."

"The devil I am!" she yelped in outrage. "Alynwick, dear God, pay attention to what you're doing. I can hear Sheldon struggling for air."

"Sheldon, is it?"

The sound of tussling, of fine wools brushing together, came to her ears, and she thought about throwing herself forward, hopefully between them. But if she fell to her knees, or worse, the floor, it would cause even more of a scene.

"Here now, what's all this fuss about?" The masculine growl that came next Elizabeth was relieved to hear.

"Sod off, Sussex," Alynwick muttered.

"Come now, my lord," her brother said. His voice was smooth and light, but Lizzy heard the edge of warning in it. "We needn't have such violence here."

It was a subtle warning to the marquis. The Brethren Guardians, of which her brother and the marquis were both members, did not need this sort of notoriety. Indeed, just by coming to break up the pair, Adrian was putting the Guardians at risk—because no one knew that Sussex, Alynwick and Lord Black shared more than the most polite and distant acquaintance with each other. If the marquis didn't cease this madness, then everything they had fought to keep from the prying eyes of the ton might very well be in jeopardy.

"Murder at the Musicale," Sussex drawled. "I can read the headlines in the morning papers. I doubt you're interested in giving the masses something other than sugar to sweeten their morning tea."

Alynwick growled something in that familiar beastly way of his. That was followed by another rustle, a rasping gasp and a brush of masculine-scented air that swept past her—Alynwick being shaken off his lordship.

"Apologies, Sheldon. I am quite certain that the Marquis of Alynwick did not mean to introduce himself in such a way."

"The hell I didn't!"

"My lord," Elizabeth whispered, moving a step toward the rasping earl and reaching out for what she thought might be his arm. "Are you all right? Can I summon a footman to fetch you something? A drink, perhaps?"

"Don't even think to touch him in my presence," said a dark, menacing voice in her ear. The sound made her shiver, as did the mysterious scent of his Scotch-laced breath washing over her. "If you doona want him torn tae pieces, leave him be."

She didn't want this—the marquis standing behind her, crowding her—and she stiffened, discovered the safe barriers she always erected when she found herself in his company. "You are nothing but an animal," she snapped, careful to make certain no one but Alynwick could hear her outburst. "Unhand me this instant." But the brute wouldn't listen, and instead pressed closer to her, his big palm cupping her elbow in a fierce grip.

When he next spoke, he seemed to have put some measure of control on his anger, for his brogue had all but disappeared, leaving behind a silky English accent that worked its way along her body.

"Animal, am I? Should I throw you down now and cover you, as befitting the animal I am?" he whispered.

She would not encourage his wicked behaviour with an answer. But Alynwick was never one to back away from a challenge, or wickedness.

"In the animal world," he growled, "the alpha is the leader. He must exert his power and let everyone know he is in charge—and *he's*," Alynwick said of Sheldon, "trespassing on my hunting grounds."

"This isn't the jungle, and your laws have no jurisdiction in the ton."

"You think not?" he purred. "The ton especially is a jungle, a feeding ground for prey like yourself. I'm merely exerting myself as chief predator."

Oh, she wished she could say what she really wanted to, and wish him to hell for the scene he had created and was bent on pursuing. But she was a lady, and must act the part while every eye of the ton looked on.

"Shall I call for your carriage, perhaps, Sheldon?" her brother enquired of the earl. Then his voice changed, as if he were looking in the opposite direction. "Lizzy, Lady Lucy approaches. She'll escort you to *our* carriage. The evening festivities, I am afraid, have come to a rather abrupt cessation."

Before she could sense any movement or sound, Elizabeth's arm was taken firmly in hand, and she was whisked away with a rustle of silk, amidst shocked gasps from the Sumners' scandalized guests.

"Let me go at once," she demanded in a low voice, but the marquis didn't hear her, or at the very least pretended he hadn't, as he all but dragged her out of the salon and into a place that was much cooler and quieter.

"Whatever barbaric law you subscribe to, Alynwick, I am not one of your subjects. Unhand me."

Silence. But his hold strengthened on her elbow, and his pace increased, so that she was forced to hurry her steps to keep up with him.

"You devil," she explained, trying to disguise the alarm in her voice. "You'll make me fall with this pace!"

"Shall I carry ye, then?"

"Don't you dare, you heathen!" she spat breathlessly. "Where are you taking me, pray?"

"Someplace quiet, where I can thrash you in private."

Her mouth dropped open in protest, but no words emerged. Only Alynwick and his fiendish ways could render her speechless and gauche. She hoped he hadn't seen her expression, or the way she could barely keep up with him.

"This will have to do," he muttered.

Her world was one of black obsidian, and she could not tell if he had brought her somewhere equally as dark, or merely shadowed. It was quiet, she knew. The distant clang of silver and china told her that they were closer to the servants preparing the midnight luncheon, and farther away from the salon. Whether they were in a room or a hall, she could not tell. She hated not knowing, of being blind to everything, when she had never been anything but these past twelve years. That she was not in control while in Alynwick's company sent a jolt of panic down her body. Of anyone, she most feared being vulnerable when he was near.

The wall was cool against her neck and bare shoulders as he swung her around and pressed her against the plaster. She sensed him before her, his heat, the scent of his body. He loomed over her, his heavily muscled, tall frame standing so near her short, voluptuous one that she was forced to share the very air with him. She should lift her chin up, an act of defiance. Try to meet his gaze head-on. But she had no knowledge of her eyes, and what they might do, where they might be directed, and she would not give him a glimpse of her weakness, no matter how fleeting it might be.

So she stood quietly, willing her breathing to slow and become controlled. Her head was lowered, her face averted, turned away from him. His breath kissed her skin as she maintained her stance, knowing she was not meeting his gaze, but showing him indifference. He touched her, the faintest graze of his fingertips along her cheek, and she struggled against him, pushing away from his touch. It only made him press closer to her—obscenely closer, for she could feel the way his abdomen moved against her gown with each of his breaths.

"Say something," she declared, despising the fact that she couldn't see his face and expression. Was he looking at her? Smirking? Having a good laugh at her expense?

"What would you have me say?"

In a fit of frustration she stamped her foot. "How could you!" she demanded, thinking of how she must have looked to the Sumners' guests as he dragged her out of the salon. "Oh," she whispered, "what have you done?"

"Protected you," he replied. "Sheltered you from the company of one who could never know you—not like how I know you."

Refusing to pay any heed to the last of his statement, or the intimacy that seemed to be created between them, Lizzy forged on, thinking it best to steer him away from any reminders of the past. "Whatever were you thinking to do such a thing? Have you grown so uncouth?"

"Truth?" he murmured, and she refused to melt at the sound of his silken voice.

"Are you capable of speaking it?" she taunted.

"Aye. Are you capable of hearing it?"

Snorting with indignation, she motioned for him to continue. She did not, however, expect him to whisper into her ear, "I thought I might carry you off, back into my den, where I would play with you, paw at you, before devouring you whole."

She shivered as she felt his hand brush along her gown. "And there is quite a bit to devour, isn't there?" he went on. "You've turned into a right armful, haven't ye? Plump as a Rubens' model, ye are," he said, his deep voice rumbling in his chest. His comment only made her more vulnerable—and incensed. *Churl!* To speak of her figure in such a way was positively unforgivable. She had gained a few stone over the years, it was true, but it was grossly ungentlemanly for the man to mention it.

Using some of her anger, she said in a haughty voice, "I demand to know what you are about, sir. *The truth.*"

"And I demand the same. What the devil," he growled back, "are you about?"

"Not that it is any of your concern," she sniffed in her best matriarchal tone, "but I am at a musicale, enjoying myself. I didn't realize it was a crime."

"Oh, aye, 'tis a crime, all right, looking the way you do, making every eye in the room turn your way. Making them stare at the picture you present."

She gasped, unable to help it. Such a cruel, cold bastard. She was a mature woman who could think what she wanted, say what she desired, and what she thought of Alynwick was nothing but the truth. She, more than anyone, knew just how cold and cruel, and every inch a bastard, the Marquis of Alynwick truly was.

His comment was beyond shocking, and she had to struggle to put herself to rights. She was an independent woman, a strong woman, and she would not let a member of the opposite sex demean her in such a way. She might be blind, but she always carried herself with dignity and decorum. If the occupants of that room were gawking at her, that was their problem, not hers.

Just as she opened her mouth to give him a scathing set-down, he leaned forward, and she felt a faint wave of heat against her cheek.

"How can you go about like this, knowing everyone is watching?" he growled. He was closer now, his breath fanning her mouth. She could smell the Scotch, almost taste the sweet spice on her tongue. "I canna bear to see it."

When she would not answer, he pressed closer, the heat of his body greedily absorbed by her traitorous one. His mouth was even closer now, next to her ear, his voice almost a caress. "You show too much, Lady Elizabeth, reveal what is meant to be kept hidden, to be indulged and shared only with one that may appreciate the gift."

"As I am completely blind, my lord, I have no idea what you are talking about. Just what am I showing?"

"I refer to the garment you have chosen to arrive in."

"What could be the matter? It is an evening gown, sir. Or have I had the misfortune to leave the house without my dress? Is that it? Am I naked?"

"You might as well be for what little it covers up."

His voice had changed. It still held anger, though she could not fathom why, but there was something else there, and she reached up, smoothed her hand along her throat, to discover for herself what atrocity Alynwick saw displayed before him.

"That gown," he rumbled in a dark, seductive voice, "is an invitation to sample what you so willingly display."

She stiffened at his absurd statement. "I have no notion what you insinuate is being displayed."

There was a smile mixed with the edge in his voice. "Lass, you ken damn well what I mean."

His body shifted, and hers jumped as if being lanced with a lightning bolt as she felt the smooth texture of his nails grazing the mounds of her décolletage. *Oh, God, he's running the back of his hand along me.*

"Such a sight, lass, makes a man dangerous," he murmured, though Elizabeth could hardly hear him for the roar of blood in her ears, and the outrage that made rational thought impossible. "Such a display is just what a man needs before he dies."

His lips followed the path of his fingers. Those seductive lips of his, which could pleasure and tease, or thin with cruelty, were grazing her chin, working down the column of her throat as he gently inserted his fingers into the cleft between her breasts. "Oh, aye, to die in arms such as this, and to be buried in such soft, lush flesh, is what every man should wish for."

"You are drunk, sir," she cried, her fingers fisting in the folds of her silk gown.

"Not too drunk, luv," he drawled before flicking the tip of his tongue in the hollow of her throat. "No' so far in my cups not to be able to pleasure ye the way yer asking for by wearing this gown and revealing all this creamy flesh."

"It was not for your benefit, I assure you," she retorted, but he only chuckled as he lowered his head and allowed the silken ends of his unbound hair to cascade over her bare shoulder.

"Nevertheless, lass, I'll take what I can get."

Determination paid off, for she waited, breathless, as Alynwick slowly dragged his mouth across the expanse of her bosom. When she could see him in her mind, she raised her hand and struck him hard against his cheek, the sound a loud crack in the quiet.

"I am asking for nothing. You, on the other hand, are asking for another sharp slap."

He laughed, reached for her wrists and raised them high above her head, holding her captive. She was stunned by his reaction, shocked that he had not been at least startled by the sound slap she had given him.

"Do it again, Beth," he rasped, and the name on his lips—the only lips to have ever called her that—made her struggle in his hold.

"Again," he said, almost panting. "Touch me again."

"You are a degenerate!" she spat, but he only held her wrists tighter. "You disgust me." How could he still be aroused? she wondered. And she truly felt ill, thinking that he might have taken some pleasure from that slap, and her present struggle.

"I might meet my end tonight. What can you give me in case my death might come to pass?"

"A good kick in your nether regions if you do not unhand me this instant. Besides, you will not die tonight, or any other night, for the devil doesn't want you in his realm, because you are even more evil and wicked than Lucifer himself!"

"Aye, I am, and I've come to give you a taste of that wickedness."

"I have never been tempted by your evil bent."

The air stilled, and she bit her lip—but it was too late. "Oh, aye, lass, you were once. You were tempted and torn asunder by it. Should I remind you what it was like to sin with me?"

He pressed up against her, his mouth found hers and he claimed her fully—not softly, beckoning, but hard and strong. His mouth twisted over hers, opening, parting her lips. Stealing her breath as he stroked his tongue inside, commanding her with deep sweeps as that insistent, searching tongue mated with hers in a fierce joining.

Oh, that it had been horrendous and grotesque. But it was not. His invasion robbed her not only of her breath, but of her thoughts, and the inner voice that reminded her that she had once followed him down this very same path, and he had abandoned her, left her alone and ashamed on a road that led nowhere but to heartache.

"Beth," he groaned as he broke away and buried his face in her throat. "I dinna want this night to be like this—dinna want more sins heaped on me before I go to that field."

"Is that it, then?" she snapped, pushing him away. "You thought you ought to give me a kiss to make it all better? To placate what is left of your tarnished honour?"

"I didn't want to die with things left unsaid. With you thinking... Well, with the way things are between us."

"You are fighting some idiotic duel over some tart you've bedded, and you're afraid you might lose? And before you go to hell you want to be forgiven?"

"No, I want to apologize."

Lizzy stopped him from saying anything else. "Save your breath, Alynwick, because it's useless."

"I'm sorry, Elizabeth. This may be the last time I can tell ye—"

"I don't give a damn about how sorry you are, or that you have at last come around seeking forgiveness. And furthermore, I will take this moment to relieve you of the misapprehension you are labouring under. I do not care, and have not cared for a very long time, whether you live or die, Lord Alynwick. I only regret that it will be someone else's bullet that may put you out of your misery, and not mine!"

He let her go then, and she moved past him just as she heard Lucy's voice calling to her. He stopped her, wrapped his strong fingers around her upper arm, holding her close to his body so she could feel his chest move with each breath, feel the movement of his mouth against the shell of her ear. "Come the morrow, if I am left alive upon Grantham Field, be assured that I will come for you. We have unfinished business between us, and I intend to end what we have started here tonight."

"You had your chance, my lord," she retorted. "You didn't want it then any more than you do now."

"So little you know," he said, and she could tell he had whispered that between set teeth. "You couldn't possibly even begin to know what I want."

Lizzy stilled for a fraction, warred for the briefest instant before saying, "It is of little consequence what you desire, Alynwick, for now I find I no longer want you."

CHAPTER THREE

I NO LONGER want you.

Was there a more painful phrase in the English-speaking world? Iain didn't think so. He'd been hurt, his heart smashed open, bleeding, upon hearing those words. Now, hours later, he still bled, the severed vessels opening every time he heard that hated sentiment repeated in his turbulent thoughts. Even closing his eyes, he heard her, and saw her, too—the way she had stood up to him, back straight, regal chin tilted at the perfect angle to relay feminine hauteur. She had not been playing coy when she had told him that. She had been speaking the truth, a truth born deep in her soul. And hours later, the bleeding continued, and the pain of that reality shattered whatever illusion and pitiful hope he had been desperately clinging to.

Most horrible, for him, was the realization that he had not even known he'd been clinging to anything, much less hope. But comprehension had dawned the minute Georgiana had challenged him about regrets. It had been then that he realized he harboured the sentimental emotion.

For the first time in his life he had not run from the knowledge, from the feeling that made its presence known. He'd accepted it, and by the time he had arrived at the Sumners' musicale, he had actually claimed it, welcomed it. But with that revelation, so foreign to him, and yes, terrifying to admit, had come the heartache of knowing that Elizabeth had washed her hands of him.

She didn't want him. And he had never stopped wanting her.

"Miserable existence," he muttered as he lifted the bottle to his mouth and drank heartily of the Scotch. He deserved no less, he knew. But somewhere inside him he had always believed that Elizabeth York understood him. Knew deep down the extent of his flaws and the defects of his personality. He had always thought that she accepted that about him, and had forgiven him his trespasses all those years ago, like the angel he not only thought her to be, but *knew* her to be.

But his angel had teeth—and claws—that had effectively eviscerated him tonight. By God, what had he been about, doing what he had? Demanding such things? He knew better than to let the years of hunger for her get the best of him. And they had.

He'd been in a murderous, incredulous rage when he'd first glimpsed Elizabeth standing beside the earl. A living, breathing darkness had blanketed him, and while he wished he could feign ignorance as to its cause, he knew better. The carpet had been torn from beneath his feet, and landing flat on the ground had winded him. A sort of red mist had gathered and clouded his sight: rage stemming from the shattered hope that one day he might find his way back to her.

It had always been a comfort to him—a perverse comfort, because he was a capricious man who took pleasure in such selfish thoughts as the one he had long clung to. In his mind, there was still time, still a chance that she might one day be his. Elizabeth did not go out in Society. She did not accept men's arms and stroll about salons with them. In essence, there was no other man in her life. No golden male to rival Iain's black soul. And the knowledge had always comforted him.

Selfishly, he wanted her to stay free of courtships and such. It gave him hope. And tonight, when he had been feeling strangely melancholy and…alone, he had needed Elizabeth. Needed for them to find their way to one another again. And that… Well, that had been all dashed to the farthest regions of hell.

Seeing her with Sheldon—the smile, that was not forced nor feigned—had ignited in Iain something unholy. Some damned monster that gnashed and snarled and struck out with huge, clawed hands.

She had been happy, and he had been more than unhappy to see her that way. Misery, the old saying went, loves company. Iain had believed that Elizabeth and he shared the same misery, the same unrequited longing. A love denied, but that would not die despite the cloying darkness that threatened its light.

But tonight had made clear that she did not share his misery. He'd been confronted with the fact that he was a fool. That he had taken the one thing in the world that had ever meant anything to him and tossed it away like a child's toy, only to be outraged when another had come by to pluck it from the sand.

Iain had toyed with Elizabeth, cast her aside and left her to find her own way in the world. Sheldon, that bastard, had been the one to find her, to pick her up and marvel at the treasure she presented.

Love unrequited. Love denied—and spurned. Iain felt the stab of pain where his heart should be. Pressing his eyes shut, he sought to banish the sensation from his awareness.

If he were any sort of gentleman, hell, any sort of decent human being, he'd slink away with his tail between his legs and never look back. But he wasn't decent. He had the pride of a marquis and a bloody Highlander. Everything inside him screamed to take what he thought rightfully belonged to him, honourable or no.

It's only fair, you bastard, a taunting voice inside him jeered. *You're getting a taste of your own medicine.*

And it was a damn bitter pill to swallow. One best diluted with a good single-malt Scotch.

"God save us, you're foxed!"

Iain held up the crystal decanter as he studied Black entering his carriage. He didn't have the patience for the earl, not tonight. Friends or no, he couldn't stomach the earl's happiness, which seemed to radiate from his every pore. "Good and drunk," he replied in a slurred voice. "Thought I'd give that fat, pompous Larabie a bit of an edge tonight. Lord knows he'll need one."

"You cannot meet him like this. I doubt you can even walk."

"I can, too," he drawled, before taking another sip. Black snatched the decanter, spilling some of the amber liquid over Iain's greatcoat, which was open, revealing his kilt and sporran. Black's dark brows rose in question, and Iain gave a foul hand gesture that should have made him feel better, but only made him realize he was verging on pathetic.

Christ, he hoped he'd die tonight and save himself the mortification of living another day to lock eyes with Elizabeth York, the haughty spinster of Sussex. *The angel of your very sinful dreams...*

The Sussex Angel, she had been called then, the year of her come-out. She had been, too. From the first moment he'd laid eyes on her, he'd wanted her. Part of him wished to bask in her goodness, her innocence. The other part had wanted to corrupt her, to drag her from the light and immerse her in sin.

She was still a damned angel, even approaching thirty. How could she still possess those beautiful, artless grey eyes and that pure, pale flesh? She was fair and perfect. He was black and corrupted. And damn him, every thought in his head kept coming back to her tonight, and the realization that he had finally allowed himself to admit to something that she spurned. That she no longer desired. *That would not fucking die!*

"What the devil are you doing here, besides irritating me?" he demanded in a churlish tone. "Thought you'd be ensconced in your chambers, enjoying the virtue of your marriage bed with your lovely wife."

"Don't," Black growled, "mock what I have with my wife. You will never understand the sanctity to be found in bed with a woman who is the other half of your soul."

He wanted another drink, and to tell the pompous Black to go to hell, but he sneered instead. "No, in fact, I will not. I don't have a soul, ergo there is no other half wandering about, waiting for me to get into bed. No arms waiting to hold me when I arrive home."

"And whose fault is that?" his friend demanded.

"I'm done with this conversation. Why are you here, and not Sussex?"

Folding his arms across his chest, Black watched him through the dim shadows of the carriage's interior. "Sussex sent a missive around. It was terse and to the point. He stated he couldn't make it, and requested that I come to be your second."

With Lucy Ashton. That's where His Grace was tonight. Trying to get a hand up the beauty's skirt. Thrown over for a woman and a toss, Iain thought, and grunted in amusement. Although he couldn't reasonably think such a thing. Sussex wanted the lovely Lucy Ashton with a blind, consuming need. It left a bad taste in Iain's mouth, knowing the determined duke would one day have her, and he himself would be forced to sit amongst those two couples and watch them, their sickening love cloying the air with an unfashionable and most disagreeable completeness. Especially when he knew he'd still be tupping whores, and longing for Elizabeth in the darkest, loneliest hours of the night.

"As your second," Black continued, allowing his gaze to rove across Iain's drunken form, "I must make it clear that you are in no shape whatsoever to meet Lord Larabie on the field of honour."

"Honour?" he snorted, aware how disgust dripped like venom in his voice. "There is no honour in this match. I slept with his wife in the attempt to find out information about our enemy. There is no honour in bedding another man's wife."

"And yet you do it with alarming frequency."

"I never pursue them," Iain growled, focusing his gaze outside the window. "They come to me."

"And that makes it all right?"

He shrugged. "I don't expect you to understand."

Leaning back, Black settled himself on the bench, stretching his long legs out before him. "I know why you do it."

That caught Iain's attention, as did the conviction he heard. "Like hell," he growled, but Black only shrugged, then met his gaze through the moonlit shadows.

"You want to punish them. The wives, for pursuing you, for so readily forsaking their vows. And you want to hurt the cuckolded husbands by showing them how poor their choice in wife was. In a way, it's a sense of honour for you, an absolution, if you will. Those that participate with you in the carnal act, in your opinion, deserve what they get, because they have been so dishonourable as to break their marriage vows in the first place. In your own way, you have a code of honour, and while you would never admit to it, you hold the vows of marriage as something sacred. I am correct, aren't I?"

"You just said I would never admit it, so why bother to ask?" he grunted.

His friend grinned, making Alynwick want to plant his fist in his face.

"This bargain you have with Larabie's wife is eating at your soul."

"I know what I'm doing."

"I don't doubt it, but I do doubt that you realize what the cost of this endeavour will be."

"I suppose my mortal soul and all that rot. God, Black, you've become an irritating pontificate since your short marriage. Sod off, and pass me my Scotch and the pistol."

"You don't have to do this."

"If you don't hand me that blasted duelling pistol, I'll put the bullet in you!"

With a sigh of reluctance, Black reached for the wooden case. Iain couldn't help but notice his friend had not agreed to the other request. The decanter remained out of reach, unless Iain was inclined to spring from the bench and sprawl overtop Black to reach for it. He'd rather be hung naked in the middle of Piccadilly than lower himself before his friend and fellow Brethren Guardian.

Grunting, he accepted the pistol. "It's not loaded."

"I know. I have visions of you tripping down the carriage steps, falling to the ground and triggering the blasted thing before we can get you to walk your paces."

Iain glared at him. "I do believe I would have done better with some scoundrel from the East End as a second."

"Then you should have procured one. As it's one minute before the designated meeting time, I will have to do."

"Bloody hell," he growled as he stood to leave the coach, "what could make this night worse?"

The carriage door suddenly flew open, to reveal the glinting end of a pistol and a set of dark eyes blazing with hatred. Both were aimed at him.

"Oh, good evening, Larabie," Iain drawled. "I see your wife is correct. You do have a habit of firing off early."

Behind him, Black groaned. Alynwick grinned. If he was going to die, then damn it, he was going out with a bang, not as a self-pitying weakling.

"You think you are so amusing, Alynwick," Larabie snarled, "but I will make you regret what you have done to me. I will take great delight in blowing you away."

Alynwick flashed a wicked smile. "Now you really do sound like your wife. She said the very same thing to me last night."

"Now, then, you've got wind in those sails."

Elizabeth paused on the landing of the curved staircase, her hand on her companion's arm. Her fingers were trembling, and Lizzie knew it was not from exertion—she was bloody quaking with fury. "And what does that mean, Maggie?" she enquired coolly, which only made her longtime friend laugh.

"Oh, you've got his bluster, all right. Your father used to storm around like a ship in a hurricane. You look just like him, I vow."

"Oh." She hadn't meant to be in such a foul mood upon entering the house. She thought she'd rid herself of the insolence and anger that had ruled her on the carriage ride home. Poor Lucy had been forced to sit in the carriage in complete silence while Lizzy brooded and her brother tackled his own thoughts.

And they both had the Marquis of Alynwick to thank for that.

"Come now, let's go on up and you can tell me all about it. It can't be that bad."

Yes, it could. And it would only get worse, because Elizabeth knew she could not confide in Maggie. This was her secret. Her own scandal to bear.

All those years ago she could have confided in her companion, but hadn't; she'd been too embarrassed at being so easily taken in by the marquis. So she had chosen to hide her shame, and to not think of how foolish she'd been.

In the ensuing years, she had been rather successful at forgetting her stupidity, her gullibility. But that had changed tonight, when Alynwick had cornered her, towered over her and turned her into a melting pot of heated flesh.

So much for the mature, controlled woman she had always believed herself to be!

"Now, then, what's got you blustering?"

"Nothing," she murmured as Maggie ushered her into her bedchamber. "I am just not used to Society, that is all."

"Was it a trial, then?"

"That would be too banal a description. I felt…" Elizabeth struggled for the right word. "An outsider, I guess."

"It will come," Maggie said as she pulled the pins from Elizabeth's heavy hair. "You've been gone from it too long, is all."

"Apparently not long enough," she found herself muttering, thinking of her run-in with the marquis.

"Perhaps if you shared your worries, that might help soothe them."

Lizzy laughed despite herself. "Believe me, Maggie, there is nothing anyone could say to make me feel better. I never want to think on the matter again."

"Well, then, there is no sense brooding over something you don't wish to share. I can't help you if you don't want it. Now step out of that gown if you please, the buttons are already undone."

Practical, strong Maggie. She knew how to get what she wanted from her charge, and it was not with cajoling. Normally, Lizzy might have indulged her companion's curiosity, and even solicited her sage advice. But not in this. This matter must never come to light.

Stepping out of the gown, which pooled around her legs, Elizabeth reached for the bedpost she knew was directly before her, and held on. She was growing calm, as she always did in her room, where everything was as it should be. Where she could move about with freedom, knowing she would not trip over something and hurt herself, or worse, destroy some priceless family relic. In her room, she was not disabled. She was not an invalid. She was just plain Elizabeth York.

A thumping sound followed by a little whimper greeted her, and she smiled, closed her eyes and allowed the warm tongue awaiting her to brush against her cheek.

"Little mouse," she whispered as she buried her face in her spaniel's soft fur. "Still up?"

Rosie, her pregnant springer spaniel, whimpered as Elizabeth spoke nonsense into her long floppy ears. Adrian had bred her with another springer in the hopes that her offspring might prove as useful as Rosie herself. It was amazing, but true, that Rosie very often acted as Elizabeth's eyes, guiding her away from furniture and objects in the way. It was Adrian's hope that he could train the pups to help others like Elizabeth.

"That dog has been waiting for you on the bed for hours now," Maggie said as she unlaced Elizabeth's corset. "Poor lamb, she's as big as a house and couldn't manage the jump up by herself."

"So you helped her, even though you think it's sacrilege for an animal to be on a bed."

"Or the settees, or that grand leather chair of His Grace's," Maggie reminded her. "Aye, I helped her. I couldn't resist when she looked at me with those sad eyes of hers."

"She is the most adorable and loving creature, isn't she?" Elizabeth murmured as she released her hold on the bedpost and snuggled against her beloved pet. "Yes," she murmured, "I love you, too, sweet."

"I wouldn't let her lick my face," Maggie muttered, and Elizabeth could almost see her lips curled in distaste.

"Well, they're the only kisses I am liable to receive, so I shall take them," she teased, but Maggie merely grunted as she pulled the corset from Elizabeth's breasts and tossed the silk-and-steel garment onto the bed. Her companion liked to claim that Rosie was a nuisance, but Lizzy knew she had a soft spot for the dog, regardless of what she wanted people to believe. Maggie might give the impression of being a commander, but inside, she had a very kind heart and a rather romantic soul. But she'd given it all up to stay and live with Lizzy. More than her lady's maid and her eyes, she had been a substitute mother, a nurse and was now a treasured friend. Lizzy could not have gained any measure of independence if it had not been for her. People thought it a testament to Lizzy's own courage and drive that she had accomplished so much despite her blindness, but really, it was because of Maggie's strength, her untiring nature and unrelenting belief that Lizzy could succeed. She owed much of what she was to her companion, who had been with her since Lizzy was fifteen and Maggie barely eighteen. They could have been sisters, and despite the difference in their social status, got on as if they were family. At some point, Lizzy was going to have to once more bring up the topic of her friend living her own life. The trouble was, Maggie was every bit as stubborn as she, and would hear none of it.

"Now, then, you're down to your chemise. Why don't you sit at the dressing table and I'll brush out your hair?"

With one last nuzzle, Elizabeth left the dog and turned, making her way across the room without assistance. She found her way to the table and slowly lowered herself onto the waiting chair.

"I met a gentleman tonight," she said, trying to keep her thoughts away from Alynwick and what had transpired between them at the musicale.

"Did you now? Must be a handsome gent for just the mention of him put those roses in your cheeks."

Smiling, Elizabeth flicked her hair over her shoulders. "I've blushed more tonight than I did when it was actually acceptable for me to blush."

"Nonsense, 'tis a woman's right to blush whenever the spirit moves her. Nothing to do with age or steadfast sensibilities."

"I allow it was rather nice," she said, recalling how it felt to walk beside a man who was not her brother, or her brother's friends. "Lady Lucy assures me that he is most handsome—and tanned."

"Tanned?" Maggie mumbled. She had hairpins in her mouth again, Lizzy could tell. "What proper English gentleman allows his flesh to get tanned?"

"A perfectly improper one, I think," Elizabeth answered, chuckling when Maggie gasped in surprise.

"And you, an innocent speaking like a coquette!"

How she wished she could see Maggie's expression. In her heart she knew her companion was not shocked by her frank speaking, but was actually smiling. Maggie was not an old matron. She was in the prime of her life, and must occasionally think of the opposite sex.

"I am nearly thirty, Maggie. Coquettes are young women who flirt and flit about. I am the furthest thing from one."

"What would you know of improper gentlemen?" Maggie asked, and Elizabeth lowered her sightless gaze to her hands, folded neatly in her lap. *Quite a bit, actually,* was her first response, but she bit it back, knowing Maggie would be standing behind her, watching her face in the dressing-table mirror.

"Nothing, other than they can be rather enticing, don't you think?"

"I cannot say," Maggie scoffed. "Myself, I think I would prefer a nice gentleman to a rogue that made me blush."

Elizabeth laughed. "You're a terrible liar, Miss Maggie Farley. You'd throw over a nice 'gennleman' any day for a rogue. Do not bother to deny it. I can hear the excitement in your voice. You're enticed by the very image."

Maggie tsked. "This is proper talk for two respectable ladies?"

"No, it isn't, is it? But just once I think it might be all right to be completely unrespectable, don't you?"

"Indeed, I do not."

"Oh, Maggie, you will not give an inch, will you?"

"Only an inch, mind," she allowed as she pulled the brush through Elizabeth's long, thick hair. "I will admit I hope you invited him to call. I would like to get a glimpse of this tanned improper gentleman. And I shall give you a good accounting of him. Not that I doubt for a second that the mischievous Lady Lucy did not do so!"

Lizzy smiled at the memory of Lucy's hushed descriptions. "She did indeed. But I would like to see him through your eyes."

"I confess I am eager to relate my accounting."

"And you shall. I expect him to call any day."

The brush was replaced on the table and Maggie's strong hand gently wrapped around Elizabeth's upper arm. "Well, then, to bed, Beauty, if your prince is calling."

"I didn't say it would be tomorrow."

"He'd be a fool to let any length of time pass till he next saw you. You are much too beautiful to risk losing. Why, there might have been other gentlemen present who desire to call upon you."

Just one, and he was the most improper man of all. Alynwick took no notice of the rules of their world. He cared about nothing, no one, other than himself. Elizabeth would not fool herself into believing that the scoundrel wished to call upon her. He observed none of the proprieties. No, what Alynwick had been about was ruining her evening with Lord Sheldon. For what reason, she could not fathom, other than he had always enjoyed making sport of her. And she had allowed it—for a time. What Alynwick did not realize was that she would no longer tolerate his interference in her life, her friendships or indeed, any possible courtships.

He could go hang for all she cared.

"'Night, miss," Maggie murmured as Elizabeth settled back against the fluffed-up pillows.

"Maggie," she found herself whispering, "what is the time?"

"Nearly two, miss."

"And dawn?" she asked quietly as she turned to face the window she could not see out of. "What time does it arrive, now that we are in the midst of November?"

"Thinking of your gentleman caller, by chance?" her companion teased.

"Perhaps." But she wasn't. For some ungodly reason she was thinking of a mist-shrouded field and tendrils of early morning light flickering off gunmetal.

"Dawn will arrive by six. There is no need to fret. I will wake you with plenty of time to help you prepare."

Maggie's departure was silent, with only the click of the closing door alerting Elizabeth to the fact her companion had departed. Gathering Rosie close to her, she ran her hands through the spaniel's long, silky coat.

"I won't sleep tonight," she whispered to the dog. "Damn him, he's robbed me of another perfectly decent night's sleep."

Rosie made a little growling sound as she struggled to get comfortable. Despite the blackness that shrouded her, Lizzy turned to face her bedroom window. Beyond the glass, she could see in her mind's eye the black, sooty grime of London. The town houses and the spire of churches and the dome of Saint Paul's—all memories from when she'd possessed sight.

She saw a field covered with a thick white blanket of frost, and tendrils of mist hovering over the ground. In the breeze, wool greatcoats flapped, and she heard pistols fire, the shots cracking through the silent air, leaving grey smoke twirling upwards from the barrels.

She imagined the scene a hundred different times in those long hours she lay silently in bed, but it was always the same. The colour of blood had swum before her eyes, and the prone body of a man was revealed with the parting of the crimson.

It was Alynwick. And despite her attempts to deny it, her heart ached at the very thought.

Unable to withstand the images she saw in her head, she felt around her nightstand, searching for the drawer pull. Finding it, she opened the drawer and lifted out the little leather journal that lay hidden inside.

Opening the cover, she allowed her fingers to trace over the brittle vellum page. She had found the diary of her notorious ancestor Sinjin York years ago, while playing in the attic of her family's country house. She hadn't understood what it was until she was older.

Once she discovered that it was a very detailed account of Sinjin's illicit affair with an unknown woman whom he called "My Veiled Lady," Elizabeth had been on a quest to discover the woman's identity.

She had lost her sight before she could, and now she was left with only the memories of passages she could no longer read.

But tonight, for some reason, she took comfort in the feel of the familiar brittle pages, which she knew held Sinjin's flowing script. And words that had captured not only her imagination, but aroused her womanly needs— needs she had always imagined sharing with one person.

4th May, 1147—Carpathians.
I have taken up the cross for my kingdom in the fight to protect Jerusalem and all of Christendom. My army is amassed, and a truce, however tenuous, has been reached between myself and the French king, Louis VII, whose army has joined with mine.

We will march to Bucharest, where we will meet with the German emperor. Then on to Byzantium, where I pray we will be allowed a peaceful crossing. I have received a missive from the Byzantine emperor, Manuel I Comnenus, who will guarantee our safe passage.

We leave on the morn, the 6th of May, the feast day of Saint George. The priest that travels with me will not hear of crossing the woods and mountains on the eve of Saint George. For at nightfall on this day it is believed that all things evil have full sway. The priest is old and superstitious, but I relent for the peace of my men, who are swayed by the tales of village peasants and gypsies, who fill their minds with talk of unnatural creatures that roam unseen around us.

I must remind myself that the Carpathians are a wild and untamed place, far removed from my beloved England. If I close my eyes I can still see the rocky coastline of Yorkshire, smell the brine of the North Sea and taste the salt on my tongue.

My memory turns to Isolde, whom I treasure above all things on earth. She was fearful of my leaving; however I allayed my lover's fears by telling her to remember me—my voice—for it will comfort her in the months ahead when she is alone. I assured my beloved Isolde that God will not forsake me on the field of glory, for which I fight for in His name. I shall return to her, the Crusades won, my heart still beating for her. I cannot help but wonder what she is doing, if she is sitting beneath the night sky thinking of me, as I am thinking of her....

Elizabeth had memorized that passage, just as she had all the other thrilling pages that followed. At first she had thought the diary merely an account of Sinjin's travels from England to Jerusalem, and the events of the Crusades. And perhaps in the beginning that was the intention. But she had no sooner turned the page and read the next entry, than she'd been drawn into Sinjin's private world of love, lust, obsession and sin....

17th May, 1147

Entered Constantinople. Reached an amicable arrangement with the Seljuk Turks. The men are nervous, fearing an attack from the Seljuks, who have been known to make alliances with the infidels. Spirits are low, especially now that it seems our priest has gone mad, possessed by some unseen thing, rambling about an unholy aura that follows us. He claims he sees that aura hovering over me—a warning, he claims, of temptation and sin. The man is mad, and I have dispatched him with four men to Sighisoara, where he will embark on a journey back to England.

The men believe the priest's ramblings, and it is more and more difficult, what with the constant fatigue and heat and very great thirst, to appeal to their rational minds.

Tomorrow we leave for Edessa, where we will rest for a few days and regain our strength. Then I shall follow my Templar brothers, who will bring us to the Holy City and our fate—the fight to keep Jerusalem in Christian hands.

—Addendum; early dawn. I dreamed of a woman. Not Isolde, but a temptress, covered in jewels and a veil. She whispered to me, beckoned

to me in my sleep to a land of exotic pleasures. I awoke with the memory of the priest's wild eyes as he gave his dire warnings to me. Some sinful temptation was following me, and it would be my ruination.

My brethren must never find out about Isolde, nor must they ever discover my dreams of the woman, for I have taken my Templar vows of chastity. But I am only a man. Man was not made to be celibate. The Dukes of Sussex were born to love women, to pleasure them with bodies honed by fighting. And I have my fair share of desires. Even now, my body is hard and aching, with images clouding my judgement. Not images of beautiful Isolde, but the mysterious woman of my dreams.

I cannot help but think that this journey to the Holy City will change everything I have ever known—everything I am. I suspect it will not be the war we wage that does so, but instead, the woman of my dreams, whom I know awaits me in Jerusalem. Perhaps I am cursed as the mad priest claims, but no curse could prevent me from moving heaven and hell to find her.

No power on earth to prevent him from moving heaven and hell to find his beloved... Elizabeth wished she could find a man who felt that way about her. Silly, naïve dream, she thought as she clutched the diary to her breasts and allowed herself to slip into sleep. She owed it to Sinjin to discover this Veiled Lady. To reward his passion and devotion by learning their story, and perhaps one day recounting it to her nieces and nephews. For she did not dare think of her own children. She would not have a story like Sinjin and his lover. She had long ago given up that dream.

Move heaven and hell... She thought of that, heard it whispered in a dark, velvety, caressing voice, and saw the eyes of the devil himself. If only *he* had thought that way all those years ago.

CHAPTER FOUR

"Now, Larabie," Black growled as he came to his feet behind Alynwick. "This is uncalled for. Allow us to emerge from the carriage, and your second and myself will commence with officiating this duel—utilizing the proper rules."

"Why should I?" Larabie snarled as he kept the barrel of the pistol raised to the spot between Alynwick's eyes. "The bastard has never played by the rules before. Defiling a man's wife," he grunted. "I should shoot off your bollocks instead of your head."

"Larabie," Alynwick drawled, "let us see if you're man enough. Pull the damn trigger."

"I wouldn't," Larabie's second advised. "At that range, you'll have the bastard's brains splattered on your coat."

Larabie's slow smile was downright chilling. "Good. I'll have my wife wash her lover's blood and guts from the wool. Would serve the bitch right for what she's done to me."

"Gentlemen…" Black's voice sounded much too resigned, and dare Iain say it, bored. "At this close range, we shall all be sprayed with Alynwick's grey matter, considering he has some, of course."

If Iain hadn't been watching Larabie's trembling hand, and the softly bobbing barrel of the duelling pistol aimed at his head, he would have turned and sent his friend a glare.

"Let us be reasonable," Black murmured as he carefully shifted his tall body forward, filling up the door space of the coach. "A few paces out into the pasture, and then we may commence."

Larabie suddenly whirled, warning Black away. That was when Iain saw his chance and took it, wrestling the pistol from his opponent. He had not expected it to be loaded—and he had certainly not expected to hear the ear-shattering crack of a bullet blast in the silence of the night.

Time seemed to shift, to stall, as Larabie's jowled face grew white. With a smile born of arrogance, Alynwick waited to watch the earl's expression turn from shock, to pain, to terror. It didn't. Instead, Iain felt the burn of his own skin being torn apart. Then the heat of his blood seeping out, onto his shirt. The force of the bullet threw him back against Black, who caught him, covering his body with his own.

"You ass," Iain rasped as he clutched the sleeve of Black's coat. "Isabella will hang me by my bollocks if you get hurt."

"Shut up," Black muttered as he efficiently placed Iain on the damp ground. "The doctor!" he ordered, and Iain saw the tips of Larabie's boots and those of his second move back, making way for the physician.

His body burned, the pain was substantial, and he suddenly was thankful that he had sat in his carriage for hours, drinking himself into a stupor. It had numbed the pain somewhat, and made it so he had not cried out, either in surprise or discomfort. He would not give that fat, fucking Larabie the pleasure of his weakness.

"I trust you are satisfied," he said, trying to breathe as normally as possible.

"Honour was met," Larabie's second announced, and Black all but flew between the small space that set them apart, confronting the man with his fist knotted in his cravat.

"Honour was not met," he snarled. "Larabie shot him in cold blood. None of the rules were adhered to. It wasn't a fair duel."

"It wasn't fair of him to bed my wife!" Larabie roared, and Iain, not wanting to hear the earl's pompous voice a second longer, rasped and waved his friend back over.

"Let it go," he murmured as Black knelt down beside him. "I don't think it's fatal, anyway. Besides, I plan on playing this up to the lady. Surely she will see to it that I am well compensated for this business."

"Damn you, this plan of yours is going to hell."

Iain shrugged and winced in pain as a tearing burn made its way down his left arm. "Shoulder, I think. Bloody bastard is lucky it's my left."

"Make way, gentlemen," the physician ordered. He set his black bag down on the damp grass beside Iain's head. Alynwick's coachman had taken a carriage lamp and was holding it over them, allowing its soft glow to illuminate the scene. Above him, Iain could see Larabie's jowls quivering. To his left stood Black, his expression the colour of his name. The doctor pulled at Iain's coat, revealing the soaked shirt beneath.

"Well, will the bastard live, or shall I make plans to leave for the continent tonight?" Larabie muttered.

"Shoulder wound," the physician announced. "There's no need to flee the scene, my lord."

"Lucky bastard. Like a cat, he is. But one day, Alynwick, you'll use up those nine lives, and I hope that when you are on the ninth and final one, it is my bullet that sends you straight to hell. Come along, Sheridan," the earl ordered. "It is time to return home to deal with my wife."

"Into the carriage, my lord," the physician instructed. "I shall follow in mine. The bullet must be removed and the wound cleansed."

"I thank you," Iain growled as Black hefted him up from the wet grass, and none too gently, either. "My man will see to it."

"You keep a surgeon at the ready, do you?" the physician said with offended hauteur.

Iain laughed at the thought. Sutherland was no doctor. He was barely a valet. But he was a hell of a villain, when Iain found himself in need of one.

"Well, then," the doctor muttered with a snap of his leather satchel. "I shall bid you good-night."

"You shouldn't have ordered him away," Black snarled as he all but dragged Iain up the carriage stairs. "Your injury is extensive. What if Sutherland can't manage it?"

"Then I should think that butler of yours," he gasped as he fell onto the carriage bench, "would do nicely."

"Billings is at home with my wife, keeping her safe. I am not having him removed to tend you and your stupidity."

"Fine, then," Iain said as he let his head fall back against the squabs. Dawn was slowly rising in the distance, and he closed his eyes as blood continued to pump from his shoulder. "Take me to Sussex House," he said, his voice sounding distant to his ears.

"Sussex House?" Black enquired. "What for? Patch yourself up first before we descend upon Sussex."

"Damn you, man!" Iain roared. "Honour a man's dying wish. Take me to Sussex House, to Elizabeth," he heard himself murmur. Thankfully, he passed out before he could hear Black's response.

ON THE EDGE OF Grantham Field, amongst the trees and the fog, stood a town coach with four gleaming black stallions. No one saw it, for he did not want them to. He was not ready for them yet. But soon… Soon the Brethren would be his.

"Did you expect this?" his companion asked as she smoothed her delicate hand up the length of his thigh.

Indeed, he had not. Alynwick was always the wild card in the troika that made up the Brethren Guardians. A hotheaded Scot, and a man who barely had any control over his base desires and his animal rage.

He had thought the marquis would simply blow the earl away, but instead, Alynwick had been wounded.

A measure of glee swam inside him. Alynwick was wounded—considerably so. It would make things that much easier with Alynwick out of the picture, even temporarily.

Patience, he told himself as the placket of his trousers fell open, and he was gripped by a knowing, skilled hand. Patience always paid off in the end. He had waited a long, long time for this. And soon, he would be rewarded.

Soon, the Brethren would belong to him—to Orpheus.

"Take me," she whispered, and he rapped his walking stick against the carriage, sending the vehicle lurching forward.

"Soon, pet," he mumbled. "I have something to do first. A little surprise for His Grace."

"It's not like you to be so kind," she murmured as her lips worked their way down his neck.

"I'm in the giving mood," he mumbled, thinking of what he would do. "And Sussex will be the benefactor."

IN THE END, Black ignored his request, which was so typical of him. The bastard always did whatever he wanted.

Instead of taking him to Sussex House, Black carried him, half-conscious, from the carriage and into Iain's own town house, past his shocked butler, whose harsh, indrawn breath echoed off the fourteen-foot-high ceiling, and all the way up the ornately carved, curving staircase to Iain's bedroom, where he dropped Iain onto the bed as though he were a sack of grain. Only then did Black rouse Sutherland.

Shortly after, his valet stumbled into the room, wiping the sleep from his eyes. "And what scrape have ye gotten yourself into this time, my lord?"

"What does it look like?" he growled. "I'm bleeding onto the sheets."

Sutherland grunted when he saw the extent of the wound he was expected to work on. "Won't be a pretty sight after I'm done, my lord."

"He's too pretty now," Iain heard Black state in his characteristic sombre voice. "A little mark to remind him of his arrogance should be his reward for this night's business. Patch him up, Sutherland."

"The ladies will only find the scar more endearing, I'm afraid."

"Yes. Peculiar how many ladies find something of merit in Alynwick."

"I'm awake and can hear every damn word you're both saying."

"Good," Sutherland muttered as he tore the blood-soaked shirt from Iain's chest. "Then you know I'll make a botch of this shoulder. But you'll live."

"Scotch," he demanded, before saying, "I don't give a damn what it looks like, just stop the bleeding."

"You won't be saying that once you have a look at my handiwork, I'll wager."

"For Christ's sake, Sutherland, I'm not a vain man."

"I wonder if you'd be claiming that if it was your face I was to work on."

"Well, then I'd look like the devil on the outside, just as I am on the inside, wouldn't I?"

Sutherland quirked a thick auburn brow. "Yer in one of those moods tonight, I see."

"Get on with it, or I'll drag myself out of this bed and find someone more inclined to work, instead of prattling like a maid."

The sound of the crystal stopper popping out of the decanter was music to his ears. However, the roar he let out when Black poured a good measure of the liquid gold onto his shoulder was not.

"Like bloody hellfire," he gasped between gritted teeth, stiffening under the burning onslaught. "And there's cheaper stuff to be used for medicinal purposes. That's a twenty-five-year aged single malt, Black, and you've pissed it away for no good reason."

"I assumed saving your hide from a stinking purulence would be reason enough."

"The inferior brands can do that as well as any of them."

Black merely raised one laconic brow as he peered down at him from the side of the bed. "I'll leave you to your duties, Sutherland. Nothing more to drink for his lordship, no matter what he says or threatens you with. I'm tired of lugging him about tonight. I want him to walk into Sussex House on his own two feet."

"Right, my lord."

Iain glared at the door as it slammed behind Black, then turned to give his valet a wrathful glare. "Cease coddling the damn wound and sew it shut. Or better yet, heat the poker and singe it closed."

It would match the brand on his chest, the one that had

been seared upon his flesh when he had been anointed as a Brethren Guardian. Iain had stoically endured the pain, making his father press the glowing brand harder into his skin, trying to break him. But Iain had always been as stubborn as a mule and had refused to do anything but look up into the spiteful eyes of his father and dare him to do his worst. He had suffered silently beneath his initiation. He could withstand the same now.

"I will not burn you," Sutherland said with disgust. "Barbaric thought. I'll sew you up good and tight and hope for the best."

"Much more expedient with the poker. Use it."

Sutherland ignored him as usual. And unable to provoke a fight to give himself something to fix upon other than the pain, Iain thought of pleasure. His thoughts drifted back to the hours before—at the Sumners', when he had clutched Elizabeth's voluptuous curves to his hard body.

A man could make a meal out of her. He certainly wanted to. An image took hold, and he barely felt the straight needle prick him, diving under skin and tissue, grabbing more flesh before being pulled tight, tugging the ragged edges of his wound together.

Closing his eyes, he thought of Elizabeth, her long, sable hair unbound, spilling in velvet waves upon a glistening mahogany dining table. Naked, pale, full curves outlined against shining veneer, beneath the delicate glow of a chandelier. She was surrounded by wine goblets and tiered plates of grapes and strawberries.

He sat at the end of the table, sipping a dark merlot, studying the landscape of her body, the way it arched and curved before him. He would wait—would make her wait—as he watched her. He would talk to her, suggest wicked, lascivious things he wanted to watch her do. She would respond to his voice, would be helpless to stop the movement of her body along the table. Her lips would move and part, her breasts… He groaned, not in pain, but pleasure, as he thought of the way her breasts would bounce and sway. He'd have her on her knees, palms planted on the table as she crawled to him, amidst rolling grapes spilling from overturned silver dishes, and streaming rivulets of red wine snaking from toppled goblets. He would watch her, unable to take his gaze off her breasts, the turgid nipples, the way her shining hair moulded to the sway of her full, rounded hips.

"Lower" he would command, and she would respond, as she had once responded so beautifully to his voiced commands. In this fantasy, it was no less true. Lower… And she would raise her hips, lower her breasts till they just scraped the table with their pointed tips. He'd watch the red wine cover her nipples as she crawled, and the wine drip from them.

Licking his dry lips, Iain watched his fantasy play out in his heated mind, the drops of crimson wine slipping from elongated nipples, the slow, seductive crawl on her knees to him, the feel of his cock, so hard, so throbbing, released from his trousers, his hand fisting it…. Then the movement of his body, the lowering of his head, his lips beneath her breast—so close, waiting for the next drop of wine to slip effortlessly onto his tongue. Her sigh when he drew her into his mouth and suckled, as he pleasured himself… He could come just imagining it.

"I believe, my lord, that we are all finished."

Reluctantly, Alynwick pulled himself from the fantasy to see his shoulder bandaged in white cloth. One glance down the length of his body to his tented kilt made him close his eyes with a groan.

"Whatever you were thinking about, my lord," Sutherland said knowingly, "it worked. You didn't flinch once."

Two hours later, Alynwick sat in a large chair before the Duke of Sussex, with yet another tent in his kilt as he thought of the images that had flowed through his vivid, fevered imaginings while Sutherland worked over him.

How easy it was to conjure the image of a fair Elizabeth, naked, crawling toward him, red wine staining her body. In his mind he had been seated like a sultan before a harem girl, studying her—his possession. He loved to watch, and there was no woman he found more fascinating than Elizabeth York, with her exterior of innocence, and the eagerness of a harlot. He'd once watched her in the grass, watched the undulations of her body beneath his roving hand as he made her come with slow, knowing caresses and whispered words that were far too indecent for any well-bred young lady's ears.

She had been younger then, less full than she was now. She'd been beautiful to his eyes, but now... Now he'd give what remained of his soul to see her body, all full, voluptuous curves and soft planes, with secret places for his hand to touch, his lips to caress. He'd had only a glimpse of it last evening, and he wanted more. So much more. To say he was hungry for her was an amusing understatement. He was *starved* for her.

He groaned, wiped his palm along his unshaved face. He was damn hard, sitting before Sussex while thinking lurid thoughts of the duke's sister. He really was an unrepentant rake to debase the innocent sister of his friend with his lascivious dreams and erotic wishes.

"What's with you?" Black demanded of the silent duke. "Are you ill?"

For the first time, Iain took in Sussex's haggard appearance, and felt some measure of pleasure. His Grace looked nearly as worn as he did this morning.

When he and Black had barged into Sussex's study not more than ten minutes before, they had roused the duke from his sleep on the couch. Sussex had nothing to grumble about; he had not been shot in the shoulder. It was then that Alynwick recalled he had some unfinished business with his friend.

"What the devil d'ye think ye were doing, fobbing me off at Grantham Field?" he asked indignantly, his anger getting the better of him and allowing him to slip into his brogue. "Ye were supposed ta be me second!"

"No," Sussex growled impatiently, "one of us was supposed to be your second, and because you showed up at the Sumners' musicale drunk and itching for a fight, I had to bodily remove you from said musicale. Ergo, I was not able to perform as your second, since I wanted to shoot you my goddamn self!"

"I wasna drunk," Alynwick grumbled, wishing he could forget about the scene he'd created at the Sumners'. "Itchin' fer a fight, aye, but no' drunk."

"Careful," Black said with some amusement, "your cultured English accent is giving way to your heathen Highland one."

Black was hardly helping. And the bastard seemed to be taking an extraordinary amount of enjoyment out of it all. Iain rarely allowed himself to fall victim to his brogue. All the more evidence that something was ruling him, and it was not the coldhearted calculations he was notorious for.

Sussex's steel-grey eyes settled on him once more. "Surely you did not believe that it was the thing to do to be your second after the stir you caused at the Sumners'?

Everyone saw what happened, and how I had to remove your arm from Sheldon's throat!"

"Get at yer point, ye windbag," he snapped, hating the earl's name being mentioned. Iain had purposely tried to forget that Elizabeth had been in that room hanging on to the arm of another man. And by the looks of things, bloody well enjoying herself.

"My point, you infuriating brute, is this. We are not supposed to be friends, or even acquaintances, in the eyes of the polite world. We're to pretend that our own private circles do not cross, so no one will suspect that we are acquainted—in ways we have all vowed never to reveal. And then you stroll in and force my hand, making my sister the object of ridicule and gossip, and you wonder why I didn't come and perform as your second? The reason, you Highland ninny, is simple—because no one would believe it! No one would think it plausible that we were out for a pint, met up and I just merrily agreed to travel at dawn to some godforsaken farmer's field to aid you in putting a bullet hole in someone, when not four hours before you were importuning my sister and nearly killing the Earl of Sheldon!"

Black's gaze volleyed between them, then he groaned as the truth of Sussex's revelations sank in. "Alynwick, you didn't. Good God, you did, didn't you?"

Iain was not chastised, and more to the point, he was ready to fight again. "You didn't force me away from anything," he sneered. "I *allowed* you to tear me off that piece of trash."

"And how do you know anything about Sheldon," Sussex growled, "when your face is constantly gazing into the bottom of a whisky decanter?"

Iain lunged over the desk, ready to tear his friend apart, but Black caught him by the coat and hauled him back. "None of that, now," he grunted as he tossed Alynwick into the chair. "Stay!" he shouted, pointing at Iain as if he were a biddable canine when he tried to stand up again.

"I'm no' a bloody mongrel to heed yer commands."

"Really?" Black straightened his waistcoat and resumed his seat. "You look like something that's been roaming the street for weeks. Where did you go after I left you in Sutherland's care?"

He'd gone to find Lady Larabie, that's where. But he'd been too deep in thought to do anything but regale the lady with the gossip of his fight with her husband. Contrary to Larabie's boasts, the man had not returned home to deal with his wife, but instead made his way to his club in St. James's. That had left the lady free to dally, but dallying had been the last thing on Iain's mind. In a strange mood, he had sought out Georgiana for something else entirely. Comfort perhaps. Solace. She'd provided nothing of the sort—only petulance that he did not seem inclined to pleasure her. He was literally sickened by it, sitting in her overly ornate little parlor fending off her roving hands, when all he really wanted was to lay his head in her lap and feel her feminine fingers run through his hair while he pretended he was with Elizabeth. But it had all been to no avail. The lady was not capable of solace, and he had left, disgusted with himself for desiring such a thing. Iain Sinclair did not need anything from anyone—most especially sanctuary in a woman's arms.

With a sigh, he answered, "You doona want t' know where I was."

"By the stench of you, I think I already do."

Iain sent Black a glare, aware that he appeared debauched. But he wasn't. He was restless, mindless. There was a sickness ruling his thoughts, and if he had the courage to look through the darkness inside him, he'd be able to name the illness. He was heartsick, his soul crying out for the one remedy that could cure his illness. *Elizabeth*.

But she did not want him, or the love that he could no longer deny.

Sliding deeper into the chair, Iain allowed his hands to riffle through his hair. He wanted his bed, the cool, crisp sheets, and he wanted the images of Elizabeth burning his brain. In his fantasies he could have anything. Even Elizabeth back again.

"Good God, Alynwick, what the devil were you thinking, coming to the Sumners' and stirring up that scene?" Sussex continued, his considerable arrogance pricked. "It'll be in all the gossip rags this morning, and we don't need that kind of exposure. Damn you!"

Sulking, Iain stared out the window, thinking of last night and the scene that had greeted him. A smiling— *glowing*—Elizabeth standing beside a man who was looking down upon her with far too much interest. "A provocation, I believe." He was under control now, his brogue banished. "I was never good at resisting taunts."

"Taunts?" Black asked quizzically as he looked from Alynwick to Sussex. The duke shrugged.

"I told you," Alynwick growled with quiet menace, "to leave her out of this."

"We're afraid, old boy, that neither of us understands a damned thing coming out of your mouth," Black drawled.

"Yes, whom are you referring to, and what was this taunt?"

"Elizabeth!" Iain said it with such a snarl that Sussex sat back in his chair. "Damn you both, don't you know the trouble she can get into? It could make matters worse for us. She has no place in this affair. She should be at

home, beneath a wool blanket, sitting by the fire, where nothing and no one can touch her!"

Black and Sussex stared at one another, confusion written all over their expressions, but Iain didn't give a damn. So be it if they discovered that he was unable to think of anything other than Elizabeth this morning.

"Dear me," said a sweetly feminine voice from the doorway. "All this roaring and fighting has awakened the entire house."

Iain stiffened at the sound, but kept his gaze focused on the grey streaks of daylight breaking through the rain clouds. He was not yet ready to see her, to feel the onslaught of emotions when he looked into her lovely and haunting grey eyes.

"Elizabeth, do come in," Sussex ordered.

"I'll be on my way, then," Iain muttered, while he rose.

"Really, Alynwick, don't be so childish. Do you think I am naive? I know exactly what you think of me, my infirmity and my limited skill in aiding your cause. You don't have to go slinking off because I've overheard you talking about me."

It was like a knife to his heart. He never wanted to hurt her. Never again. "My apolo—"

"I don't require that, either," she said. "Because it's a lie. You aren't sorry. It's what you feel. Don't bother to deny it."

"You have no idea what I fe—"

With a slight wave of her hand, she effectively cut him dead, and he knew the expression on his face was one of shock and outrage.

"Do carry on," Elizabeth ordered. "I only came for a cup of tea. Mrs. Hammond claims to have brought you a tray, and I don't want to wait for another tray to be sent up."

Black did the honours pouring, and Iain watched as his friend carefully passed her the cup and saucer. Her morning gown, a crème-colored silk-and-lace confection with long, fluttering sleeves, was at once prim and proper, yet so damn enticing. It made him want to slowly pull the tie of her wrapper loose to discover what wicked thing she wore beneath.

"Now, then, keep it down, if you please, or the servants will be privy to everything. I heard two maids giggling as I approached the study. No doubt they were spying. As an aside, Lucy and I will be meeting today. It's likely she'll come here, so I hope the three of you will make yourselves scarce, because I plan on quizzing her about matters."

"What matters?" Iain demanded. He hated how Sussex allowed her take to part in any Brethren discussions. It wasn't safe.

"That, my lord, is none of your concern. Seek your own clues to this case, and I will seek mine. Now, then, come along, Rosie," she said regally. And obeying her ladyship, Elizabeth's spaniel nudged her in the right direction, away from anything that might impede her regal exit.

"Damned female," Iain grunted bitterly. "A curse and a pox on headstrong women who won't be led by a man."

"I daresay you'll have half the women of London sporting pox marks and curses, Alynwick."

Iain scowled at Black, but continued to watch as Elizabeth disappeared through the door. The thought of her being hurt while trying to aid them in the search for Orpheus sent fear through him. Iain Sinclair, Marquis of Alynwick, feared nothing—except losing Elizabeth. Even though she did not belong to him, and likely never would, Iain took comfort in the fact that he could see her, listen to her, stand back and quietly watch her, and think of the impossible—all the things he would do and say to her if she was his to possess. If he couldn't see her, if she was taken and no longer a part of his world, he wouldn't survive. His stolen looks and dreams of her sustained him.

No, Elizabeth must not be allowed to be part of this mystery that surrounded them. The danger was too real, and the thought of losing her much too painful. But before he could speak his mind, and protest her involvement, Black interjected.

"Now, then, gentlemen, if you please," the earl murmured as he sat in the chair opposite Sussex's desk, sipping at his tea as though he were a damned prince. "The task of the duel is done, the objective reached and our mission can commence," he said smoothly. "I acted as second, performed a credible act, and now it is all water under the bridge."

"Oh, go to hell, Black," Alynwick muttered as he sank farther into the matching chair. "You're being a self-righteous bastard, and I'd love to shove my fist into that smug face of yers."

Black's black brows rose over the rim of his teacup, and Sussex groaned, closing his eyes.

"Be that as it may, we need to go forward from here. What is our next move? Sussex, have you learned any more about the coins, or Orpheus?"

"As a matter of fact I have, just last night—"

"Your pardon, Your Grace," his butler said from the doorway.

"What is it now?" Sussex groaned, sending the butler, Hastings, scurrying behind the wooden panel, only to peer around it.

"You have a caller."

"What?"

"A caller. A visitor," Hastings clarified.

"Now? At this hour?"

"Your Grace?" the butler discreetly cleared his throat. "Shall I send her on her way?"

Before Sussex could answer, a flurry in emerald-green velvet trimmed in black satin swam through the door, causing Sussex's butler to grow white with horror.

"And what is the meaning of this?"

Iain watched as Lucy Ashton stormed into the room, cornering Sussex in his domain.

"I do not," she spat, "respond to this sort of blackmail. Oh, good day, Lord Black, Lord Alynwick." She dropped a quick but polite curtsey, then turned once more to face Sussex, before either of them had a chance to rise from his chair. Iain watched her slamming a folded piece of paper on the desk, wondering where her ire sprang from.

"You, Your Grace, may offer me an explanation."

Sussex waved his hand, silently telling them to bugger off, but Iain was not inclined to honour his wishes. At the duke's lethal glare, he and Black reluctantly started to leave.

They were strolling across the study when Mrs. Hammond, the Sussex housekeeper, screamed with such a bloodcurdling howl that they all went running into the hall.

"Your Grace," Mrs. Hammond shouted. "Oh, good God in heaven! Your Grace! You must come!"

They found the plump housekeeper, her white linen cap askew, running breathlessly down the hall from the kitchen, her arms flailing.

"What is it, Mrs. Hammond?" Sussex enquired, catching the woman by the shoulders.

"There now, lass," Iain murmured. "Take a deep breath and tell us. It canna be as bad as all this."

The housekeeper's brown eyes were wild with fear. Shaking her head, she looked from Iain to the duke. "It can, your lordships. It can be worse. Oh," she cried into her apron. "It's over there, Your Grace, at the door to the kitchen gardens. A dead body—oh, I shall never recover!"

CHAPTER FIVE

SUSSEX WAS FIRST TO REACH the kitchen, with Iain hard on his heels. Alynwick had the very unsettling image of Elizabeth lying crumpled in the back garden, her body twisted in an unnatural position. It made him want to run to find her, to knock Sussex out of the way out of fear and desperation. Iain's throat was dry, his breathing ragged, and in his mind he frantically called her name. *Beth...!*

The garden door was open wide, and a wheelbarrow heaped with dried leaves and twigs sat on the flagstone path.

"What is the meaning of this?" Sussex growled, his boots ringing shrilly as he ran. When he reached the barrow he stopped, frozen. Blue satin spilled from it, rippling in the early morning wind. Iain closed his eyes and whispered a prayer of gratitude. It was not Elizabeth.

Sussex brushed the leaves away, and the face of a woman was revealed, pasty white and bruised, and unfortunately, dead. "Anastasia," he whispered.

Iain heard Lucy gasp behind him. Saw over his shoulder that Elizabeth, still wearing her morning gown and wrapper, was hastily making her way down the hall with her pregnant spaniel waddling beside her, guiding her mistress away from a rosewood table. On top was an enormous bouquet of hothouse flowers and a silver salver filled with correspondence that sat precariously near the corner of the table, where it might catch on Elizabeth's sleeve. Stepping back, Iain went to her and took her arm none too gently. He was trembling, still thinking of the vision of her lying dead on the flagstones. Her damnable independent streak would be the ruin of her, not to mention the ruination of his sanity.

"Unhand me, Alynwick!"

"How did you know it was me?" he asked incredulously, unnerved, and more than curious about how she was able to discern it was him from all the others present.

"I can smell you, if you must know!"

Something primal and visceral ran through him as the intimacy of her words hit him. "You know my scent?"

He hadn't meant for his voice to be almost a growl, nor had he meant to pull her roughly to a stop. But now that he had her, her elbows cupped in his palms, her lace wrapper smashed up against his chest, he wasn't going to apologize.

Looking down at her upturned face, he saw surprise and wariness in her gaze. How long it had been since he'd allowed himself to look deeply into her eyes? They were perfect, a stormy grey, the black pupils large, the left one a bit larger than the right. A lush sweep of curved black lashes blinked slowly. He could see himself reflected in her eyes, and selfishly was relieved that she could not see his lovelorn expression—the hope that something more than animosity might grow between them.

"How do I smell?" he asked, his voice quiet and a bit hoarse. She softened, yielding the slightest fraction, and he bit his lip at the way her breasts pressed against him. Resisted the urge to wrap his arm around her waist and slip his free hand beneath her wrapper to cup her, to pull at her nipple, preparing to draw it into his mouth.

"Like the woods," she said, her voice not at all steady

and sure, "at twilight. Musky, earthy, with the taste of cedar and the crispness of night."

Twilight had always been her favourite time of the day. When she had started losing her sight, the glare of the sun had always diminished her vision. But come night, and the dark blues, grays and mauves of evening, Elizabeth saw everything clearer, sharper. He had purposely made love to her for the first time at twilight so that she might see everything he did to her.

It had been in the woods, on the Sinclair plaid, that he had taken her. Had watched the night fall upon her naked body, which glowed pure and innocent beneath the silvery moonlight and his large hands. How he wanted that back—to have her once again beneath him!

Frowning, she tried to pull away, but he held her tight.

"Stay." One word, said with the hope of a man struggling to hold on.

"No."

She pulled away, but he reached for her again, forced her to accept his arm. As they walked out into the early morning sun, he took in the scene, described what he saw to Elizabeth, who suddenly seemed to be holding on to him, not the other way around.

"Good God, a woman? Dead?" she gasped.

"Yes," he whispered. Sussex was speaking.

"Who is it? Good Lord, how did she come to be here, in our kitchen garden?" Elizabeth demanded.

"Shh, let's listen," Iain whispered. "Your brother is investigating the body now. I see recognition in his eyes. Sussex," he called out. "Who the devil is she?"

The duke didn't answer.

"She's still warm," Lucy whispered beside them, and Iain watched as she crossed herself, shuddering. "And look." Lucy pulled a folded letter from the woman's lax fingers. Iain read the missive over Sussex's shoulder, then reached for Elizabeth, unconsciously wrapping a protective arm around her waist.

It might have been the redhead. We crossed paths, but I thought I'd give you one final warning. Send another spy to my club, and the redhead will suffer a fate far more painful than this one.

It could very well have been Elizabeth, Iain thought, and despite her resistance, he lifted her into his arms and carried her back into the house, for fear the madman might be still lurking in the garden, might see her and fix his murdering gaze upon her. This had gone too far. It was much too dangerous for her to be allowed out of sight. She needed protecting.

"You will not aid Sussex anymore in our search for Orpheus, do you understand?" Iain demanded as he carried her deeper into the house, away from the horrible crime on the kitchen step.

"You will not tell me what I can and cannot do, my lord."

"I can and I am. You will cease meddling."

"Meddling? Your arrogance is not to be borne!"

"Nor is your reckless disregard for your safety!"

"Reckless disregard? Oooh!" She seethed, struggling in his hold. "How dare you, sir? I'll have you know that I am extraordinarily careful…."

She trailed off, and out of curiosity he glanced down at her and saw a loathsome expression cross her face. "It's not that you are worried about my safety, is it? The truth of the matter is you don't believe I can be any help at all because of my blindness. You think me an inconvenience. A hindrance."

"That is not it."

"Put me down. At once!"

He obeyed her. Not because he wanted to, but because there was something in the way she said it that gave him pause.

She turned to him, signaled for Rosie to come to her, then tilted her chin in defiance. "I do not need your protection or your protestations. I don't need you. I *never* needed you."

And then she turned away, haughty and beautiful, and begging to be picked up and carried off to her room and ravished until her words were not refusals, but entreaties.

"I will protect you, regardless of what you say or how you feel," he quietly vowed. He had said that once before, and he had failed miserably. But this time he meant it. He would protect Elizabeth even if it killed him.

"LIZZY, WHAT BRINGS YOU here?" Sussex asked sleepily.

With arms outstretched, Elizabeth waved them in front of her, trying to search for any obstacles in her way.

"Your valet said you had a headache. I wanted to check on you."

"No, keep going straight, otherwise you're going to crash headlong into the bedpost."

She was relieved that Adrian had not bothered to stir himself from the bed to help her. She'd had her fill of overprotective men who sought to stifle her with help, reminding her of how she was nothing but a disabled nuisance.

"There. If I plop down here will it be on a chair or a stool?"

"Dressing chair."

Lowering herself, Elizabeth felt around with her hands for the rounded edges of the seat. "There," she said, while she artfully arranged her skirts, hoping she appeared appropriate sitting there, wondering what she was wearing this morning. She had been too irate over Alynwick's demands that she keep her nose out of Brethren business to enquire about the colour of her dress. It was taffeta, she knew, just by the way it sounded as she arranged the long skirts. A grosgrain taffeta; she could feel the nap beneath her sensitive fingertips. Other than that, she had no clue what Maggie had dressed her in.

"You look lovely in that shade of yellow."

"Thank you. I was wondering what color this gown was."

"The hue reminds me of a summer day."

"Good heavens, brother, I do believe that Lady Lucy's penchant for description is rubbing off on you."

"Do you? I had rather hoped that it would be the other way around—that I might be rubbing off on her."

"And what makes you think you are not?"

"Because she made it known, in no uncertain terms, that she finds me rather loathsome."

"Posh," Lizzy said, waving away her brother's worry. "Lucy is confused, is all. She feels for you, Adrian. I can sense it. She doesn't loathe you at all. She is merely trying to understand what it is you do to her. Besides, we had a chat over tea this morning, after that horrible business was concluded, and she asked me a few questions about you."

"Really?" The covers rustled, as though he was sitting up. "What questions?"

"I am not at liberty to share our discourse, but suffice it to say that I think you have captivated her, despite her best intentions not to notice you."

"And when did you become an expert in affairs of the heart?"

"After the stacks of penny dreadfuls Isabella and Lucy have been reading to me these past weeks."

"Ah," he said, laughing. "Advice from overwrought literature. You are indeed an expert."

"Mark my words, Adrian. Lucy will be your wife, and will fall head over heels in love with you. Every bit as much, if not more, than you love her."

She was met with silence, and she listened for the sounds in the room. Nothing. Adrian must be lying there, hands folded behind his head, studying her. Drat the man, he was too observant. She never could hide much from him.

"Lizzy?" he murmured, and she heard the silent question in his voice.

"I only came to find you, to see if you might need anything."

"Well, here you are," her brother drawled, sounding amused. "Risking life and limb to check on me and my aching head. Isn't that what you claimed?"

"Indeed. How is your head?"

"I took a sulphur tonic and it is much improved."

Curling her lips, she said, "I thought I smelt something foul upon entering this room, but felt it was impolite and far too personal to point it out."

Adrian laughed again and she heard him settling back onto his pillows. "And what of the other questions, Lizzy?"

She never could fool Adrian. There was a time, when she was much younger, that Adrian had been nothing but a thorn in her side. He'd been mean, taunting, but then he had grown quite ill, and was whisked away by their father to a remote estate. It had taken months for him to heal from his ailment, and when she had next seen him, he had been a changed man. Kind and thoughtful. Protective without being overbearing, and so very, very understanding of her needs. She had been completely blind upon his return, and she frequently lamented the fact that she could not see his face. See the man he had become.

"Let's have the real reason, Lizzy. Out with it."

Shrugging, she fidgeted with her hands. "I came to ask about Lucy. I wondered, with the events of the morning, how she was. She seemed rather determined to avoid the topic with me."

He sighed. "I sent her home with a footman to protect her. I read the note to you, so you know the bastard might have just as easily killed her—the redhead in the note, no doubt—as opposed to Anastasia. And the thought of it chills me to the core."

"Yes, Anastasia," Lizzy murmured, thinking of the lady who had been murdered and presented to them in the back garden. "Imagine, Lucy crossing paths with that monster."

"I'd rather not. I've barely slept thinking of it, and how it might have been her, her red hair spilling from the wheelbarrow, the bruises on her lovely neck."

"She is safe, and I have no doubt she will remain thus. She seemed unnerved to me. I doubt she will go searching for trouble, or any of those occult meetings and séances she has been dabbling in."

"I shall have to find a way to believe as you do. But, Lizzy, I'm terrified. I have only you to confess it to, but I'm frightened to the marrow of my bones that this man we hunt might strike again before we find him. He knows so much about us—the Brethrens, our father…."

"As to that, I have questions, Adrian."

"I knew you would."

"What did you tell the servants about Anastasia?"

"I lied, of course. Said that she was an actress from

the opera who took an unnatural fixation with me. She killed herself because I would not have her. Seems a bit vain and sanctimonious, but the staff knows that I am nothing if not a stickler for proprieties. They believed my reluctance to begin an affair with an opera dancer. They accepted what I told them, and will carry on in their service, and silence, as they always have."

"But you were saddened by the tale. I hear it in your voice even now."

"I wish I did not have to malign her reputation after death. Seemed such a cruel, unforgiving thing to do, to claim her to be something she was not, just to save my reputation."

"Not only your reputation, but the knowledge of the Guardians. She would understand, I think, Adrian."

"Yes. She would. She was that sort of woman. I only regret that she knew such suffering in her life."

"She was Father's mistress?" she guessed. The woman would have known no kindness, no softness from their father. No man was more cold, more unforgiving than him.

"I heard your gasp when I announced her name. I thought perhaps you knew her, or of her."

"No, I didn't. I guess it was merely a sound of shock. Father never struck me as the sort to keep a woman. How did she bear it, do you think, suffering and enduring him?"

"Theirs was a strange relationship. She loved him. And in his own way, I think he…cared for her. His style of caring, anyway."

"I never knew. Never saw her, or heard him speak of her."

"Wives and daughters are not supposed to learn of a man's mistress, Lizzy."

"You did."

"That was...different." His voice was quieter, more mysterious now. "Circumstances beyond my control, I'm afraid. I shielded the secret from you because I knew it would hurt you, cause you pain when you thought of your—our mother being betrayed."

"I never knew, yet somehow, whoever killed this woman put a connection together between you and her."

"To Father, and by extension me. God only knows how he discovered Ana's connection to the house of York. Because of it, I've added extra security within the house, and outside. I won't leave you vulnerable, Lizzy, while I am trying to solve this mystery."

"Yes, of course. Very unnerving to discover what happened this morning, and on our own doorstep. Poor Anastasia, I hope she's at peace and did not suffer much."

"You seem to be bearing up rather well, considering the circumstances."

Lizzy shrugged. She was hiding it well, she supposed. But it was rather unnerving to be blind. How would she tell if anything was out of place? How would she know if an intruder had gained entrance into her home, or loomed over her while she was asleep, with a knife pressed to her throat?

"Lizzy, what is really on your mind?"

Frowning, she tried to put the pieces of the puzzle together. "She was helping you, wasn't she—with this Guardian business? You allowed Anastasia to assist you."

"I didn't ask her to, Lizzy," Adrian said softly. "She wanted to and would brook no refusal. She informed me that she had a direct entrance into the club, that her lover knew Orpheus. I agreed to it because it's been the closest we've gotten to him, except for Alynwick's—" Her brother coughed, stopping midsentence.

"Alynwick's what?" she demanded.

"He has, er, a connection to someone who frequents the club."

"Some notorious tart, I'd wager," Lizzy said haughtily, but the bitterness in her voice betrayed her true feelings. Damn Iain for making her still feel anything for him. "It must be Lady Larabie, then."

"What? How can you know of that?"

"Oh, come, brother, I am blind, not stupid or hard of hearing. I heard the gossip about him and the newly wed Lady Larabie. I also learned there was to be a duel. From the sounds of him this morning, he must have escaped it unscathed."

"Lizzy."

"No matter. Alynwick's life and what debauchery he makes of it is none of my concern. What do I care if he is killed for his adulterous deeds? Good riddance, I would say. The scroll he keeps as part of the Guardians' treasure could easily be given to you or Black, and instead of three Brethren there could be two perfectly capable souls."

"What is it with you two? If it isn't him demanding that I keep you out of matters, it's you voicing your distaste for the fellow. What happened to make you notice one another, when you have never bothered with each other before now?"

Elizabeth felt herself stiffen. Adrian was coming too close to the truth.

"Alynwick said I was to stay out of Brethren business. In fact he demanded it. I won't have it, Adrian. Who is he to demand anything of me?"

There, she'd said it, the real reason for her visit. Heaving a sigh, she waited for her brother's answer.

"Normally, I would say he is an ass and order you to ignore him, but in this case, I have to agree. It's become personal, and whoever this Orpheus is, he knows of Lucy and my feelings for her. I'm distracted, Lizzy, and I can't be worrying over both you and Lucy. Seeing Anastasia this morning... Well, I couldn't survive if it were you or Lucy."

"I'm not an invalid, Adrian, to be coddled and cosseted."

"I didn't say you were, and I'm not treating you as one."

"He is."

"He, who?" Elizabeth could hear annoyance in her brother's voice.

"Alynwick."

"Well, he is being a royal pain, what with the scene he created last night."

She didn't want to think of last night and how he had humiliated her. She had enough anger ruling her now, without more fat added to the fire. "He is purposely leaving me out. He practically shoved me from the salon this morning when all of you were discussing the murder and what was to be done. As a consequence I didn't hear what my role was to be."

"You don't have one, Lizzy."

The blow was instantaneous, and it hurt. "You're listening to him! I can't believe it! Alynwick of all people? Adrian, you traitor!"

"For once he has a valid point. Lizzy." Her brother sighed. "We cannot avoid the obvious. You're at a disadvantage and it makes you extremely vulnerable."

Jumping up, Elizabeth fisted her hands at her sides. "I'll hinder you, is that it?"

"Of course not."

"While you and Black and Alynwick are out searching for the monster who killed Anastasia, you want me home, where you don't have to worry about your blind sister tripping into danger. Well, Adrian York, I am not completely useless," she snapped, storming off.

"Lizzy, get back here."

"I only thought to help," she said, hating the sadness in her voice. "What else is left to me? I have no husband or children to occupy my time. I can't see to paint or embroider, or read, or decorate. I can't even shop without another set of eyes escorting me. I have nothing, Adrian. *Nothing!*"

"That's not true."

"Oh, do not lie to yourself, thinking you are making me feel better. Lies only make me feel worse, for I know they are spoken out of pity. The truth is, I have never complained about my blindness or bemoaned my fate. I always had the Brethren Guardians to make me feel worthwhile and capable. I had you and Black to talk to, and I was involved in discussions, in the history of our ancestors. I was a part of the group, and it kept me happy. Now you are denying me the one thing that made my life worth anything."

Whether she was intended to hear his sigh, Elizabeth did not know. But when her brother spoke, it was with a sense of resignation.

"Black and Alynwick have left to bury Anastasia's body, and then they are to search her dwelling. They'll be back this afternoon. Perhaps you might sit with us and hear what they've discovered."

"I might as well be a dog you are throwing a bone to. It's an appeasement."

"It's a compromise, Lizzy."

"No, thank you. I shall be busy this afternoon, entertaining Lord Sheldon at tea."

"He's calling, is he? I knew he would. I will speak to you tonight, then, and tell you what I have learned about the murder. But that is all, Lizzy. I won't allow you to do more than that. Witnessing what this fiend is capable of, I won't throw you into danger—even if you did possess sight. I won't risk it. You can rail and scream, and the answer will remain the same. You are not getting directly involved."

Reluctantly, she nodded. "I suppose this is all I can hope for, isn't it—bits and scraps of information you wish to share with me?"

"For now, Lizzy."

"Stay safe, Adrian. And do protect Lucy."

He groaned. "She'll be the death of me."

"But it will be a pleasant death, won't it?"

"Aye, it will."

Elizabeth laughed at the smile she heard in his voice.

"Lizzy," he called as she made her slow progression across the room. "It's out of love that I said it, you know. I want you safe, and it's hard enough for me to keep everyone I love safe."

"I would be selfish not to acknowledge how grateful I am that everyone cares about my well-being. However, hoyden that I am, I bristle at being protected. I might have to accept your decision to keep me apart from Brethren business, but I don't have to like it."

"Lizzy, you have always been a part of the Guardians, and accepted as one of us. But that was before, when it was just talk, and secrets, and keeping the relics safe. There was no real, tangible danger. But now there is, and it's a nasty business. It's real, Elizabeth. Life and death, and not one of us is willing to risk your safety. Whatever you may think, Black keeps Isabella far away from danger, and any discussion of the Guardians. I plan to do the same with Lucy, if she ever consents to be my wife. You should not feel singled out, or abandoned."

She felt like weeping. Strange how she hadn't felt so hopeless and helpless since the summer her eyesight had left her. Lizzy experienced those same feelings, searching and struggling, wondering how to go on and where she might fit in. She understood Adrian's concern, really, she did, but her brother didn't realize that it was quite easy for Isabella and Lucy to be kept sheltered. They had not been born into a Guardian family. It was not their birthright. And more importantly, they had other things to keep their minds occupied. Isabella had a home and a husband, and one day children, and Lucy had the potential. Lizzy herself had none of that to offer comfort or stimulation. She was alone, and being with the Guardians, discussing it all, taking part, had been like a family to her. She was not alone then. Not incapable.

"You are always a part of this, Lizzy," her brother said quietly. "I hope you know that. That you will always have a place with me."

Yes. A thought that was comforting, yet bittersweet. Adrian would always take care of her, and she would always be protected, the blind sister, the blind aunt, living amongst the family he would have.

There would be nothing of her own. No life to lead apart from that of sister, sister-in-law and loving aunt. It made her absolutely miserable, and guilty for thinking this way, when there were women out there who would give up their souls for the kind of life she had.

"Good morning, brother," she replied, hoping he didn't hear the sadness in her voice. "I hope your head feels better."

"And enjoy your tea—but not too much, Lizzy. The only hasty nuptials I am eager to announce are my own."

"Silly man," she said, smiling. "It's just tea."

"A lot can happen over tea and crumpets, Lizzy. Believe me."

CHAPTER SIX

HOURS AFTER THE DISCOVERY of Anastasia's body in their kitchen garden, the house seemed to settle into a semblance of calm. The servants were too loyal, too well trained, to discuss the matter with anyone, but still Lizzy feared the implications for not only her brother, but the Brethren Guardians. Those implications had her fidgeting and on edge. Not even Maggie's pampering for Sheldon's impending visit seemed to calm her thoughts. What if the woman who had been killed by Orpheus's hand had been Isabella, or Lucy? How would Lizzy have borne it, the loss of those friendships? Or what if it had been Sussex? How in the world would she be able to get on in life without Adrian by her side? She had come to depend upon him. It had not always been that way between them. But after his convalescence he had morphed from a spoiled aristocrat to a caring man and devoted brother who had become her lifeline. She could not lose him.

No, Orpheus must be stopped before he could take any other lives—especially the lives of those she loved so dearly. She only wished she had the ability to stop him herself. Would that she could! But she couldn't. She wouldn't even be able to identify him, or know if he stood nose to nose with her. Some assistance she would bring the Guardians! she thought with a snort. She was an intelligent, honest female. She knew her limitations. It was her heart that would not admit to them.

After her talk with Adrian, she felt more resigned to her fate than ever. He was correct, of course. In the past she had been part of debates and discussions, of stories passed down from their Templar ancestors. They had never fought a true enemy. Not until Orpheus. She was not equipped to help them, or protect herself. How it stung, to admit the truth.

"Now, then, miss, you're looking radiant and composed. I daresay your *gennleman* will be gobsmacked when he sees you."

"Maggie, you're a wonderful balm for a nervous soul," she replied, not feeling any sense of composure. She was still rattled by the dead body that had appeared that morning, and what was more, she was horridly nervous about what lay just beyond the closed door in front of her.

"Now, there's nothing to be worried about. That nasty bit of business this morning is done and over, and should be far from your thoughts. You sail right on into that room with Rosie here, and don't let him see your uneasiness. Everything is out of the way. I made sure of it myself. You'll make a grand entrance, just like a queen, and there will be nothing to cause you to stumble."

Nodding, Elizabeth smoothed her damp palms down the sides of her skirts. She was nervous. More than nervous. She was bloody terrified. It was one thing to indulge in a short stroll around a salon with dozens of eyes watching her. Quite another to entertain a man—alone.

What will he think of me?

She had not been able to stop asking herself that question all morning. And now, after the early morning's excitement, she was even more rattled. She must act calm and cool and collected. Neither she nor her brother could afford to make her caller suspicious of anything. She just hoped that Alynwick would not be back for hours, giving

her plenty of time to entertain Sheldon, and have him depart before Alynwick and Black's return. The marquis,
she acknowledged, had been somewhat of a loose can-
non that morning, and after last night's debacle she had
no wish for him to meet up with Sheldon in the hall. The
less Alynwick knew of her appointments and visitors the
better. The man had no right to interfere with her life,
but it seemed that part of being a Brethren Guardian was
protecting and smothering the blind sister of one of their
group. How she despised Alynwick's overprotective and
arrogant commands, which she was still seething over.

Letting out a long breath, Lizzy forced the marquis
out of her thoughts. She had worried about him on that
desolate field with a gun pointed at him. It had robbed
her of sleep, made her forget his past betrayal. But this
morning he had seemed as fit as ever—and as surly. She
had regretted almost immediately that she'd given up
hours of sleep worrying over the beast. But then, it had
not been all wasted, for she had put those hours to use
by thinking of Sinjin's journal and trying to piece the
puzzle together. Who was the Veiled Lady whom Sinjin York had loved until his dying breath? It had been
her obsession to discover the woman's identity the moment she had finished the diary. Of course, at that time
she had fancied herself having the same sort of clandes-
tine romance, only her Lancelot had turned out to be a
toad—with warts.

Now that it seemed likely she would be cast aside,
unable to aid the Brethren, she needed something to do.
Perhaps focusing all her attention on the diary and the
identity of the woman would bring her some measure of
accomplishment. At least it would give her something to
ponder during the day.

"Now, don't fret about a thing," Maggie was saying,

drawing her from her thoughts. "I'll be in with the tea tray, and I'll set you up all proper. His Grace has gone into his study, and has asked not be disturbed. I shall attend you, but I'll sit out of the way while you have your visit."

"There really isn't a need for you to chaperone. I'm quite firmly a spinster." Besides, it would be terribly uncomfortable to sit through this first visit while her companion watched. It was already going to be damned difficult to entertain, knowing a woman who had been connected to her father—and Sussex—had just been murdered. It was even more disconcerting to know that Lizzy was completely unable to help them in capturing the murderer. Even Lucy had been of some assistance. Lucy, who was new in their little group. It had chafed Lizzy a bit, listening to Lucy and Alynwick discussing facts and evidence. Evidence Lizzy could not see. Facts she could not supply, or provide a reasoning for.

It was not like her to be envious, but that morning she had been, and in truth, still was. That morning she had felt like an outsider. A weakling. And those feelings of inadequacy and disability plagued her still as she stood immobile, regretting her decision to allow Lord Sheldon to call on her.

"There now, quit wringing your hands in your skirts. You're wrinkling the taffeta. In you go, miss, and lift that chin high."

She was thirty years old, she reminded herself. Not some green girl. She did not need to allow herself to sink into melancholy because of hurt feelings. No, she had to stand tall, to be the woman of strength she had always been.

"Wish me luck?"

"Luck?" Maggie scoffed as she gently urged her forward. "You've no need for luck. A woman makes her own luck. Besides, you look absolutely radiant."

Smiling, Lizzy heard the click of Rosie's nails against the marble floor. With a quiet snick a footman opened the door for her, and she felt the reassuring pressure of Rosie's muzzle pressing into her thigh.

"Shall I lend my arm, Lady Elizabeth?" a voice asked in low tones.

It was her most favoured footman. "Not today, Charles. You understand, don't you?"

"Indeed, my lady." She could hear the smile in his voice. "Knock 'em off 'is feet."

She would indeed, she thought as she gathered her confidence and breezed into the little yellow salon that was her favourite room in the mansion. The windows faced east, and she liked to feel the sun on her face as she sipped her tea. The colours, she knew, were warm and cheerful, reminding her of a summer's day, rather like the dress she was wearing.

Already her spirits were boosted. The sun was out, she realized as she stepped into the room. And he was there. She could smell him, the scent of masculinity and shaving soap. He was close, she knew, and when she heard the scrape of a chair against the floor, she realized that he was immediately to her right. She stopped, allowing Rosie's head to gently nudge her to the left.

"Good afternoon, Lady Elizabeth."

Lord Sheldon. His voice was soft, mellow, like a fine vintage wine—smooth and decadent.

She curtseyed and said, "My lord." Rising, she extended her arm, and he took it, wrapping his fingers around her elbow, steering her across the room to where she felt the curved wooden arm of the settee.

Lowering herself onto the cushion, she took extra care

to look controlled, yet elegant—and not blind. More than anything, she did not want to appear disabled and dependent during this, their first visit. First impressions, she knew, were lasting. It was one thing to stroll about a salon with him, but quite another to get through a proper afternoon call.

"Astonishing," he said, and she could hear amazement in his voice. "That little spaniel nudged you along, all the way."

Patting the empty cushion beside her, Elizabeth heard the scratching of Rosie's paws against the chintz fabric. Grasping her gently about the middle, she hefted her up, and smiled when Rosie inelegantly flopped down beside her, giving a little sigh of relief, or perhaps annoyance. Sheldon joined Lizzy in a laugh.

"Poor darling, she is in the family way, I am afraid."

"I can see that," the earl replied as he pulled a chair across the floorboards, closer to the settee. "Her time must be soon?"

"I believe so. Sussex says within the month."

"I've never seen an animal do such a thing. She was guiding you, wasn't she?"

Nodding, Elizabeth dragged her hand through Rosie's fur. "She was. My brother trained her, and he hopes her pups might be just as agreeable as their mother to this sort of training."

"I must speak with him about this. It sounds like a venture that could benefit many. I wonder if he could do anything with my retriever? He's a dashing fellow, but rather disobedient. Terrible habit of jumping, and breaking lead to go haring off into the forest."

"Sussex has a way with animals, that is for certain. I am quite sure he would be more than happy to explain his methods."

"I will ask him."

"I should like to meet this retriever of yours. He sounds positively naughty."

"He is. But he has the most affectionate face. Makes it rather difficult to reprimand him."

"I adore animals. They have such perfect instinct, don't they? And they care for everyone, no matter how many times you scold them."

"They do, indeed. Jack, my retriever, travelled with me from Egypt. I'm afraid he's having some difficulty fitting in. But I hope it will pass soon. And it would be my honour to introduce the two of you. Perhaps you might even teach me how to scold him."

Lizzy laughed. "Not likely. I'm much too inclined to spoil and coddle. Just look at Rosie here, sprawled out on my settee. And worse, she has positively commandeered Sussex's leather chair that sits before the hearth in his study. No, I am the last person to teach any amount of discipline."

"Well, then, I shall have to try to prevent myself falling victim to his lolling tongue and sparkling eyes. And I will still introduce you, and pray he doesn't jump up and knock you to the ground."

"Oh, I am rather sturdy, my lord. Besides, I'm used to dog hair and sticky licks. I am made of stern stuff, I daresay."

"Indeed, I do believe you are, Lady Elizabeth. I detect a steel core in you that few women could boast of."

What a lovely compliment, Elizabeth thought as the salon lapsed into polite silence, broken by Maggie rolling the tea cart into the room. "Tea, Lady Elizabeth."

This would be the test. How would his lordship react when she could not perform the task of hostess?

"How do you take your tea, Lord Sheldon?"

"Just black if you please."

Nodding, she asked, "And a square, or biscuit?"

"You know," he replied, and Elizabeth had the feeling he was not addressing her, but Maggie. "Why not leave this with us, and I shall pour and prepare Lady Elizabeth's tea?"

"Why, that's very good, my lord."

He had won her companion over with that, and was well on his way to winning her, too.

When Maggie had retreated, Sheldon turned to Elizabeth and asked, "How do you take your tea?"

"One cube of sugar and a generous dollop of cream, please."

"You have a sweet tooth," he remarked, and she could hear the teasing in his voice.

"I do indeed."

"Now, how shall I do this? Hand the cup to you, or set it on the table before you?"

Cocking her head to the side, Elizabeth sat silent for a moment.

"Lady Elizabeth," he said, and there was a great deal of embarrassment in his voice. "I... Forgive me."

"No," she admonished, her voice soft even to her own ears. "Forgive *me*. I was just taken aback, is all. It is so very nice to be asked how one should deal with my impairment, instead of skirting about it as if it didn't exist."

"I don't want you burned, and, in truth, I don't want you to put an end to my call because of my ineptness."

She flushed; she knew she did. Her cheeks must be crimson. "If you will, place a biscuit on the saucer, and the handle of the teacup to my left, and place it in my hands. That would be perfect."

He did as she instructed, and she flushed again when

their fingers brushed. She heard the catch of his breath—
it echoed hers—and a pleasant warmth infused her.

The air stirred, followed by the sounds of Lord Sheldon settling into his chair and taking his cup and saucer in hand.

"Darjeeling?" he enquired as he sipped the brew.

"My favourite. I hope you don't mind it."

"No, of course not. The flavours remind me of the
East. When I was in Jerusalem I enjoyed my tea infused
with cardamom pods, and a hint of sugar. It is not unlike this Darjeeling."

"Oh, it sounds wonderful. When you next come to
call I'll make certain to serve the tea with cardamom."

Lizzy heard him chuckle. "I have a supply at home.
I shall bring it."

"And I'll provide the tea."

"It all sounds very polite, Lady Elizabeth."

"Please, call me Elizabeth, or Lizzy. All my closest
friends do."

"Very well, Lizzy. Then you must call me by name.
Julian."

It suited him, she thought as she carefully raised the
delicate cup to her lips. It was a strong name. A very masculine name, with a hint of sensuality to it.

Be careful, Lizzy, she warned herself, *you're falling too
fast.* And she needn't remind herself what happened the
last time she'd fallen headlong into something like this.

"It's a lovely day today. I wonder how many more can
be in store for us with winter approaching?" her visitor
murmured.

"Yes, I can feel the sun shining on my face. Such a
treat for November."

"November in Egypt is always sunny and hot. Sandstorms are prevalent, as well. The golden sands whirl up in circles and cover every surface imaginable."

"Is that just in the desert, or does it reach the cities, too?"

"Lizzy, I may safely assure you that sand has a way of reaching every nook and cranny—and I do mean *every*."

She laughed. "My governess used to have a fit of vapours when I would come home from the sea. I had an affinity for castles, you see, and thought nothing of plopping myself down in the sand to play. Of course, only damp sand will do, and damp sand makes a hash out of ladies' stockings."

The chink of china told her he had rested his cup in the saucer. "I can see you, you know. Sitting in the sand, black hair plaited beneath a straw bonnet, and scoops of brown, wet sand marring your gown."

"I wanted to wear britches, but my governess swooned at the thought."

"Harridan, weren't you?"

"Indeed," she said with a smile. "Not a perfect young lady as I ought to have been." Her father had berated her for that, and her mother had pleaded with her to act as she should. But Lizzy had always been of an independent mind. Despite her father's numerous violent outbursts, she had refused to cower—or cow to his demands.

"How long have you been in England, Julian?"

"Only three months."

"Do you miss the East?"

She sensed him shrug, heard the way his toe seemed to tap against the carpet. "I was a small boy when my parents left England. I barely remember it. The East has been my home—it's what I know best. But I am growing to enjoy England, and London, especially," he said, his voice dropping, "since strolling with a lovely young woman last night."

Her smile, she knew, would appear modest and shy. She was flattered and embarrassed, having no experience with compliments. Her one and only dalliance had not been this way. It had been wild and frenzied, full of pent-up longing and animal needs. It had not been polite and flirtatious. The man had been the furthest thing from a civilized gentleman.

"You said your parents took you there when you were young. What was the lure for them?"

"My father was a diplomat. Second son, you know, so he needed a career. He loved travel, as did my mother, and different cultures had always been an obsession of his. So he packed us up and moved us to Cairo, where he was the highest ranking diplomat at the British Embassy. It was," Sheldon said with a fondness in his voice, "a childhood that every young boy should experience."

"You sound like someone I know," she said, unable to hide her frown. "All full of adventure and intrigue—but only for boys."

Julian laughed. "My apologies, Lizzy. I should have said 'a childhood any child—male or female—should experience.'"

"Only if you believe it."

There was a pause for a brief, tense second. Elizabeth could not regret what she had said. As a female, she had been left out of too many things in life, things that her younger brother had been entitled to, things he did with Black and Alynwick simply because he was the eldest male of the family. While Adrian had been encouraged to experience the world, she had been expected to stay home and learn how to play the piano and embroider cushions and plan elegant dinners. She hadn't wanted any of that.

She'd wanted to don a pair of britches and boots and a billowing white shirt and ride the deserts of the East on a black, glistening Arabian, just as Black and Alynwick and her brother had.

It was grossly unfair, the limitations that English society put upon the female sex.

"I have uncovered a truth about you, Elizabeth," Julian announced. He didn't sound at all perturbed by it. "You're a feminist."

"Not a feminist," she clarified, "but one who simply believes in equality. There are many females equally capable as any man—at least in heart, drive and intelligence."

"I do believe in equality, Elizabeth. For instance, I think it would be perfectly wonderful to have you accompany me to the East, riding beside me in the desert, meeting the tribes, tactfully negotiating peace and trade."

"You flatter me, my lord."

"No," he said, and she heard his cup being set on the table. "Not flattery. I'm not one for insincerity. It's true. A man could enjoy so many more facets of the world if he could bring along a partner who suited him in every way. There's only so much enjoyment to be had with your mates, after all."

Flushing, she picked up her biscuit and nibbled on it. Lizzy knew what he was referring to, and she knew she was blushing. Yet she could not deny she found his forward way of speaking pleasing. A woman would know where she stood with him. And she respected that. An open honesty.

"I have not had a conversation like this in... Well, I don't think I ever have," Sheldon commented. "At least not with a lady. It's rather refreshing."

Indeed it was. Their talk seemed so natural, flowing

from one topic to another, as if they had been friends for ages, not just new acquaintances. She had quite forgotten to be nervous.

"Now, then, I know you believe in the equality of the sexes, but what else, Elizabeth? Tell me something about yourself, something no one else knows."

She couldn't. That would shock him, and most likely turn him away. Elizabeth York was considered an angel among women. She couldn't very well admit that Lizzy York was a harlot who had risked all for a torrid love affair that had left her ruined and shattered—and disgraced. "I'm a bit of a bookie, I'm afraid. When I possessed sight, I had my nose in a book all the time. Since then, I have my companion, Maggie, read everything to me."

"I enjoy reading, as well. Although my skills at reading aloud are a tad rusty. I shall have to practice if I am to impress you at all while reading to you."

She glanced away, despite the fact she could not see him. He was saying all the right things, making her thoughts fly high and her body warm.

"When I was younger, I enjoyed anything about the Knights Templar," she blurted out. Oh, why had she said that? She was quite losing her head!

He paused, moved his chair closer. "Did you? I have a fondness for them, too. In Jerusalem, I studied them, and came across some evidence that they might possess the Holy Grail."

Why had she opened up this discussion? Lizzy asked herself. She must steer him away from it, and any mention of a chalice—or a possible connection to the house of York. The last thing they needed was for Julian to discover that her ancestor had been a Templar, and had been charged with the duty of shielding a chalice from the world.

"I found some rather interesting information on a golden chalice, and a group of Templars who reportedly were given sacred relics to protect," Sheldon was saying. "In fact, there were three of them, although there are stories that there were actually four. There is a considerable amount of evidence—and speculation—that they had a hand in building the Templar church."

"Really?" Her voice sounded strangled, and the biscuit she was nibbling on was turning to dust in her mouth.

"I've discovered a very strong connection to the three Templars and the Temple Church at the Inns of Court."

"How interesting." She had not heard that, about the church. Strange. She wondered if Sussex knew of the connection.

"In fact," Julian said, his voice filling with excitement, "I have a grant from the British Archaeological Society to investigate the crypts below the church. There's an array of underground tunnels and networks—so typical of the Templars. I mean to discover the secrets of that church, and the Knights who built it."

She hoped the horror did not show in her eyes. "You're an archaeologist, then?"

"I am. As the son of a second son, I never expected to come into a title. I needed a vocation, and living in Egypt, well, I was fascinated with archaeological digs, and their finds. I knew that delving into the earth and raising long-buried and forgotten relics was my future. My father died five years ago, and when my uncle died this past spring, the title came to me. I never expected it. And when I learned I was to be an earl, I never expected to be able to indulge in my love of archaeology.

But that's changed now. I'll begin working in the Templar church next week."

Her mind was reeling. Not only with the implications for the Brethren Guardians, if Julian were to stumble on something about them, but herself, as well. Perhaps the earl could help her with the discovery of the identity of the Veiled Lady. He could be her eyes. They could work together…. She knew there was nothing in the journal to implicate the Guardians. There was absolutely no mention of them or the relics in the book, which was a diary recounting Sinjin York's illicit affair with a woman who was his soul, or so he claimed.

"Elizabeth, would you like to come with me one day? I realize that most women would find it tedious and dirty, but something tells me you might be very keen to experience a dig. It's not the Egyptian desert, but it might be exciting all the same."

Biting her lip, Elizabeth had to stop herself from jumping up from the settee and flinging herself into Julian's arms. Oh, how dearly she wanted to join him. To learn of his discovery right alongside him. To be asked to help, and not told to stand back and stay safe. She had been sheltered and protected too long.

"I would love to, Julian."

"Fantastic! I shall make the arrangements, then. Do I need to ask Sussex for his permission?"

"No indeed. I am nearly thirty, and he's almost three years younger. I daresay I do not need his permission." She sounded rather indignant.

"All right, then. I shall send around a missive, outlining the details. Your companion will read it to you, will she?"

"That will be delightful. And of course Maggie will read your missive and pen my reply."

"Lizzy." He coughed, cleared his throat. "The dig is not until next week. I was hoping...that is to say, might I call on you before that?"

"I was hoping you would," she said, while her face flamed red. "I find your conversation vastly enjoyable."

"Just my conversation?"

There was an awkward pause, while Lizzy struggled to respond. She was out of her element here. She'd never entertained a gentleman, a potential suitor before. It had not been like this with her lover. They had known each other forever. It had been Alynwick, of course, who had swept her off her feet and claimed her body and soul. Alynwick whom she had spent a summer making passionate love with. Alynwick who had betrayed and hurt her. After that summer she'd stayed alone and apart.

The silence, she realized, was much too long. She needed to answer, but did not know how. Alynwick had taken the lead in their affair, and she had blindly followed. He had been the teacher and her the eager, apt pupil. She had never learned how to answer such a question as the one Sheldon was asking. And God above, she did not want to get it wrong. She wanted to do what was right, reply just as a lady of their social sphere would. Not as a woman who had spent a summer in shame.

"Elizabeth, you said that your friends frequently describe things to you."

"It's the only way I am able to see. I had the gift of sight for the first eighteen years of my life, so I am able to recall many things, and picture them if they're described to me."

"I see."

There was something in his voice that made her grow still, made her listen for any change in his breathing, or the fidgeting of a finger against his teacup, the tap of a toe....

"Forgive my impertinence, Elizabeth, but last night you informed me that you were the sort of woman who says what is on her mind."

"And so I did." She was nervous. Something was wrong. Perhaps she should have just admitted to him that it was more than their conversation she found enticing.

"I, too, prefer to speak plainly. I am open and honest, and feel that I must be that way with you."

And here it was. It was coming, and much sooner than she had anticipated, given how easily their conversation seemed to start and keep flowing.

"Did Lady Lucy describe my features to you?"

"What?" Caught by surprise, Elizabeth gave a little cough as her teacup wobbled precariously in the saucer. The air stirred, and the cup and saucer were efficiently removed and placed on the table. Rosie made a stirring noise, and it was only then that Lizzy realized Julian had picked up her pet and carefully placed her at the end of the settee, so that he could occupy the cushion next to her.

Her pulse fluttered at the base of her throat. She didn't know what to do, where to turn her head. It was rude, she knew, to not turn to him, but she could not. He was too close, and she did not know where to set her gaze.

"Elizabeth." He reached for her hands, which she'd folded in her lap. His finger brushed over her knuckles, making her face flame once more.

"Last night, when we were introduced, did your friend have the opportunity to describe me to you?"

Her brow furrowed in confusion. "Yes."

"And was her description...flattering?"

Tilting her head, Lizzy tried to figure out what he was asking. "She said you were tanned."

"I am. Regrettable in polite society, but unavoidable in Egypt and the Holy Land."

Smiling shyly, Elizabeth looked away. "Intriguing for a woman who has never been out of England."

Capturing her chin with his fingers, he turned her face so that she must be looking directly at him, for she felt his breath on her cheek.

"Did Lady Lucy make me out to be someone you might…fancy?"

Elizabeth could hardly believe he was speaking of such things. At her hesitation, he moved closer, reached for her other hand.

"Would you care to see for yourself?" he asked, and brought her palms up to his shoulders.

"What of you?" Her voice was much too husky and breathless. "What did you…when you saw…"

"I thought you the most beautiful woman I have ever seen, and I knew that I must be introduced to you."

"From across the Sumners' salon?" she asked, teasing him.

"No, from the street. I saw you months ago, walking with your brother, and I knew then that I would find a way to introduce myself to Sussex—and then you."

"So, you knew before last night that I was blind."

"Yes."

"And it did not deter you from asking me to stroll with you?"

"Deter me? After months of attempting to wear down your brother and soften him to the idea of introducing us? God, no," Julian murmured. "I am a man of eight and thirty, Elizabeth. I have put callow, youthful years behind me. I see the world differently, and how I see you… Well, it is with a man's eye, and a man's appreciation."

"The blindness is hereditary. My mother had it, as did

her mother. Thus far, the males of our family seem to be spared. But I couldn't guarantee—"

"Shh." Gripping her hands, he gave them a soft squeeze as they lay on his shoulders. "Elizabeth, you do not have to warn me away."

"I speak as I find," she said, her voice barely a whisper.

"Then speak of what you find when you look at me."

Reaching for her hands, Julian lifted them from his shoulders. Lizzy allowed her fingers to caress the strong column of his neck, then the hollow of his throat.

"Strong," she whispered as her fingers crept over his jaws. "Sculpted, like a statue. Angular. Masculine."

He swallowed. They were sitting so close that she could hear it.

"Your lips." Slowly she allowed the tips of her fingers to skim over the soft, supple flesh. "You have a mouth made to give pleasure."

"God, yes," he said, drawing her closer by wrapping his arm around her waist and pulling her gently toward him. They were both mature adults, her firmly on the shelf. There was no cause to be coy, and there was no reason for him not to let her know he appreciated her comments.

"They are not firm and grim, nor cold and cruel."

"No, not cruel," he answered, and allowed her further exploration, over his cheeks, his nose, to his eyes, which were fringed in long lashes. He allowed it, withstood it as he held her tight.

"I think I see a very handsome man," Lizzy announced. "Indeed, a man whom I could very well fancy."

CHAPTER SEVEN

IAIN PEERED THROUGH the narrow opening in the door. Blood curdling in his veins, he widened the crack a fraction more and took in the scene before him.

Elizabeth, nearly sitting upon Lord Sheldon's lap, his arm indecently wrapped around her waist as her generous bosom pressed forward, forcing the man to lift his chin or bury his face in her décolletage.

They were whispering to each other, Elizabeth's fingers tracing over Sheldon's face as she discovered him through her fingertips.

Iain had seen her do that before, but never had it been this intimate, this erotic. He was a bastard for watching, he knew. Even more of a bastard for what he was about to do.

He'd left Sussex and Black back in the duke's study, discussing the details of what they had discovered in Anastasia Lockwood's house—which amounted to next to nothing. He had excused himself, his friends barely looking up from the papers they studied as he left the room.

He hadn't been able to stay away from the salon, knowing that Sheldon was here, and that Elizabeth was "entertaining" him.

They looked so perfect together, and Iain was alarmed to see it. In his mind, it had always been himself he imagined sitting next to her. In her life there would be no other man. But he was a conceited and selfish fool to believe it. He knew she must hold nothing in her heart for him, nothing but a deep, abiding hurt and loathing. Had she done to him what he had done to her, he would be eaten alive with hatred.

She smiled, and Sheldon, still holding her wrists in his hands, pressed in, head angling, mouth lowering. A reckless jealousy engulfed Iain, blinding him to anything but his own needs—and the desire to have another chance to make Elizabeth his. It had been burning in his mind since last night, when Georgiana had made him realize the biggest regret of his life: walking away from Lizzy. He wouldn't do it again. Facing the prospect of dying, Iain had finally allowed himself to admit the truth. He wanted Elizabeth York. *Needed* her in his life. He would not give up until she was his.

"Ah, the tea. I wondered where to find it."

Elizabeth gasped in a most satisfying way, and Sheldon looked up in shock. Then the earl's eyes flashed with something akin to violence. "You," he said with a snarl.

"Yes. Me. What the devil are you doing here, Sheldon?"

"I was invited," he snapped. "And it seems you are not."

Iain smiled, but it was not one of warmth, but that of a man sizing up the enemy. In Sheldon's eyes, Iain saw flickering memories of what had transpired between them last night. Good. The man was remembering….

"My lord, please," Elizabeth chided. "Take the tea and leave."

"Why, when the entertainment seems to be so much more enjoyable in here?"

Sheldon lunged up from the settee, towering in an impressive rage. Something like admiration lit Iain's belly. This man deserved her if he was going to stand up and fight the person who had tried to choke the life out of him the previous evening. Unfortunately for Sheldon, Iain wasn't giving up his claim to her.

"What do you mean by coming here, my lord?" Elizabeth demanded.

"Am I not welcome?"

"You are not," she snapped. "You know very well where Sussex is, and he always has a well-stocked tea tray there."

"Perhaps it's not Sussex I'm searching for."

Elizabeth frowned, and Iain felt a measure of guilt about creating such a scene. But the monster inside him seemed to goad him on when he saw how Sheldon put a steady, reassuring hand on her shoulder.

"You're making the lady uncomfortable, Alynwick. I think you should leave."

"Me? Make the lady uncomfortable? I've known her for decades. Perhaps you, Sheldon, are making the lady uneasy. Perhaps *you* should leave."

"Ooh, damn you!" Elizabeth cried, and Sheldon didn't seem to flinch at her language, or her unladylike outburst. Bloody hell, he was perfect for the strong-willed Elizabeth. Plus he was far nicer than Iain, and much more a gentleman.

He really should leave them be. Elizabeth, after what he'd done to her, and what life had given her, really deserved some measure of peace and happiness. But damn it, he was certain she could find it with him. She had once before. He just needed to find a way to make her trust him. Make her see that he'd been wrong and stupid all those years ago.

"Julian, perhaps you should leave and let me manage this."

Iain arched an eyebrow. Things had progressed quickly

if they were using first names. The knowledge left a rather sour taste in his mouth.

The men exchanged gazes from across the room, and Iain had no difficulty deciphering Sheldon's silent glare. But he agreed with a brisk nod. Turning to her, Sheldon reached for her hand, carried it to his mouth and placed a kiss on her knuckles. "Thank you for the tea. I don't think I've ever enjoyed an afternoon more."

She blushed beautifully, the tops of her breasts turning a delicate pink. At one time Iain used to make her blush, used to make that silken flesh above her bodice flush like a pale pink rose, and now, to see another do so, made him want to smash something.

"I hope you will call again soon," she whispered.

"I was hoping this evening, if you will receive me?"

"I'd like that."

Another kiss on her knuckles, this one lingering, and then he said quietly, "Till this evening." With a glare in Iain's direction, he picked up his hat from the table and breezed past him, but not before he sent Iain a look of warning. It was not over between them. Far from it.

The door closed quietly behind the earl, and Lizzy wasted no time in berating Iain. "Get out. You had your say this morning, and you will be happy to know that I am now banished from contributing to your little group. You've had your way, and now there is nothing more to be said between us."

"I disagree. There is plenty more to be discussed, if the little scene I stumbled upon is any indication."

"How dare you!" she snapped.

"How dare I what? Interrupt a most improper kiss during an afternoon call?"

"As if you have any idea of what is proper. You're utterly indecent, Alynwick, and I will not have you coming into my salon and judging what is moral and immoral."

"You've only just met, or so Sussex tells me. Who knows what Sheldon's true motives are? He might be casting about for an heiress, and you've one of the richest dowries in the ton. Or perhaps he's looking to gain favor with Sussex, who is known for being rather kind and indulgent, using his powers of influence, persuasion and fortune to help those in need of a leg up."

"Oooh, you filthy beast," she railed, jumping up from the settee. "Of course there must be motivations behind his call! Of course, for what other reason could there be for him to come and visit a blind spinster?"

Iain winced. He had not meant it in such a way. He'd only meant to make her realize she knew nothing about the earl. "You know that's not what I was implying."

"Oh, yes, it is. Just because you came to me with motivations does not mean every man thinks the same way. Not every male on this earth uses people for his own selfish gains and pleasure."

That hurt. Like a hammer being swung against his chest. But he deserved nothing less. He *had* used her. Shamelessly.

"You live your life in darkness and sin," she declared. "You've forgotten human kindness and decency. You've forgotten what it is to care. You haven't been around in over a decade—"

"That most certainly is not true," he growled, but she dismissed his comments with a wave of her hand.

"You've floated in and out, coming and going as it pleases you. But you've not been present, Alynwick, not in any meaningful way, most certainly not in my life since that summer day you lifted my skirts, took your pleasure and left me alone in the grass."

A muscle in his jaw was twitching. He did not want to stand there and listen to her recriminations, no matter how accurate they were. He despised hearing them, hated himself for doing what he had all those years ago, but most of all, he loathed what he saw in Elizabeth's beautiful grey eyes.

"You have had no place in my life—by your design— for twelve years," she said through tight lips. "To enter this room now, when I am entertaining a gentleman, goes beyond the pale. You have no rights. No say. No reason to voice any concerns or objections about the matter. You had that right once, Iain," she huffed, her body now stiff with righteous anger, "but you didn't bother with it then, and you cannot now."

"I know." What else was there to say? What excuses could be made? If he truly wanted another chance with her he must be honest. To be the polar opposite of what he had been all these years. "You're right, Beth," he said, and closed his eyes, savouring her name. The name only he used. The name he whispered when he was on top of her, pleasuring her, driving himself deep inside her. He'd whispered it in her ear, "Beth…Beth…take more… all of me…" and when she did, when she'd widened her legs and pulled him in deeper, he had whispered, "My Beth," and had meant every word. She was his. Would always be his.

"What?" she demanded. Her expression was one of confusion, and he couldn't blame her for it.

"You're correct, of course. I have no right to think of you at all, do I? I shouldn't give a damn whom you invite to tea, whom you sit with on the settee, whom you blush for. But damn me, Elizabeth, I care. I care so much that I could have dragged him off that flowered atrocity and beaten him to a bloody pulp for just making you smile, when I've never given you cause to do anything but frown."

"What game is this?" she demanded. "Oh, how I despise not being able to see your face and the lies in your eyes."

"No lies. I swear."

"You swore you'd never hurt me, either. But that was soon forgotten, abandoned in the wake of the other lies you told, and the ones you forgot."

"I want another chance." He blurted that out, the words sounding almost desperate to his ear, the suave seduction he was famous for suddenly evaporating like smoke.

The air was heavy, taut, until she cried, "Absolutely not!"

There was no brooking the point. No hesitation in answering, either. Elizabeth was a woman who knew what she was about. She had convictions and morals, and stood for everything he wasn't.

He wasn't ready to give up, however. Nowhere near, he fumed as he took a handful of steps closer to her and reached for her. He'd taken his jacket off, leaving him in his waistcoat and shirtsleeves. His arm hurt like the devil, throbbing like an unrelenting demon. Scotch would have taken care of the pain rather nicely, but he'd had too much last night, and today... Well, today he had made plans to change. To be someone worthy of Elizabeth York and her attentions. He'd wanted this audience with her, to tell her that he meant for her to forgive him, and that he would do everything to earn that forgiveness. And he hadn't thought it would be sincere if Scotch was filling his veins.

Instead, he'd gritted his teeth against the pain while he and Black buried Anastasia, and again now, when Elizabeth's hands locked around his arms, squeezing his biceps so that she might steady herself. The wound was seeping again. He could feel the heat, the stickiness clinging to the fine linen sleeve.

"Don't struggle," he breathed, pulling her closer. "Don't—" But she pushed away an inch, her hand leaving his arm as she brought her fingers to her nose. The tips were covered in blood.

"No, don't!"

But it was too late. Her tongue came out, tentatively tasting. His blood coated her lip, and she frowned. Worry replaced anger, and something wickedly carnal and base stole over him. Iain swooped down, capturing her mouth with his.

His blood tainted her own sweet taste, and again the primal sensation swept through him as he wrapped his arm around her waist and pulled her voluptuous form against his unyielding one. She was soft and womanly, her belly cushioning him, embracing his hardening cock. He was breathless, but unable to stop the kiss to draw in air, for fear she would pull away.

She hadn't responded yet, but the animal in him would wait—didn't care, it seemed. All he could think about was Elizabeth, her fingers tipped in blood and her tongue coming out to taste them—taste him.

He was ravenous, his mouth twisting overtop hers, and when she gasped, he sank his tongue deep into her mouth, searching for hers, stealing her breath. There was no seduction, no rhythm or finesse to this kiss. It was uncoordinated, full of pent-up passion. Raw.

Kiss me! The words chanted over and over in his head, a merciless pleading. *Melt for me.... Sink with me to the carpet.*

Unable to resist, Iain moved his hand to her breast, cupped her, squeezed, groaned at the heavy weight of her in his palm, the taffeta-covered flesh spilling from between his fingers. He wanted that flesh in his mouth, wanted to lift her breast to his lips, suckle her voraciously. Wanted to make her tremble and cry out—come with only his mouth on her luscious breasts.

"Stop," she cried, pulling away.

"Nay, I canna do it," he groaned, wincing as he heard his brogue, thick and hard as he buried his mouth in her neck and nuzzled her fragrant skin with his lips. His fingers were soothing her breast, where he prayed he had not gripped her too hard. "Doona ask me to."

"You're bleeding."

"It's no bother," he growled, and ducked his head, searching once more for her mouth.

"Iain, for God's sake, *stop!*"

If he hadn't already decided to turn over a new leaf, he would have pressed on, heedless of her protests. He would have kissed her until she forgot she was protesting. But this wasn't the way to win Elizabeth back. In fact, it had never been the way to win her in the first place, but that was the method he had used. He'd overpowered her with a seductive onslaught that an innocent like her could never fight against.

Forcing himself to stop, he stood still, breathless as Elizabeth once more brushed her fingers over the sleeve of his left arm. "From last night, I assume?"

"Aye."

"I cannot say I'm happy to hear you were wounded, but really, if you'd quit getting into the beds of married women, you wouldn't find yourself in these predicaments."

"What recourse am I left with when the one bed I want is not open to me?"

"Now you're just being ridiculous. You're like a child

with a toy. You've seen someone express interest in me and now you want to play, to see if the toy is really that interesting, or if it should be thrown to the back of the wardrobe. And you should know, Iain, that I'm not interested in playing with you. Now, let's find someone to look at your arm. Did Sutherland mend this for you? Perhaps you should have had a proper physician sew you up."

She was rambling as she led him from the salon. Before they reached the door, Iain pulled her to a stop.

"You're not a toy, Beth. You're the best gift I've ever been given, and I didn't take care of you like I should have. But I will. You'll see. You'll come back to me and I will unwrap you with such care that you will never break again."

"You've lost too much blood if you think I will ever allow anything like that to ever happen again. What is done is done. It's a part of the past. Now, then, let's get you to someone who can actually see what the devil is going on with your arm. As much as I once wished you dead, I cannot say that I still desire it, at least not here, today, bleeding on the carpet in my favourite room."

His voice softened, and he brushed back the loose strands of her hair that had fallen during their kiss. "Well, then, that's a start, isn't it, my Beth?"

THE WIND PICKED UP, riffling through Iain's hair. The November day had turned to twilight, the forthcoming winter making its presence known by the bite of the breeze and the scent of coldness in the air. He should be back home, in his study, indulging in a glass of Scotch while seated beside a blazing fire laid neatly in the hearth. But his curiosity and instincts had gotten the better of him, and instead of staying home tonight and nursing his aching shoulder, he found himself here.

Iain hadn't been able to help himself. The urge to discover everything he could about Sheldon, and his plans for Elizabeth, had been gnawing at him all afternoon, and into the evening. Try as he might, he could not erase the image of her seated beside the earl, her gentle fingers traversing the man's face. They had forged a connection that afternoon, and it terrified him. What if he was too late? What if Elizabeth had deep and abiding feelings for the earl?

No, the word whispered in his mind. He would not think that way. Not allow it. He couldn't—*wouldn't*—lose her. And so he had waited in an unmarked hackney outside of Sheldon's town house, and watched. And waited. Only to find himself following the earl, who had only newly arrived in England. Iain wanted to know this man's secrets. Knew he had them. *Every* man had some sort of secret or another he wished to hide.

While Sussex and Black were discussing the evening's plans for attending the Adelphi Theatre in search of Orpheus, Iain was supposed to be seducing Lady Larabie, and discovering what she knew of the mysterious enemy they were trying to find. But Georgiana was the furthest thing from his mind tonight. So, too, was any business he might have a duty to perform on behalf of his friends. Orpheus and the Brethren Guardians could wait. Discovering what the Earl of Sheldon was up to could not.

Burying his chin in the collar of his woollen greatcoat, Iain watched from the shadows as the Earl of Sheldon gambolled up the stone steps of the British Museum, carrying a satchel. It was getting on in the evening—nearly eight. Well past closing time. But one light blazed softly in an east-facing window, indicating that someone was still inside. A caretaker, perhaps. But if it was only a custodian, what was the earl up to, climbing the steps?

What are you about? Iain silently questioned as he watched the man. *Who are you?*

Upon Sheldon's approach, the double doors opened only enough to permit the earl to slide through. With a cautious look around, the man behind the door peered left and right before closing it softly.

Iain had no idea who had opened the door to Sheldon, but he did know one thing: the earl needed to be watched. There was something about him that pulled at Iain's gut. He had not survived this long without listening to his infallible sense for trouble.

"Shall I go then, my lord, and search his place?"

Sutherland. What would Iain do without the man? He was far more use to him as a spy than as a valet. There was no job Sutherland wouldn't do for him. In fact, just that afternoon, Iain had had his valet staked out at the House of Orpheus, the place where their nemesis appeared like a damn magi, and disappeared just as quickly. Iain had wanted to know whether the infamous Lady Larabie had come for a visit. She had not, but someone else had. Nigel Lasseter.

The man had meant nothing to Iain, but he'd stored the information away, to be pulled out at a later time. Now, it seemed, was the time. Nigel Lasseter had funded a research trip to the Holy City for one of the medieval museum curators, a Mr. Wendell Knighton—one-time suitor of one Isabella Fairmont, now Lady Black.

Knighton had somehow discovered the legend of the Brethren Guardians, and also the fact that the Guardians protected three relics fabled to hold secrets to a power no mortal should possess—a pendant, a chalice and a scroll. Knighton had stolen the pendant from Black and the chalice from Sussex, then had been mysteriously murdered—shot to death on the steps of the Masonic

Lodge. Iain and the others had found the relics and hidden them away once again. But they did not learn how Knighton had discovered that the fable of the Guardians and the relics was true.

The man they called Orpheus was involved in Knighton's murder and, they suspected, was the person who had aided Knighton in discovering the artefacts. Orpheus's identity was a puzzling, frustrating secret. The man knew too much about the Guardians, too much about Sussex and his father, and the mistress the old duke had kept for years. Enough to murder Anastasia in cold blood. But who he was, and how he was connected to all this, eluded them. The man was cunning, well protected and, it seemed, beyond the reach of Iain and his cohorts.

There had at one time, Iain knew, been a fourth Templar in the Brethren Guardians, but he had been betrayed by the other three, his body left on the desert sands in the East. Could it be possible that someone wanted them to believe this Orpheus was a descendant of the fourth Templar? Did Iain even believe it, or was the discovery of the Brethren Guardians just lucky happenstance? Was there something housed within the museum that contained the Brethren legend? Had Nigel Lasseter discovered it? Had someone else?

It was an unsettling thought, to have such a savvy, knowledgeable snake in their midst who could confound three of the most suspicious and cunning minds in England.

What they needed was more information. Something was missing—some nefarious piece of the puzzle that was the glue to all the other pieces. But what was it? Iain had no idea. He only knew that the three relics were safe, and in their possession. He had a link to Orpheus through Georgiana, a link he must use before Orpheus slipped once more beyond their reach, and God forbid, harmed one of them or their loved ones.

Iain could not help but draw a line connecting Sheldon's after-hours visit to the museum and knowledge of the Holy Land with the fact that Nigel Lasseter had once paid for an expedition to Jerusalem. Lasseter obviously had interest in Templar lore and crusader artefacts. He also frequented the House of Orpheus. The logical conclusion was that the common denominator in this mess was Nigel Lasseter—and now, perhaps, the Earl of Sheldon. It was the only thing Iain had to go on at the moment.

He thought of Sheldon, who was far too interested in Elizabeth for his peace of mind. Now that his suspicions were aroused, Iain knew he couldn't afford to let the man out of his sight.

"Well, my lord," Sutherland asked again, while cupping his hands together and blowing his hot breath into them. "What will it be? Want me on my way before the gent leaves the museum, and I'll report back to you?"

"No," Iain murmured, still watching the facade of the museum, and the flickering light in the window. "I'll search his house."

"I don't mind. I've a knack for it."

"No, my friend. I'll do it. It's…personal."

Sutherland's eyes suddenly lit with understanding. "So I was right. This has nothing to do with that hussy yer bedding."

"How do you know?" And he wasn't bedding the hussy—not anymore. Not after last night, and the cold, sick feeling he'd had upon seeing Georgiana. He had finally allowed himself to admit the truth—that he loved Elizabeth and wanted her back. It was the only thing he seemed able to focus on at the moment.

"Because you would no' stick your neck out for the likes of her, or others of her kind. You wouldn't say it's personal. What you have with her is the coldest, most impersonal thing I've ever seen."

"You talk too much, Sutherland."

"You only say that when I've pricked a nerve. It's that lovely of yours, isn't it? Somehow she's involved."

"You don't know what you're talking about."

"I don't, eh? Well, I know what I see, and it's that protective gleam in your coldhearted gaze. I saw it only the once, the night I came across you and the enchanting Elizabeth York going at it like animals. You jumped up, covered her with yer plaid, and when you turned back to me, you had the very same look in your eyes as you do now."

Iain turned to his valet. "Oh? And what look would that be?"

"The one that says 'I'll rip yer bollocks from ye and stuff 'em down yer throat if ye even look at her, or think ta touch her.'"

Closing his eyes, Iain slowly turned his attention back to the museum. Sutherland was not done talking, however.

"He wants her, does he?" his servant asked. "Does the gent know he is about to be torn to pieces by the mad marquis for daring to take something that belongs to him?"

"I only want to learn his secrets."

Sutherland snorted. "You want to tear him limb from limb, then show up at the lovely's house and display for her what you've done. After which you'll carry her off to her bedchamber like some feral animal marking a mate." The valet smiled. "Like any Highlander worth his mettle would do. Stake your claim on the lass, then, my lord. You're well overdue."

"Is there anything I can't hide from you, Sutherland?" He sighed in irritation.

"Aye, you can. Up until now, you hid your heart. I've been wondering all these years if you even had one. Now, I see it's lain fallow in your chest, and has just begun to beat again."

Indeed, it had. He had never wanted to risk it, not after what he had done to Elizabeth all those years ago. He hadn't wanted to pull the damn organ from the depths he had buried it, lest it hurt like it had when he had turned his back on the only woman he'd loved. The only woman he would ever love.

Now that it had begun to beat again, Iain finally accepted the fact that every beat was for Elizabeth.

"Watch him," he ordered. "We'll meet back at the house, and you can tell me every move the bastard makes. I want to know who he leaves with, how long he stays there. If he carries anything out, or if he makes another stop. I want to know *everything,* Sutherland."

"Aye, I know how all this works. Off you go, me laird, and wreak your hell upon him."

Oh, yes, the Earl of Sheldon would know the meaning of hell and pain when Iain was done with him.

THROUGH SHIFTING SHADOWS and weak light, Orpheus studied his accomplice. He was perturbed. There was a flaw in his plan, one he had not anticipated, and one that could potentially cause him a great deal of trouble. This newest development made him want to lash out and choke the life out of someone—anyone.

His web was unraveling, but like a diligent spider, he

would reinforce the weakness and continue weaving, preparing the silken threads to capture his enemies.

"Have Alynwick tracked," he snarled as he lifted the flap of the blind just enough so he could see out the window, without being seen himself. "Find out what he knows. What connection he has put together. And what nuisance he'll be with the girl."

"As you wish, my lord."

"And don't pander to me in that snivelling way of yours," he snarled, baring his teeth. "I'm in no mood for it. Keep him in your sights at all times, or you'll pay dearly for failing me, do you understand?"

"Of course. Indeed, you make yourself very clear, as always."

"Always was a slippery, conniving bastard," he muttered. "Never trust a Scot, even if they give the appearance they're nothing but lecherous drunkards. Always had it in him," he whispered, more to himself than anyone. "I saw it that night, those dark eyes looking up, hatred and spite blazing in their depths. I knew then that he would not be complacent until the final blow killed him. And even then he'd spit in your face before tumbling to hell."

"I know what will do the job," his accomplice murmured. "I know the blow that will kill him, and keep him from destroying our plans."

"Then by all means use it."

"Of course."

He was not relieved. Not one bit. There was still another factor he had not considered. One misstep and it would be ruined. Goddamn it, he had thought the man dead, never to haunt him again. But he'd been wrong, the man was alive.

Either that, or he was staring into the face of a ghost. One of many who no doubt would plague his existence until he left this plane for the next.

CHAPTER EIGHT

IT WAS DARK IN THE STUDY, the curtains drawn, whether to keep out the drafts or to hide something, Iain didn't know. It had been remarkably easy to find his way into Sheldon's town house, an ancient monstrosity in the heart of Cavendish Square. The windows had the original Georgian locks that were child's play to pick. By the look of it, the previous earls of Sheldon hadn't given a damn about thievery. By all accounts, neither did the current one, or he would have had every lock on every window replaced.

A growl outside the study door alerted Iain to the fact he was not exactly alone. He wondered what sort of beast was in the hall, snarling at the door. It wouldn't do for the animal to alert a footman. But, then, the master was out, and when the master was out, the staff played games. Iain knew that from firsthand experience. He'd caught his maids with the footmen more times than he cared to remember.

The growl was followed by a whimper, and the rhythmic slapping of a tail hitting the floor. No guard dog that was, for certain. Still, the damn thing was going to attract unwanted attention, and Iain had no desire to be caught standing in the middle of Sheldon's study by the butler.

On the desk, an oil lamp was burning low. He tsked... neglectful servants. Probably meant to shut it off, but in their haste to partake of the time the master was out, were too hasty in their tasks, and only turned it down.

Or perhaps the master himself had been in a hurry. Either way, it was fortuitous for Iain. No time wasted fumbling with matches.

Turning the lamp up just enough to chase away the shadows, he slowly looked around the study. It was inordinately neat and tidy, with nothing cluttering the surface of the desk. Leather-bound books filled the bookcases, while glistening dark walnut walls gave a nod to the ancient aristocrats who peered down soberly from their portraits. On the surface the room looked like many other male sanctuaries he had been in, but there was something here that bothered him. It was too damn neat. No man, gentleman or no, was this tidy.

Sheldon was hiding something. There could be no other conclusion. It was far easier to detect if something was askew or missing if everything was scrupulously kept, and the clutter normally acquired in a gentleman's study was nonexistent.

It also made it much easier to search.

Deciding to make use of the small time he had, Iain began quietly opening the desk drawers. Nothing other than loose sheaves of paper, writing instruments, blotter and inkwell, sealing wax and a gold seal bearing the coat of arms of the earls of Sheldon were to be found. With a muttered oath, he turned to the bookcases, pulling out tomes and peering behind. *Nothing.*

It was apparent that everything in the room was from the previous earl. There was nothing intimate or personal belonging to Sheldon, giving away no clues, nor any impression of the man.

The tidiness, however, still struck home. It was almost as though Sheldon was an officer on campaign, with all his belongings tucked neatly away in a tent measuring no more than half the size of this room. Not even a cuff link or the burnt end of a cheroot in an ashtray was present. Not even a decanter of Scotch or brandy, Iain thought mulishly. He could use a drink to settle the mounting frustrations he felt as his gaze roved over the walls and the hearth.

A silently ticking pendulum clock perched on the mantel was the only decoration in the room. It was an exquisite piece, a campaign piece, Iain noted as he lifted it up and studied it. The kind of piece that was an heirloom, passed down from father to son.

Tipping it over, Iain studied the bottom, ran his finger over an uneven edge, and tripped a false panel, only to see a shadow inside.

The sound of the front door opening and slamming shut, along with the dog's wild barking, informed him he had run out of time. Replacing the bottom, he set the clock back on the mantel, then extinguished the lamp. Iain dashed to the window and quickly jumped out, shutting the pane mere seconds before the earl sauntered into the room. Peering back through the glass, he saw Sheldon stop in the middle of the study, frozen, then look carefully around the room and tilt his head as if sniffing the air.

The dog was running circles around him, jumping and barking, begging for attention. Sheldon reached out and scratched the animal behind the ears, his gaze landing directly on the clock, the gold pendulum swaying back and forth. The satchel he wore slung over his shoulder was slipped off and placed haphazardly atop the desk. The canvas flap opened, allowing parchment rolls to spill out of the bag.

Etchings... Iain squinted, trying to make out the drawings. Elevations of some sort, he thought, and his eyes widened as he saw the Templar cross in the corner of one, and beside it, the Cross Lorraine—a cross with an

extra vertical bar, which had always been a heraldic sign
to mark the dukes of Lorraine. It was also used within
Freemasonry to denote a member's degrees.

Fascinating. Iain could not drag his gaze from the
symbols that seemed to entwine with his and the other
Brethrens' past. This could be no coincidence.

Taking brisk steps, Sheldon crossed the room to the
hearth, placed his hands on the clock and adjusted the
angle of it, his brows furrowed. Perplexed, thinking…

Sheldon knew. It was as if Iain could hear him say
Someone has been in this room....

The earl moved to the window, and Iain pressed back
against the redbrick, blending into the night that surrounded him. He was in the garden, with little moonlight.
Sheldon would not be able to see him. But that didn't stop
the earl from standing at the window for an inordinately
long time, gazing out into the vast darkness. Finally, he
moved back, pulled the curtains closed. It was then that
Iain walked down the street to the waiting hackney.

"Sussex House," he demanded. He had a blazing desire to check on Elizabeth, and to fill Sussex and Black
in on his discoveries.

ONE, TWO, THREE, one, two, three… Cautiously, Lizzy
made her way about the salon in slow steps, her arms
not outstretched, searching for danger, as they should be,
but curved, as if preparing to go around someone's shoulders. Not just someone's, she thought while she moved,
keeping time in her head, but Lord Sheldon's.

It had been years—more than a decade, she reminded
herself—since she'd waltzed. She hadn't dared to attempt
it. But something had propelled her to do so this evening.

One, two, three, one, two, three… Yes, the rhythm was
coming back, and she sensed that she was far enough

away from any objects that might impede this imaginary dance.

One, two, three... It was almost automatic now, and with the added protection of being in Sheldon's arms, well, there was nothing stopping her from accepting his proposal to dance, if one should ever come. This proved it—she was capable of moving through the dark, able to be led, and to trust that the one leading her would not send her into danger.

Smiling, she picked up the pace, gliding as if she were clasped in a pair of strong arms, being whisked around a ballroom. She twirled, giving it a go, then sensed, too late, that she had misjudged her whereabouts in the room, and her proximity to the hearth.

The loud crash of the scuttle and poker smashing against the marble hearth reverberated around the room with such a clatter that she knew everyone in the house would hear it. Stopping, she tried to reach for the rest of the tumbling objects, but promptly tripped over the hem of her gown, sending herself careening forward into what she prayed was not the marble pillar of the hearth.

After landing with a thud, her hands skidded along the smooth floor, her body following, only to be stopped by the impact of her forehead against the immovable pillar.

If she could see, she knew her vision would be swimming. Stars would be bursting behind her eyes. They were there, she knew; she just couldn't see them. But she could sense the immediate vertigo, the nausea rise up and the pain of her head—not to mention her damaged pride.

Stupid, stupid fool, she thought as tears stung her eyes. What nonsense was she trying to prove—and to whom?

"Beth!"

She groaned when the door was flung open against

the wall, making her already pounding head throb more painfully.

"Good Christ," said a voice she did not want to hear. "What the devil happened?"

"Go away," she moaned as she brushed her hand across her skull and immediately felt a sticky warmth on her fingers. "Just leave me be."

"Like hell," Alynwick grunted, and she felt him lean over her, the scent of his body burning her nose, the heat from his chest comforting. Immediately she struggled against it as she felt her skirts being brushed aside. "Christ," he whispered, his voice unsteady, "your gown was only inches from the fire." He shuddered. "You could have gone up in flames."

She pictured it, her prone body igniting, the satin of her evening gown lighting up as fire snaked along her body. And all because she'd wanted to see if she could waltz. Vain, silly creature. So very greatly in need of his protection. Even though she would not thank him for it.

"Hold still," he snapped, and she heard him reach into his jacket pocket for a handkerchief, then delicately brush loose strands of hair away from her brow. "You're bleeding," he murmured. "Let me have a look."

"Get. Out!" she enunciated in a clipped tone.

"Are you dizzy?" he demanded. "Can you sit up?"

"I can manage myself, thank you," she muttered as she struggled to sit upright. Moving her shoulders caused her to wince and hiss in discomfort. His hand, so warm and large, landed between her shoulder blades, supporting her.

"Let me look," he repeated.

"Can't you understand you are not wanted here?"

"Settle your feathers," he whispered against her ear. "There is no need to act all pricklish. You're injured."

"I'm mortified! Can you not allow me to wallow in my own stupidity in peace?" she said, her bravado deflated.

"I'll not leave you alone."

"Wonderful. So I am to endure further mortification in your presence, is that it? You *are* a devil, Alynwick," she snapped.

Her head hurt and her body ached. Her pride, well, it was damn near decimated. Bad enough she had fallen, but to be rescued by Iain, to know he saw her in such an unglamorous position, sprawled out on the floor, was more than degrading. It was appalling, not to mention utterly unacceptable.

"What the devil were you doing, and so close to the hearth?"

"Just help me up."

He did as she commanded, but he did not release her. Instead he held her, steadied her, not by the arms, but by wrapping his arms around her waist and holding her close.

"Lady Elizabeth?"

She groaned again. Maggie. And she would discover her wrapped in Alynwick's lascivious arms.

"Your mistress has fallen. Summon the doctor."

"Right away, my lord."

Elizabeth could envision Maggie bobbing a curtsey and rushing to do his bidding. "No!" she cried, trying to shake off his hold. "I'm fine."

"You're bleeding, miss," Maggie said worriedly.

"It's only superficial. I just need a wet cloth."

Silence. She could imagine that there were shared looks between her companion and Alynwick, and she hated that she couldn't see them, could not tell what transpired.

"Very well," Iain muttered. "If you would be so good,

Maggie, as to get me some supplies, I shall tend to the lady in lieu of the physician."

Elizabeth gasped in outrage at his suggestion, but found herself moved effortlessly to a settee, and lowered gently onto its cushions.

"I shall accept the doctor." She sniffed, trying to find her shield and pride so she could brandish both before him. But it was a useless endeavour, for they were both still lying on the marble floor where she had fallen.

"Too late," he said as he took the cushion beside her. She was sitting upright, and felt a little bilious. She'd give anything to lie down, but would not give the maddening Iain a chance to be smug—and correct. "Your companion has already left the room, and now there is no one else here but me. Lucifer."

She almost smiled at that quip. Almost.

"Why are you here at this time of night? Shouldn't you be out doing something wanton and depraved?"

"How do you know that I haven't come here for that express purpose?" he teased.

Sucking in her breath, Elizabeth tried to ignore him. "Sussex is not in."

"You don't think I've come here tonight to be wanton and depraved with Sussex, do you? My, how much of a degenerate you think me."

He was teasing. She heard the laughter in his words, in the silky voice that seemed to slide along her flesh.

"I think you a *proliferate* degenerate."

"Yes. I know." There was no further teasing in his voice. The light banter had been replaced with something that sounded rather akin to pain. But for one to feel pain, one must have a heart, a conscience, and Iain possessed neither.

"I can't tell you where my brother has gone. You suggested that I be kept out of Brethren affairs, and Sussex has lost his mind, believing you correct. But I was told that he made a hasty escape after learning that Lucy had not been home since this morning. I do hope nothing has happened to her, especially after the events of today."

"I am sure she is well. Sussex will find her."

"He's been gone for hours. Took Black and Isabella with him. I suspect he's gone to the House of Orpheus, but again, he would not tell me. He only said he would return soon."

"It's a good thing, then, that I came when I did. You should not be alone. Now, come closer and let me see you," he demanded.

"You're not touching me," she announced. "Besides, I'm perfectly fine. And it's unseemly for you to be visiting in the evening when my brother is out."

"And why is that?" he murmured.

"You know perfectly well why. It's the evening, Alynwick. You know what people will think if it gets out that you have been over in the evening while my brother is not at home."

"That we are having sex, is that it? You fool yourself, Beth, or perhaps you forget the fact that one can fuck quite adequately in the daylight during a polite morning call."

She blushed at his crass language, and he laughed.

"Morning or evening. Either way, people will wonder what it is I am doing here. It's the way of the ton."

"Oh, your language," she muttered, but winced as the pain in her head worsened. "You try my patience to no end." *And desolate my heart.*

To hear what occurred between them debased to something done in a brothel made her want to retch.

With an annoyed-sounding sigh, he reached for her,

pulled her closer while ignoring her gasp and struggles, and tilted her head, to what she perceived was the light from an oil lamp, for she felt the flickering heat on her cheek, smelled the scent of the burning oil.

"You were waltzing."

The words, spoken so softly, stopped her cold. "You were spying on me!" she accused in outrage, but with typical Alynwick indifference he did not seem at all chagrined to be caught intruding upon her privacy.

"For whose arms were you risking life and limb?"

"None of your concern."

She felt him brush up against her, then dab at her brow with his handkerchief, which was covered in his scent, and did nothing but stir her unease.

"You're already starting to bruise. I wish I could have arrived sooner, caught you before you fell."

"I wish you had not been spying in the first place!" Straightening her spine, she winced in pain before she could check the emotion. Alynwick was already leaning back, his deft fingers trailing across the skin that was revealed by the neck of her gown.

"You're bleeding here, too—and bruised. Let me see."

"I think you have seen enough for one day, my lord. I thank you for picking me up off the ground. Now if you would be so kind as to take your leave, Maggie can see to my war wounds."

"I have no other appointments for the evening. I am happy to linger and assist you."

"Well, I do have appointments," she growled. "Now take yourself off."

"Ah," he said, and there was a wealth of knowledge in that one word. "Shelly must be coming by. An evening call? How sordid, Elizabeth."

"Lord Sheldon," she corrected. "And yes, he is. And I

will die ten thousand deaths if he arrives and I am looking like this."

"Looking like what?" he murmured silkily as he tugged a few strands of hair that were already falling from her coiffure. "Like you have been well and truly tumbled?"

"Like I have tripped and fallen like a blind fool," she snapped, pulling away from him.

"Never a fool, Beth," he said, and she hated—and adored—the way he said her name. "Shall I take you in my arms and waltz with you?"

"Certainly not."

"Shall I just take you in my arms, then?"

"I am not a child, my lord."

"I know. One look at your body and no man could think you a child. But still, I have the mad urge to kiss away your pain and make you feel better. I could, you know." His voice was a deep rumble as his finger traced her collarbone. "I could take away the pain, replace the ache with another sort of ache, a thrumming heaviness, one of yearning deep in your core." His hand slowly glided down, to where her breasts were pushed high beneath her bodice. Sinking one finger into the cleft, he slowly moved it up and down, intimating the carnal act she remembered all too easily.

"I could bend you back and pleasure you, and you wouldn't even feel the scrapes between your shoulders as you lay against the settee, because you would be too far gone with the feel of my mouth and lips tasting you… parting you." With his thick finger he did just that, parted her breasts, creating a space for his tongue to flick and lave and circle, intimating another act he had performed on her once so long ago. He had a beautiful mouth, a skilled tongue that shocked yet excited her. She had been mortified by what he had done, but not enough to make him stop. No, she had only opened wider to him, and lowered her hand to his hair, so she could feel the movement of his head against her.

Oh, God, she was breathing too fast, her breasts responding to his touch, her body liquefying with the silky, tempting voice of the devil. "I know how it will be—how I will find you beneath the heavy layers of your skirts. So wet, Beth, thick and drenched and ready for me to slide inside and make you moan with the pain and pleasure of a climax that I will hold just out of your reach, until," he murmured, "you call my name and ask me to make you come."

She was already wet, her breasts heaving at the provocative words. In truth, she was nearly there, and he knew it, felt his knowing smile against the crest of her breast. She frowned, wished she could glare at the man. "You are positively indecent and insufferably arrogant."

"I know, and secretly you love it, I think."

"There is nothing secret I feel for you."

He was about to respond when providence saved her. Maggie had arrived, making a great fuss as she carried her ointments and potions into the room. Elizabeth heard the thump of linen hit the table. Miraculously, she was able to grab hold of her riotous emotions and hide them behind a steady voice.

"Goodness, we're not performing surgery, Maggie. It is nothing but a simple cut."

"It's begun to drip down your forehead."

Immediately she raised her hand to her head, and only managed to smear it more. "It's drying."

What a sight she must look. And in front of Iain Sinclair, who no doubt was dressed impeccably and looking far too handsome, while smiling smugly as he thought

how easily her body capitulated to his words of seduction. It was enough to make a very composed woman
want to scream and pull at her hair.

"Allow me."

There was nothing else to be done but to sit quietly and
permit Iain to fix the mess she had made, especially with
Maggie looking on. She heard the cloth being dunked
in the water, the drops raining back into the bowl as it
was wrung out.

"Sit back, Elizabeth," he commanded, "and rest your
head against the settee."

She did as he asked, only because she could not possibly manage herself, and to have him sitting there watching her muddle through the painstaking operation would
be too much to bear. So she permitted herself to lean
back, and allowed him to bend over her and hold the
cloth against her forehead.

"There's ointment here, my lord. A soothing mint
salve. I see both her palms are reddened and scraped.
They'll need ointment, too."

Contrary as she was, Lizzy curled her fingers, con-
cealing her palms. She needn't have bothered, for he left
the cloth on her head and began to pry her fingers loose
slowly, one by one, until both her palms were revealed
and his finger was grazing the tender flesh.

"Friction burn," he murmured. "You must have slid
on the carpet before landing on the marble."

She burned. But it had nothing to do with the carpet,
and everything to do with the way his finger slowly caressed her palm, making intricate little strokes, erotic
circles that started out wide and narrowed into soft little
brushes of his fingertips. He had done the same movement before, but it had not been her palm he had stroked
so expertly, but the pale pink of her areola, stopping only

when he had reached her hardened nipple. She could not fight back the memory or the way her body recalled that illicit pleasure. Did he remember that afternoon, lying beside the brook in the long grass? Did he remember how he had picked up a green reed and watched avidly as he teased the tip of her nipple with the end of it? Good God, she could not forget it, or what had followed!

The ringing of the doorbell made her jump. The cloth fell from her head and onto her bosom with a sloppy wet sound, while her fingers wrapped reflexively around Iain's hand.

"Oh, God," she groaned. "What time is it, Maggie?"

"I will see to it, miss," her companion answered. "You just repair yourself here and I shall set things to right out there."

"I suppose it could be worse," Elizabeth muttered, forgetting she was not alone. "He could have been here when I was lying on the floor, splayed out like a felled deer."

Iain's laugh as he took the cloth and tossed it into the basin did nothing to make her feel better. "Indeed he could have, but then he would have been gifted with the sight of your bottom in the air, and the hem of your gown up around your knees. No man should gain that gift so easily."

She snorted. *He* had. And much easier than that, she reminded herself.

"Your forehead has stopped bleeding," he mumbled as he dabbed her brow once more. "Although it's bruised. You might even have a black eye from it."

"Lovely. I shall tell Maggie to inform my caller that I am indisposed."

"Coward."

She went rigid on the settee. She knew he watched

her, his dark eyes scrutinizing her face. "I am no coward," she growled back.

"You never were before," he challenged. "So why now?"

"Because my forehead is cut, my eye black and no doubt my gown is dirty. It is hardly the way a woman wants to present herself to...to..."

"Her lover?"

Elizabeth swallowed, bristling at the word, uttered in Iain's velvet voice. "Caller," she clarified.

"Little coward," he whispered once more, but this time he said it as he raised her hand to his mouth.

"I am not!" she hissed as she felt him press a kiss into the tender flesh of her palm, then followed it with the supple glide of his tongue.

"Yes, you are. You try to wish for what awaits you outside this room, when you are really wanting what I whispered to you—what we could do here if you allowed me to lay you back and press my body into yours, to put my lips to all those secret places I want to taste, those places you want to hold me to. But you're too afraid, too cowardly to admit that you wanted it a few minutes ago—wanted it so desperately. And you still do."

"How dare you!" She snatched back her hand, but Iain leaned forward and recaptured it. This time when he touched her, it was not with his lips or his tongue, but with the soothing salve Maggie had brought.

"I do, indeed, dare much. But you, Elizabeth, are worth it."

"Such flattery, Alynwick. I have heard it before from you, and have learned it is meaningless. I don't want to talk like this. I don't want you speaking to me in such a fashion."

He shrugged. She felt the movement beside her. "All

right, then, we shall discuss something else—for now. Why *were* you practicing the waltz?"

She sighed, feeling defeated. "Because I thought he might one day ask me to dance, and I wanted to make certain that I could manage it without doing something like this—only in front of a couple hundred peers."

"Do you not trust him to protect you?"

"Of course," she said indignantly.

"No, you don't. Else you would not have tried this stunt by yourself."

"Oh, do cease talking," she barked, hating how he so easily consumed her thoughts and strength. "And finish quickly."

"If me finishing quickly makes your visit to him all the more precipitous, then you may be assured that I shall take my own damn time."

"Why do you toy with me?" she demanded. "Why, when you come here, can you not leave me be?"

His fingers stilled against her palm for the briefest second before he reached for her, trailed his thumb along her jaw, tipping her head until she knew her sightless eyes were settled on his face. She closed her lids, tried to turn away, but he held her still.

"Don't look away," he whispered, and there was such anguish in those words that she opened her eyelids—still unable to see—and wished she could barter her soul for the chance to see him looking at her once more. "I can't see you, you know that."

"Yes, you can. You can see me sitting here with you, on this settee, our knees touching, my fingers on your pale skin. You can imagine my expression—it's one of horror, and terror, because I am thinking of you quitting this room, and me, and walking to him. I canna bear it,

Beth," he groaned. "Everything inside me screams that it's wrong."

"It isn't," she said, trying to keep her voice from trembling. "The only thing that is wrong is being alone in this room with you. It was wrong when I allowed you in all those years ago. It still is wrong."

"Nothing is wrong between you and me. It's been the only right thing in my life."

He had no knowledge of the pain he had wreaked upon her—the regret, the hatred she had felt for being weak and silly and naive. It had been the worst decision of her life, allowing him to take her body and soul, and yet he sat here, claiming it had felt right to him. Then why had he left? Why had he allowed his wedding banns to another to be read in church? Why had he bedded her, toyed with her and walked away without another glance?

"I believe I am mended," she said, her voice controlled. She rose from the settee, slowly, regally, not allowing him to see how much discomfort she was in, or how she foolishly wanted nothing more than to stay on the settee with him. Foolish, impulsive female. She could not fight him like this. She could never withstand the slow, sensual onslaught that had always been her undoing. She would not survive it again when he walked away from her.

So she would resist. She must. Although she never would have believed it would be so easy to find herself falling once again. Not after his betrayal, after the pain he had inflicted upon her. How weak willed she was when it came to him, when he offered her the sweet seduction she still thought about deep in the night when she was alone, her body aching for the affection of another. When she yearned to be touched.

Steeling her thoughts and gathering the strength to

stiffen her spine, she said, "I thank you for your assistance, my lord. Good evening."

As elegantly as possible, Elizabeth picked her way across the room to the door. In her mind she recalled the placement of the furniture, which hadn't changed since she'd lost her sight—Adrian had seen to that. It was a relief to know she would not make a fool of herself yet again in front of Iain.

"So the little lamb runs from the big bad wolf."

Her hand twisted on the knob, but she didn't pull open the door. Without turning back she said, "The lamb is little no longer."

"But she still fears the wolf."

"No, not fears. She is aware. She knows what the wolf is capable of, and she wishes to give him a wide berth so that he may go his own way."

"The wolf won't give up."

"The lamb will not allow herself to be destroyed by him. She narrowly escaped the last time."

"Beth…"

How had she not heard him rise from the settee and cross the floor? It was impossible, especially with her heightened hearing, but here he was, his chest to her back, his groin fitted into the softness of her bottom as his palms flattened against the door, closing it with a soft click.

"Last night in Grantham Field, I faced death, and unlike others who have stared it in the face, I did not see my life and what I had done flash before me. I saw you…. Every moment we had spent together, every mental picture I have of you, I saw, and I had an epiphany. I realized that it is your face I see upon rising every morning, and the last thing I see before going to sleep. You are my first thought and my last—of every day."

"Don't do this," she begged as she lowered her head and let it rest against the cool wood. "Please."

His hand slid down the door, only to rest against her shoulder while his fingers toyed with the strands of hair that had fallen loose.

"Don't go to him," he breathed against her neck. His lips found the pulse there, and he sucked it gently before coming up to whisper in her ear, "Stay with me, Beth. Let the wolf come to the lamb."

"So that he may what?" she asked, her voice shaking, her body trembling.

"Taste you." He kissed her neck, drew his tongue up along her throat. "Place his hands on you and rediscover you. Fit himself inside you and find heaven once more."

"And the lamb will be left then, the wolf satisfied, free to roam as he pleases. No, Iain," she whispered. "I did that once. I won't do it again. What we had..." She swallowed. "Well, it wasn't good enough to allow me to make the same foolish mistake twice."

He growled then, nipped at her neck, tugged with the tips of his teeth on her earlobe. "We were young then, inexperienced. We're adults now, Elizabeth. I assure you, I can make it so damn good for you that you will want to come back to me again and again."

"A lamb led to the slaughter. No, Iain. I am through dying a silent death every night. I have forgotten you. And you... Well, you forgot me, too. Our futures are different and separate."

"If you go to him, Beth, I swear I shall never give you a moment's peace with him. He won't have you. He cannot give you what I can."

She laughed, a small, bitter sound that escaped her throat. "I hope he cannot, for I have had enough of shame and heartache. And that, Iain Sinclair, is all you ever gave to me."

Shocked, he loosened his hold on her, and she used the moment to open the door and slip out to the hallway, where Maggie was awaiting her. "It wasn't him, luv, but a messenger he sent with a note, conveying his apologies that he could not visit. Business to attend to, he claimed. But he sent by a book for you. He thought you might enjoy it. I'll read to you, if you like," Maggie whispered. "Now let's get you changed. Are you well?" she queried. "You do look pale, and your breathing isn't at all right."

"Just get me away from him," she gasped as she took Maggie's hand and held on tightly.

"Who?"

"The wolf in the room."

CHAPTER NINE

THE BRISK MORNING WALK and the bracing November wind did nothing to cool his ardour or his mind's wanderings, Iain thought irritably. He hadn't been able to sleep, his dreams consumed with images of Elizabeth hurt and bleeding—replaced only by the memories of how she had looked when her breathing changed, her lips parted and that arousing flush spread over her décolletage when he had said those erotic things to her. Not even the fact that she had injured herself practicing the waltz for Sheldon was enough to dampen his arousal—for it had been Iain who had reduced her steady breaths to hard rasps. His suggestions that had fueled the images Elizabeth hid from him behind her sightless eyes. But they had been there, mental pictures of the two of them locked in an amorous embrace. She longed for it, the reunion of their bodies, the reconnection—rediscovery—of a passion that had been too long denied.

Making love to Elizabeth had been a pleasure he had never experienced again. Making love to the woman she now was would be something he knew would shatter his soul.

There was more to this fixation. The passion, yes, the desire would never wane. But there was a need to know her as he had never taken the time to know her before. He wanted more than a physical connection with her. He wanted a bond. A friendship. He wanted to know her soul as intimately as he had once known her body.

He had no idea where to begin, how to forge a meaningful relationship. He was essentially a loner. A man who kept his thoughts and feelings private. Who preferred to hide behind meaningless sex and empty passion, for fear he had nothing to offer anyone, least of all Elizabeth. He had his love, an inner voice reminded him, but what use was it when that love had caused her nothing but pain?

Strolling along Bond Street, lost in his thoughts, Iain absently nodded in acknowledgement to the familiar faces that seemed to swim before him. It was sunny, albeit cold. There was a bitterness in the air, the kind that was common during harsh winters in the Scottish Highlands. A storm was brewing, he sensed as he tilted his head back and inched his hat higher onto his brow so he could see the slate-grey sky above him. The clouds were almost black, the blue skies of summer replaced with a grey backdrop that only made the clouds more ominous looking. It was the sort of morning that made one want to linger in bed, listening to the crackle of a fire in the hearth while making slow, lazy love to a woman. Not just any woman, he thought as he paused to look into a store window, but one who was a constant presence in his life. A woman who would be found in his bed every night. Who would live with him, share the ups and downs of life. The pain, the pleasure, the sorrows, the joy.

A slow, relaxed loving was only achieved with a partner whom you could turn your most intimate secrets and dreams over to. A woman you believed in, trusted. One you didn't have to keep up your guard around, but who allowed you to sink into her with no other thought than pleasure, and connection, and the sharing of bodies and whispers, and love. Love... Yes, he wanted it, and it scared the hell out of him, because he knew it might be too late for him to find love with the one woman who made him want to reach out and taste it. Who had made the surly Iain Sinclair wish he still possessed hers.

Beth's innocent love. He'd possessed it once, and he hadn't cared enough to keep it safe, hadn't thought for one second that he might bitterly regret its loss. But he did. His regret ran to unfathomable depths. He'd lost himself, his humanity, when he'd turned from that love, and now he wanted nothing more than to crawl from the depths and search for the love he knew had never died between them. It was there, tangled and entwined like the roots of an ancient oak, reaching deep. Anchoring to the ground. He was bound to Elizabeth in the most elemental of ways, just as she was to him.

He knew it, acknowledged it. Now he needed to find a way to make Elizabeth see it, to make her take that blind leap of faith into the world that awaited them, and forget the past.

Snorting in amusement, Iain shook his head. He'd become a blathering romantic without his Scotch. He didn't like it, this exposure of his true feelings and dreams. Gazing into the window, between the gold lettering, he stared, unseeing, wondering how long it had been since he had allowed himself to think of anything other than drowning his past in Scotch, and the willing body of any woman who would have him.

The memories numbed him. He no longer wanted that life. It was while facing down death that he'd realized he very much wanted to live. Wanted to love and be loved.

Now, Iain wondered what had brought him here to Waters and Whites on this cold morning. What had him pausing on his mindless walk through Bond Street to peer

into the window of the famous jewellers? He was not in
the market, as it were, to buy, but something had made
him stop. Something made him want to go in.

Reaching for the handle, he opened the door. The tin-
kle of bells above him rang out clearly, causing the el-
derly man behind the counter to glance up.

"Good day, my lord."

With a nod, Iain moved into the small shop and began
to peruse the glass cases. It was warm inside, with the
iron stove in the back pumping out heat. Gas lamps hung
suspended from the ceiling, their flickering light radi-
ating onto the glass, making the contents in each case
sparkle—a dazzling array in an otherwise bleak, cold
day.

It was several minutes before the shopkeeper came
over to him. With a slight cough, he forced Iain's attention away from the piece that had caught his eye from
the window.

"I am Waters, proprietor of this store. Might I be of
some help, my lord?"

Slowly, Iain's gaze dropped back to the moonstone
necklace that had kept him mesmerized for the better
half of five minutes.

"She's a beauty, isn't she?" Waters murmured. "The
finest specimen of adularescence from Ceylon."

"Stunning," Iain replied as the shimmer of the bluish
stones reflected in the play of light from the window, and
the black satin cloth it lay upon.

"Do you wish to see it out, my lord?"

"I do."

Waters reached into the case and slowly lifted the
necklace. It was large and outlandish, and made for only
one type of woman—someone with an expanse of pure,

unblemished skin and a magnificent bosom to nestle the large cabochon between her breasts.

An image of that woman quickly flashed in Iain's mind as he skimmed his fingers across the gems and the silver filigree that curled like lace around the stones.

"Adularescence, you called them," he murmured. "I thought them moonstones."

"Adularescence is what we call them in trade, my lord, but they are indeed known as moonstones. Ceylon is the finest place on earth to find them. See how they shimmer a pale blue? One only has to touch, and move, perhaps play with the gems to see the spectrum of glimmer and light and the scale of color, from very faint white to a mysterious blue. Very lovely on a woman's neck, my lord."

"Yes." Iain swallowed hard. He could imagine Elizabeth in something like this. A dichotomy of ethereal elegance and feminine sensuality. The moonstone was a perfect gem for her.

"Are you familiar with this stone?"

"No." He shook his head. "But it caught my eye from the window as I was passing by."

"You've a very fine eye, my lord. This necklace is remarkable. It is said that the moonstone was created for a woman to entrap a man. There's a good bit of mystique and magic that surrounds it. Many cultures the world over, especially in India, regard it as a holy gemstone with magical properties. They call it the dream stone, and the wearer is said to be gifted with beautiful visions the night through. In Arab countries women are known to wear moonstones sewn into their garments, because in their culture they're a symbol of fertility."

"And in the slightly less exotic English culture, Waters?" Iain asked, amused by the man's enthusiasm for his profession.

The shopkeeper's smile was catching as he glanced down at the necklace. "With its soft shimmer, and the way the light playfully, almost sensually changes with the movement of a woman's neck, I think it the most decadent of stones. It's a lover's stone, made to entice a man to follow the tantalizing glimmer over the throat and bosom. Any Englishman worth his salt should be entranced by a woman in moonstones."

"And if this Englishman doesn't want every man to be entranced?" Iain said, with a lilt in his voice.

"Oh, I think said Englishman could manage to keep the others from his lady. Besides, I think it's in a man to flaunt his possessions, as barbaric as it sounds. He wants to show off what he has, and what others may only wish to have."

"Aye, how true that is."

"Any woman can wear diamonds, but it takes the right sort of female to carry off moonstones to their full effect. Have you such a lady in mind?"

He did, and it was insane to even think of purchasing something like this for her. Yet he couldn't imagine another woman in London wearing it; certainly no one could carry it off the way Elizabeth could. With her pale skin, black hair and grey eyes she would be stunning in it, especially with the bodice of that low-cut, twilight-coloured gown she had been wearing at the Sumners' musicale to frame it.

"I fancy this piece the most," Waters murmured as he, too, was caught up in the display of light and luminescence. "You'll think me a sentimental fool for saying this, but I've hoped it would someday find its way to the right woman—and man—who can appreciate the beauty of it."

"I'm that man," Iain muttered. And how he could appreciate not only the necklace, but Elizabeth wearing it.

"If it is a matter of cost—"

Iain waved aside the comment. "Cost is of no consequence."

"I'll leave you, then, shall I? To think about the necklace?"

"Yes."

Would she wear it? Would she think it utterly ridiculous that he would buy her something like this? After everything that had happened between them Iain had no right to give her such a thing. *A peace offering,* his mind said in a hopeful whisper. It was rather elaborate for that.

But this was Elizabeth. She had always been different from the other women of his acquaintance. There had always been something about her that reached far down inside his soul and touched him where no other person ever had.

Waters moved silently away, and Iain saw from the corner of his eye how the man was making himself busy arranging a row of diamond and ruby rings in a case that was farthest away from him. Now alone, he was free to lift the necklace and allow it to dangle from his hand. The sunlight hit it and he tilted his palm left to right so he could study the shimmering light projected from the stones.

Elizabeth would be utter temptation in the twilight while wearing this. Irresistible. In his mind, he could visualize the way his fingers would look outlining the stones as they rested against her neck, saw the path of his lips skimming across the necklace, and Elizabeth's throat. Yes, how erotic it would be to play with her while she wore it.

"You know how much I adore diamonds," said a

deeply feminine voice from behind him. "Moonstones are so… Well, let us just say that only *women* wear diamonds."

Iain caught Waters watching him with curiosity as he lowered the necklace to the counter and confronted Georgiana.

"I hope I'm not ruining a surprise," she murmured as she pressed close to him. "But I thought I might let you know that necklace wouldn't do for me, darling."

He had to continue the charade, had to make her believe that he was totally besotted with her, when what he really wanted to do was wring her neck.

"I am dazzled by pretty things, and all things glittery, Georgiana. I merely got caught up in the fascination of it, is all."

Her smile made him feel as though snakes were slithering over his body. "And do you find me dazzling, my lord?"

He could not bring himself to say the words, so instead gave a discreet nod, which made her laugh.

"Come, you have to see the ring Larabie bought me—a forgiveness gift, you see."

Larabie was a fool to part with even a pound of his money on this creature. And what the blazes was his lordship doing, providing her with a gift upon this occasion? She had been the one caught in a scandalous embrace! Poor Larabie, he was doomed—blinded by his wife and her manipulations.

Iain almost felt pity for the man, but then, if Larabie wanted to be blind to his young wife's actions, so be it. Iain could never respect a man who allowed his wife to rule him that way. But then, who was he to respect anything, when he lived the way he did? After all, it had been Iain Larabie had discovered in a shadowed alcove with his wife.

Well, not for much longer, he decided as he dutifully followed the lady's swaying hips, which were encased in a dark purple satin-weave morning gown. Once he had what he desired from her, he would leave, and she would move on to someone else, and Larabie would be left to fight more duels and provide more tokens of his forgiveness.

"Mr. Waters, I trust my husband has been by today?"

The man inclined his head politely, but Iain noticed how he glanced at him from the corner of his eye with a glint of distaste.

"Indeed he did, madam. Allow me to run to the back."

Iain noticed that Waters first replaced the moonstones in their nest of black silk before fishing in his waistcoat pocket for a ring of keys to lock the case. They shared an unspoken comment as they looked at one another across the room. Water's expression, one of betrayal, said, *I thought you someone of worth, and now I know you're not.* Iain's was one of resignation.

He would not buy this creature anything, he thought as he watched Georgiana bend over the glass cases. She was excitedly showing him which ear bobs and necklace she wanted next—whether from him or her husband.

Georgiana was the sort of woman who demanded and took. She would not appreciate the idea of a man stopping on the spur of the moment to purchase something he could not stop himself from fantasizing about her wearing.

Elizabeth, he knew, was never demanding. She would enjoy a gift picked out by someone other than herself. There was an intimacy to a man thoughtfully choosing the right piece of jewellery for his woman, whether she be his lover or his wife. Iain found it rather rewarding to peruse the cases in such a fine establishment and choose something that seemed made just for her.

It would be too easy to have a woman come in and demand this or that, and for him to toss out his calling card and have the bill run up, and his secretary drop off a draft. That would be cold and impersonal, rather like Georgiana herself.

"Oh, here it comes." She suddenly squealed with pleasure as Waters emerged from the back room carrying a little red box. "It's absolutely stunning. I don't know anything that could top it, except perhaps—" her smile was coy as she gazed back into the case "—that wonderful diamond choker." She fluttered her lashes, and Iain felt a rise of impatience and annoyance.

"Madam, your ring." Waters produced the box and carefully opened the lid with a little creak of the leather.

Georgiana gasped and squealed again, and Iain forced himself not to roll his eyes.

The ring was enormous, full of clusters of diamonds, with a large emerald-shaped diamond in the centre. "Its total weight is five carats, correct?"

Waters nodded. "Yes, my lady."

Slipping it on over her glove, she marveled at its size. "Lovely," she said as she waved her hand about, so the gemstones flashed in the light. "Thousands of pounds, wasn't it, Mr. Waters?"

The man cleared his throat, and Iain studied the ring on her finger, feeling curiously devoid of any sort of response. Ostentatious and gaudy, the ring did nothing for him. Nothing like his visions of Beth in that necklace.

"It was a truly integument gift, Lady Larabie," Waters agreed with something more of politeness than the lady possessed.

He could afford to purchase such a ring as that, Iain mused, but what was the point, when it meant nothing? It was just to appease, to toss literally thousands of pounds out the window.

"I'll take the moonstones," he blurted, shocking both Waters and Georgiana.

"But I don't like it," she said with a pout, then seemed to recover as she recalled how she must look to Waters. "I mean, I told you that your lady and I have remarkably similar tastes, and if I do not care for the piece, then I'm quite certain she will not, either. I'd hate for you to waste your money on something that will only lie hidden away at the bottom of a jewel box. Or worse, require the inconvenience of a journey back to return it. Now, if you are interested in parting with some of your money, then permit me to suggest that you begin looking at this lovely diamond choker."

"Waters, the moonstone."

"Well, then," Georgiana said with a little huff, "I suppose I should be off."

"Good day, Lady Larabie."

Iain watched her make a grand exit out of the shop and into the carriage that waited on the street for her. He was aware of how Waters watched him as he carefully wrapped up the necklace in a black velvet pouch.

"Do not fret, Waters, the necklace is going to a lady of rare beauty, exceptional elegance and purity. The harridan who just left will never possess it."

Waters's smile could only be called sly. "As I said upon your arrival, your lordship has a good eye, and dare I say it, an uncanny instinct."

Iain nodded and reached out for the pouch, which was tied with a satin ribbon. Then he handed Waters his card, instructing him to send the bill around that afternoon, and Iain would see he was paid immediately.

Before Iain was out the door, Waters called out to him. "I do hope that I shall one day meet the lady who has been so fortunate as to have you purchase this for her."

"I hope so, too, Waters. And then you might have occasion to fit her for my ring."

CHAPTER TEN

"I HEAR CONGRATULATIONS are in order."

Slowly, Elizabeth strolled alongside Lord Sheldon, her hand on his arm, as Maggie walked a discreet distance behind them. Jack, Sheldon's retriever, pranced beside them, his panting interspersed with the sound of his paws crunching the gravel, and the jangle of the lead.

It was a crisp morning, the wind carrying with it the promise of something more biting by the afternoon. She could almost smell snow in the air, and the remnants of the morning's cold, clean frost blanketing the grass.

The breeze whispered against the short bonnet veil she had worn to hide the large bump and bruise on her forehead. Maggie had said her eye was not black-and-blue, but merely shadowed beneath. Still, Lizzy hadn't wanted to draw any attention to it.

Vanity and pride, she thought as they walked the quiet paths of Hyde Park. Who knew she had a good measure of both?

"Yes, they are," she answered, thinking back to that morning, and Sussex awakening her in bed with the news. "How did you hear of it so soon?"

Sheldon's laugh had a rich timbre. "I literally ran into His Grace dashing down the steps of your house, as I was jogging up. He seemed in great haste to get to Lady Lucy's—or rather his fiancée, as he called her."

"Yes, all excitement, I'm sure," Elizabeth replied neutrally. Her brother had compromised Lucy last night. Lizzy had barely been awake when Sussex had announced the news. The wedding would take place on the morrow—nothing grand, but private, in the salon of Lucy's father's—Lord Stonebrook's—town house in Grosvenor Square.

While Elizabeth had never doubted Adrian's success in making Lucy Ashton his bride, she was well aware that her brother's sense of honour had been shoved to the side, if he had, indeed, compromised her friend as he had stated. She couldn't help but wonder what Lucy was feeling this morning. Lizzy had been friends with her for only a few weeks, but in that short time they had become very close, each of them sharing intimate secrets with the other. She had known Lucy long enough to realize she would not look kindly upon a fait accompli marriage. It wasn't the way either of them would wish to embark upon married life.

Lizzy had wanted to go with Adrian to see Lucy, but he'd refused, stating only that he needed to speak with her in private, and reassure her that he had not intended for them to be discovered last night—at the House of Orpheus of all places.

Elizabeth had been quietly stewing as she breakfasted alone. Before Alynwick and his outrageous suggestion of keeping her out of Brethren business, Sussex would have told her the circumstances of how he and Lucy had found themselves at Orpheus's infamous club.

But that morning, her brother would not speak of it, only to tell her that he had found Lucy safe, and that they were to be married. "This afternoon, Black and Alynwick are to meet here," he said. "You can come into my study, Lizzy, and discover the facts then. I must be off.

I have a special licence to obtain, and a woman to convince that marriage to me will be a dream of a lifetime."

Elizabeth had every intention of attending the gathering, but then Lord Sheldon had arrived, requesting that she join him for a walk around the park, and she decided it was silly to sit and stew when the sun was finally shining and a handsome gentleman was requesting she spend some time with him.

Besides, she and Isabella would be calling on Lucy this afternoon for tea, and she would find out all the details Sussex thought he should deny her.

"I hope they'll both be happy," Sheldon said as he deftly steered them to the left along the curving path.

"I have no doubt they will," she answered. Tipping her face to the sun, which had finally chosen to shine, she smiled, basking in the warmth that penetrated the lace. "What a lovely day it is."

"A bit crisper than yesterday," he replied, "but all the same, rather refreshing. This will be my first winter back home since I was a child. I can hardly wait to see the snow."

Inhaling the cold air, Elizabeth claimed, "You won't have to wait long, I think. The scent of it is in the air."

"Can you smell it? Truly?"

He sounded a little astonished, and she gave a small smile, enjoying how he did not seem to shy away from the fact that she was blind. "I can. I have a heightened sense of smell, and hearing, too. It's very common for those who have lost a sense to discover the remaining ones more defined."

"I've heard of the coming fall scenting the air, but never snow in winter."

"Here. Stop for a moment and close your eyes."

He did, and when she was sure he stood quiet and still

with his eyes pressed firmly shut, she said, "Now, take a deep breath and bring the air into your lungs."

He did as she requested, drawing the breath into his chest. "The air does have a scent," he allowed. "And a taste I was never aware of before. But whether it is of impending snow or not, I cannot say."

They began strolling again, and Elizabeth allowed her gloved fingers to sink into the woollen sleeve of Sheldon's coat. "When you see those first few flakes, my lord, go outside, close your eyes and draw in the air. You will find that it smells the same as it does now."

"I will, Lady Elizabeth, if only to prove that my nose is not abysmal in skill."

They laughed, and Jack began to jump and pull in excitement at the sounds they were making. "Down!" Sheldon barked, and the dog complied immediately, settling back into a pace the animal, Elizabeth knew, felt was too sedate.

"Poor old Jack, I'm slowing him up."

"Nonsense. He just has to learn not everything is a race."

"He is young, yes?"

"Not yet two."

"Ah, yes, just a pup, then. Full of vinegar, young dogs are. I have no doubt he'll settle in."

"He's doing much better than I thought he would," Sheldon said, and Elizabeth heard pride in his voice. "In Egypt he had the run of the desert, catching whatever he desired. But now he's been confined to strolls and manicured parks. This is his first 'real' walk in the park. Normally by now I would be doubled over, out of breath after chasing him along the paths. The devilish creature has an inordinate fondness for ladies' hems, I'm afraid. He's forever tugging at them, thinking it a grand game.

When they shriek in dismay, it only makes him want to play more."

"Poor Jack." Elizabeth laughed. "It's rather like being a woman, all caged up and forbidden to let her hair down and race in the wind atop a gleaming horse. Stuffy old rules, aren't they, Jack?"

The dog panted harder, and she fancied he was gazing up at her, his tongue lolling heavily, as if he understood that in her he had found a kindred spirit.

"Yes, they are stuffy rules, as you say." Sheldon's voice grew deeper, more thoughtful. "Do you ride, Elizabeth?"

"I used to, and when we are in the country my brother takes me riding with him. We can't, of course, in the city. Rather unseemly for a lady to share a saddle with a gentleman, even if it is her brother. Besides, it's safer for me to ride astride, and that would send the matrons of the ton into fits of paroxysms if they were to see me that way, looking like some wild creature from the moors."

He laughed at the mental picture she created. "Yes, I can see your point. But something tells me you would welcome a late-night ride or early dawn jaunt through the mists of the park, your hair blowing in the wind."

"Oh, yes. It would be grand. I assume you are used to riding hell-bent through the desert on a magnificent black Arabian?"

"Once or twice," he admitted. "But it would be a rather novel thing here in England. Would cause quite a stir if one was discovered being so reckless, and informally dressed, for I prefer nothing but boots, britches and a linen shirt when I ride."

She could see him quite clearly on his horse, white shirt billowing in the breeze, against a backdrop of golden sand dunes. Why were only men allowed such luxuries? she thought with a sigh.

"Indeed it would be rather scandalous here in London. That is why I only risk the scandal in the north, where there are none but sheep to tell on you."

"Ah, yes. Quite. Nothing much but sheep, and amazing scenery up there, isn't that correct?"

"That's what makes it perfect."

"Your family's home is near Whitby, I understand."

"It is. I used to run down a path from the estate that led to the beach. Tides can be a bit unpredictable there, but it was a fantastic spot for fossil collecting. Are you a collector, my lord?"

They kept up their pace, and Elizabeth enjoyed listening to the sounds of life going on around her. Jack was pulling again, and Sheldon was tugging on the leash, keeping him in line. When the earl was satisfied that the dog was minding him for the moment, he answered, "I am a collector. But then I think it's a bit of a compulsion with archaeologists. We love to discover objects, but are loath to give them up. In my private collection, I have artefacts from Jerusalem, and a large number of Templar relics. Like you, I've been fascinated by the order since boyhood. I spent nearly a year working in the Holy City on a Royal Archaeological expedition at Temple Mount. That is where I discovered the story of the three Templars I told you about yesterday."

"Oh, yes," she murmured, her voice growing faint. She fought the urge to nibble her lip nervously.

"As a connoisseur of Templars, Elizabeth, have you ever heard such a story before I shared it with you?"

"No, I'm afraid I haven't." She was thankful for the veil, and the way it would shield the lie in her eyes. "Although I am aware that there are many stories and theories that link the Templars to religious artefacts. But none seem to hold up to any kind of intense scrutiny. After they were disbanded and murdered, so few remained of the order that their stories and artefacts have disappeared, much like the order itself. I doubt we shall ever really know the truth."

"I believe very strongly that story of the three Templars is true. But what I'm most fascinated about—driven to find out, really—is if the tale of the fourth Templar is true. I have found some credible evidence that he did exist, but what happened to the quartet, I do not know. I only know that his body was discovered in the desert. Murdered. And the remaining three were gone, never to be heard from again. So, too, were the relics they were carrying out of Jerusalem when they fled the Holy Land for the safety of Scotland."

"So the story of the fourth Templar stops there with his dead body, does it?"

"No, indeed it doesn't. It goes forward quite a few centuries, in fact."

Tiny hairs on her neck stood at attention. The story of the fourth Templar, she had been told, was a work of fiction. A fairy tale. There had only ever been three Templars who formed the Brethren Guardians: Sinjin York, her ancestor; Haelan St. Clair, the Marquis of Alynwick; and Drake Sheldon, the Earl of Black. She paused, her brow furrowing in thought. It hadn't occurred to her before. Was it possible that the Sheldon surname was in any way related to this matter, and the earl's title? Or was it merely coincidence? Still, her companion's cryptic revelation drew her deeper into the story of the fourth Templar, who was supposed to have been murdered and betrayed by the three Brethren, many generations removed.

She had thought it only a medieval tale, but now there seemed evidence that it was more truth than fable. And perhaps a reason why this Orpheus fellow knew so much about the Brethren, and the relics? If, indeed, the trail of the fourth Templar did not die out, was it possible that Orpheus was part of his lineage? Was he seeking revenge upon the Brethren for wrongful deeds done to his ancestor? Seemed rather unlikely, but still, she must share this information with Sussex. It might very well be of help. Although it did not really aid them in understanding how Orpheus had connected their long-dead father's past mistress to Sussex.

"The archaeologist in me," Sheldon continued, "would give a king's ransom to find the religious relics they smuggled out of the East. For certain, there was a chalice." He paused, then said quietly, "And a scroll that reportedly was hidden within the Ark of the Covenant."

Oh, dear... Already he knew far too much for her comfort. The York family had been entrusted with the chalice, and Alynwick's family kept the scroll safe. The latter, as far as she knew, was the most important relic, for it was inscribed with the ways to bring all three artefacts together, and in a ceremony of alchemy, and black magic, give the person who possessed all three unimaginable power. Power that was never meant to be in the hands of a mere mortal.

If one believed in such things, of course. And Elizabeth, despite her good common sense, did.

"Do you think the Temple Church might hold any information about these relics you seek?"

"I hope so. What's more, I think it might house clues about the identity of the three Templars, and where the artefacts might be."

"Oh." She most definitely needed to warn Sussex about this.

"Perhaps with our shared interest, we might discover the story together, Elizabeth."

How she hoped not. She could not allow him to unearth anything about the three Templars, or her connection to them. In a desperate bid to make him think of other things, she asked, "How versed on the Second Crusades are you?"

"Very," he answered. It was said with a great deal of pride. "It's my speciality. When in Jerusalem I unearthed a Templar cache of coin and jewels, hidden beneath the catacombs of Temple Mount."

"No doubt hidden to keep it out of the greedy hands of King Philip."

"Indeed. Philip IV was in dire need of funds at the time, and with the wealth the Templars had amassed, they were a prime target for his avarice and cruelty."

"The Templars were in possession of enormous wealth and property, not only in the Holy Land and Eastern Europe, but Western Europe, as well," she stated. "Philip was furious when he learned the Templars were shipping off their riches to faraway places to keep it safe. I heard, in fact, that many scholars believe the most priceless of their treasures and relics were sent to the New World, to a remote part of Nova Scotia. Which is quite a claim in itself, for if it is true, that would significantly predate the first explorer to land upon the New World's shores."

"You are very knowledgeable, Elizabeth."

She shrugged, careful to make sure she did not lose contact with his arm. "It's a topic that is very near and dear to me. I find the Templars a fascinating study, a dichotomy of chivalry versus cruelty, the vows of faith, poverty and chastity clashing with ambition, wealth, a lust for a war that saw thousands of men, women and children die, all in the name of God. It seems a never-ending conflict of the good in humanity versus its uglier side."

"Jerusalem, and Temple Mount in particular, mean so

much to so many in our world. To the Jews it is the site of Solomon's temple, to Muslims, it is fought over for Mohammed, and to Christians, it is claimed for God and his son. With that much passion and devotion for one place comes both the best and worst sides of the human race. And the Templars were no different. They fell victim to their humanity."

"Yes, I think you're right. A sacred place for so many, but with different meaning for all. Tell me, where is this cache that you unearthed?"

Sheldon grew quiet for a moment. When he spoke, his voice took on a rough and dangerous edge. "Stolen, I am afraid. I was working one evening in a tomb where a religious relic was supposed to have been hidden. I discovered it while reading the confession of a tortured Templar during the Inquisition of the Templars."

"What was this relic?" she gasped, unable to help herself. She felt his stare, the way he turned to watch her profile, which thankfully was concealed by the veil.

"A shroud, covered in red stains. Believed to be Christ's burial shroud. The Templars reportedly took their vows before it, and spent their night in prayer and contemplation the night before taking orders."

"And did you find it?"

"I did not. I was struck from behind before I could get very far in the excavation. The blow was intended to knock me out, but I fought my attacker, and saw who it was."

"Who was it?" she asked breathlessly, intrigued and excited.

"A colleague of mine, Mr. Nigel Lasseter. Bloody hell, I taught the bastard everything I knew about excavation. Oh, pardon my language, Elizabeth."

The world seemed to be pulled from beneath her feet, and she felt her legs give way, unable to support her.

"Here now," he said softly, "I've got you."

"I tripped over a stone, I think," she said, her entire body now trembling. *So close...* It seemed strangely compelling, yet utterly frightening how things appeared to be drawing them together, linking not only their interests, but their pasts. Like sacred geometry, there was a force drawing the lines, and somewhere in the middle they would find answers to what they each were seeking.

"Well, I have you now," he said, holding her close. "You're safe."

"Is everything all right, Lady Elizabeth?" Maggie asked, as Sheldon slowly released his hold of her arms.

"Yes, just a stone, I think, Maggie. I am quite all right, thanks to Lord Sheldon's remarkably quick reflexes."

"Shall we return to the carriage, Elizabeth?" he asked.

"No, no, we mustn't. Not yet. I have far too many questions to quit this walk."

He laughed. "Very well. Let us continue on."

They resumed their stroll, and Elizabeth sorted through the facts she was hearing. This was not the first time that Nigel Lasseter's name had come up within the circle of the Brethren Guardians. Lasseter had a personal connection with Wendell Knighton, who at one time had been the suitor of Isabella—now Lord Black's wife. Knighton had wound up murdered, by, her brother believed, the man who called himself Orpheus.

What an eerie kinship, Lizzy thought. Nigel Lasseter connected to Sheldon, as well as to Black via his wife's dead suitor.

Sacred geometry at work once more. If she possessed sight, she would have drawn it out. Shown the lines, the connections between souls who hadn't even known each other or crossed paths until only a few weeks ago. How strange… The Temple Church was considered a building displaying the proportions and theories of sacred geometry, and Sheldon was going to do a dig there, searching for the story of the three Templars. As well, Sheldon had a deep and personal connection with Lasseter. All of a sudden, her mind could not keep up with the many lines it was drawing and connecting.

"You are deep in thought, Lizzy," Sheldon said. "What questions do you have for me?"

"What happened to Mr. Lasseter?"

"After beating me senseless and leaving me for dead, he left Jerusalem with the cache. He's been selling it off, a few pieces at a time. That is all I know. Well, that, and I have heard he is here in London."

Something in his voice told Elizabeth Sheldon wasn't fully telling the truth. She could hardly be angry at him for that, though, for she wasn't telling the truth, either. They were merely protecting what they thought they should. Perhaps she should admit to him that Lasseter was, indeed, in London. But if the earl took to searching for him, he might discover information that would lead him to draw lines between Lasseter and Isabella's old suitor, and possibly the Brethren themselves. And that she could not allow, so instead, she pretended ignorance.

"And the shroud? Did you ever discover it?" she asked, trying to get back to a safer topic.

"It wasn't there, but I found a piece of the True Cross."

"The one that the Bishop of Acre reportedly carried into battle at the Horns of Hattin?"

"The very one. The one Saladin captured, and then ransomed back to the Crusaders when the Muslims surrendered the city."

"What was it like?" she gasped, wishing she could

have been there, working beside him. To touch something of such historical importance… She couldn't imagine it.

"It was in poor repair, falling apart, really, but it was wrapped in cloth with the description of what it was. Holding it in my hands was the most gratifying moment of my life. Even more so than finding the Templar cache."

"Where is it now?"

"The British Museum, with the new curator of medieval studies. I delivered it there myself."

"How rewarding it must be to discover such fascinating objects. To learn of people and civilizations that have not been heard of for centuries."

"It is. It's why I am so thankful that I have been granted access to the Temple Church. I did not want to give up my profession, but knew I had a responsibility to my family to honour and uphold the title. I am fortunate that for a while at least I will be able to wear both hats. I *will* discover the full story of the Templars, Lizzy. I've vowed to, and when I make a promise, I never go back on it. Even if it is only a promise to myself."

Elizabeth knew she would somehow have to prevent him from fulfilling that promise. There was one way, she mused, that might distract him from it, at least for a short time.

How she hoped this would help dissuade him from thinking over much on unearthing the secrets of the Brethren Guardians. "Well, I have in my possession a diary from the Crusades. It belonged to a Templar knight, and it's an account of his affair with a mysterious lady."

He stopped, shocked. She heard his startled breath. "Are you quite certain? The Templars took a vow of chastity and poverty."

"Yes, quite sure. The entries are rather…detailed. What is more, the woman in question appears to be one of wealth and rank. Their affair was kept secret, not only because of his vow, but to protect her identity, as well. You see, forbidden from both sides."

"Fascinating. Who was she?"

"That is the mystery, I am afraid. She is only identified as the Veiled Lady. It's been a goal of mine for many years to discover her name. Thus far, I have not been successful in my attempts to lift the veil of secrecy, as it were."

"And the knight?"

This was where she must lie again. "Oh, I have no idea, really. I just happened to come across the book years ago in an old, musty bookshop. Some pages are missing, and the writer never discloses his identity. I suppose because he had taken a vow of chastity."

"I suppose. Wouldn't be quite the thing for a Templar to be discovered entwined in a torrid affair."

"No, seems rather dangerous."

"It is real, not a clever fake?" Sheldon asked, his voice sounding excited.

"Oh, no," she said, "not a forgery, but a very real, authentic diary."

"I would love to see it. If you would permit me, of course."

"Well, that is…" Why, why, why had she brought up the diary? Lizzy mentally blasted herself. What a mess she was digging. She'd meant only to distract the earl, and yes, perhaps she was thinking of her own selfish desires—to discover the identity of Sinjin's lover. Out of any of her acquaintances, Sheldon was the most likely to aid her. And yet she had just invited him to possibly discover more about her and her family than she had ever wanted.

"Elizabeth?"

Biting her lip, she murmured "Oh, yes. Yes, perhaps you can see it one day."

"Maybe I can aid you in discovering the woman's identity?"

"Well, that is to say…" What was there to say? She'd opened Pandora's box! Her loose tongue had done this. But maybe he would be put off. Or maybe having him help her with the diary was a means to keep him close, a way to make certain he didn't discover anything about Sinjin, or his connection to her and Adrian.

"Lady Elizabeth," he drawled, reaching out to squeeze her gloved hand. "I would assist you in anything. Anything at all. And I do insist. I must have a peek at this mysterious diary. How about tomorrow, hmm?"

"REALLY, LUCY, I think it's just wonderful that you're finally marrying His Grace. It's a brilliant match."

Lizzy took a careful sip of her tea, while listening to Lady Black attempt to soothe Lucy's ruffled feathers for at least the tenth time since they'd sat down.

"You wouldn't say that if you were the one forced to marry him, Isabella."

"Lucy!"

"It's perfectly all right, Isabella," Elizabeth interjected. "There is no need to protect me. I might be Adrian's sister, but I'm a woman first. No woman wishes to be seduced into marriage. You were seduced, were you not?" she teased.

"Oh, now you are just fishing for gossip!" Lucy hissed, but Elizabeth could sense a change in her voice. The anger was abating, giving way to teasing. Always a good sign.

"Well, I for one would adore discovering those *on dits,*" Isabella murmured, while reaching for a biscuit.

Lizzy could hear them sliding on the plate next to her. "Do share, Lucy."

"No, I don't think I will."

"So cruel, especially when you took such delight in the scandal that Black and I created. And now to be so mean as to not allow me to share in yours." Lizzy could almost see Lady Black pouting dramatically.

"Oh, all right."

Lizzy recoiled at the thought. "No, really, Lucy dear. I do love Sussex, but not enough to hear about his seduction of you."

Lucy had the generosity to laugh. "I would have spared you the most gruesome details, Lizzy."

"Thank you for small graces. Now, then, perhaps you might share with us how in the world you found yourself in the House of Orpheus last evening."

"Much too droll, I'm afraid, and besides, speaking of it reminds me of my impending nuptials. I don't want to think about that right now."

"All right, then what shall we discuss? The new penny dreadfuls?"

"Well, since we're talking of seduction, tell us, how goes it with the mysterious Lord Sheldon?" Lucy suggested. "Very neutral territory, isn't he, Isabella? Neither one of us will be at all offended, Lizzy, by the sordid details."

"No seduction going on at all," she said with a small smile. "But he does share a lot of my interests, and he's a very amiable man whose conversation is most fascinating and enjoyable."

"And of course the fact that he's titled, rich, handsome—*and tanned*," Lucy announced loudly, "is all second to his eloquent...tongue."

Lizzy shook her head in mirth. "You are too bad. You

will give Sussex fits, I think. He needs that, to share a good laugh. But, no, to answer your question, Lucy, none of the above have really factored into my opinion of the earl."

"Oh, that's disappointing," Isabella murmured. "When Lucy told me of the earl squiring you about I had such high hopes."

"I'm sorry to disappoint you."

"Oh, pish," Lucy snapped. "That's claptrap, Lizzy, and you know it. Where are the stories of breathless kisses, heaving bosoms…dark, dangerous secrets…"

"No heaving bosoms here, I'm afraid. And no secrets."

The air in the room fairly crackled, setting Elizabeth's nerves on edge. Were Lucy and Isabella sharing knowing looks? She had to know.

"What silent signals are you sending to one another, hmm? I can feel them, you and Isabella shooting each other telling glances."

"Oh, nothing," Lucy said, sounding very sly. "I was just wondering if there might be heaving bosoms, but not necessarily heaving for Sheldon."

The air crackled again, through the heavy silence. Lucy would not give an inch, but Isabella took pity on Elizabeth and broke the stillness.

"Ahem!" She coughed, clearing her throat. "I'm not quite sure if you know this…. Well, of course you don't know…." She giggled, and it was so strange a sound coming from her friend that Lizzy arched her eyebrows in surprise. "Oh, dear, I'm really awful at this sort of thing."

"Go on, Isabella," Lucy encouraged. "Tell her."

"Well, Lizzy, I feel obligated to tell you something that my husband strictly forbade me to, and which I expressly promised not to repeat."

"Then you probably shouldn't," Elizabeth said a little uneasily. What the devil was going on?

"It involves you, and in fact… Well, in fact, I've already repeated it to Lucy, terrible wife that I am. But I only did it because, well, because it involves you and a certain someone, and as your very good friend, I feel obligated to share it."

Lizzy was sweating now. What could it be?

"The night of Alynwick's duel, Black stood up with him as his second. Unfortunately, things went awry and Alynwick was shot."

Relieved, Elizabeth waved away her comment. "Oh, I already know that."

"But did you know that Alynwick's *dying request,* as my husband put it, was for Black to take him to you?"

Lizzy promptly coughed on a mouthful of tea. Wheezing, she covered her lips with the back of her hand. "He said what?" she gasped.

"Black said he was rather insistent upon it."

"So, what is going on with you and the mad marquis, Lizzy?" Lucy asked as she gently swatted Elizabeth between her shoulders, helping to stop her coughing. "You cannot fob us off now, you know. For I saw you with him, that night at the musicale, and there were definite smouldering looks and heaving bosoms."

"You can't be serious!"

Lucy pressed forward and reached for Lizzy's cup, taking it from her. Together, both she and Isabella reached for her hands, holding them tightly in a friendly grip.

"You told us you had an affair, years ago, with the marquis."

"And I'm repenting my loose tongue," she snapped, feeling horribly embarrassed.

"Oh, don't be. Ours is a sisterhood. Secrets are shared

and kept. There's no worries, Lizzy. But what Isabella and I are getting at is, well, with your blindness, you don't see what we do."

"And what is that? My abundance of cleavage spilling from my bodice, which you attribute to the presence of Alynwick, of all people?"

"No, Lizzy, we see the way he looks at you."

"Oh, yes, with a capricious amusement, and disdain."

Lucy—at least Lizzy believed it was her hand—stroked her fingers soothingly. "Lizzy, the Marquis of Alynwick is a man very much in love—with you."

"Nonsense." Oh, how that one word came out trembling in fear. And, Lord help her, an absolutely absurd sense of hope.

"We want to tell you what he looks like when he's around you. His eyes never leave you. When he talks to others, his eyes are so dark and cold, but when he sees you they light up, and they linger. They roam over your body, and there's nothing but the most passionate—*loving*—expression in them."

"Even Black has noticed and commented upon it, Lizzy."

"No." She shook her head. "No, he's such a good liar. If you could only have been there, seen his eyes, and the lies he hid so well. No, it cannot be true. I won't believe it."

Hands squeezed hers. "I have seen the same implacable expression in Black's eyes when he pursued me, Lizzy. I have seen the same in Sussex's gaze when he looks upon Lucy. Alynwick has the same look. He will not be deterred. He wants you back. He looks as though he'd die to have you back."

"No!" Lizzy jumped up and accidentally upset the tea tray. "Oh, my goodness, I'm so sorry." She started fumbling about, but Lucy and Isabella stopped her, hugged her as tears began to scald her eyes.

"You're our friend and we want your happiness. Trust us to help you, Lizzy."

"You don't understand," she gasped, "He *broke me!* I...can't allow it again."

"All right," Lucy whispered, hugging her tightly. "I can see you're not ready. But we will be here, Lizzy, when you are. And for now, say you'll trust us enough to believe what we see. The marquis... Well, whatever he was once is not the man he is now."

"You don't know the whole story," Elizabeth whispered, keeping her eyes squeezed shut. "No one does. Only me. And all I can say is... Well, he took every dream I ever held in life and tore them from me. I'll never forgive him for that. *Never.* What I suffered was unbearable."

"I've seen much suffering," Isabella said as she hugged Lizzy close. "I've despaired. Have wanted to give up. But God doesn't give us anything we cannot handle, Lizzy. And oftentimes, when it all seems too much, He sends someone to help us through it. Just remember that, hmm?"

"I'll try, but it's much easier to hate than to live on false hope. And that's all Alynwick has ever been able to offer."

CHAPTER ELEVEN

"GOOD GOD, abducted and brought to the House of Orpheus?"

Nodding, Sussex didn't take his gaze off the letter opener he was busy twirling in his hands. "Yes. My future wife did not return home yesterday morning after I sent her with a footman, *and* after I had made it all very clear as to why I demanded she obey me in this matter. Apparently, the dead body she witnessed dropped at my doorstep was not enough to induce her to obey her future lord and husband. The infuriating woman decided to disobey me and visit a psychic instead."

Iain couldn't help but grin at the perturbed duke. No one disobeyed the express edicts of His Grace. But it seemed one waiflike redhead found great pleasure in doing so. "As I said before, Sussex, a curse and a pox on headstrong women who won't be led by a man."

"Indeed." The lines around Sussex's mouth were grim. "It seems that she has been to this psychic before, and felt quite safe alone with the woman. She ordered the footman to wait in the carriage for her. When she entered the conveyance after conducting her business, she was grabbed from behind and rendered unconscious by a cloth over her mouth that had been doused with ether. When she awoke, it was to find herself on a bed in the House of Orpheus."

Iain was speechless. He could well comprehend the

rage that must have ruled Sussex, not only because Lucy had expressly disobeyed him. The terror he must have experienced upon discovering her missing would have been all-consuming. "How did you learn of her whereabouts?" he asked.

"The footman I assigned to her, God bless his determined Cockney soul, traipsed from the scene, where he had been dragged from the carriage and beaten, to Sussex House. He was the one to inform me that he had awakened just in time to witness Lucy being carried inside the Adelphi."

"He couldn't identify the kidnapper?"

Sussex shook his head.

"Well, at any rate, I hope you rewarded the man for walking a few miles in that state."

"He's making his recovery in a guest chamber as we speak. The moment he remains conscious for more than a minute, I shall grant him whatever he wishes. I shudder to think of what might have come out of it if he hadn't been able to get back and tell me."

"And how was it, exactly, that you became leg shackled to the girl?"

Sussex smiled faintly, obviously indulging in a very private memory. "Suffice it to say the matter is a private one."

The priggish Duke of Sussex, caught in a compromising position? Iain could hardly credit it. He had always thought the duke a passionless man, more concerned with propriety and honour than the baser elements of a gentleman's makeup.

Knowing he would not get much more out of Sussex in regards to his hasty engagement, he enquired, "Did she see him? This Orpheus?"

"No, she did not. I was hoping you might be able to

shed some light on the matter. Did you see Orpheus yourself? You did say you were meeting Lady Larabie last evening at the club."

Feeling guilty, he glanced away, out the study window to the sun-filled garden. "I sent around a missive with my regrets," he answered. "My shoulder didn't seem up to it."

There was no reason for Sussex to learn Iain had decided to forgo a nauseating evening with Georgiana discovering all he could about Orpheus, for one spent trailing the Earl of Sheldon. His Grace had made it perfectly clear that he liked Sheldon, and worst of all, that his sister liked the man, as well.

"I trust you will consider pursuing the matter of Orpheus while I am away on my honeymoon," Sussex mumbled, drawing Iain from his thoughts. "I know it's poor timing to leave London with everything going on, and his deuced ability to befuddle us, but I cannot help it. I must leave with Lucy, and hopefully then our hasty marriage and the inevitable scandal that will arise out of it will quiet down, so that when I return in a few weeks the furor will be over and I may take up my place alongside you and Black. I'm afraid by staying in London I risk the chance of being seen by others. We don't need questions right now. Plus, I would like to ensure Lucy's safety, and I think that's best served at my estate in Yorkshire."

"Rest assured that I will. And if Black would tear himself away from his wife, and their bed, he might be of assistance, as well."

Sussex grinned for the first time since they'd sat down to discuss things. "You underestimate the lure of one's bride, I think."

Iain groaned. "Et tu, Brute?" Shaking his head, he studied the duke, all lovelorn and distracted. "You're not going the way of Black, are you? Besotted fool that he is."

"I've already gone. You know that. I've made no secret of desiring a match with Lucy. And now I have it. I won't let anything stop it. You'll understand one day, Sinclair, when you allow someone into your heart."

Iain shrugged, knowing that someone already resided deep within the damnable organ. "Perhaps."

"I do have a favour to ask, Alynwick."

The seriousness of the duke's voice caused him to look up sharply. "Yes?"

"Elizabeth. She has flatly refused to accompany Lucy and me to Yorkshire. She claims she would be nothing but a burden, and a nuisance to a newlywed couple. She won't listen to reason, I'm afraid."

Iain had been feeling decidedly melancholy—even angry—since learning of Sussex's impending nuptials. Not because he disliked Lady Lucy or the married state, but because he had known that Sussex would take Elizabeth with him, and the thought of her being gone so far away was more than he could bear. Now, discovering that Elizabeth refused to go, Iain found his mood much, much lighter.

"You want me to watch over her."

"Would you? I know you don't get on well, but I don't trust anyone else with her safety. Black is too busy being besotted by his wife, as you say. I need someone with a clear head. Someone who won't be distracted."

How little Sussex knew of him. One glance at Elizabeth, and he would be completely, thoroughly distracted. He was distracted from the topic at hand now, just thinking of how he would have every affordable chance to wear her down... To make her see him as he now was. A man wanting forgiveness, desiring a life with her. A man who would do his damnedest to be worthy of a woman such as her.

"You may be assured, Sussex, that I will keep Elizabeth safe."

"I know you will. I worry, however, especially after the murder of Anastasia. I am forced to take Rosie with me. Her whelping time will be soon, and I need the expertise of the breeder at my estate. Elizabeth relies on Rosie, and I rely on the dog's acute hearing to alert us to any trouble. I can't help but think how vulnerable Elizabeth will be here alone, with only the servants to keep her safe. They have no real understanding of how dangerous our lives have become."

"I will keep her safe." It was a solemn vow.

Sussex must have heard it, too, and glanced up, a militant gleam in his eye. "Keep an eye on Sheldon, as well. He's been around two days in a row. I think it rather obvious, his infatuation with her. I don't know the extent of Elizabeth's interest, but I would take no risk there. I don't know him well enough, and despite the fact I rather like him, there is something I cannot quite put my finger on."

Senses alert, Iain straightened in his chair, noting the stiffness in the duke. "What has you questioning the earl?"

Sussex had always possessed a remarkable instinct in regards to duplicity. It amazed Iain that the duke had never guessed at Iain's, in regards to his sister. That Sussex had never discovered he'd seduced and deflowered the virginal Elizabeth, when he had always believed the sin all but tattooed across his face, left Iain oddly nervous, and guilty.

Sussex waved away Iain's question and placed the jewelled letter opener on a leather blotter. "As I said, I cannot quite pinpoint it. He seems on the up and up, but there is something there. Intangible as it may be, it is still present. I don't think I'm wrong here, although I wish to hell I was, if for nothing but Elizabeth's sake."

Not looking up from his polished boots, Iain mumbled, "I followed him last night."

Only then did he dare glance up, to see Sussex's grey eyes narrowed and fixed firmly upon him. How much like his sister he looked, with the same coloured eyes glaring at him.

"It's the truth of why I cried off with Georgiana last evening."

"And what purpose did you have to follow him?"

"You are not the only one possessed of good instincts, Sussex."

The duke relaxed a bit, settling his large frame in the leather chair, and waited for Iain to share the tale. "Well? Did you discover anything of worth?"

"Our guts seem infallible, for his activity last evening raised more questions than answers."

Sussex pressed forward again, his expression dark. "Explain."

"I followed him to the museum."

"He's lived in the East all his life. Perhaps he had a longing to visit a decayed mummy. You know, home sickness and all that."

Iain did not care for Sussex's sarcasm. He was wound tightly this afternoon, and was in no mood to humour the duke. "It was well after closing time. What's more, someone was watching for his approach, because he had hardly rapped upon the doors when they were opened, allowing him entrance."

"Interesting."

"He was carrying a canvas satchel."

"I wonder what was in it?" Sussex said, already knowing that Iain would have discovered the contents of the bag.

"Drawings of elevations, scrolls of them. And what is more, on one of them there was an image of a Templar cross, and beside it, most curiously, was the Cross Lorraine."

Sussex sat back in his chair, and Iain could almost see the duke's brain processing the information. "A coincidence, perhaps. The Templar cross is quite common. A romantic symbol that many use."

"On sketches of elevations? That's a stretch, isn't it?"

Sussex frowned. "I suppose, but hardly enough to condemn him."

"There's more. In his study, housed in a pendulum clock, was a rolled piece of parchment that was hidden beneath a false bottom."

"You broke into the man's house!"

Iain sent the duke a look of annoyance. "I don't do things by half measures. You know that. Of course I searched his house. But he returned before I could discover what the paper was. But it was hidden for a purpose."

"Damn it, Alynwick, you take too many risks!"

"And you don't? Allowing Elizabeth to be…" God, the word *courted* would just not form on his tongue "…to be visited by a man we know nothing about. A man whose appearance back in Society leaves me more than suspicious, especially since the arrival of this Orpheus, and all the other inexplicable things that have happened. Damn it, Sussex, admit it, you've been blinded by your desire for Lucy, and now things have gone too far."

"*You're* taking things too far, Alynwick."

"We've not been suspicious enough."

"Your focus should be on Lady Larabie, and getting

close to this Orpheus. You're the one who came up with the damn plan, who informed us that the lady knew him personally. Orpheus is the key to the whole mystery, and it's the lady's assistance we need to get close to him."

"He isn't the entire mystery, Sussex. Have you forgotten Nigel Lasseter?"

His friend stiffened. "What do you mean?"

"Sutherland was hanging about the theatre yesterday upon my orders. I asked him to watch for Lady Larabie. I've grown suspicious of the witch, and wanted him to discover all he could about her comings and goings. He did not see her, but he did discover Nigel Lasseter going into the theatre, by way of the back alley. Interesting, don't you think, considering he was the patron who paid for Wendell Knighton's trek to the Holy City? And now Knighton is dead…. And to enter through the back, as if he owned the place. It was not at night, when the club is in full swing, but during the afternoon…."

Releasing an expletive, Sussex wiped his hands over his tired face, then tossed back his head and groaned. "Another damn puzzle, and yet another piece we are supposed to fit in. You're right, of course. I've lost my perspective. *Damn it!*"

"Love, I suppose, is an immovable force. Even it can supersede Brethren demands and duties. Although I highly doubt our merciless fathers ever allowed the emotion to surpass their love affair with all things Brethren."

Sussex's gaze flickered to his. There was pain in those grey depths. Naked, haunting pain. Iain couldn't help but wonder if Sussex saw the same stark misery reflected in his own gaze. "In our fathers' lives, nothing took precedence. It was always Brethren Guardian duties and honour that came before everything. My pain has made me foolish, so that I don't think things through as I ought to. I hope my ineptness was not the cause of Anastasia's death."

"I doubt you could have prevented it. I've sent Sutherland out today to see what he can discover about Nigel Lasseter. I've also—" Iain shuddered at the memory "—sent a missive around to Lady Larabie, who will receive me tonight. Leave it to me, Sussex. Enjoy your new bride for the next few weeks, and when you return I shall have news for you."

"You will keep your word in regards to Elizabeth?"

"You have it. I will be her constant shadow. No harm will come to her, I vow it."

"Adrian!" a high-pitched, breathless voice called from the hall. "I must see you. This instant."

Ridiculously, Iain felt his heart jolt, then run wild at the sound of Elizabeth's exclamation. Shifting his weight in the chair, he was suddenly conscious of the velvet pouch hidden in his breast pocket. He'd nearly forgotten about the necklace he'd purchased for her that morning, and the daydreams he had of placing it around her throat. Now they were back, those intimate, sensual images, and he waited, barely breathing, to watch her make her grand entrance.

What a bloody hopeless sap he'd become.

The door opened, and there she was. Iain sucked in his breath at the sight of her, wind in her sails as she breezed into Sussex's study on the arm of a footman. Panting and waddling, Rosie struggled to keep up with her mistress.

Elizabeth's cheeks were pink, her pure skin glowing in the sunlight that streamed through the window. Her voluptuous curves were encased in a dark blue, form-fitting coat edged in black bear fur, her delicate hands covered in black kid leather. In one hand she carried a book, the oxblood-coloured leather spine of which was cracked and peeling with age.

Atop her head she wore a jaunty little hat with blue and black roses, and a beguiling black veil that only added to the sensual mystique of Elizabeth York. Angel on the outside, succubus on the inside. Damn it, how the demon within him wanted her with a ruthless, dangerous need that completely consumed him.

Before he faced death on Grantham Field, Iain had been able to bury that need. To use the savage control and discipline his father had made him acquire to bury his feelings for Elizabeth where they could never be found, or disturb him. But something had changed that night. Like Pandora's box, the long-ignored feelings had sprung free from their hiding place, bringing chaos and fury, and a sickness that clung to him. Every thought, every decision was made with a purpose to reunite him with Elizabeth. For the past few days he'd felt as though every breath he took was for her. Always her. *Only her.*

And now here she was, robbing him of breath and speech, and the brutal self-control that hid everything he was. Elizabeth had done this, taken a wild, snarling wolf and turned him into a damnable, drooling lapdog!

Before, the very idea of allowing himself to fall so easily, to be vulnerable to another human being, would have sent him lashing out, reeling against feeling anything. Surprisingly, he did not feel angered by the fact that Elizabeth had softened his hard edges, but rather he was grateful for it. It had been a long time since he'd allowed himself a modicum of truth in regards to his feelings, but in this, he had to be honest. He had never stopped caring about Lizzy and her well-being. Had never stopped desiring her. Had always loved her, knowing she held nothing inside for him but a seething hatred he all too well deserved.

Iain had always feared his love for her, feared examining his feelings about loving another—so fiercely, and not having the same feeling reciprocated. She could have no idea what it was like to lie in bed at night and ache for another, to love only one other on earth and know that person did not feel anything in return but contempt. Did she know how lonely he was? Could she imagine his guilt, regret, the hatred he held for himself and his actions twelve years ago? Could she fathom that he, the Mad Marquis, the Aberrant Alynwick, could harbour such deep sentiment, a love that would cross oceans of time, even lifetimes? A love that would never die?

Would she believe him if he told her all this? If he exposed his feelings to her, and in doing so, exposed himself to her ridicule and rejection?

How did one take such hatred and turn it into love? As she stood before him, he pondered that, questioning how he could take something dark and forbidding and make it pure and desirable. He'd give away his fortune, his title, all his earthly possessions for one chance to make Elizabeth see it—his worth. His love.

He didn't know how to pray. He was not a man of religion and faith, despite his vocation as a Brethren Guardian, but he swallowed hard, closed his eyes and silently pleaded. *Please, give me one more chance to earn her forgiveness. Let me love her well, like I should have all those years ago. One more chance at redemption, and I shall do whatever You ask....*

"Thank you, Charles," Elizabeth said, as she excused the footman. "I shall call for you when I am ready to go upstairs."

"Very good, my lady." The footman bowed and promptly

left. Elizabeth stuck out her hand, indicating that Sussex should relieve her of the book she carried. Unable to help himself, Iain stood, pulled the ancient tome from her hand and said, "Good afternoon, Elizabeth. Might I say, you are looking lovely today."

The book fell from her fingers when she realized she was not alone with her brother. The little flutter at the base of her throat increased as she smoothed a gloved hand over her midriff, drawing Iain's gaze, and his lascivious imagination.

"Good day, my lord," she answered, recovering with admirable aplomb. "Forgive me for interrupting."

"Your company is always most welcome."

He recovered the book from the floor, scarcely taking his eyes off her, or from the way she was slowly unbuttoning the clasps of her coat, revealing the blue gown she wore beneath.

Sussex was watching him, and unfortunately noting how Iain's gaze unavoidably slipped to the expanse of bosom that came enticingly into view. Her bodice had a lace insert, with just a hint of flesh showing beneath. It drove him mad, looking at it, wondering what it would be like to pull it out and press his lips to her skin.

Tossing the book onto Sussex's desk, Iain reached for her hand and assisted her to the chair he had been using. Then he carefully put distance between them by standing before the window so he could watch her—discreetly, of course.

"Lizzy, at last you're home. How was your walk?" her brother enquired.

"Wonderful." She smiled, her breathlessness growing. "Highly informative."

"Oh?"

"Who were you walking with?" Iain suddenly demanded, his voice too authoritative. Sussex shot him a glare, and Iain ignored it.

"Why, Lord Sheldon, of course." She smiled sweetly as she said the man's name, and Iain's vision was suddenly awash in crimson.

"All afternoon?" he said hotly. Damn her, she was a menace to his nerves, and temper.

"It was only for an hour, and Maggie was with us. For heaven's sake, my lord, I need not answer to you. You are not my brother or my father. You're...well, nothing to me."

Oh, how he wanted to stride over to her, lift her out of the chair by her shoulders and remind her just what they had once been to each other.

"Well, then, Lizzy," Sussex began carefully, sending a questioning glance in Iain's direction. "What has you rushing in here before you've even removed your bonnet?"

Settling herself comfortably in the chair, Elizabeth began removing her gloves, finger by finger. Did the woman not understand how unbearably erotic that was to a man? Iain wanted to throttle her. How easy it was for her to tease him. But it had always been like that, him watching her, studying her from afar and absorbing everything she said, every look, every word, as though she were water and he a lowly sea sponge.

How his father must be laughing in his grave at his weak-willed son. A son he had always accused of not being from his loins. *"No son of mine would have such an unnatural affection for a female. You're weak, boy. A disgrace."* The mighty Marquis of Alynwick would never allow a woman to break him, or so he had boasted numerous times to Iain. *"A woman weakens a man, boy,"* he had always claimed. *"Never lose your head over them.*

You're in control, not them. Once you give females any power, you're doomed to having your bollocks forever in their grip."

He had listened to that misplaced, idiotic advice once before, and it had brought him nothing but years of misery and empty debauchery. His father might have enjoyed living his life in such a way, but Iain could not.

"I have very important news," Elizabeth announced, her voice suddenly quieting. Iain had to press forward to hear her. "I trust there is no one else here, besides him?"

Elizabeth's pale hand waved negligently toward Iain and the window where he was standing, gripping the sill so tightly his fingers were turning white. The little she devil, what she did to his temper!

"You are at liberty to speak freely, Lizzy. It is only the three of us."

Nodding, she cleared her throat, straightened her spine and pressed her gloves together before laying them across her lap.

"Were you aware that Lord Sheldon is an archaeologist, brother?"

"No, I was not."

Sussex sent Iain an odd look, one he ignored as he ground his teeth together. How he loathed knowing she had spent her time with the man, when Iain had done nothing all day but think of her. Think of last evening on the settee, when he had cared for her injuries and whispered all sorts of indecent things to her. And it hadn't only been him that had been affected. She'd been aroused. But she had rebuffed him despite her body's obvious response.

"Well, he is. And one of his interests is the Templars."

That made Iain straighten up and listen closely. He

and Sussex shared another quick glance, and then the duke said, "Go on."

"It appears that he spent time in Jerusalem, excavating the catacombs of Temple Mount. He found a cache of Templar coins and jewels. And…" she paused, wet her lips with the tip of her tongue "…a story about three Templars who were charged with the task of removing three sacred relics from the Holy Land."

"Bloody hell," Sussex groaned.

Iain could barely contain his own anger. He knew if he railed out against Sheldon, Elizabeth would baulk. Would take up the bastard and protect him, just to spite Iain. And she had every right to do so.

"Lord Sheldon has not yet discovered the names of the Templars, nor has he discovered what the relics are, although he did say he suspects a chalice might be one of them. And a scroll…" She trailed off.

Sussex groaned again and Iain cursed, while Elizabeth continued.

"And that's not all. Sheldon knows the story of the fourth Templar, and he believes it's credible. What is even more alarming is that he has been granted access to the Temple Church at the Inns of Court. He plans on digging up the crypts beneath looking for evidence."

"I told you I didn't trust him!"

Elizabeth shot a mutinous glare in the general vicinity of Iain's voice. "And I told you to stay out of my affairs, my lord."

"Affairs, is it?"

She looked away, her cheeks colouring brilliantly. "I believe he does not know much more than that."

"Did he ask you questions?" Sussex demanded. "Was he fishing about for anything?"

"No. In fact it was really just a conversation that began

because we were talking of our interests. However, I was alarmed enough to come to you. We might very well have a problem, Adrian."

"Might?" Iain growled. "Good God, there is no might about it. The truth is we have a very great problem."

She sniffed, a sound of pure disdain. "Perhaps we might finish this conversation alone, brother."

"No, Alynwick stays. He'll be left here to deal with things after I am married tomorrow. He deserves the right to know it all. And what he might be dealing with."

Reluctantly, Elizabeth nodded, still looking straight ahead though her hands were nervously fidgeting with her gloves. "He has invited me to attend a time or two while he excavates the crypts in Temple Church. Naturally, I accepted."

"I think not!" Iain exclaimed. "Are you out of your mind?"

"No, indeed. In fact, I am rather firmly planted in it. I do have a brain, my lord, and it functions for other things beyond the commonly accepted female accomplishments. Naturally—" she turned her head to address Sussex "—I accepted because it will provide me with any information that Sheldon might happen to discover in the crypts. I can, of course, immediately relate them to you."

"She's right, of course," Sussex muttered. "And if it is all very innocent, Lizzy will not be in any danger."

"And if it's not innocent?"

Sussex's expression went pale, but Elizabeth blithely waved her hand. "It's a matter of curiosity, I believe. Lord Sheldon is an archaeologist, and the story of the Templars is a very enticing one. He only wants to discover it and solve it."

"And publish it in every damn journal out there."

Shrugging, Elizabeth said, "Then we shall have to

think of what is to be done, if and when he arrives at that point. Speaking of points," she muttered, "I fancy we have another very interesting point to discuss."

"And what is that, Lizzy?"

"Lord Sheldon, it seems, has had a very nasty run-in with one Mr. Nigel Lasseter."

The room went still. Iain heard the breath leave Sussex's lungs, and the two men exchanged alarmed glances. "Oh?" the duke said.

"Remember that Templar cache of treasure I told you about? Well, apparently Mr. Lasseter was working at the time in Temple Mount alongside Lord Sheldon. One night when Sheldon was working, he was struck on the back of the head. He fought his assailant, and was able to see who it was. Nigel Lasseter. The man left Sheldon for dead, and made off with the cache. Sheldon informed me that Lasseter has been selling off bits and bobs of the treasure ever since. However, I don't believe that his lordship is aware that Lasseter is now in London. He mentioned merely that he had heard Lasseter might be in Town. Nor do I think he knows of Lasseter's sponsorship of Knighton's expedition to the Holy City. I did not tell him, nor did I confirm anything about Lasseter."

"You were right not to tell him, Lizzy. And to come to me with this."

"I thought it all very much reminded me of sacred geometry. You remember, brother, how Father would always move around the chalice, hiding it, using shapes on a map that had meaning. In my mind I noted all the names and places of things that have happened, and mentally drew the lines, connecting everything. I think if you place the names in a certain order and connect the lines, you will have something. Although one must possess sight to see it."

Iain's rage was replaced with a swelling pride. Elizabeth York had always been the loveliest, most angelic creature he had ever known. He had desired her not only for her looks, but her voluptuous, luscious body, and the way she had allowed him to use it for his pleasure. She had become even more lovely in the ensuing years, her body more enticing. The promise of a beautiful, wanton sensuality sparkled in her eyes. But at this moment, he thought of none of that. Only stared at her, marvelling at how damn intelligent she was. The beauty of the organ hidden beneath the beautiful face. *What a beautiful intelligence you have, my love.* He might have said the words if Sussex wasn't present to hear them.

"Sacred geometry," Iain murmured admiringly.

"Yes, my lord. The Templars were the ones to use it, a knowledge that of course was passed down by the Freemasons at Solomon's temple. Today it's used by the Masons. All very relevant to our situation, don't you think?"

"I don't need to think, for you have clearly done so for us. I don't believe any of us would have reached that conclusion."

"Yes, well," she muttered, her smile chilling, "this is what happens when you relegate able-bodied minds to the corner because they are of the wrong sex."

She would not let it go, and Iain smiled, admiring how fierce and stubborn she was.

"Well, that is all," she said, before carefully rising from the chair.

Sussex reached for the bell cord, signaling for a servant. "I don't like this, Lizzy," he warned. "It could be very dangerous. We know very little about Sheldon."

"I've never felt threatened in Lord Sheldon's company. This is truly the only way to discover what he knows, and what he might learn. And despite what some of you think, I *can* be of some assistance."

"Lizzy," Sussex groaned in warning, but was interrupted by his butler.

"Your Grace, you rang?"

"Yes, Lady Elizabeth is ready to go upstairs. Call for Charles, will you?"

"At once, Your Grace," the butler said, before bowing.

"Oh," Elizabeth said. "One more thing, Adrian. I had tea with Lucy this afternoon after my walk. She really is quite down in spirits. I informed her—vowed, really—that you would make a most loving, honourable and caring husband. Please do not make a liar of me."

The duke laughed. "I will not. You'll see, Lizzy. I promise to make her the happiest woman on earth."

"I told her that. She didn't reply, but in my mind, I could see her frown in dismay. You do have your work cut out for you. But, then, anything worth possessing is worth traipsing the levels of hell for, isn't it? Especially a woman's love." Lizzy's smile was brilliant. "My book, please."

Iain reached for the leather tome, then for her hand, allowing his bare fingers to slide down hers, skin to skin. The light, fluttering touch was so unbearably erotic that her breath caught as he placed the book in her hand. He noticed what it was, and tipped his head to the side, studying the intricate heraldry work on the spine. What was she doing with this?

"Thank you, my lord." Her words were clipped, her tone anything but gracious.

She had known it was him passing her the book, and he wondered if she had smelt him once more. The thought set the animal in him purring. As he held her hand in his, while they cradled the book together, his mind conjured up the very delicious image of Elizabeth lying on top of him, her hair loose and unbound, dragging over him, cocooning him as she worked her way down his body, traversing him with her nose, smelling him, tasting him, listening to his demands.

My God, I would crawl through every dominion of hell, if only to have you once more.

A deep voice cleared, then coughed, forcing Iain to release her hand. The footman was waiting, and reluctantly, Iain placed Elizabeth's hand on the servant's forearm.

"My lady?"

"Yes, I'm ready, Charles. Adrian, will I see you at supper?"

"Yes. You will."

Iain could not take his eyes off Elizabeth as she disappeared from the room with the footman.

"I trust, Alynwick, that you will know what to do about Sheldon?"

"Indeed, I do."

And he did. He'd see to it that she was never alone with the earl—and that she did not lose her heart to the bastard. *That,* Iain silently fumed, would once more belong to him.

CHAPTER TWELVE

"YOUR HANDS ARE COLD," Maggie noted as she took Elizabeth's gloves from her. "And you're pale, too. Does your head still pain you? It's terribly bruised. Darker even than this morning."

"No, my head is quite sound." Her pride still stung however, but that was nothing new. She had developed an excess of the vice since losing her sight. There was nothing worse than being thought of as an invalid, when one was in perfectly good health and capable of still doing *some* things for oneself. "I will admit, however, that I am a bit chilled." Elizabeth vigorously rubbed her hands together to get the blood flowing once again. "The wind was rather biting at times this afternoon, wasn't it?"

"Indeed it was."

"I would wager that a storm is approaching. I could sense it on my walk."

"Yes. The infamous stroll," Maggie teased. "Common sense would say that you should have ended your jaunt about the park much sooner than you did. But when the heart is engaged the head is never listened to, is it?"

"Maggie," Elizabeth said with a laugh. "You are very unsubtle."

"Am I?" Lizzy could hear the feigned innocence in her companion's voice. "Perhaps I should just come out and ask, then?"

"That would be far too bold of you," she teased.

"Let me overstep my bounds, this time."

Laughing, she gasped, "*This* time?"

"I'm only wondering what the two of you were talking about all that while. I swear, my tootsies were throbbing by the time you turned about and declared it time to make our way back to the carriage. I nearly wept with relief."

"I'm sorry. I didn't know your feet were paining you. You should have told me."

"And brought an abrupt end to your visit with that fine-looking gentleman? How selfish."

"Is he fine, Maggie?" she couldn't help but ask.

"As tanned as any infidel or Caribbean pirate, I wager. And hair that is kissed by the sun. Devilishly handsome, especially when he glances down at you and smiles."

Elizabeth felt a touch giddy, and stemmed the silly reaction. "Lucy mentioned he was tolerable."

"Tolerable?" Maggie cried. "Why, I daresay he's more than tolerable! He is really quite handsome, and very kind about the eyes, if you don't mind my saying. And gentlemanly, too. He helped me down from the carriage, you know. Most fine *gennlemen*," she drawled, "can't be bothered seeing to the assistance of the help."

"He has stolen your heart, has he?"

"Nonsense. I'm just trying to throw yours into his keeping, is all."

Elizabeth did not have an answer to that. It was much too soon. She liked Lord Sheldon, very much. They had many interests in common, and seemed able to converse with friendly ease and teasing banter, which was always a good sign. And there was no denying the blooming attraction, at least on her part. But she had been taken in before, and could not afford to be so rash this time around.

Elizabeth listened to the sounds of her companion rustling about her room. Maggie must have tugged a bell pull because there was a slight rap at the door, followed by the sound of the upstairs maid.

"You rang, miss?"

"Build the fire, if you please," Maggie requested. "Lady Elizabeth is chilled."

"Right away, ma'am."

Elizabeth immediately pulled a face. She did not like it when people fussed over her. She was blind, not frail and dying.

"Oh, don't do that," Maggie commanded. "Don't give me that sour expression. There's been many a hearty soul brought low by the cold. I daresay many that are heartier than you."

"You fuss too much, Maggie."

"It's my duty."

"Fibber, it's your delight to vex me."

"Never," Maggie said with good cheer. "That's enough wood for now, Agatha. On you go."

When the door closed behind the maid, Maggie let out a long, aggrieved sigh. "That girl. Wherever did His Grace find her?"

"Someplace dark and dangerous, and most inappropriate for a young woman of her years, is what he told me." Sussex was always out, prowling the streets of the East End, trying to save as many souls as he could. Elizabeth supported his endeavours in any way she could.

"Well, they must have very dirty hearths in the East End, for she's made quite a mess of the embers."

"If they have burning hearths at all," she reminded her companion. "Besides, I can't see the embers, therefore they aren't bothering me."

"Well, they're bothering me. I'll have to have a word with her."

"Give her a chance, Maggie. She's only held the post

for a fortnight. Besides, I don't want her thinking I'm a harridan. I quite like the girl. She's friendly and she doesn't walk about as though I were a fragile china doll ready to shatter into shards. Let her be, if you please."

"Very well. Now, then, what do you wish to wear for supper?"

"Something comfortable. It is only Sussex and I tonight, and I'm quite sure it will be a short evening for us both."

"Yes, His Grace's wedding day is tomorrow. Everyone in the household is so very happy for him, and seems genuinely fond of Lady Lucy. She'll make a good duchess, and a good mistress to the staff."

"Yes, she will." Lizzy smiled fondly as she thought of her friend. "And I will be happy to call her sister."

"I'll begin the packing tonight, then."

"Oh, no, didn't I tell you? I won't be joining Sussex in Yorkshire. I'm staying behind in London."

The long silence told Elizabeth all she needed to know. Maggie, like her brother, thought it a miserable idea. With a groan, Elizabeth flopped back onto the bed and curled against Rosie, who was sleeping deeply.

"Is that really wise, my lady? You've always accompanied His Grace."

"His Grace was never on his honeymoon. Maggie, trust me, the last place I should be is traipsing along with Sussex and Lucy while they honeymoon. Imagine it, my being dependent upon them, and them just starting out their lives together. No, there will be many more years ahead in which I shall be a burden to them. I *will not* be one on their honeymoon!"

"You most certainly are not a burden!"

"You know what I mean. It's not as though I am completely independent. I will need assistance, Maggie. And you would be there, too, but you know my brother. He hovers, though he thinks he does not. He dotes, too. The only person he should be doting upon is Lucy."

"I wonder if you're all too pleased to stay in London because of a certain someone?"

Fear temporarily gripped her. Was Maggie referring to Alynwick? No, of course not, she thought, shaking her head. Maggie could have no knowledge of her past with the marquis, or the strange feelings he had begun to earnestly churn within her. For so long she had been safe from him. He had kept his distance, and their conversations, although short and strained, had always been polite—and disinterested. And now they were anything but. *He* was anything but distant. For the past few days he'd been a constant presence within her home, a beautiful, sensual, *unwelcome* visitor in her dreams. Damn the man, she smelt his scent in almost every room of the house.

This was just another example of how Iain affected her. Maggie was insinuating Elizabeth would be happy to stay in London because of Lord Sheldon, but all that came to mind was Iain.

How dangerous he was to her peace of mind. She had refused to think of him in that way for years, and now could hardly stay focused on the innocent conversation she was having with her companion, without images of Iain, and the supple glide of his fingers along hers, intruding. She could be dead and buried, lying in the cold ground, and still vividly recall the sensation of those incredibly skilled fingers trailing over her body. Every inch of her discovered, and she had allowed it. She couldn't allow it again. The first time, she'd been innocent. Had naively believed everything he had said. Falling victim to his skilled seduction was no fault of her own. But to fall again, when she was supposedly older and wiser... Well, she would deserve everything she got, then, wouldn't she?

"You look knackered, lying there atop those pillows. Why don't you rest for a bit before dinner?"

How kind Maggie was to leave her alone, in bed, with tumultuous thoughts of Iain to torment her. Lizzy had spent a perfectly pleasurable afternoon with Sheldon, indulging in a wonderful conversation with a man she knew she could quite easily feel something very strongly for, only to come home and have every memory, every feeling for him wiped clean, with the sound of a voice and the touch of a hand....

Damn you, Iain Sinclair....

Without awaiting her reply, Maggie left her, the quiet click of the door signaling her departure. Rosie heard it, gave a little growl, then immediately stretched out again, nuzzling her muzzle into Lizzy's palm.

"Elizabeth?" Her companion had returned.

"Yes?"

"Allow me to overstep my bounds once more, and say that Lord Alynwick is a very handsome man, too. I daresay even more so than Lord Sheldon."

"That is far too bold, Maggie Farley."

"Perhaps, but I thought it needed saying. He cares for you, Elizabeth. It's ablaze in his eyes, tattooed on his face."

"Maggie—"

"Enjoy your rest." The door clicked quietly shut again.

"What am I going to do, little mouse?" she whispered to her faithful spaniel. "What a simpleton I am for even giving the man a second thought. You think me silly, don't you?"

Rosie answered her by licking her wrist.

"Yes, you wish I would cease bellyaching about him.

I'm sure you're quite tired of hearing his name, and my complaints."

With a growl, Rosie rolled onto her back, paws bent.

"I suppose it's only fair I reward you for your listening skills and nonjudgemental ways."

Rosie's groan of delight when Lizzy started rubbing her cumbersome belly made her laugh. The small dog shifted on the bed and Elizabeth heard the rustle of the book against the coverlet.

She should be thinking of the diary, and how best to obtain Sheldon's assistance, without giving away Sinjin's name or his involvement with the Brethren Guardians. Perhaps she should put the earl off, tell him that she had misplaced the book and could no longer find it. But she did dearly wish to know who the woman was, and turning down Sheldon's offer of assistance would make the attempt of discovering the woman futile.

Perhaps Lizzy should have Maggie read it, see if there was any reference to Sinjin's name, or anything that might give away his identity. She could instruct her to tear out those pages, but then she'd be destroying a treasured family heirloom.... Bloody hell, there was no winning in this mess! Still, tearing out the pages might be the only way, if Sheldon pushed her to show him the book. But, then, she thought, why would he? To him, it was merely an interesting anecdotal piece of history. He shouldn't insist, but should, in fact, accept her excuse that she could no longer find it. Of course, that meant giving up a set of knowledgeable eyes that might very well have aided her.

The quandary of what to do left Elizabeth irritable and frustrated. How she wished she could read the book herself, those passages she could no longer remember by heart. The diary was very intimate, and she found herself wondering if she was even prepared to share such a thing with Sheldon. He was a scholar, of course, and she was certain he would read the diary as such. But could she? It might make things…strange between them. Might create something that she was not quite ready for. Not yet, anyway. It might, she mused darkly, make her think of Iain Sinclair. It always had in the past. That book had made her want what Sinjin and his mystery lady had shared—and she had wanted it to be with Iain.

Stupid, stupid, stupid…

Too keyed up to rest, she found her thoughts tumbling in a circle. Unable to keep them at bay, she felt like she was racing against the wind, trying to outrun them. But the past would always be there, haunting her.

Carefully she rolled to her side, reached for the thick post at the foot of the bed and gripped it, holding herself steady. In four steps, she knew, she would be before the long looking glass. It had been a gift from her mother, a piece she had brought with her from France upon her marriage to Elizabeth's father.

Lizzy remembered its shining rosewood frame and scrollwork edges. The legs were turned, carved with ornate roses and clamshells. She wondered if the mirror was warped yet by age, or spotted with black marks.

She remembered the piece as being decadent, a frivolity to delight a young girl who enjoyed dressing up in her mother's hats and evening shoes and tromping about her dressing room as she watched the Duchess of Sussex prepare for an evening out.

Despite her blindness Elizabeth could still picture herself standing before the mirror, her short, chubby body drowning in her mother's ball gown and gloves.

She'd soon grown out of that chubbiness and into a body that made her violently self-conscious. She had matured far too early, her mother said, and Elizabeth used to hide in her room, crying herself to sleep, despising the voluptuous curves that she possessed, and none of the other girls of their acquaintance did.

Her mother had been losing her sight then, and Elizabeth longed to hear her remark upon her looks, even though she knew her mother was disappointed that she had not inherited her French beauty or slim figure. It would mean, at least, that her mother could actually see her.

What would she think of me now?

Her mother had died from a terrible fall down the staircase at a ball she had been hosting months after Iain deserted Lizzy. Elizabeth's own sight was swiftly diminishing at that time, and she recalled how, weeks before the accident, they used to sit quietly in the salon together, contemplating their futures. She had known that the blackness engulfing her mother would soon come to swallow her as well, and it did, taking her hostage.

Smoothing her hands over her body, Lizzy wondered if she had grown to resemble her mother. Sussex claimed she looked like their father. She had not wanted that, for the duke had been so cold and removed—and so very ashamed of her. She wanted to have nothing in common with him, least of all the cold austerity of his looks.

What did others see in her? Her hair was black, she knew, and long. When it was unpinned, she could feel it hanging around her hips. When Maggie brushed it out for the night, she often commented on how shiny it was, like a pelt of sable, and perfectly straight.

Her eyes were grey. They hadn't changed with her blindness, Maggie assured her. Lizzy often wondered if she looked blind. It was a tiny fear of hers, to have wild, wandering eyes that were not focused or steady. She wondered if people averted their gazes from her when she spoke to them. She would never know if they did, and had always feared that they might, leaving others to observe her conversing with the top of a head, or an ear— or worse, a back.

Was she beautiful? She didn't know. When she had sight she had thought herself a strange-looking creature, with hair so dark and skin so pale. Her grey eyes often made her appear downcast and melancholy. Her lips were full, she knew, and her cheeks always plump, like the rest of her.

She was nearly thirty now. The last time she had seen her reflection, she'd been nineteen. How much had she changed? Did she have lines around her eyes? Her mouth? Was her body enticing, or just doughy? Would she see a mature woman in the reflection, or would she see remnants of that sad, lost young woman?

Her hands, of their own volition, slid along the curve of her hips, which her gown could not conceal, and over the rise of her belly, the soft protuberance beneath her corset, and up to the bodice of her gown.

She felt the curves, sensed a woman's body, but could not decipher if it was the sort that was becoming to men. Impotent frustration rose like a fury inside her. She was not vain, not at all, but there were times in a woman's life when she wanted to see her reflection and gaze upon herself, to discover the woman she was. What others saw in her. Lizzy had no idea what appeared in the looking glass. No sense of identity, or person...

"Wondering what he sees when he looks at you?"

She started, gasped, nearly screamed until she felt the heat of Iain's chest against her back. The firm grip of his large hands anchoring around her waist as he slowly brought her rigid spine to rest against the long length of his body.

"Shall I tell you what he sees? What any man sees?"

"Don't." Oh, her voice sounded breathless and weak, and so very unconvincing. She thought back to that afternoon, to Lucy and Isabella, and she only felt weaker, thinking of what they had said. What they saw in Iain's gaze.

"Let me be your eyes, Beth."

The whisper of her name, the name only he used, was at once so arousing and powerful, yet like a sword to the heart. How could one be aroused, when slowly but effectively being stabbed to death?

"G-get out before you are discovered here."

"No one will discover us."

"Maggie—"

"Is sound asleep in her room. She left the door open and I noticed her napping as I crept by. Your brother is lost in thought over his impending nuptials. There is no one to discover us."

"The servants, my maid…"

"I've locked the door. It is only you and I and a very exhausted Rosie in this room."

"You have no right to come here, none at all!"

"I think I do."

"Well, you're wrong."

"I only wanted to make certain you were safe."

"And why shouldn't I be? This is, after all, my home."

"You are determined to thwart my attempt at being a gentleman."

"No, to prevent any more lies that spring so easily from your lips."

His hand was hot, burning through the bodice of her gown. "All right, then. The truth. I came up here to find you because I could not stay away."

Elizabeth snorted, trying to find level footing. "Not likely. You have some other motivation up your sleeve."

"Perhaps. Maybe it's that I want to kiss you again. To see your body naked in this mirror, with my hands covering you. I want, Beth," he whispered darkly next to her ear, "to see myself sink deeply inside you. To watch you accept me."

"No."

"Slowly, penetrating deep, softly, lazily, until the past is gone, purged from us both."

That, she could not allow. She was not good at hating. Forgiveness and understanding came too easily to her, she feared, and knew it would be all too simple to forgive him for the past. To *want* to allow him that kiss. Or worse, to wish he would take the decision from her, and just do it. Yes, that… She had always gravitated to that aspect of him, the dominant part that always knew what she wanted, and wouldn't allow her to run away in fear.

Swallowing, she gathered her courage to fight him and her body's natural instincts. "I am not at all interested in your kisses, my lord."

"Are you not?"

How smooth and dark his voice was, whispering into her ear. The man knew she lied. It seemed she couldn't hide anything from him.

"What of Sheldon's kisses?" he asked grimly. "Are you interested in his?"

"I don't see what concern that is of yours."

"Everything you do concerns me. Everywhere you go, everyone you visit, everything you do…or dream."

"You make things out to be there that aren't."

"Is that so?"

"Of—of course," she stammered, despising how she felt obligated to gift him with a reason for spending time with Sheldon. "He has agreed to help me discover the name of someone in a diary I found."

"Ah, yes, the book you were carrying."

"Sinjin York's personal diary. There is a mystery in it."

"And Sheldon, you think, will help you discover it? What a mad scheme."

"It's not a scheme," she snapped.

"The truth, Elizabeth. What game are you playing?" Iain said, his voice growing angry. "What purpose will it serve to bring Sheldon where he doesn't belong? Where he can only create havoc, and not solve the mystery? Leave him out of it. Why risk the safety of the Brethren Guardians by showing him this book?"

She didn't like Iain's tone, or the way he just seemed to think it was his right to command her, to bend her to his will.

"What possible help could he be to you?"

"He's agreed to be my eyes," she replied tartly.

"I could be your eyes, Beth."

She would not tremble...*would not*.... "I doubt you could be of any assistance." No, he would be a liability to her, a menace.

"And you think he can aid you, is that it?"

"Yes."

"He can't. And it would be more than dangerous to think he could. To show him that damn diary."

"Of course he can help me," she sniffed.

"No, love," he whispered. "He can't. But there is one person who can."

She was not his love. Had never been his love. "Oh? I suppose you know one who will better serve me, then?"

"Me."

"Your arrogance astounds me," she snapped irritably. "What makes you think you can help me?"

"What makes you think I can't?"

"You've never been interested in helping anyone before. It is not in your makeup to care, to want to come to the aid of another."

"You are partially correct, Elizabeth. I am arrogant and selfish, and, no, I haven't cared about helping anyone, except one person. You."

"I doubt that. You wanted only one thing from me, and you got it, and promptly walked away. Let that be enough."

His body stiffened behind her, and she wondered if she had hurt him, or if it was his considerable pride that baulked at the reminder that he had been nothing but a horrid rake and unscrupulous seducer to her. He had never cared. If he had, he would not have said the things he had to her.

"Let me help you with the diary."

"No, Lord Sheldon has offered, and I have accepted. You are free to pursue your own vices, and no longer have to involve yourself in anything I'm doing."

"I've been involved in your life, Elizabeth, whether you have noticed it or not, for a very long time."

She struggled against him, fighting against a warmth that refused to fade. How she wished she could send him on his way, but she was weak and inconstant. The wicked creature who always found him irresistible was much more insistent than the woman of good sense.

"You've said your piece. Now it is time to leave."

"Not yet. You haven't answered my question," he said quietly, his voice wrapping around her in the dark. "What is your purpose in standing here before this mirror?"

"None of your business." She could not weaken. *Could not.* "You have no right to know my thoughts."

"I know it for the truth, that I should never be allowed

into your life, that I have no right to assume I should be. Yet I cannot help but think it is my concern. After all, I have tasted you, have brought you to shuddering climax. My body has been deeply inside yours. I know you as no man ever has, Elizabeth. We have a connection, and although you want to deny it, to ignore the fact, the bond between us remains—neglected and dormant, perhaps, but like a bud in spring, is ready to awaken in the heat."

Her head was swimming. "I will never allow you back in."

He sighed, and Elizabeth felt his chin drop to the juncture of her shoulder and neck. He needed a shave, for his jaw was covered in a night beard. The devil slowly brushed his chin against her skin, abrading her, sensitizing it, and her womb responded with a deep ache of want.

Blast him, not even a kiss, only a small grazing touch, and she was already aching inside. She closed her eyes against the knowledge, the realization that she was weak and wanton.

"I am already there, aren't I? Already so deep inside you. Just as deep as you are inside me. The past might lie between us, but there is something there beyond the hurt. Isn't there?"

She refused to answer. Couldn't. Didn't trust herself to speak for fear she might say yes, or even nod in agreement. No man made her surrender, made her give up her control like Alynwick.

"Damn, but you smell so good," he murmured as his palm, large and firm, moved from her waist to make a slow progression over her stomach, her ribs, the valley between her breasts, where the tips of his fingers toyed with the bow on her bodice. "I can smell you, the building desire, the struggle within. I remember it from all those years ago, the heady musk of your excitement. The outline of your body before the window. The way it made me feel to look at you, to know you were mine. The way I took you…" His lips brushed softly over her flesh. "The way you gave yourself to me."

Once before, they had stood like this in the dark of night, when he had crept into her room. She had been watching for him from her window, and he had silently come up behind her, captured her around the waist and tore off her night rail and wrapper, rendering her naked. He had made love to her like that, with her naked and on her knees, her hair fisted in his hand. Him, behind her, fully dressed, breathing hard—exciting her. He had possessed her, and she had allowed him to. Had given him everything she had, and he'd taken it. Like a man starved, he had greedily consumed her.

"Tell me what you were searching for, standing before this mirror?"

Shaking her head, Elizabeth pressed her lips together. She refused to answer, to give words to her vulnerability. But he knew… Somehow the soulless, callous Alynwick always could read her thoughts…. Knew what she wanted, what she yearned for her. He proved her correct when he said, "See yourself through my eyes, Beth."

Coward. Weakling. Silly wanton. No, she could not allow him to show her what she was. She had no wish to see how quickly and easily she could succumb to him.

But, oh, God, his fingers, hot on the bare flesh of her bosom, felt so good. Their trembling against her, the sweep of his mouth across the bounding pulse of her neck… It felt too good to resist, and she allowed her head to fall back against him. It had been so long since she had been touched. She'd had so much of him before—his mouth, his hands. His body moving inside hers. And then he had left, abruptly withdrawn from her. His touch had been a living thing, a life, and when he had gone, it had been like a death. Hers.

How she longed for this in the night. To be stroked. Held. Caressed. There was nothing to rival a lover's soft, reverent touch, and it had been sacred to her. He had made her body his, a supplicant only too willing to obey with just a touch. Then, like all masters do with their slaves, he had tossed her aside when she was no longer of any value to him.

"You are so beautiful." His lips moved over her neck, his chin over her sensitive collarbone. "You cannot imagine how lovely, Beth. Every man's dream. My most wicked, erotic fantasy come to life."

"No." She shook her head, protesting not his assessment, but the way she felt herself falling against him, the way her arm rose up over her head to clutch at him. She could not stop the action, nor prevent the tears that started to well behind her closed eyes.

So much pain…. Her heart was aching with it, with the memories of his betrayal. It was mixed with the onslaught of pleasure, so acute, so overwhelming. She was literally trembling with it, her body awakening after years of feeling cold and dead. It wanted to reach out to him. *To live.* The inner struggle was tearing her apart, and she could do nothing more than rest against him and pray…. Pray that he would not destroy her once again.

"Just the other night, I dreamed of you, pale and naked, crawling to me, your body covered in red wine—your curves, the tips of your breasts. You were wanton and beautiful, seductive. And I was your slave, Beth."

"Iain." She wanted to beg him to stop, but could not say the word.

"Beth…Beth…" His voice was hoarse, calling to her from a place that sounded far away. But he was here; she felt him, the gentle, seductive slide of his lips along her throat. The moist heat of his breath, the hardness of his erection pressing into her bottom. An erection he took no shame in, but pride, for he crushed it against her, made her feel it. Want it.

It was insupportable, to know soul deep that it was wrong of her to take any pleasure in this. To allow him any liberties. But she was mortal, and mortals were conceived in sin. She was at the mercy of her humanity now, not her mind. Even her free will had been stolen the moment his fingers touched her, awakening her like a dormant tree in the spring sunshine. And the first tear slipped down, unchecked. Oh, God, what was she doing?

"Don't cry…my Beth." He could hardly believe that hard rasp was his voice. But it was. "My love, don't."

Her eyes were closed, her head tilted back, her face averted so he could not see her, only feel the slow slide of a tear that slipped unbidden from the corner of her eye, down her cheek and onto his lips.

Holding her tighter to him, his heart pounding, Iain tried to find words, the words that would make her feel safe in the arms of a monster who had ruined her. But he couldn't. Only after they had made love had he felt able to talk to her. Words had never come easily. His childhood had been one of solitude and silence, and he was comfortable with that. But Elizabeth had always made the silence unbearable. And when he had finished making love to her, he would lie down beside her and hold her, and together they would talk about everything, anything. For him, the conversations after were every bit as intimate as the acts they shared. He still felt that way, and could not summon the courage to just talk, and hold. There were walls around them, walls that had never been there before.

If he could only tear them down…

"I want to see you."

She shook her head, denying him.

"Yes, let me."

Carefully he dragged one corner of her bodice off her shoulder. She was beautiful there, rounded and soft, her skin as luminescent as a pearl, as pale and alluring as moonlight. Brushing his face against her, he listened to her breaths, turned his cheek against her and swiped his tongue, circling the delicate ball of her shoulder until the circles became smaller and he was sucking her, watching her—them—in the reflection of the mirror.

Beautiful angel, he thought as he pulled the bodice of her gown down as low as he could without unbuttoning the back. He didn't dare move her, for fear it would break the spell that had woven around them. For there was a spell. Iain had never felt anything like it. A wondrous sensation that slowly wrapped around them, binding them together, thoughts, wishes, dreams merging. Becoming one. He had to see her, to watch her, and she wanted him, his hands over her, covering her. Her body spoke, and his understood the silent command.

The mounds of her breasts were exposed, pushed up tightly by the constriction of her corset and bodice. He wanted to touch, to see her naked—stroked by his hands. To kiss. To pleasure her until her tears were ones of sexual satisfaction.

"Iain…"

Her voice was soft, a whisper. *Frightened.* He should whisper back to her. Tell her it was all right, that he would keep her safe. He wouldn't leave, wouldn't turn his back and walk away. Never again.

His fingers gripped her skirts, inching them up in a slow slide that tormented him. He could not look away, especially when the pale stockings came into view, followed by the rounded curves of her thighs. There were layers of petticoats, and white lace frothing beneath his hands, and Elizabeth's fevered breaths rasping against his neck, all coalescing into a beautiful, sensual frenzy that was whipping up like a tempest inside him.

He would have her. Right now, on the floor, lying before the mirror.

Slowly, he placed his thigh between her legs, wrapped one arm around her waist, anchoring her to him, then lifted her thigh to rest over his.

"Open to me."

The sweet exhalation he heard was made all the sweeter by the sight in the mirror. Elizabeth wore no drawers. Beneath her gown she was naked, bared, exposed to his gaze. And his hand, trembling, left her knee, slid up the soft expanse of her inner thigh until his palm cupped her, felt the heat and moisture. He touched her and watched her response in the mirror—the parted lips, the tip of her tongue creeping out, until he caught it in his mouth and sucked, opened her lips wider, kissed her with everything he had as he circled his thumb over her, feeling the slick flesh beneath his fingertip, the quiver of her body, the long beautiful sigh of a lover surrendering.

Her fingers were in his hair, tugging and pulling. The kiss turned deeper and his fingers smoothed down her sex, stroking her, building her up until he slipped them inside, filling her. He felt and heard the vibration of her moan.

"Beautiful, beautiful Beth, evening has fallen, the blues of the sky filtering in through your window. You are temptation in the twilight and I can no longer resist you."

"You must, Iain," she murmured, pulling away from

him, the blue of her gown slipping away from his black trousers, until all of her was concealed from him.

He pulled her back, turned her in his arms and lowered his mouth until he could place a kiss on the apex of her breast. "Do you really want that, Elizabeth? For me to leave you like this? Aching? When I could so easily appease you?"

He reached for her hand, kissed the tips of her fingers, and lowered it between them, fitting her palm over the engorged length of his cock. Closing his eyes, he dropped his head until it was resting against hers. He kissed the bruise and small cut on her forehead, savoured the feel of her pressed against him. Impossibly, he was growing harder and thicker behind his trousers.

"Beth…" He cupped her face in his palms, tilted it up and brushed his mouth over hers. "Take it. Let us find our way back to each other. Let our bodies say what we cannot, or will not, allow ourselves to tell each other."

Cupping him, she stroked the outline of his stiffness with her thumb. He was damp behind his trousers, ready to spill, ready to tear open the fastenings and free himself into her palm. "Beth." It was a deep, painful plea, said against her mouth. "Take me."

The barest second of hesitation flashed between them. He was aware of holding his breath, of pressing his cock into her, of murmuring next to her ear, "Take it all, Beth, take it deep inside you."

"No, Iain." Her voice held a steely conviction. "No."

"It's what we both want."

"No, it isn't." She did not look at him, but instead twisted in his arms, averting her face. "I am done with you. Quite done."

"Are you?" he demanded, anger rising up inside him.

"Well, that is unfortunate, Elizabeth, because I have not even begun with you."

He left then, afraid his pride, arrogance and fear would rise up, take over, and he would say something damaging and reprehensible. It was just another block in the road, he told himself. A fight she knew she must wage, and one he knew he must wear down. She would give in, would allow him in; he just needed to give her time. The right inducement.

As he left her, he saw the book on the bed and reached for it, opening it. This was the way. The secret to unlocking Elizabeth.

"Don't waste your time with Sheldon on this diary," he announced suddenly. "He can't help you. But I can. I will. I have knowledge of the Veiled Lady you seek."

"For a price no doubt," she snapped.

"Yes," he answered. "A price. It won't be so steep that you can't pay it."

"What if I don't want to? Pay the price, that is?"

"How badly do you want to know who she was, Elizabeth? How badly do you want to know *her* story?"

He left her like that, a nearly impossible feat. He wanted nothing more than to go back to her, drag her to the bed and kiss her, love her, mend the past until it melted away and there was nothing but a future between them.

"Let me know when you're ready to begin."

"I will never agree to it, you know."

"You will."

She had to. It was the only chance left to him. Seduce her with a love story that defied centuries. A love story that mirrored their own.

CHAPTER THIRTEEN

THE DOOR OPENED on the third violent rap of the brass knocker.

"May I be of service?" The steely eyed, pinched-mouthed butler looked down the long length of his nose in hauteur.

"Tell Sheldon the Marquis of Alynwick is here to see him."

"His lordship is not in this evening."

"My apologies. Perhaps in my attempt at politeness, you did not understand me," Iain snarled as he placed the toe of his boot on the step to prevent the butler from slamming the door in his face. "You will go now and inform Sheldon that Alynwick demands an audience, and if he denies me, I will tear down this door and any other door that keeps him from what I want. Is that understood?"

The butler sniffed. "Very well, my lord. If you will wait here." The door slammed shut.

Iain was left staring at the black painted door and brass knocker in the image of a lion's head. It took no more than a minute for the butler to return and open the door to him.

"His lordship will see you immediately."

Shrugging off his greatcoat and hat, he handed them to the butler, who passed them along to a footman before he escorted Iain down the long, mahogany-panelled hall to Sheldon's study.

Throwing back the doors, the man announced in tones that conveyed immense distaste, "The Marquis of Alynwick."

Sheldon glanced up from the middle of the floor, where he was busy attempting to make a black dog sit still.

"Jack!"

Sheldon roared the name, but the dog came bounding over to Iain, his tail wagging so voraciously that his whole back end was swaying.

"Down!" Iain ordered when he jumped up on him. The canine obeyed, much to Sheldon's obvious surprise. Iain petted the animal behind the ears as a reward for listening. The dog licked his hand as though it were a sweet.

"Jack, go lie down."

Reluctantly, the dog obeyed, prancing to a blanket on the floor near the hearth.

"Forgive him. He's just learning his manners. But from what I heard of you at the door, you're not one to be impressed by good ones."

Setting his teeth together, Iain fisted his hands at his sides. "I'm not a pandering, toadying aristocrat, no. Why waste time on niceties using double entendres when a succinct statement derives far more satisfactory results?"

Sheldon watched him, his gaze steady and knowing. "I am neither pandering nor toadying, either. I've spent too many years in the East, dealing with those who do not care for the British way of evasiveness and betrayal hidden behind gentility. Sit," he commanded, motioning to the chair before his desk. "Drink?"

Overnight, it seemed, a bar had been set up. There hadn't been one present last night when Iain had searched the study. "No, thank you."

"Tea? Brandy? *Scotch?*" he asked, his gaze sly, as if

the bastard knew Iain's tongue was hanging out for a wee dram of *uisge beatha,* the water of life. But he'd be damned if he took anything from the Earl of Sheldon.

With a shrug, Sheldon poured himself a large measure of brandy from the decanter on a side table, then took a chair behind his desk. Setting the glass down, he moved a pencil over onto an unrolled piece of parchment, manoeuvring the tip so that it rested against the Templar cross fixed on the corner, ensuring Iain's gaze would be drawn to it.

Cunning scoundrel...

And this was the sort of man Elizabeth had spent her time with? The man she had thought to share Sinjin's diary with? Sheldon was as dangerous as a two-headed cobra.

"You will forgive the disarray of my study, I hope. I have had a locksmith in today to add new locks to my windows, and the maid has not yet been in to clean up the workman's wood shavings."

Iain refused to allow his gaze to slide to the windows. He would not give any confirmation to the answers Sheldon was seeking with his veiled statements.

"Infidels, thieves and murderers abound in the metropolis," he replied. "It's good to watch your back."

"Indeed." Sheldon sat back in his chair, reached for his brandy and took a leisurely sip. "Although years spent abroad have given me an edge, I think. They have a way about them, in the East. A certain relish and technique for subterfuge, ambush and revenge. One picks that up quite quickly when one is raised amongst them."

"I wouldn't know. I was raised by a Highland clan in the wilds of Scotland. We Scots have our own way of vengeance and retribution."

"I shall have to remember that."

"See that you do."

Leaning forward, Sheldon replaced his glass atop the desk and ran his tanned hands across the parchment, fanning them out so that the paper lay flat. "To what do I owe this somewhat expected visit?"

"You know very well what is on my mind."

"Lady Elizabeth York."

"You're a quick study, Sheldon."

"I only state the obvious, a trait we share, I think. We share something else, too. The fact that Elizabeth York is on both our minds." He glanced up, his gaze daring Iain to refute the truth. "Isn't she?"

Iain's eyes dropped down to Sheldon's hands. He had a horrid, gut-wrenching visual of those dark hands traversing the pale curves of Elizabeth's naked body. It made him grit his teeth and strive for control. Especially when he still had the scent of her clinging to his fingers.

What he was doing was underhanded, most especially to Elizabeth. But a desperate man would do anything. Even cut off his arm. And Iain was desperate enough to do just that. Although he had tried, unsuccessfully, to make himself believe that this visit was part of his duty to Sussex and Black, and the Guardians. As such it was his obligation to investigate Sheldon and discover what he knew about their order. But he was here for Elizabeth, his Beth.

"Leave her be, Sheldon."

The earl cocked his head, studying him. "You think I'm toying with her, or that I mean to harm her?"

"I don't know your true intentions."

"They aren't to hurt Elizabeth, I assure you."

"*Lady* Elizabeth," he muttered between set teeth.

From the corner of his eye, he saw the dog's head

come up. Senses alert, the animal watched them, obviously aware of the very dangerous hostility in the air.

"All right, then. Lady Elizabeth. She's a remarkable woman. I've never met one like her. I could spend hours talking to her."

"You have, it seems," Iain growled.

"What has she told you?"

The question was asked in a mild, almost artless way that spoke volumes. In trying to seem relaxed and almost uncaring, Sheldon was revealing a great amount of anxiety.

"She has not told me anything, but I was with Sussex when she informed him of your little stroll this afternoon."

"Ah."

He would not have Sheldon thinking that Elizabeth had gossiped about him, or that she had been purposely questioning the earl to extract information that she could share with them. He still didn't know who or what Sheldon was, and he would not have Elizabeth in danger.

"So Sussex sent you over here, did he?"

"No, he did not. I came on my own volition."

"Because you love her."

It was not a question, but a boldly stated fact. One Iain would not deign to answer, because when he admitted it, when he finally said the words aloud, the first person to hear them would be Elizabeth.

"You came here tonight to tell me to stay away from her, is that it? You've discovered that she and I share much in common, and that I have requested she join me on my latest expedition."

Sheldon slid the etching closer to the edge of the desk so Iain could see it. "Elevations of Temple Church. I'm sure Elizabeth told you of my interest in the Knights Templar, and the artefacts and mystery surrounding them."

"She did. What I'm wondering is what you stand to gain by bringing her there with you."

"The pleasure of her company? The excitement of sharing a find with someone who understands my enthusiasm? Elizabeth has just as much zeal as I for the Templars. Or did you not know that?"

Christ. The bastard was perfect for her! The thought nearly knocked Iain from his chair. How he hated to admit such a thing, but it was there, staring him in the face. The Earl of Sheldon was everything Iain wasn't—kind, gentlemanly, well-read; everything a woman like Elizabeth should want in a husband and more. They shared the same interests, they talked with ease—but they could not possess the same elemental passion that Iain and Elizabeth held for each other. That was a rare phenomenon, a meeting of souls and hearts, and every other ethereal thing he could think of. There was simply no way Elizabeth could feel that—could allow herself to feel that—for another man.

Suddenly, Iain narrowed his eyes. "What are you about, Sheldon?"

Surprised, the earl held up his hands. "As you can see, I have nothing to hide, Alynwick. I'm an archaeologist with a love of Templar lore. I came into my title quite accidentally, and have been in England only a short time."

"I've asked around about you," he said, "and there is precious little anyone knows about you, or your time spent abroad."

"I don't doubt it." The bastard didn't even look surprised that Iain had taken it into his head to investigate him or his past. "My family is a very small one, and since my father spent much of his time in the East, the few connections and friendships he had while growing up here have all but disappeared."

"Convenient."

"If a bit lonely."

Iain decided to ignore that statement, and the image of Elizabeth filling that void for Sheldon.

"While there were few who knew me, there was no end to the people willing to impart to me what they knew of the Mad Marquis." Sheldon's hazel eyes flickered up from the pencil he was holding, landing on Iain. "Like you, I decided after you nearly choked me to death at the Sumners' musicale that I did not, indeed, know enough about you."

Iain should have expected no less, but still was shocked. Not that anyone wouldn't relish the idea of gossiping about him. But he hadn't thought Sheldon the type to go searching for information. He'd believed him bookish, concerned with literary salons and art—not the type to exert oneself to investigate a man's past, or break into his study.

The earl was a puzzle. And Iain loathed puzzles. He definitely had no patience for them.

"And what did you learn?" he asked in a bored tone. "Anything of use, or was it all the usual nonsense, a digest of my sexual escapades?"

"There were any number of those. I confess you put the most virile of the male species to shame by your prowess. But I found something of interest there."

"I doubt it. I'm only exciting when it comes to my sexual appetites and the scandals they create. Other than that, the ton doesn't give a damn."

"You were raised by an abusive mother."

Iain had murder in his eyes, he knew, as his gaze narrowed on Sheldon. How had he learned that?

"Your parents separated when you were young. Your father left you in her care, having no need of you until, it can be presumed, he desired to mould you into his heir. Your mother's father was the laird of the Clan Sinclair. The old man was a tyrant and so, all the accounts say, was his daughter."

It had been the main attraction for his father, his mother's innate strength. He'd wanted that bred into his son, so that when it came time to take his place, not as the Marquis of Alynwick, but as a Brethren Guardian, he would have a backbone of steel.

His father had known what his mother was like. How she raged at any imperfection. She was not maternal. Not soft and loving. She had raised Iain to be immune to any emotion, and when her lessons did not work, his grandfather had taken over the task.

Most of all, Iain had learned to be selfish and self-serving, putting his desires before anyone else's. A legacy that most parents would cringe away from, but not his. They'd relished it. He was strong in both body and mind. He needed no one. Not even them.

"When your grandfather died on a deer hunt, you took his place as laird. You were ten. Your first act as chieftain was to see to the removal of your mother to another house—in Sterling. Far, far away from you."

She had deserved it, damn it. He'd been ten, and yet she and the chieftain still beat him. He could never please her, so he'd pleased himself instead and sent her packing. He never saw her again.

"You were laird for six years, and a highly regarded one. Courageous and strong, and respected by the other chieftains. They saw quite a promising man in that youth. Then one day your father rode into the Highlands, whisking you away. When you returned, there was nothing left of the young laird. In his place was a man made of stone. A statue as cold as marble and as immovable as granite."

What precious little Iain had managed to salvage of his soul after he'd had his mother banished, his father had swiftly destroyed, leaving him an empty shell. A devil in human flesh.

"You are his image, I am told. Cruel. Cold. Selfish. Bent on getting your wishes whatever the costs or collateral damage."

Yes, he was, but he was trying damn hard to change that. To be the man he desired to be, not the replica of his father.

"Well?" Sheldon demanded.

"Someone has been very chatty, I see. But it hardly matters. Maladjusted families are a dime a dozen in the ton. It hardly signifies anything. Besides, I could have told you that I was a merciless, coldhearted bastard and saved you the trouble. Who told you?" he asked, wondering how Sheldon had come by it all.

"You have very shoddy locks on your study windows."

"You bloody bastard." Iain bolted from his chair, and the earl rose to meet him.

"We are even, aren't we? Don't bother to deny it. I know you broke into my study last night. I could smell it—Elizabeth. The scent is on you now. The same scent that marked the air last night."

Suddenly, Iain was terrified for Elizabeth. What if Sheldon was truly their enemy? What would he do to her? "What are you hiding, Sheldon?"

"I would ask the same question of you, Alynwick. What do you hide, and Sussex? And Lord Black, for that matter?"

"Go to hell!"

"I found it, you know. Your boyhood journal. Who

knew you were the sort to pour your soul into a book? I thought you more the type to lash out with your fists and smash things. Heartbreaking, really, reading it all. Although it made me understand the man—how you turned into an unfeeling brute."

Panic raced through him. Unable to burn it, he had hidden that journal beneath the floorboards of his bedroom. Not too far from the scroll his family had been entrusted to keep safe for all eternity. Had Sheldon found that, too?

"Your name, Sinclair. It is really St. Clair, isn't it?"

"Of course not." The hairs on his neck stood straight up. Who *was* Sheldon?

"I researched it, you know. At the museum. I traced a Templar out of Jerusalem, a Haelan St. Clair. He fled to his native Scotland, where he was a chieftain of the Clan St. Clair. For some reason he garnered the notice and generosity of the king. He was given the title of Alynwick. At the same time, the clan of St. Clair quietly changed their name to Sinclair, a bastardization started by the English, but used for convenience and secrecy. But why, it's not known."

To keep the clan safe from those who wanted Haelan St. Clair persecuted. To protect the scroll and the Brethren Guardians so no one could follow their trail from Jerusalem.

"You are the direct descendant of Haelan St. Clair."

Iain saw no reason to deny it. It would only make Sheldon want to dig deeper. "Aye. I am. It was over seven hundred years ago. What significance is it now?"

Sheldon glanced down at the elevation drawing on his desk, his gaze lingering over the Templar cross and the Lorraine cross emblazoned there. "Haelan St. Clair was a Templar knight who was charged with the task of protecting a sacred relic from the Ark of the Covenant."

Iain fought to maintain control, at least the outward appearance of it. Damn it, Sheldon had stepped much too close to their little group, and the history of the Guardians. Dangerous man, the earl was.

"I hardly believe in medieval stories of chivalry, and I have no use for religion. Besides, I didn't come here to talk of Templars and ancestors long since turned to dust. I came to tell you that if you see Elizabeth again, you'll be putting your life in danger. Do you understand me?"

"I genuinely care for her."

"I genuinely don't give a damn."

"My interest in her is noble, honest. I would make her my wife. Are you suggesting that your motives are as pure?"

"I do not suggest anything. I state. And you can be damned sure that my intentions are my own, and I won't let anything stand in the way of them. You've been warned, Sheldon," Iain growled, pointing his finger at him. "Carry on with your dig, and whatever else you're trying to unlock, but leave Elizabeth alone."

He turned to leave, pulled violently on the door and yanked it open, stopping only when he heard Sheldon call his name. "You know, Alynwick, if she really wanted you, she would be yours. But she's not, is she?"

"Sod off."

"I won't fight over her like two rabid dogs. I won't do her the disservice. I'm man enough to allow her to decide for herself. Are you?"

Slamming the door shut, Iain fumed all the way down the hall. Bloody, arrogant ass. He'd love to rip the prat's head off and feed it to his dog!

IF SHE REALLY WANTED YOU, she would be yours....

Smarting at Sheldon's words, Iain viciously tugged at the ends of his tie. *If she really wanted you...*

She did, damn it. He had felt that desire in her body. But Elizabeth's desire wasn't all he wanted from her. He wanted her heart. Her love.

Damn Sheldon for finely dissecting his emotions and shoving them down his throat. He should have been furious—and frightened by the ease with which the earl had discovered all he had about him and the Templars. That, far above anything else, should have made him feel this violent. But that was far back in his mind now. Clouded by everything Elizabeth. At least Sheldon had not found the scroll. That had been the first thing Iain had checked on upon returning home.

"You are in a fine mood this evening," Sutherland observed.

"I'm miserable, aye," Iain grunted as he drank a long swallow of whisky. "Bloody miserable. You'd be, too, if you had to face an evening like the one I'm about to."

"Then why do you do it, allow the Lady Larabie to come to you?"

"Because I must. More than my soul rests on her knowledge of Orpheus. The lives of those I love and care most about are relying on me to find a way to discover all I can about our enemy. Lady Larabie claims a personal friendship with Orpheus. She dangled the carrot of introducing me to him, and I've taken the bite."

"Is there no other way to find the man?"

"No. He's a damn magician, popping up when he desires, and hiding more often than not. Georgiana has promised an introduction, and that's all I need to assess our enemy and make plans to destroy him. I need a face to the name, and without her help, we can't get close to him. It's not as though he wanders about his club, surveying the wickedness that goes on there. He hides, and it's only through Lady Larabie that I can corner him. In truth, she has me by the bollocks."

"She's taken what little of your soul remains, I think."

Tired, Iain sighed, finished off his drink and placed the glass firmly upon his desk. "Don't I know it. You're dismissed for the evening, Sutherland." He only wished he could so easily dismiss the events of an hour ago, when he'd confronted Sheldon in his lair.

"My lord—"

"Don't." He held up his hand. "I know what I'm doing. It's not like I haven't entertained a woman for my own motives before. In that, Sutherland, I'm not a novice."

Turning his back on his valet, Iain made his way to the salon, where the lady with the black veil sat awaiting him. For some reason, looking at the veil reminded him of Elizabeth's Veiled Lady, and the diary he needed to pull out of its hiding place.

"Forgive me, I was finishing up business."

Folding the veil over her bonnet, Georgiana rose, greeting him with the sleek smile of a cat. "I have missed you between my thighs, my Highland beast."

He was nothing but a rutting animal to her. A stud to pleasure her. So far, she'd gotten far more out of him than he had her. He took no pleasure in her, their passion, their bed sport. He would not do so again. No matter what she did, or pleaded with him to do. He had vowed to himself that he would get Elizabeth back, and he would. Goddamn it, he would. And he would not soil his heart and soul—and body—with this creature before he did so. He would not come to Elizabeth dirty.

"Undress me," Georgiana ordered, coming to him,

running her hands over his chest. "I want you to take me on the settee, then your desk...in a chair by the fire."

Closing his eyes, he pretended that her touch inflamed him, when really he sought to hide the revulsion in his eyes. He didn't want this. Not Georgiana, not this mindless act. Not after what he'd shared with Elizabeth. He still felt the embrace, the feel of her in his arms, the heat of her core wrapping around his fingers. There had been more in those shared minutes than there would be with hours spent fornicating with Georgiana.

"Your arm," she purred, and he heard very little genuine sympathy. "I hope it's up to the task tonight?"

"That, and another most important appendage."

Her eyes glowed with delight. Hiding a wince, he moved her away from him. Her perfume was cloying, choking him. Lord, he needed another drink. He noticed she wore the ring that Larabie had purchased for her. It made him think of the necklace he had placed on his dressing table. He'd watched it in the gaslight as Sutherland shaved him, imagining what it would look like encircling Elizabeth's throat.

He wanted to make love to her with her wearing nothing but that necklace.

"Already so hard," Georgiana gasped, stroking him. "That's what I adore about you, Alynwick. You're always up for it."

It was time to push for what he wanted, and he wouldn't get it by playing coy games any longer. It was time to be the beast that Georgiana was so fond of.

He allowed her to stroke him, pulled her closer and looked into her eyes, challenging her.

"Yes?"

He tugged her even nearer, pressed her against the wall, crushing her against it, his body pressing into her back so she could not see the lie in his eyes. "I want to fuck you," he breathed hard against her neck, "tonight, at the club, with everyone watching us. With all eyes on you and me."

"I thought you'd never ask," she murmured, her body trembling in desire. "Let us be off—quickly."

ORPHEUS WATCHED HIM through the throngs of bodies that writhed at his feet. Alynwick was there, a woman tugging him along. He would stay and watch the show, for Alynwick's lover was quite lovely and, he knew from experience, fucked like a succubus. He wanted to watch the Scot handle her, to match her—break her, even. Another time he might have joined them, but he was not quite ready to meet the Scot. Not yet. Soon. He was preparing to meet them all and send them to hell.

His rightful place in the world was returning to him. There was just one small matter to see to. Elizabeth York. He laughed, rose from his chair, then skimmed his hand appreciatively along a woman's breast. She had been waiting for him, trying to catch his attention, but unlike Alynwick, he was not ruled by his cock.

"Lovely," he murmured. "Really, rather perfect. But, next time."

He patted her and brushed beyond her, thinking of how pleasurable it was going to be to watch the mighty Marquis of Alynwick fall to pieces when he gutted Elizabeth from throat to muff, and let her fall to Alynwick's feet, her life's blood pooling, flowing....

YEARS AGO, when Iain had been trying to drink and fuck himself into oblivion, the House of Orpheus would have been his home. It was everything the depraved Alynwick would have desired. He would have lost himself here, allowed himself to drown in the debauchery, to die in sin.

Women of all shapes, sizes and colors paraded about, wearing nothing but masks to shield their identities. The club was filled with a decadent, opulent feeling, a glittering essence that made the debauchery seem somehow more elegant and erotic.

Perhaps it was only the heavy incense filling the room that made him think such things. The aroma was sweet. Heady. Opium? Whatever it was, it made him relax a measure, made the air and his blood thick, sluggish.

Leading him through the orgy, which appeared to be in full swing, Georgiana tugged at his hand and gazed back at him over her shoulder, her eyes glowing with sexual intent, the promise of meeting Orpheus a seductive lure she had cast for Iain to follow her from the carriage to the club.

He was not even hard. And he didn't plan on becoming so, either. He had only one purpose in coming to the club, and it was not to dally with Georgiana, despite the promise in her eyes.

"Here," she murmured, stopping him. They were near a corner furnished with pillows and mats. It was not the center of attention, but could very well be, with the silk hangings and pillows. Georgiana, it seemed, was intent on making it so. She had discarded her cloak and was now unbuttoning the gold gown she wore. The cleft of her breasts came into view, and from the corner of his eye, he saw another masked gentleman stop kissing a woman, only to leer at Georgiana as she slowly disrobed.

"It looks like you will have to fight for me," she cooed as the gown slipped to the floor and she stepped out of it, completely naked and kissed by the glow of the candles that surrounded them.

He can bloody well have you, Iain thought with disgust.

"Lovely creature," the man all but panted as he watched her sultry, catlike moves.

With a detached eye, Iain watched Georgiana's sensuous progression toward him. He could not help but think of his fantasy—of Elizabeth naked, crawling to him—and comparing the two. What a difference. Elizabeth's generous curves and welcome aroused him like nothing ever had. Especially Georgiana's overt sexuality. Iain realized he much preferred Elizabeth's angelic veneer, which hid so much passion. If only he could make her feel safe enough with him to release it.

The man was now on his knees, his arms wrapped around Georgiana's calf, his hands smoothing up over her slim thigh, mouth wandering wantonly over the flesh. Her fingers slid into the man's hair, almost patting him like a dog as her gaze locked with Iain's.

"Ménage à trois?" she asked in her most seductive voice.

"I don't share with other men."

He brushed past her, and she laughed, calling out to him, "Foolish man, you have all along."

Iain didn't bother to stop and question her accusation. She had been a means to an end. Nothing more. Georgiana could take whomever she wanted to her bed, because he was done with her. He was here, and somewhere in this place of hedonism, Orpheus was hiding. This had been the goal all along, the prize to be won after wooing Lady Larabie. This is what Alynwick had sold his soul for. He could no longer play the lady's games. Couldn't wait for Georgiana to deign to bring him to Orpheus. It was now, it had to be, because he could no longer go on selling himself to the woman.

Leaving the main room, Iain entered a dimly lit corridor. The activities had already begun to spill out into the halls. His progress went unnoticed by the writhing bodies, unheard over the sounds of ecstasy. Turning left, he entered a corridor that was not lit by candles or gas lanterns. Obviously, the darkness was supposed to be a deterrent, but Iain had never been afraid of the dark.

Opening the first door, he saw it led to nothing but a bedchamber. A quick glance around told him it was part of the club's erotic arsenal, not a private space belonging to Orpheus.

The next three chambers were much the same, except the last one held a particular scent, a man's cologne. Someone had just been in this room. The moon was bright, spilling into the chamber from the window, affording Iain a small amount of light in which to search the space. The walls were panelled in a dark wood, the room furnished, but not in the same decadent way as the others. The cologne seemed stronger near the wall opposite the window and door. There wasn't a table or chair, or desk, where someone might have sat. Nor was there a picture or mirror that they might have stood before. That could mean one thing.

Sliding his hands over the walls, Iain searched for any uneven panels, and was rewarded with the feel of a small metal lever. Carefully, quietly, he pulled it, and saw a portion of the panel give way, opening slowly with a soft groan of protest. The opening was not large, and he had to crouch to make it through. Straightening, he saw that he was no longer in the club, but a labyrinth of dimly lit halls.

Following the corridor, he had a sense that he was moving downward, each twist, each turn giving the impression of descent. He could hear the raucous cheers and laughter coming from the Adelphi Theatre, which was beneath the club, but in the same building, confirming his suspicions that he was, indeed, going down.

Ahead, he heard a door open, then quietly close. He walked faster, making certain his boots did not ring out on the wooden floors. Beyond the bend, doors lined both sides of the hall. He paused briefly at each one, seeking the lingering scent of cologne.

At the third door on the left the cologne was strongest. There was something else as well, something musky and earthy—old. Cracking open the door, he saw a sliver of light, the back of a man with long black hair streaming over his shoulders. He was removing his evening jacket, reaching for a crimson banyan, which he shrugged into, knotting the sash tightly around his waist.

Nigel Lasseter.

Iain felt a rush of triumph. He had the bastard at last. And by the looks of things, the way Lasseter moved through the secret parts of the club with ease and confidence, Nigel *was* Orpheus. The pieces of the puzzle began to snap into place. Nigel must have been using the wealth from the Templar cache he had stolen from Sheldon, and was now using the club as a cover. Clever bastard to recoup his expenses by creating an establishment that charged hefty dues to become a member. The risqué club was exactly the thing to attract the most bored in Society, which usually happened to be the richest.

The next piece that so easily fit was that Lasseter must have discovered the story of the Brethren Guardians, because he had unearthed the fact in Jerusalem, while excavating with Sheldon. And if Lasseter knew of them, then Sheldon must also.

Quietly, Iain moved forward, watched as Lasseter disappeared through another door, softly clicking it closed behind him.

"I wouldn't, guv." Iain heard the cocking of a gun at the back of his head, just as he was about to step into the room. "Slowly now," the thick, Cockney voice said smoothly. "Turn slowly with yer paws up."

Iain slowly turned to face his captor. His eyes widened in shock when he saw a second man with a gun pointed to the temple of none other than the Earl of Sheldon.

Sheldon's eyes went almost as round as his, but he quickly shielded them from the interested gazes of the guards.

"Now what the devil are ye two up to, wanderin' Mr. Lasseter's halls?"

"What does it look like?" Sheldon demanded in a very strange, sotto effeminate voice. "We were to meet up in private. Obviously, we took a wrong turn somewhere." Sheldon's eyes sent Iain the message that he had better play along, or they were both going to have their brains blasted out of their skulls.

"Were ye now?" The guard holding Sheldon looked amused and disgusted all at once.

Damn Sheldon for this ruse. Iain would rather fight and get it over with. But he supposed the earl's idea was satisfactory—for now. Iain wanted the element of surprise when he cornered Lasseter, and tussling with his guards wasn't conducive to an ambush. He just hoped that Lasseter couldn't hear the commotion. Not that Iain couldn't handle himself, but he preferred not to in front of Sheldon. He still didn't trust the bastard, and finding him here, in Orpheus's club, only made him more suspicious.

"Is that right?" the guard asked, pressing the barrel of the pistol into his flesh. "You have an assignation with this bloke?"

Iain cleared his throat. "Yes, an assignation." No point beating about the bush. He did warn Sheldon that he didn't insinuate, he stated. "You understand the circumstances, don't you?"

The man with the gun poised between Iain's eyebrows sneered. "Can't says I do, guv. Unnatural, them urges. But yer kind seems to have them enough."

Iain shrugged. "All that paddling from the schoolmasters. Changes a man." He swore he heard Sheldon chuckle.

"Yeah, well, two big blokes like ye should be givin' it to the ladies."

"Yes, well," Sheldon interjected in his ridiculous voice, "we prefer the company of each other. Perhaps you might show us a back way out? As you said, quite unnatural, our relationship, and against the law, as a matter of fact."

"No' to mention the fact that my wife is in the main room. She has no idea of my...inclinations," Iain provided.

"Is she now? Poor miss, I should take her in hand."

"Crawley," the other guard—the nervous one—warned as he eyed Iain's height and the breadth. "No need for offence."

"Yer right. I could have a bit of skirt and muff whenever. But what these blokes 'ave, well, that don't come too easy now, does it? How much for our silence and yer safe removal?" Iain's guard demanded with cunning eyes.

The other guard motioned with his head to the chamber behind Iain. "We should take 'em to Lasseter."

"They're two flash boys bent on a bit of buggery. What the devil would Lasseter do with them, besides watch?" He chuckled. "Maybe you'd like that, eh? A third to yer party?"

"Ah, no," Iain grunted, recognizing a chasm he did not want to explore.

"I'm rather shy," Sheldon provided, seeing the same

difficulty Iain did. "Doesn't always work when I'm nervous, if you get my meaning?"

"Understand," the man named Crawley leered. "Sometimes the mast just doesn't want to rig up the flag."

This was becoming utterly ridiculous. "I have a hundred pounds on me now. Will that suffice?" Iain asked.

Crawley's eyes lit with interest. "That'll do."

After the transfer of money, the guard motioned both of them forward. "Hands on yer head, and follow my directions."

Guns aimed at their vitals, the guards steered them down the long curving corridor, down a long flight of stairs to another door. Crawley fished in his pocket for a key ring and fitted an old-fashioned skeleton key into the lock. The door swung open and the cold night air swept in, raw and fierce in their faces.

"On ye go," Crawley announced. "And don't come back."

The door slammed shut behind them, and Iain heard the key turning in the lock. They were in an alley, the same alley, he suspected, where Sutherland had witnessed Nigel Lasseter entering the Adelphi Theatre.

Turning his head, he studied Sheldon through the dim gaslight that filtered from the Strand. "I can beat the information I want out of you here, Sheldon, or we can take this someplace more civilized and a tad bit warmer. Either way, you're not leaving until I learn every damn secret you're hiding."

CHAPTER FOURTEEN

IAIN SAT BEHIND HIS DESK, a large snifter of Scotch—his second—in his hand. Sheldon sat across from him, eyes watchful, but certainly not afraid.

"Why the hell did you come up with that particular ruse?" Iain said irritably.

Sheldon smiled at the memory, no doubt having a good laugh at Iain's expense. "What is it that concerns you, Alynwick—that your reputation might suffer? I doubt the guards knew your identity, unless, of course, you frequent that establishment regularly?"

Iain glared at the man, but Sheldon waved aside his ire. "I see you are in no mood for jests."

"What was your first clue?" he growled.

"Well, it seemed to me to be the most expedient way of incurring their disgust and getting us out of their sight. Plausible as well, considering what I saw in that main room."

"Are you?"

"Am I what?"

"One of...those," Iain muttered.

"Hell no!" Sheldon declared. "I'm a hot-blooded male who spends it on women, thank you very much."

"Not on Elizabeth," Iain said, staring down the earl. Seeing that Sheldon understood his point, he relaxed a measure. "The question begged asking. You came up with the idea rather quickly, and your act was highly convincing. Done this sort of thing before, Sheldon?"

The earl took a long swallow of Scotch, and Iain grinned when it made him cough. Aye, an effeminate, indeed.

"I suppose there's no keeping anything from you now."

"No, there's not. So don't bother to deny it. Your fate was sealed the second my eyes landed on you. I was going to have you, Sheldon, whether you desired it or not."

The man's eyes lit with fury at the double entendre, which really was in poor taste, but which Iain found rather amusing, and still could not quite wrap his mind around. He'd played many parts over his lifetime, but never that of the aristocratic tosser.

"First and foremost, my lord," the earl sneered, "let me make this understood. I quite adore women and have absolutely no designs nor interest in you. Or any other man, for that matter."

"What a relief, Sheldon. Your act was so damn genuine that I began to wonder."

"Well, don't. No doubt that crafty mind of yours was already calculating that my interest in Elizabeth must be platonic, what with my proclivities, which naturally gives you the advantage."

"It was leaning that way, yes."

"Well, I hate to disappoint you. I am still very much interested in Elizabeth—in *that* way."

"Bastard."

Sheldon smiled, raising Iain's ire. "But Sebastian de Montfort is a persona I frequently employ. He's come in very useful over the years."

"What?"

Reaching into his jacket pocket, Sheldon fished about, making Iain stiffen, wondering if the earl was going to pull a weapon on him. But instead, he tossed an object across the polished veneer of his desk.

"Detective Inspector Julian Wentworth."

Iain's gaze flew to the silver crest of Scotland Yard, then back to Sheldon. Interesting... He had thought him many things, but never a detective. Iain didn't know whether to be alarmed or relieved by the information.

"Did you suspect?"

Iain shook is head. He slid the badge back to Sheldon, who pocketed it once again.

"Good. Then no one knows, and I'd like to keep it that way, Alynwick."

"Then you had better start speaking," he suggested. "I am all ears."

Taking another drink of Scotch—this time a sip— Sheldon finally sat back in his chair and contemplated Iain.

"You've been an admirable adversary, although it was never my intention to have you as one. Imagine my surprise when I discovered my study had been breached. And that you were the culprit."

"You've poor locks, Detective. A novice could have picked them."

"No, they couldn't have. And you're not a novice. I knew that the moment you put your elbow to my throat. You knew the most vulnerable spot on a man, and with one quick press you could have fractured the cartilage and eviscerated my larynx and trachea, killing me within seconds. I knew then that I had to find out more about you, and what complication you might be to me and my case."

"The Scots can be savage when provoked, and you provoked me."

"You took me by surprise, Alynwick, and I'm not easily surprised. Ask my superiors, they'll tell you. I'm thorough, methodical, meticulous and I can always outwit an enemy. But you… You have the brawn, brains and cunning of a jungle beast."

"Thank you, but I'm still not letting you see my naked arse."

Sheldon grinned and shook his head. "You won't let me live that down, will you?"

"Never. That voice… God, it was like being in a salon with all those tosser artists."

"How do you think I came by it? I studied them most carefully. I can also be a convincing Arab, with a little kohl and dye for my hair."

"What are you doing in England? What is this case you speak of? Are you truly an earl, or are you yet again posing as someone you're not?"

"A fair question. I am the legitimate earl, but as a son of a second son, I never expected to inherit. My father was a diplomat, but he was also high in Scotland Yard. He trained me. I attended a special branch of the Yard at the embassy. Highly secret. I trust you won't tell of it?"

"You have my word."

Nodding, Sheldon plunged on. "I became a sort of spy for British and Arab affairs. As a cover, I became an archaeologist, which allowed me a large and varied contact with the Arabs. I had a great interest in archaeology, but it was always a cover for what I loved more, espionage."

"Explains how you so easily dug up the skeletons in my family closet."

"Partly. I had some help from Special Branch. Your father was on their watch list for decades, and they themselves had acquired quite a bit of information on him. I merely helped myself to it. I needed to see if you were in on Lasseter's scheme."

"And?"

"There's no connection with you. But there was one with Black."

Iain narrowed his gaze, senses alert. "What sort of connection?"

"Actually, it was with Lady Black."

"You will tread very carefully, Detective. The lady is a good friend, and wife of a man whom I consider a brother."

Damn, his tongue was getting loose, but he could not allow Black or his wife to be maligned. Damn Brethren Guardian secrets. He was tired of them.

"Lady Black, when she was Miss Fairmont, was being courted by Wendell Knighton, curator at the museum, and a protégé of Nigel Lasseter. It was Lasseter who funded Knighton's expedition to the Holy Land, because Lasseter himself could not return, not after what he did to me. He feared that I might be alive, you see, after he left me for dead. He would never dare set foot in Jerusalem after that, so he needed someone to do the work for him. That's where Knighton came in, a young man eager to make his mark not only on his profession, but the world. Lasseter could not have begged the devil for a better or more eager dupe."

"And where is it you come in, Detective?"

"I was preparing to leave Jerusalem. By then, I had heard all I needed to know of Lasseter, and my revenge, while sanctioned by Scotland Yard, had become rather personal. When Knighton mysteriously died, I knew it was Lasseter. The man will kill whomever gets in his way."

"In the way of what? What does he want?"

"I don't know. I never could reason it out. While he

pretended to be my friend, Lasseter kept his secrets close to his heart."

"What has this to do with the House of Orpheus?"

"I didn't know of the club until tonight—when I followed you. You see, the lady you were with, Marie Lalonde, was Lasseter's lover and fugitive accomplice. Naturally, when I saw you, I had to discover your connection to her."

"Marie Lalonde? I'm sorry, Detective, but I've never met a woman by that name."

"I believe she goes by the name of Georgiana Larabie."

Admiration lit Iain's eyes. "I thank you, Sheldon. You've saved me an evening of inconvenience, for I was planning on investigating the most duplicitous Georgiana myself."

"Oh, she has raised your suspicions?"

"Indeed." He'd known the bitch was hiding something, and here it was Nigel Lasseter all along, his enemy. Orpheus himself, the man she had promised to take him to. Obviously, he had played right into their hands. He'd been a fool, and it didn't sit well with him—not at all.

"Might I ask how she raised your guard, my lord?"

"No." Taking a sip of Scotch, Iain set the glass back onto the desk and thought through his plan. "I sense a breach of hostilities between us, Sheldon, at least temporarily."

"Yes?"

"I can only give you my word of honour that what I was doing with Lady Larabie was nothing to do with her time spent in Jerusalem with Lasseter, or any crimes she committed in France. You'll have to trust me that if I discover anything that might aid your case, then I will share it. Until then, I must keep my own counsel."

"That's fair, I suppose. Should I keep my own counsel tonight, and not share with Elizabeth whom I saw you depart with?"

He wanted to hate this man, but the bloody determination he saw in Sheldon's gaze made Iain admire him instead. "I know how it looks, but nothing happened. Elizabeth…" He swallowed hard, thinking of her, thinking of her with Sheldon. "I'd never do anything to harm her. Her…opinion of me at the moment is not very good, and while I will admit that I deserve it, I do not deserve to be labeled for something I didn't do. I did not betray Elizabeth with Lady Larabie."

"Fair enough. I believe you."

Nodding, Iain motioned for Sheldon to continue. "Tell me about Lasseter, and your connection with him. I'm afraid your explanation has been somewhat convoluted and I am left rather confused by the whole matter."

"Forgive me. I had assumed that you would know. I told Elizabeth the story of my connection to him."

"And you thought she would spill your secrets? Detective, your opinion of her is rather low, is it not?"

Sheldon had the grace to blush. "In my experience, there are few true, honest people in this world."

"In mine as well, but you will find that Elizabeth York is one of the few good ones out there. She is an angel, and can be trusted with a man's life. The secrets of his soul."

Sheldon studied him in the gaslight, and Iain had the urge to hide in the shadows. But something shifted in Sheldon's gaze. A perception. An understanding. He spoke no more of Elizabeth, but instead continued his story.

"My business with Nigel Lasseter, who is a French émigré and wanted for a string of robberies in France, began in Jerusalem nearly three years ago. He made his way to the Holy City, where I was working as an archaeologist at Temple Mount. I was investigating a rebellion plot involving the Turks, while disguised on a British dig. Lasseter befriended me. He was interested in excavating, and had a real obsession with the Templars. We struck up a friendship because I, too, have a genuine love of Templar lore. At that point I had no knowledge of his past. We discussed at length the Templars, and their methodology for hiding sacred relics, money and escape routes. He was especially interested in those—in the Templar method of building underground crypts and tunnels."

"Why?"

"I believe it was something I said that piqued his interest. I mistakenly informed him of how the Templars' preferred mode of hiding their cache was in their crypts."

"Ah, I see. So he somehow persuaded you to allow him to assist you."

"Worse," Sheldon muttered, and Iain saw the anger and shame in his eyes. "I didn't just allow him to assist, I showed him how to excavate. How to find the gems of the Templars."

"And then?"

"I came across a cache. Lasseter wasn't with me at the time, but I brought him later to show him what I'd found. Along with the treasure there was a scroll outlining the story of three Templars. He became very excited about it. Almost…possessive, I would say. He waited for me to dig up the entire treasure, and when I did, he accosted me one evening in the tunnel, tried to stave my head in with an excavating pitch and leave me for dead. I fought him, and was winning until darling Marie came to save the day for Lasseter. She brained me with a large rock, and I fell to the ground. I'm sure they thought me dead. It took me months to recover."

"So Lasseter and Marie stole the cache and began selling off pieces to fund their return to England."

"Exactly."

"You said you told this story to Elizabeth. Why? What interest would she have in it?"

"I was hoping to discover if either you or Sussex had any connection with Lasseter. I already knew there was a very thin connection to Black. I did not learn of your link until tonight, till I saw you with the woman I know as Marie."

"You will not find more than that, Sheldon. I personally guarantee it."

"Well, when I woke from my extended sleep, I informed Special Branch of what had happened, alerting them to the fact that I believed Lasseter to be on the run, and most likely headed to London. Where else can one get lost in the throngs of humanity?"

"And they separated," Iain mused. "They knew Scotland Yard would be looking for two people, a man and a woman."

"It would appear so. And in the meantime, Marie found a new persona, and was able to dupe poor old lecherous Larabie into marrying her. No doubt Larabie is unwittingly supplying Lasseter with money to keep afloat." Sheldon sat forward and peered into Iain's eyes. There was an implacable determination in his gaze. "I want him, Alynwick, and Marie, too. I want them to stand trial, to suffer for their crimes."

"I want him as well, but for something very different."

"Tell me."

"I can't."

"Is it illegal?"

"No." How could he confide in Sheldon about the Brethren Guardians? He couldn't. Absolutely could not betray Black and Sussex, no matter the cost. But he did need to know how Lasseter knew so much about them, and what he was planning on doing with the information. "You will have to take my word for it, Sheldon," he said at last. "My reason for wanting him is my own. If I get him first, I'll hand him over to you after I'm done with my questioning. If you manage to get him before me, I ask only that I am allowed to interrogate him—in private."

"And you swear to me that there is nothing more to it than that?"

"The matter is a long one, Sheldon. A matter of family, and secrets. But as far as I know, nothing illegal. And nothing to do with what he did in France, or what he did to you."

Sheldon sat back and studied him thoughtfully. "I'll let you keep your secrets, Alynwick. For now. But at some point I fear that they might all come tumbling out."

"Then I shall have to deal with it, won't I? Until then, I will keep them to myself."

Rising from his chair, Sheldon stuck out his hand. "To a temporary truce—in this matter."

Iain accepted the handshake, knowing they shared a truce in the business of Lasseter and the House of Orpheus. But the matter of Elizabeth, he knew, was far from settled.

"HAVE A CARE, Elizabeth. The steps are uneven and crumbling. There now," Sheldon said, clasping her hand carefully. "Two more steps and you'll be standing on the floor, which is really quite uneven, so you'll have to hold on to me."

The smell of earth and mould burned her nose. The sound of water tapping against stone echoed in the distance. Jack's bark ricocheted off the walls, which she imagined were curved medieval arches carved into the stone. Here she was, beneath the Templar church, where no soul had ventured in hundreds of years. What secrets awaited discovery? What treasures were to be found?

How she wished she possessed sight so that she might see the great arching caverns, the crypts made of stone, complete with effigies of knights who had served hundreds of years ago.

Jack barked again, only this time he took off running down the corridor, his paws scratching against the dirt and stones.

"Jack!" Sheldon growled, then called, "Jack, come back here!"

"Oh, dear, has he run off?" Elizabeth asked. She heard the whoosh of the flame from Julian's torch, knew that he had lifted it high in the air to illuminate the passageway. The atmosphere was damp and close, heavy with the scents of earth and mildew. Elizabeth held her free arm out to the side and found her fingers touching a slick stone wall.

"It's very narrow, isn't it?"

"Indeed, typical of Templar buildings. Designed to take only two abreast," Sheldon murmured as he carefully led her along the uneven dirt floor. "But the etchings are incredible, Elizabeth. Preserved and intact from the sands of time. It's as if they were entirely forgotten. And maybe they have been, for all we know."

"I can hear your excitement," she said, smiling. "I can feel it."

"Discovery. There's nothing like it."

"No, there isn't. I can almost sense what it must have been like for you when you discovered the Templar cache in Temple Mount."

"Nearly as exciting as this." He held her hand tighter,

moved her gently to the left to avoid an object on the ground. "I'm so glad you allowed me this. I know it's early yet in the day for calls, and with your brother's wedding this afternoon, well, I thought there was no better time, especially since you'll be leaving for Yorkshire. I knew you wouldn't have another chance to visit Temple Church."

"Oh, no, I was most happy to be invited." She had needed this diversion. She hadn't slept well last night, with her thoughts focused on Iain and what he had done to her in her room, before the mirror. And worse, what he had made her feel. Try as she might she hadn't been able to stop thinking of him, not even when she had attempted to concentrate on the diary, and recall the passages that had once kept her so amused. When a few of the entries did come to mind, they only made her think of Iain, and their past, and the things he had whispered in her ear. Things that might become their future, if she allowed herself to fall once more.

"How long will you be gone?" Julian asked, drawing her from her memories.

"Oh, I'm not going to Yorkshire. I've decided to stay in town."

"Indeed?"

Smiling, she reached out and smoothed her palm over the rough edges of the stone wall. "Yes. I didn't want to be a killjoy to Lucy and Adrian on their honeymoon."

"How could you ever be that?" the earl asked, and Elizabeth heard the way his voice dropped, became husky in the quiet. Suddenly she was nervous. And uncertain.

"Here, move your hand over an inch." She jumped like a startled doe at the contact of his warm fingers. She should never have come today, but she had wanted to escape the house, her room, her thoughts of Iain. And

Sheldon's offer to tour the crypts of Temple Church had seemed like just the thing to take her mind off her worries. But now, having him so close, feeling his hand guiding hers over the elevated carvings, seemed far too intimate and disturbing.

"It's an image of a Templar," he murmured. "No name, but the etching is fully intact. There's even an emerald in the hilt of his sword."

"Beautiful." She breathed the word as her fingers came into contact with the emerald, which felt as large as a grape.

"Yes. It is. Come, there is more to discover by the looks of it."

Lizzy followed, holding on to Sheldon's arm as he led her deeper into the cavern.

"While we walk, tell me more about this diary you have, Elizabeth," he suggested as he took her hand and began guiding her once more down the dirt path of the crypt. "I've been most fascinated by the opportunity to aid you."

And here it was. The time had come. There was nothing to be done but to lie to Julian. It was the only way she could avoid arousing his suspicions, keeping him from making a connection with her family and the three Templars.

"As I said, I found the diary in a little shop. There is nothing to identify the knight, other than he was a Templar away on Crusade. It outlines an affair with a woman he met while over there. Very little is given about her identity other than she was a great beauty, and a lady of renown and influence. He writes that many men bowed to her."

"Could it have been the King of Jerusalem's sister?"

"Baldwin IV's sister, Sybilla? Why would you ask?"

"She was known to have had many lovers, and was often intrigued by the Knights Templar."

"I hadn't thought of that, although I feel it unlikely. The diary does not explicitly say that the woman escaped the Holy Land with him, but there are accounts in the diary that led me to believe the writer had occasion to see the woman throughout his life. It was a great source of agony for him, as they were forced to endure separate lives, their love a secret."

"It cannot be her then, for her story is well documented. She did not leave the Holy Land during her lifetime."

"A very good guess, however. I do think that the woman was from the East, because he often praised her olive skin, ebony hair and dark eyes. At the very least, she dressed in the Eastern style."

"Perhaps one of the king's concubines? He had a favoured one, Marguerite. Her father was of the French aristocracy, her mother a beautiful Eastern houri who became his lover. It is said that Baldwin's love for her was the most perfect love, for he never touched her, only watched her dance. He was a leper, if you recall. And to have had…well, carnal knowledge of her would have condemned her to his fate."

"Such a horrible disease, and rather kind of Baldwin, considering the times. Women were merely pawns then, even more than today."

"Empires were born through the female line back then. And Jerusalem's kings were no different."

"You know, now that you mention this Marguerite, I'm reminded of how the knight met his Veiled Lady. He claimed she appeared first in a dream. He dreamed of her for three nights, and then one evening, while supping with the king, he saw her, behind shimmering veils and a golden screen. He had pleaded with her to remove her veil, but she would not."

"We shall have to do more work to uncover this mystery. But it sounds as good a place as any to start."

Julian reached for Elizabeth's hand once more, and helped her over a bit of crumbling stone. "Now that you are not leaving for Yorkshire, perhaps we might meet to go over this diary."

"Yes, that would be lovely." Strangely, she no longer felt any excitement for it. She could not invite Sheldon in to look at it, could not let him discover Sinjin's name. Not only that, but every time she thought of Sinjin's romance, she could not help thinking of Iain and their own affair. Despite how dangerous it was to be near him, the only person she could imagine sharing the diary with was him.

What a fool she had been to tell Sheldon of the book. So impulsive, so...stupid. She hadn't been thinking clearly, hadn't thought through anything. She'd been mad, and sulking over her banishment from the Brethren. And this, she thought with disgust, was the reason Iain had been right to suggest that she be kept away. She was a hindrance. If Sheldon discovered their secret, she'd be the cause.

"You're trembling. Are you cold?"

"It is quite damp down here, isn't it?" She hated lying, but could not reasonably admit the truth—that a sudden image of Iain, his lips caressing her shoulder, had come into her head, leaving her trembling.

"Lizzy." Julian halted her, turned her slightly with his hands on her shoulders. "Do you wish to leave? I understand if you do. The place has a peculiar feeling. One of dread and oppression, I think."

"Yes, there is an ominous feeling, isn't there?"

"What do you want to do, Lizzy?" he whispered. "Go, or stay with me?"

She didn't know what she wanted. Again, her thoughts were muddled. And then it was taken out of her hands, when Julian pressed forward, lowered his head and brushed his lips over hers in a soft kiss.

"Lizzy," he murmured. She did not protest, nor did she when he kissed her again, this time parting her lips, brushing his tongue along the moist seam of her mouth. It was a very lovely kiss. A kiss any woman would be glad to be given by a man such as Julian.

"It's no good, is it?" he murmured, and she wondered if he was looking down at her with eyes that shone with regret, or anger. "It's not what you want."

"It is not that at all, Julian." Gripping the sleeves of his coat, she held on to him. Tried to steady her gaze, and diffuse the blush in her cheeks. "It's not that it wasn't good, far from it."

"It's not my lips you desire."

It was said in such a way that Elizabeth knew without a doubt that he suspected there was a rival for his attentions.

"May I speak honestly, Julian?"

"You may. I have come to depend upon your honesty, Elizabeth."

She forced herself to speak the words she had tried to run from. "I don't want to hurt you, but…" Licking her lips, she pressed her eyes shut and sought deep within for the courage to be honest with him. "I like you. Very much. Another time, perhaps…"

"We might have been lovers?" he supplied for her.

Nodding, she scraped her teeth across her lips. "I'm afraid that I have given my heart to someone else. I thought… Well, that is, I thought I had taken it back years ago, but it seems I have not. I cannot give you more, under false pretences. Perhaps later," she whispered. "But that isn't fair to you, to wait to see if I could offer more."

"And does he know he still has your heart?"

"No, and he never will. He isn't the sort of man to care for a woman's heart. I would be a fool to tell him."

"Lizzy, you would be a fool not to. Most men, you know, are rather terrified of the female heart. Perhaps he is just waiting for a sign from you. Let him know it's okay for him to come to you."

"You don't understand."

"You would be surprised," he murmured.

"I don't want to lose your friendship, Julian."

"You won't. There is more to my interest in you than the sexual. You're a bold, interesting woman, Elizabeth, and I find I enjoy spending time with you. That will not change simply because your feelings are not the same as mine. I will relish your friendship, and perhaps, in time, your feelings will change. If they do not, then I shall be happy to call you friend. I only hope that I have not ruined our open conversations with that ill-timed kiss."

"Of course you haven't." Leaning forward, she pressed her lips against him. His cheek, she thought. It was a warm kiss. A kiss designed for a dear friend.

A bark from behind them made her jump. Julian reached for her, held her. "Jack, what's this you've got?"

"What is it?"

"He's dragging something."

"Let us investigate, shall we?"

Taking her hand, Julian placed it on his arm and steered them to where Jack waited for them, panting with excitement and exertion. He licked her hand after releasing his hold on whatever he had found.

"A man's shirt. Linen. Fashionable. Most certainly not in keeping with the age of these crypts."

"Strange, you said you hadn't begun excavating down here."

"I haven't. Stay here, Lizzy. I will be right back."

"Certainly not!" she argued. "I'm coming with you."

"I don't know what is around that corner. There could be danger."

"No, Jack would have alerted us to that. If there was someone else in this crypt with us, we would have known it. There would have been a sound when Jack came upon them."

"True. Well, against my better judgement, come along. But don't let go of my arm."

They made their way along the corridor, where the scent of earth and stone became stronger. It was fresher smelling, not musty as it had been when they first entered the crypt.

"Someone has been digging," Julian announced, and Elizabeth felt him bend down, heard Jack's excited yelp. "It's fresh."

"It is a hole?" she asked.

"Yes. Big enough to put a body in."

"Do you think someone has found a Templar coffin?"

"No. I think it far more sinister than that. Come, let's go."

Jack barked again. "I think he wants to show you something else," Lizzy suggested.

"No, I want you out of here. I can come back and investigate the matter later."

Jack barked and ran off, making Julian curse. "We had better follow him. There's no telling where the devil this tunnel leads to."

They walked for what seemed like forever before they

came to where Jack stood quietly growling. The clank of metal against metal as the dog nosed about in the dirt drew Elizabeth's curiosity.

"Tools. Excavating tools," Julian murmured.

"But how?"

"I don't know, but the tunnel bends around a corner. It must lead somewhere."

"How far do you think we've walked? It seems like forever, and it's damper here. Colder. The sound of water tapping is louder with a faster rhythm."

"Tributaries from the Thames, perhaps."

"Where do you think we are, Julian?"

"We've traveled nearly half a mile, I think. We must be beneath the Strand."

A sense of foreboding wrapped around her. "This is no coincidence, Julian."

"No, it's not. Come, let us make our way back to the church. It will be getting on now, and we don't want you to be late for Sussex's wedding."

Lizzy reached out and halted him. "What are you not telling me?"

"I'm not hiding anything from you, Lizzy. But I mean to investigate this, and who might have come down here, and for what purpose."

"Do you smell that?" she asked suddenly. "It smells like...perfume."

Julian inhaled deeply. "I can't smell anything but the dirt. And mould."

"It was a delicate scent, as if it just floated past."

"Jack went by with the damn shirt in his mouth. Perhaps there's cologne on it."

"No, not cologne," Elizabeth insisted. "Perfume. And I have smelt that particular scent before."

Frowning, she tried to locate the memory.

"What a remarkable nose you have, Lizzy." He squeezed her hand. "But let us not dally here. My senses tell me that someone might be on their way back to this spot, and we do not want to be discovered."

He led her away from the tools Jack had found. Their progression was slow, and Julian's gait was funny.

"What are you doing?" she asked.

"Covering our tracks. We don't want anyone following our path."

Shivering, Lizzy whispered, "I feel like someone has just walked over my grave." Ominous. Disturbing. And so very, very real.

CHAPTER FIFTEEN

"YOU WILL SEND WORD around if you need anything? Anything at all."

Elizabeth felt herself smiling faintly at the urgency she heard in Black's voice. He was determined to win, and she was just as determined that he wouldn't, despite the fact she was weary tonight. It had been a long day, what with the morning at Temple Church and the afternoon with Adrian and Lucy. Lizzy had been distracted during the wedding, thinking of those strange moments in the crypt when she had felt another there with them... watching. Waiting. Her thoughts had travelled back and forth, from the strange notion that someone had been digging in the crypt, to Julian's kiss and the confession she had made.

She had not expected herself to admit the truth to either Julian or herself about her feelings. She most certainly had not thought that Iain Sinclair owned anything of hers anymore, least of all her heart. But that realization had come swiftly, a most unwelcome one. She knew that Iain did still have her heart. If he didn't, if he truly meant nothing to her, as she professed, then what he did, what he had offered in her bedchamber when he had held her in his arms, would not have tempted her so much, or haunted her. If she felt nothing for Iain, Julian's kiss would have affected her much more profoundly.

Yes. It was the truth. Despite his actions, his appalling behaviour, his abandonment, the devil still owned her heart, and most likely her soul. It was a realization that at once astounded her and terrified her. One thing that had come out of her long contemplation was that Iain must never learn the truth. He must never know, or have that power over her.

"Lizzy?"

The deep voice pulled her from her worries. "Yes, yes of course, I will. You know I will let you know if I need you, Black."

"Have a care, Elizabeth, and make certain the servants double-check that all the windows are locked, and all the doors. We cannot be too careful."

"I will. You may rest easy about leaving me tonight."

Black released a long sigh. "I really wish you would reconsider our offer, and come stay with Bella and me."

"I will be fine here. This is my home. Really, there is no need for worry."

"You're all alone."

"I have two dozen servants to share this house with!" she said with a laugh.

"I don't like this, Elizabeth. You should be coming home with us. Really, I should demand it."

Elizabeth heard the crinkle of Isabella's taffeta gown brushing against the marble floor. "My love, don't be a pest," she chastised her husband. "Lizzy will be perfectly safe here. Besides, we will be calling on each other daily, won't we, Elizabeth?"

"Indeed we shall. See now, Lord Black, I will be perfectly fine. I've never been ill at ease with my own company, and rather relish the idea of having the house to myself."

There was a low grumble from the earl, followed by a little laugh from his wife. "Come now, off we go," Isabella murmured, ushering him out. "Do sleep well, Lizzy, and expect me tomorrow afternoon. I wish to go to the new bookseller, and the confectioner's. I have been wanting more of that chocolate he sells."

"Of course, tomorrow afternoon it is. Until then. Good night."

When the door closed behind them, Lizzy felt herself sag just a bit.

"Looks like snow, my lady," Charles murmured as he reached for her hand and placed her fingers on his forearm. "Grey as slate the sky is."

"Is it?" She thought of how she had told Julian it would snow. She wondered if he remembered, and if he was even now looking out at the sky, marvelling at her abilities.

"Skies like that don't bode well. Me mum says she can feel the snow coming, that her bones ache with it. And the rain, too."

"How interesting. I could smell the coming snow in the air yesterday. Your mother and I could be weather forecasters," Lizzy teased.

Charles laughed at her jest, then turned her and together they walked slowly down the hall to the salon. The house was very quiet, and Lizzy wondered how she would survive weeks of solitude, when she had become used to the bustle of the house in the past month or more.

"I've prepared the hearth in the yellow salon, if that suits my lady."

"That will do very well, Charles. And tea, will you see that a tray is brought in?"

"Indeed I shall."

She felt as if she needed something to revive her. Strange how she felt so out of sorts. It was Adrian's wedding day and she should be happy for him. She was happy,

in fact. Still, something didn't feel quite right. It went beyond Sheldon's kiss, and the discovery in the crypt. It was
a restlessness, an inability to calm her thoughts, or even
focus them. Perhaps it was the secret knowledge that she
had thought that business with Iain all those years ago
over and done with, only to learn that she had never forgotten him, or taken her heart back.

"Here we go, miss. Shall I walk you to the settee?"

"I can manage from here. Thank you, Charles."

"I'll send Miss Maggie to you, then, shall I?"

"No, don't disturb her. Let her have a few more hours
to herself. I will be quite happy here until I am ready to
retire."

"Very good, miss."

The click of the door echoed in the quiet, and although
Elizabeth could not see, she still closed her eyes and listened to the gentle crackle of the logs in the hearth, and
the howl of the wind outside. Rubbing her arms, she listened to the sounds of life outside her window, the carriages rolling past, the clopping of horses' hooves. The
distant crow of blackbirds roosting in the leafless trees.

A sense of calm seemed to settle over the house.
Adrian and Lucy had been gone for hours now. Hopefully, they had already stopped at an inn and were warm
and cozy, on this their wedding night. She also hoped
that Lucy would soon realize, as Lizzy did, how perfect she and Adrian were together. She prayed they were
not spending their wedding night apart, their pride ruling their actions. When they returned from Yorkshire,
she expected to see two people very much in love, and
very happy with one another. That had been her wish,
that they soon realize how much they loved each other,
as she pulled the wishing well charm, secured with its
white string, from their wedding cake. Iain had pulled

the heart, and she found herself wondering what he had wished for.

It was just a silly custom, as old as time. The charms were a medieval amusement and did not really carry any special powers, or deliverance of wishes. And yet she knew that Iain had studied the charm, had closed his eyes and made his wish, and carefully wrapped the string around the heart and deposited the charm for safekeeping deep in his pocket.

She had both Lucy and Isabella to thank for that visual, which they had very eagerly whispered to her.

"You'll miss them, won't you?"

Elizabeth jumped at the intrusion into her thoughts, and she found herself whirling in the direction of the voice. She did not need sight to know who stood before her.

"Iain? But you left. Hours ago."

"I did. And now I am back."

"How?" Lizzy found herself frowning. "How in the world did you get in?" She knew for certain that he had not come in through the common route—the front door.

"Ah, you forget I have had special training, thanks to the tutelage of my father."

Lizzy couldn't help but arch her brows in annoyance. "It is not likely Brethren Guardian training that assisted you in breaching my home, and more likely years of scaling walls to avoid irate husbands."

He chuckled, the sound dark and devilish to her ears. "You think me an unconscionable sinner?"

"I don't think you to be. I *know* you to be." Folding her arms beneath her breasts, she glared. Whether it was in his direction or not, she did not particularly care. Her heart was beating far too fast for her comfort. It welcomed him, the lure of his presence. It *wanted* him here. *Traitorous organ.* "What do you want?"

There was a beat of silence, followed by the quiet movement of his footsteps across the room. "I thought we might share the evening together."

"Out of the question."

His voice was soft as a sensual whisper. "I wasn't asking, Beth. I was informing you."

"What right have you to do such a thing?" she gasped. She was annoyed. Perturbed. *Excited.*

The sound of his boots on the floorboards told her he was making his way slowly toward her, and her pulse skipped a beat.

"Your brother gave me the right when he requested that I watch over you while he's journeying on his honeymoon. I gave him my word I would protect you with my life. In the past, I haven't been very good about honouring my word, Beth. But in this, I mean it. With every ounce of my being."

"You *would* pick this moment to turn honourable," she grumbled. She was livid with Adrian for doing such a thing, and behind her back. But she could not condemn him for it. He was merely seeing to her safety. He was her brother, her *loving* brother. She knew that Adrian would have felt it his duty to set a plan in place for her well-being. And he would not have wanted to request it of Black, who had a new wife.

The fates, it seemed, were conspiring to keep her in the presence of Alynwick.

"Very well, you have seen to my safety. I am safe, as you can see. You may leave."

She was too addled to notice she could not smell him. He was standing right before her, a shadow of darkness, and she should have noticed his scent immediately. When he reached out and glided his fingers along her jaw, she jumped, surprised she had not realized just how close he was to her.

"I'll not leave you, not yet. I sense you do not really wish for solitude tonight."

"You're wrong."

"I see it in your eyes. You miss them already, your brother, and Rosie."

Quickly, she glanced away. She did not want him looking at her blind eyes. And she wished he had not said Rosie's name, for her eyes immediately began to well. She had not been without her pet for years, and knowing that Rosie was going to have her puppies without her own love and assistance tore at Lizzy's heart. Rosie was more than a guide dog and a companion. She was a friend. A treasured friend. And a confidante. Elizabeth would be desolate during the nights without her.

"Already you feel bereft, do you not?"

"I would have liked to keep her here, but how…" She swallowed, tried to smother her feelings. "I can't care for her in her time of need the way Adrian can—and he will see her well tended and comforted. I know that. It's just that… Well, it was the only thing to be done."

"It's never easy to do what is right by the one you love, is it?"

His statement evoked so many feelings inside her; frightening, tumultuous feelings she didn't dare give thought or voice to.

"Ah, Beth," he murmured as he wiped a traitorous tear from the corner of her eye. "No, you will not be alone tonight."

He brushed against her, reached for her hand and pulled her to the window that overlooked Grosvenor Square. Carefully, he placed her palm against the glass.

It was frigid, the chill stinging her skin as he pressed his large hand overtop hers.

"Let me take your mind off your worries, Beth. Just one night, let me stay."

"To talk," she murmured. *To stave off the loneliness...*

"Yes," he replied, his voice deeply masculine, "to talk."

Oh, what a fool she was to allow such a thing. He was a dangerous man, always had been. Yet she could no more resist him now than she had all those years ago.

"Night has blanketed the city, and with it, snow has begun to fall."

"Has it?" she asked in wonder. "I can hear the wind whipping itself into a howling frenzy, but the snow... I didn't know."

"Would you care to see it, Beth?"

"You know I can't."

"I could show you a way."

Intrigued, she could not help but turn to him, to the sound of his voice in the quiet room. "How?"

Reaching for her hand, he entwined his fingers with hers and led her from the room. In silence they made their way to the hall, where Hastings, the butler, awaited them.

"Your coat, my lord. Lady Elizabeth, allow me to aid you with your cloak."

It was a matter of seconds and she was dressed warmly, her hair covered in a bonnet, the ribbons of which Iain had insisted upon tying himself. Then he was leading her through the kitchen, and the garden door, where only days ago the deceased body of Anastasia Lockwood had been found.

"Hold on to my hand," he ordered, and Elizabeth realized he did not wear any gloves. But he had taken care to help her put on hers. The knowledge made a warmth grow deep in her belly.

"It's slippery, Elizabeth. Your hand."

She had no choice but to obey him.

Clutching his fingers tightly, Elizabeth followed him outside, gasping as a gust of wind caught at her bonnet, surprising her with its biting chill. The wind brought the first few flakes of snow against her cheeks, and she lifted her face, allowing the flakes to settle over her, and onto her eyelashes. She knew—could feel Iain's gaze upon her, watching her with his dark blue eyes.

"Can you feel them, Beth? The snowflakes?"

She nodded, bit her lip at the pure enjoyment of such a childlike indulgence. "They're melting on my lashes," she said, smiling at the feeling.

"How could they not?" he murmured as he brushed the wetness from her eyelashes. "Such an enticing place to flutter to, lie upon and melt."

She turned her head, averting her face. After last night in her room, she was much too weak, much too in danger of capitulating to a desire that he had awakened. Like a sleeping dragon, he had poked and prodded, and awakened the hungry beast inside her. She must keep her desire carefully tethered. She must.

"Shall we walk to the bench? It's beneath the trees, which may or may not protect us from the wind. But we could try it."

She should not be out here with him, but the lure was far too enticing. She relished the cold air, the feel of the snow. To know that night blanketed them, and that his world was almost—*almost*—as dark as hers.

Iain helped her to sit on the bench. The snow was falling heavier now. She could smell it, circling, the wind carrying not only the flakes, but the scent of a winter storm. This was not going to be a light sprinkling of snow, but a blizzard that would blanket the earth in a white carpet. It would be the kind of storm that made one burrow beneath the bedcovers at night and listen to the howling winds in the darkness.

"You always did love a good storm," Iain said beside her. "A marvellous clapping thunderstorm, with streaks of angry lightning, or a terrifying blizzard."

"Yes." And he used to sit with her, in the years before their affair and during it, and watch the storms with her. It had started to rain moments after he had left her lying in the grass upon his plaid blanket that afternoon years ago. She had lain there for what seemed like hours, her tears blending with the raindrops that soaked her prone form. She recalled the rumbling of thunder, the fierce flashes of lightning that forked over the rolling sea. She remembered how much hotter her tears were than the late-August raindrops.

"I always loved to watch a storm blow in, too," Iain mused. "Angry, volatile, Mother Nature unleashing her fury. So many times I would watch the sky and feel a kindred spirit to her. Inside me, the same tempest brewed. The rolling darkness, the howling winds. You used to say that my expression could turn as black as a thundercloud."

Indeed, it could. He had been as wild and wicked and volatile as Mother Nature in a tempest. It had frightened many girls off, made many young men give him a wide berth. But not her. Somehow his volatile nature had only drawn her in. Once she realized that volatility led to other fierce passions, well, she had been consumed by the paradox of him. She had wanted to save him, she thought, mentally laughing at the absurdity of it. A mere mortal did not hold off the storms, but succumbed to them. And Iain had succumbed to his.

She knew they were storms created by his parents. He had talked of them, of the years of growing up cold and alone. She understood what living a solitary life could do to people. It changed them. Her life after Iain had been solitary. And most certainly, it had changed her.

But they had never been solitary with one another. It had only ever been Iain that she had allowed to glimpse deep inside her. Only Iain she had talked to with open ease, and unguarded honesty. Despite what had happened between them, Elizabeth knew it had been the same for him. Iain had discovered how easy it was to share himself with her, and as a consequence, they had spent nearly as much time talking as they had making love. There had been more to them than the physical aspects of their relationship—much, much more. And that was why his betrayal had hurt so much. Why it had destroyed her. Had it been only sexual, she could have borne it, but it had become much more than that. It had become a union of friendship, and need, and kindred spirits.

"This reminds me of sitting on the cliffs," Iain said, drawing her to the present. "Watching a summer storm come in from the North Sea, you beside me, your hair blowing in the wind. I remember looking down at you, thinking you the most beautiful creature in the world. Your eyes were alive and sparkling, your skin flushed with the aftereffects of my lovemaking. I wanted you again, to slake the impending storm inside me. Only you, Beth, calmed the storms. The rage inside me. You still do. Even now there is peace stealing over me. Just sitting beside you, I can feel it, breathe easier. Think clearer. You have a way with me, a way that no woman has ever come close to. The rage only grew with them. Never subsided. I never watched a storm while with them. That was a private indulgence. I would stand at my window, or wander around the garden, watching the sky, thinking of you. Thinking of how I had ruined it all and wishing upon those storm clouds… *If I could only have one more chance…*"

"Iain," she whispered, unable to find the words, unwilling, perhaps, because she did not want to argue, or put an end to this moment. Yet she didn't feel she possessed the strength to withstand any intimate discussions. Thankfully, he did not press, but he did shift closer, shielding her body from the wind with his broad shoulders.

"It's a full moon tonight," he murmured. "The silver glow makes the snowflakes glitter, and the wind makes them swirl as though they were white orbs dancing in the night. The sky is white now with the heavy blanket of flakes raining down upon us. When you tilt your head up, it's blinding. You have to blink so fast to keep snowflakes from falling into your eyes. It's like powdered sugar being poured through a sieve."

She could see it so clearly in her mind, visualize the very spot where they were sitting, and how the storm was going on around them, two figures sitting side by side in the dark.

"Is your hair white with snow?" she asked.

"Why don't you see for yourself?"

He gave her no time to protest, but reached out and slowly drew off her gloves until her hands were bared to the chill wind.

"I have waited for this, Beth, this moment," he whispered as he took her hands in his and brought her fingertips to his mouth, kissing each fingertip before placing her palms on either side of his face. "When Sussex, Black and I returned from the East, I watched you as you did this—touched Sussex, then Black. And I waited, holding my breath, barely able to control my feelings, waiting to feel your touch on my face. But you did not. You made a polite enquiry after my health and left me standing alone by the hearth. And, then, the other afternoon with Sheldon, you touched him, and I was alone, and apart again. Remembering what it was like to await your touch, and then never to feel it. Beth," he whispered as he moved closer to her, "won't you touch me? See me?"

Her hands moved, unbidden. She had not commanded them to, but they were suddenly reaching for his hair, which was damp and heavy with snow. The wind took strands of it, blowing it forward, over his brow. She followed the melting flakes, revelling in the thickness, the softness of his hair, which he wore long. She had loved to run her fingers through it before. Tug at it in mounting pleasure. Snuggle into it in the shared intimacy of their loving.

Moving her hands down his neck, she explored the lean cords of his throat, the jut of his Adam's apple, and the skin of his cheeks, covered with the first dusting of a night beard. Then upwards, until she reached his forehead, felt the strong brow, the silky eyebrows, which she knew were black. His eyes were closed and, hands trembling, she allowed her fingertips to skate over his lids.

"Beth." She felt his hot breath on the exposed skin of her wrists. Heard the agony and pleasure in his voice over the quiet wail of the wind.

His cheeks were chiselled, his jaw strong and angular. She wanted to feel his lips, but didn't dare. She tried to pull away, but he reached for her, pressed her fingers to his mouth and forced her to seek the courage to touch him there. His lips were soft, his mouth lush, causing memories to return, of kisses, deep and slow and consuming. Of his mouth traversing her body, learning her, discovering her. How they'd curved in a masculine smile when he'd looked down at her after piercing her maidenhead.

He was as beautiful as she remembered. His features formidable. Masculine. "Beautiful fallen angel," she whispered, not intending to give voice to her thoughts, to the memories she had of them. But he heard her, and wrapped his cold fingers around her wrist, holding her hand to his mouth. He kissed her, breathed against her, and she felt with her free hand that his eyes were pressed shut. He wasn't looking at her. Could he not bear to? Or was the moment too powerful, too overwhelming, that he had to close his eyes in order to savour every nuance of her touch?

He was so beautiful. Always had been. And fallen so far from grace and honour. He was looking for redemption, she knew. And she was dangerously close to giving it to him.

"Beth, what do you see?" She felt his lips tremble beneath her fingers.

"I wish… I wish I could see the lies in your eyes," she answered, giving voice to the truth, and her fears. "They were there before, and I didn't see it, even though I possessed sight."

"No, Beth."

"They're there now, I'm sure. Carefully concealed by your words, the press of your lips against my hand. But if I looked deep within, I would find them. Wouldn't I?"

"There are no lies. Never again. I vow it."

How she wanted to believe him. How little it would take for her to do so. "You wanted to know what I saw, Iain? I saw a beautiful liar. You always were, you know."

"You wouldn't see lies, Beth. You'd see hopeful dreams.

Wishes. Perhaps even a prayer. But no lies. Just naked honesty, and stark need. A very deep regret, and the hope of forgiveness. The dreams of a fallen angel, as you call me, trying to find his way back to heaven. Which for him was always in your arms."

She sensed his desperation, and she tried to move away from him, to put space between them, but he would not allow it. "Give me a chance to earn your forgiveness. To make you forget the past."

"How can I when the past has shaped me into what I have become? I can't forget it, Iain, because to forget it makes me vulnerable, makes it too easy for me to slip back into being the creature I was—naïve and foolish."

"You were never those things."

"Yes. I was."

"Look beyond that, Beth. See me with your other senses. They will confirm what I'm telling you. They will show you what your eyes cannot. That I am a man desiring change. A man who wants to find himself, to give himself to you."

"I don't want to look, Iain. I don't want to see you."

"I know you still do. During the nights, when you're alone, you see me. See what we were to each other. I think you even see into the future, and that sometimes you see *me* in that future." He clasped her hands in his, his large palms swallowing hers up. "I want to make you see past my betrayal, Elizabeth, to the truth of what we had. Of what we still have. The feelings are still there, they just need a chance to come out of the suffocating darkness we've both buried them under."

It would be so easy to place her hand in his and allow him to take her upstairs, undress her, caress her. Tempt her.

"You ask for too much, Iain," she murmured. "More than I can give."

"Do I?"

Movement against her made her pause, made her stiffen as she felt him press forward, felt his body shift until his back and shoulders were pressing indecently against her belly and his head was turned, the curve of his cheek lying on her lap.

"Can you give me this, Beth? Just one moment to lie here and close my eyes, and feel you beneath me, soft and curved?"

"And what would you find?" she asked, her voice little more than a breathless whisper.

"Solace."

Closing her eyes, she bit hard on her lip, trying not to weaken against that one word. There had been no hesitation when he said it. It was as if he'd known it—what he'd desired all along, a feeling of tranquility. Peace. Rightness.

Her hand hovered over his head, her fingers itching to touch, to run her fingers through his hair, which would be damp with snow. What picture did they make, seated on this bench, a tempest of white swirling around them as he laid his head in her lap?

"Do you believe a mere mortal can change, Beth?"

Whatever he was once is not the man he is now... Lucy's words came rushing back, and Elizabeth bit her lip, forcing herself not to answer in haste.

"Or do you believe that he is forever condemned to be what he was, what he allowed himself to be?"

Yes... The word hovered on her tongue. *Yes, you are condemned. A soul cannot change.* But, then, if that were the case, she had to be honest and say that if one could not change, if one was condemned by previous actions and reputation, then she would forever be that naive, foolish girl. Not the woman she prided herself on being now.

"Beth," he whispered, then said nothing more, but reached for her hand and brought it to his hair. Unbidden, her fingers went into the wet strands, stroking and clutching as the sounds of the storm swirled around them. Such a strange place and time for this, but then, their relationship had never been predictable, or what one would deem acceptable. He had always been wild, half-tamed, always thumbing his nose at the rules and proprieties. It was what she had loved best about him, his ability to surprise her, to make her forget the world they inhabited and the expectations that world had for them. He had tempted her, taken her from her angelic pedestal and made her feel mortal, and womanly. She had only ever been herself—her true self—with Iain. Only he had the ability to set her free.

So it should not surprise her that they were seated on a garden bench in the midst of a snowstorm, the wind howling a lamenting, sorrowful sound as Iain placed his head in her lap, and her fingers attempted to give him what he desired—solace and peace.

Why she should give it to him, she had no clue. He deserved nothing kind from her. No words of forgiveness, no easy acceptance. And yet, she thought, as her fingers left his hair and trailed over his forehead, it would be all too easy to offer him that—and more. All too easy to find herself loving him again. Once more, she scoffed. Had she ever truly stopped loving him? Or had she just buried those feelings, making herself believe that she was stronger than that, and would not be such a ninny as to continue to love a man who had ruined her. Who had been so cruel and careless with that love.

Reaching for her hand, he brought her fingertips to his mouth, placing a long, reverent kiss on them.

Silly, silly fool, she whispered to herself, *he knows all the ways to make you weaken, to make you capitulate. And when you have done so, when you have surrendered your soul, and your self-respect, when you have submitted to him, what then? What solace will he provide you? What peace and tranquility will you find with him?*

Temptation was fleeting. A visceral force that came, overwhelmed, then dissipated. Shame, however, was never spent. It only grew, engulfed, encompassed, destroyed. And this, Elizabeth knew, she must never forget.

Leave him now, the voice inside her warned. *Run before temptation can claw at you. Flee before he can melt that iced corner of your heart where your love for him could so easily become thawed, and revived.* And perhaps it was already too late, she thought, as she listened to the wind, felt the snow hit her cheeks. Despite the snow and the wind and the cold, she was already melting.

As if he knew the turn of her mind, he rose from the bench, captured her hand in his and brought her up to stand before him. "The storm is quickly approaching. It's time to go in. But, Beth," he murmured against her ear, "the night is far from over."

CHAPTER SIXTEEN

THE TEA WAS WARMING, infusing her with some much needed strength. Outside, the wind howled, fierce and low, rattling the windows, while inside, the fire in the hearth crackled. On the opposite side of the salon, Iain sat, no doubt studying her from beneath his long lashes. Elizabeth could see him, sprawled, most likely, in a chair, with his boots crossed, his hands folded across his abdomen. She'd been relieved when he had not taken the spot beside her on the settee. She was still discomposed by their intimacy in the garden. He had made her want things she had scarcely allowed herself to think of, let alone believe in.

"Staff have prepared a room in the guest wing, my lord, and Charles has set out a nightshirt belonging to His Grace. I hope it will do for the night," Maggie said as she poured the tea. "It's snowing something fierce out there. Why, Charles says it's impossible to see more than a foot in front of you. Impossible to ride home tonight. The roads are as slippery as an icicle. We could not in all conscience allow you to make your way home tonight in this blizzard. There's no telling what might happen to you."

"Thank you, Maggie. Although I think I might know someone who is not feeling quite as generous as you, and would have no qualms about sending me out into this weather and my certain doom."

How correct you are, Elizabeth wanted to answer sharply, but she held her tongue and took a sip of her tea instead.

She heard the passing of china, followed by the creak of Maggie's knees as she curtseyed to Iain. She left them then, with a comment for Lizzy to call when she was ready to prepare for bed. The word made her blush, made her think unseemly thoughts, and how once she had imagined what it would be like to be Iain's wife, and await him in her bedchamber while she prepared for bed.

The door clicked shut, and Elizabeth occupied her time with sipping her tea, while listening to the rhythmic sway of the pendulum of the mantel clock. The silence was heavy, uncomfortable. She had no knowledge if Iain felt the same way, or if he sat quite at ease. Either way, it didn't matter. She would not stay here in the room with him.

"I think I shall retire," she said suddenly, unable to stand the proximity. "It's been a long day."

"I'll escort you to your room."

Strange, how she felt oddly deflated that he had not opposed her idea, or attempted to make her stay a bit longer. He seemed almost...relieved that she was leaving him. After those moments in the garden, she had expected more from him, at least somewhat of an argument.

Shrugging off the disconcerting notion, Elizabeth rose and smoothed her palms down her gown. "There is no need to trouble yourself. Finish your tea. I'll ring for Maggie."

"It's never any trouble to escort you to your chamber, Elizabeth," he drawled. He was back to using her proper name. No more *Beths* whispered in his seductive voice.

Reaching for her hand, he did not place it on his arm, but threaded his fingers through hers, holding them clasped in his. He was tugging her along, and she followed him, willingly. Their pace was slow, unhurried. His fingers clasped hers tighter as they ascended the stairs, him in front. In her mind she counted the stairs, all thirty-seven of them, ensuring she would know when she arrived at the top, so she would not make a spectacle of herself and trip, or worse, bash into him.

Once there, he pulled her along, then slowed, coming to a stop before her chamber door. Raising their clasped hands, he pressed his lips against her knuckles. "Good night, Beth," he murmured. "Dream of me, hmm?"

Before she could answer, he opened the door. "Maggie, your mistress is here. She wishes to retire for the night."

With a curtsey, Elizabeth murmured, "Good night, my lord," and promptly shut the door behind her.

"I DO HOPE HIS GRACE is safe at an inn this night," Maggie muttered as she set to undoing Elizabeth's gown. "Frightful weather. Can you hear it beyond the window? The wind howling like some demon beast in the night."

"It does sound mournful, doesn't it?"

"Aye. And you always did have a strange fondness for beasts," Maggie teased, "and for healing their damaged souls, or at the very least trying to."

"Whatever do you mean?" Elizabeth asked. Her comment was much too close to what she and Iain had talked about outside. But Maggie had no knowledge of their past. Couldn't possibly suspect that there was anything between them.

Maggie decided not to answer, but instead talked of much safer things. "Well, I daresay you enjoy this weather, but only because you're in here, tucked warmly at home, not out braving the elements. I'm glad his lordship chose not to travel back home tonight, even if it's only a few blocks away. Imagine the horses, how they would suffer in this weather. Not to mention how they would manage the icy roads, pulling that great hulking carriage of his."

"Yes, you've explained that already," Elizabeth muttered. "The weather is a convenient excuse for you to extend an overnight stay to Lord Alynwick."

"You can't send his lordship out into weather such as this!" Maggie exclaimed as she did away with Elizabeth's corset. "You'd never forgive yourself if some harm came to him."

"No, of course not," she murmured as Maggie slipped Lizzy's night rail over her head. "Besides, the weather is so terrible that there isn't a soul or carriage in sight. No one will know or even suspect that his lordship has stayed the night."

"Let us hope not."

"Well, I'm sure the weather will be all cleared up on the morrow. These storms never last more than a night. It's only November, after all."

"Indeed."

"Shall I brush out your hair now?"

"No, I'll do it. You go to bed, Maggie. You've had a very long day. I'm not quite ready for bed yet."

"You're certain?"

Lizzy couldn't help but smile. "I can brush my hair, I assure you."

"Well, all right, then," Maggie said, but there was a strange quality to her voice. "Sleep well, Lady Elizabeth."

When the door clicked shut behind her companion, Elizabeth made her way to her dressing table and sank onto the cushioned chair. Running her fingers over the table, she felt the hand mirror, the brush and comb all aligned before her. To her right was a box that housed her hairpins. For long minutes she sat silently staring at a mirror she could not see. Outside, the storm raged, and she listened, allowing her thoughts to settle into a semblance of calm.

The room was warm, the fire burning brightly on the hearth. Even from here she could feel the heat of it, the flickering flames, and envisioned shadows dancing on the walls. Skimming her fingers over her nightgown, she realized that Maggie had put a fine lawn garment on her. It had a lace yoke and delicate ribbon work. Strange for a night like this, when a snowstorm whirled outside.

She wasn't cold. Just curious. The fire was actually very warm, and soon Lizzy began to feel languid from the warmth, and the comforting sound of the wind. Lost in thought, she didn't hear the door open or close, until she heard the click of the lock.

"Maggie?"

A warm hand wrapped around the nape of her neck; the tips of fingers burrowed into her upswept hair. "Me."

Iain… Dear God, what was he doing here?

His hands moved from her neck, smoothed over her shoulders and down her arms. He reached over her from behind and grasped her hand, bringing it to her lap. Then he placed something there. Took her hand and placed it on the object he had laid in her lap.

Tracing her fingers over it, she discovered the slightly rough texture, smelled the scent of leather. It was small, square, the spine embossed with an emblem that felt very familiar under her questing fingertips.

"The Veiled Lady's diary," Iain murmured next to her as he slowly pulled a pin from her hair. A strand fell down and she felt him lift it to his face. "Open the cover. We'll read it together."

Oh, how like him to use this against her. He should

not be here, under any circumstances, but especially now, when she was dressed in nothing more than a nightgown. She was certain the flames from the hearth rendered the expensive linen translucent. She should tell him to go, but her fingers would not leave the book, only opened the cover and traced over the page. Beneath her fingertips she felt the raised edges of ink that had been set to paper. The writing felt much different than the writing in Sinjin's diary. That script had been bold, heavy, pressed deeply into the pages with a sort of repressed passion. This was lighter, more flowing, much more feminine.

"Where did you get this?"

Another pin was pulled from her hair. "I've had it for years."

"Why did you never tell me?"

"I would have had I'd known you were interested, or that you had Sinjin's matching volume."

"Who is she?" Elizabeth demanded. "How do you know this is in any way connected to my diary?"

He bent down behind her, his mouth brushing the delicate flesh behind her ear. "Soon."

Another pin. Then another. Silently, he worked behind her, until her hair was unbound and flowing around her. He took handfuls of it, let it slide through his fingers.

"So long. Does it reach your bottom?" he asked. He leaned over her, took something from the table. The brush. He began pulling it through her hair. Carefully. Slowly.

"Yes," she answered, swallowing hard. Strangely, this was far more intimate than anything he had ever done to her body.

"So black and shining. I'd like to see it against your naked skin."

"Iain."

"Shall I read the first entry, then?" he asked, subtly ignoring her and the beginning of her protest.

This she could not resist. He could brush her hair all night if he wished, if he would exchange that liberty for a glimpse into the world of the Veiled Lady.

"Yes, please. Begin."

"'He came to me in a dream.'" Iain's voice was deep, beckoning. "'A prince in a white tunic, a red cross over his breast. His hair was black, his eyes the color of storm clouds. He was everything I had dreamed of during these long days and nights of my imprisonment. He lay upon the ground, the stars for a canopy, the dying embers of a fire for his blanket. I would have given up every comfort in this gilded cage in which I had been placed, for the chance to be with him on the desert sand. But he is forbidden to me. A lover in my dreams. Yet I cannot help but think he is the other half of my soul. Even in my dream I knew him to be the one. The only person in the world who could complete me.'"

Iain had not stopped brushing Elizabeth's hair, and she closed her eyes, enjoying the soothing motion, the rasp of his voice in the quiet. "Turn the pages, stop whenever it feels right," he ordered. Then he replaced the brush on the dressing table, moved his hands to her head and raked his fingers through her hair.

She did as he asked, and she felt him step closer to her, the back of her chair the only barrier between them. But his hands... His beautiful hands continued to move through her hair, massaging her scalp.

"'I saw him tonight, through the silken veils and screens that keep us apart from the world. My face was covered as I danced. Only my eyes peered out, but my knight knew me—just by my eyes. His gaze flickered down my body as I performed for the men who had gathered. He knew my body. Had kissed it in my dreams. Had touched me as I have never been touched before. I dreamed of those touches, how his hands moved along my skin. How in the quiet of the night I retraced the path of his fingers with my own. Somehow, he knew my every wish, my every secret desire.'"

Iain paused in his massage and leaned over once more, whispering in her ear. "Another entry. Stop when you want."

It would only get more detailed, if this diary was anything like Sinjin's. She was so tempted to turn only one page. But Iain's hands smoothing down her neck, his thumbs pressing into her skin, relieving her of the tight knots, made her a bit reckless. So, too, did the idea of him reading something very naughty aloud. It was strange, erotic, to hear him read the words of a woman's secret desire. Elizabeth could so easily imagine that they were her thoughts he was whispering aloud.

Flipping through the pages, she stopped, waited to hear him speak. When he did, he was closer, peering over her shoulder, whispering next to her ear as he read the words from the diary that rested in her lap.

"'I lay awake on the pillows, while his hands—Sinjin's hands—burned a wake over my body. Inside I trembled, heated, wanted to beg for the fleeting touch of his hands on my breasts.'"

Elizabeth was aware of how Iain's palm caressed her throat, rested over the expanse of her chest as he read. Then he very slowly untied the ribbon to her night rail and parted the yoke, revealing the crests of her breasts.

"'He claims to adore my breasts, and his touch conveys that. He stares at me, watching as his palms, rough, calloused, cup me. His touch isn't enough, merely a tease. I should not be so wanton, but I want more, what no lady should desire if she were truly a lady. I want his hand engulfing me.'" Iain's breath caressed the shell of Lizzy's ear as his hot palm sneaked beneath the yoke of her night rail, cupping one heavy breast. He sighed, squeezed, then freed her breasts from the material, allowing the linen to slip down her arms. He would be watching in the dressing-table mirror, she knew. He would see her, her breasts large and heavy, cupped from behind in his palms.

"'I want his tongue on me, following the path of his hands.'" Iain nuzzled the side of her breast. His mouth warm and open, he kissed her as he moved to the side of the chair, making his way closer to her breast, and the nipple she felt curl in anticipation. "'I want him to pleasure me until I scream, until I fall apart with nothing but his mouth suckling me.'"

Iain had done that once to her. Did he remember? He found her nipple, curled his tongue around it and moaned as she arched into him. How could she deny this? Stop him? Her body cried out in pain at the thought of denying him. *Just a bit more,* it pleaded. It had been so long... so long....

But Iain was not content with that. He wanted more, he lifted her up, and the Veiled Lady's diary fell to the ground. He took Elizabeth's chair, sat her on his lap and removed her gown. She was completely naked and, embarrassed, she shielded her breasts and sex with her arms.

"No, Beth." He kissed her ear, pulled her arms away, positioned her so that her legs were open, lying over his thighs. He was fully clothed, and she felt the heat of his chest through his shirt, the woollen blend of his trousers on her bottom.

"How is it you've only grown more beautiful?" he

asked. "Your body... What a pleasure it will be to taste, to traverse these curves in the dark."

His hand skimmed over her, resting against her belly, then lower over her mons. He began to speak to her, words from the diary. Was he reading it from where it had fallen on the floor, or had he memorized the passages as she had done?

"'I ache to feel him inside me, long and rigid, filling me.'" Elizabeth felt his hand beneath her bottom, caressing her, then freeing the buttons of his trousers. Finally, the burning heat of his erection pressed against her. "'I need him, so deep inside me. Awaiting his penetration.'" That last word was whispered hotly in her ear and she squirmed on his lap, but he only held her more tightly.

"Was it like that for you, Beth, waiting that first time to feel me inside you? Awaiting my penetration?"

He was moving her so the head of his penis was nudging against the rim of her sex. His hand was stroking lazily, parting her core, allowing the edges of her sex to slip closed, then opening them again with his fingers.

"Did you ache for me deep inside? Do you ache now?"

She was breathing too fast, her chest rising and falling in anticipation, fear, and he reached for her head, held it back until it was resting against the crook of his neck. His mouth found hers, first the corner, which he kissed. His hand continued to play, his erection coming closer, nudging inside her. It made her breathe harder, faster, like a terrified virgin—not in fear that he would hurt her, but in terror of the intensity of the emotions, the desire, the very great need to feel him possess her body once more.

"Shh," he whispered, placing his hand over her chest, calming her.

He kissed her, a slow, deep kiss. His tongue was warm, circling, making the same pattern as his hand was over her clitoris. She grew taut, ready, and his hand slid from where it rested over her breast bone, down to her breast, where he tugged at her nipple while stimulating her most sensitive centre.

It was intentionally provocative. Deliberately slow. He knew how to play with her, to keep her suspended, but she wanted more, to come crashing down into his arms, her body splintering.

Brazenly, she reached down the length of her body and tried to move his hand lower. She wanted his fingers moving inside her, appeasing the ache. The way he played with her nipple only intensified that need. So, too, did the knowledge that he was fully clothed beneath her, and was watching her in the mirror, and she was left to imagine what they must look like.

Stubbornly, he refused to give her what she wanted. His fingers remained against her, playing, stroking, while she felt empty.

"Say it, Beth," he demanded, and she heard how husky and rough his voice was. Felt how his chest had begun to grow hot, his shirt dampening against her back. "Say you want me inside. Not my fingers, but this."

She shook her head when he brushed his phallus against her bottom. She did not want to fall that far. This was more than she'd ever thought to allow herself.

"Then you shall have to remain unfulfilled." He kissed her neck, drew his tongue along the column of her throat. "Empty." Another caress of his tongue. "Aching. I want to give you what you want, Beth," he said darkly, "but with my cock."

Biting her lip, she nodded, pressed her eyes shut. She needed to feel him inside, and if not with his fingers, then with what he desired. In truth, it was her desire, too. Even though it shouldn't be. She whimpered in surrender, such a weak-willed woman.

"It's not bad to want this, Beth," he murmured as he kissed her, slowly guided himself to her entrance. "It's not wicked to want to join with me."

Why, then, did she feel she was selling her soul to the devil?

She almost cried no, jumped off his lap, but then he slid into her, straight, steady and so full, penetrating her so deeply that she moaned, dug her nails into his thighs.

"Beth," he groaned as his hips moved slowly. "Take it all," he whispered. "All of me, my Beth."

She had no experience with this, this position, this complete exposure. But he helped her, planted his hands on her hips and showed her the way to move. She felt Iain's body behind her, heard his breaths which became uneven gasps.

Slowly he moved, his hips thrusting, retreating, building the rhythm, taking it from lazy to harder, more determined, more possessing. His fingers bit into her hips as he angled her, and she heard him growl next to her ear. "So damn good," he said. "You should see it, Beth, what we look like doing this, loving each other."

She grew wet, arched her back, excitement growing when she learned he was watching them. His hands left her hips, came to her breasts and cupped them, the nipples sliding between his fingers as he pulled to the rhythm of his cock, which was stroking seamlessly in and out of her.

"Yes, yes," he murmured as his body worked beneath hers. She sensed the moment he was about to climax; his body always stiffened. He drew his breath in and held it raggedly, his fingers biting into her nipples, and Elizabeth knew what she must do. She accepted one last thrust, then lifted herself off his lap as he came.

"Beth?" he gasped in surprise. He reached for her, tried to bring her back to him, then moaned, spilling his seed. She was left unfulfilled, aching. But it was far better than to be filled with any repercussions from her lapse of discipline.

Surprising her, Iain reached for her, held her close to him as he framed her face in his hands. "Why?" he demanded. He was furious, she realized.

"This madness you're suffering under. It won't last forever, Iain. Just like the last time. And I do not want to be compromised and left with something you don't want."

She would have given her soul to see his expression. She wasn't sure if it was shock or hurt, but he suddenly released her, set her away from him so he could stand. And then he left, just as he had the last time, without a word.

CHAPTER SEVENTEEN

GODDAMN HER, he was still seething when the dawn came. He had stood at the bedroom window for hours, watching the blinding whirl of snow, lost in thoughts of Elizabeth and what they had done.

He saw her upon his lap, naked, open, accepting him. She'd been so damn lush, her body welcoming him as though he had never been gone from her. He'd wanted to carry her to the bed, to stretch out on top of her and feel her curves beneath him, but he'd been mesmerized by the image in the mirror. How they looked together. He'd been enslaved at that moment, the second he slid inside her body. He'd thought of so many things, but most of all, he'd thought of what it would be like to take Elizabeth that way while she was heavy with child. And she hadn't wanted that. Had accused *him* of not wanting it, when even now he thought of how satisfying it would be to give her his seed and create a life with her.

Banging his fist on the sill, he hung his head and tried to stuff the pain back down. Pain was a sign of weakness, or so his father had claimed. Never show pain, or fear. And never tears. Iain, as far as he knew, had never once cried. To weep was weakness, and neither his mother nor his father had tolerated that failing. But he was close... so damn close to letting his fear and frustrations get the better of him. Maybe Sheldon was right. If Elizabeth truly desired him, she would be his now....

Activity in the hall told him the servants were waking for the day. He wondered if Elizabeth still slept. Had she thought of him last night? Did she relive that scene as he had? Bloody hell, he had barely a dozen strokes into her and was coming, leaving her dissatisfied. He'd planned to remedy that, knowing he could not hold back his climax. But she'd put a damper on his plans. She'd rejected him. Rejected his seed.

He'd never offered it to another before. He always wore French letters when he took a woman, and never relied on them, preferring to pull out at that peak. That moment with Elizabeth had been the first time in twelve damn years he'd been flesh to flesh inside someone, and it had felt so damn good. It had been only her he'd touched, skin to skin. And she'd denied him. But not only that, she'd denied herself, because Iain knew that she hadn't thought that way before. She'd taken him every time he'd had her, pouring into her.

A knock sounded at the door, and he called, "Enter," in a voice that was much too rough.

Charles, Elizabeth's favourite footman, peered his head inside. "Snowed in," he muttered. "Three-foot drifts by the mews. Took a dozen of us to dig it out to get food to the horses. I'm afraid, my lord, you'll be stuck here until the thoroughfares are cleaned. And as it's still blowing a white tempest out there, I doubt that will be for some time."

"What a shame," Iain said, "that I shall be forced to spend *days* here."

His sarcasm was lost on the footman. "Nothing to do about it, my lord. I'll send some of His Grace's clothes to you. You're about his size."

"Thank you."

Charles was about to close the door when Iain turned

from the window and said, "Be so good as to inform Lady Elizabeth that her presence at breakfast is requested."

"At once, my lord."

Days… Well, let's see what good he could make of them.

"YOU'RE LATE."

Elizabeth saw red when Iain spoke from the depths of the dining room. How dare he command her about like he was her…her *husband,* for heaven's sake! "This is my home, and I will dine when I'm good and ready to dine."

"You eat by nine, Elizabeth, every morning. It is nearly noon. You're simply avoiding me."

How the blazes did he know that about her? He wasn't around for breakfast normally, and she couldn't imagine that he would recall such a thing from the past. No, he was merely goading her.

Carefully, she took her seat and settled her napkin on her lap. "Charles, I'll have—"

"Charles has been dismissed for now. I'll see to your plate. Although I should think that by now the eggs are cold."

"Have you eaten?" she asked.

"No, testament to my current mood, I should suspect."

The scents of bacon and sausages and toast floated over to her. Iain set a plate in front of her. She heard another plate being placed to the right, followed by the squeaking of a chair as Iain sank into it.

"I've poured your tea. The handle is to the left."

"Thank you. I had no idea that you—"

"I've watched you for years, Elizabeth. I know how you accept your teacup, the way your plate should be ordered, with meat to the left, potatoes to the right and your vegetable to the bottom. I know you prefer red wine, and you have a sweet tooth. I also know that you would rather die by means of torture than to show any outward weakness."

"How well you know me."

"Did you doubt it?" he asked. "Did you think I would not know you as intimately as I know myself?"

She glanced away. "I assumed—"

"I know what you thought of me. What you still think of me."

Better to steer away from this conversation, which could very easily turn into a discussion of what had happened between them last night. For herself, Elizabeth had decided to deem the entire interlude a grave error in judgement, and forget about the entire matter.

"I understand the weather has made a turn for the worse."

If he was frustrated by the change in the conversation, he hid it well. "It has. I shall have to intrude upon your hospitality for a bit longer, I'm afraid." He spat the word *hospitality* out as though it were poison. Obviously, their politely strained conversation was at an end.

"Yes, of course. Make yourself at home."

"At home, shall I?" he growled, and she heard the tines of his fork hitting the china plate.

"Yes, of course. Do as you would in your own home. Although in this weather I doubt you will be able to bring your ladies by."

Silverware clattered to the table and Elizabeth felt some satisfaction for the dig.

"Is that what you think I do all day? Fornicate?"

"I don't really think upon it," she murmured as she took a small bite of her toast. "What else do you do besides chase skirts?"

"My days are filled with many activities, mostly

Brethren affairs and obligations to my clan and the Sinclair lands. There are many days and nights when I've been too damn busy to even think of fornicating."

"Well, that is very edifying."

"What do you do all damn day? Think of new ways to flagellate me?"

"Of course not. I barely think of you at all."

This was becoming very mean-spirited, she realized.

"What a little liar you are."

"I learned from the best, didn't I?"

"I can take whatever you dish out, Beth," he murmured. "I can take the pain, the way your words are intended to strip me of my flesh. I won't run and hide from you. I won't cower. Let us discuss the matter right now."

"I wasn't aware there was anything to discuss," she sniffed. "And let go of my wrist. It isn't seemly."

"It's much more seemly than what happened upstairs last evening, don't you think? Did you touch yourself, Beth, after I left? Did you complete what you would not allow me to do?"

"Stop this at once!"

He leaned in, pulled her by the wrist so that she came very close to him as he whispered, "I would have brought you off so hard you would have screamed, would have begged for it—for more of it."

"I no longer have an appetite. Excuse me."

He released her, but followed her out of the dining room, stalking her. He was so cruel, so...right. And she hated him for it. Despised that he knew that much about her. Fumbling her way along the halls, she was keenly aware that he was behind her, watching her struggle to get her bearings. He didn't help her, just stalked her like a wolf waiting to pounce on injured prey.

Finally, she found the door to the salon and opened it,

quickly shutting it before he could enter. Letting out a breath she didn't know she'd been holding, she collapsed against the wood.

"I'll let you go this time," he said from the other side of the door. "But you can't avoid me forever, Beth. We will have this conversation. You will hear what I have to say."

"Go away, Iain."

"Go away?" he said. "You ask the impossible, Beth, for I am so completely entwined with you that it's impossible for me to separate myself. If you would only rest for a moment, and not try to run from me, you would see that the same is true for you. Just as water always flows to the ocean, we're trying to make our way back to each other."

"I won't go back to you," she whispered to herself, but he heard her.

"I'm coming for you, Beth. And there is nothing you can do to stop me."

AND THEY SAID SCOTS were a stubborn lot! He had never met a more stubborn woman in all his life. She'd avoided him at luncheon, and then at dinner. It was nearing midnight and still no sign of her. Outside, the blizzard had begun to die down, but the wind still howled, causing the snow on the ground to drift. He was anxious that the brunt of the storm was over and he had wasted a day with Elizabeth. He would likely be gone on the morrow, and his plans to make Elizabeth his had gone up in a puff of smoke.

He'd underestimated her stubbornness, her resolve. Or perhaps, a voice inside him said, he had underestimated how much he had hurt her when he'd left her.

Forgiveness was a complicated ideation. So was love. He wanted both from her, but perhaps she would never be ready to give him either. There could not be love without forgiveness. And no forgiveness without an explanation from him. He feared that. It terrified him, knowing he had to give her full disclosure for his actions. He was shamed by them. Afraid that after she heard his reason, forgiveness would be out of the question.

He was a damn coward, unable to face up to his past. To the man he had been. No, he hadn't really been a man then. He'd been a spoiled, selfish fool.

Gazing about the salon, he tried to think of a way to make it right. To make it so that Elizabeth could trust him, would hear him out. He was not the man he'd once been. He'd changed, and would change more, too, if she would only give him a chance. There needed to be some sort of bridge between them, an olive branch that would help to pave the way to forgiveness. He had to ensure that the connection they had once shared flickered back to life, binding them, before he could begin discussing the reasons why he had failed her.

Sinjin's diary caught his eye, and he lifted it up from the table, held it in his hand and studied the writing within. There was a curse on the houses of York and Sinclair. No man and woman from those houses could ever fall in love, else that love was fated to die, to cause immense pain and unrequited longing. The curse had proved true for Sinjin and his lady. They had died apart, though their hearts were as one.

Iain could hardly believe what he was thinking, but he rose from his chair and carried the diary in his hand, searching for Elizabeth.

He found her in her room, sitting on the window box. She was dressed in a night rail and wrapper, and he found his gaze darting to the dressing-table chair he had occupied last night. Images of Elizabeth giving herself to him so completely gave him the courage to come deeper into the room.

"In your diary, does it mention a curse?" he asked.

"No, it does not. But I have heard of one."

"Do you think it's true, this curse between our houses?"

He sat on the opposite end of the box, facing her. She lifted her legs and wrapped her arms around her knees, hiding herself from him. A piece of his soul was chipped away. He'd done irreparable damage to her. He saw it in her eyes.

"Do you believe that no man or woman from the houses of York and Sinclair can fall in love?"

She shrugged, cast her gaze to the window, avoiding him. "I don't know. It seems that way, doesn't it? We certainly have been made miserable by our lust and the way we gave in to it."

"Is it only lust, Elizabeth?" he asked. "Do you not think there was more to what we shared?"

"Don't speak of it, Iain," she begged him. "Please don't."

"All right. Perhaps, then, I should honour my word and help you discover the secret about the Veiled Lady, shouldn't I?"

She shook her head. "No, it's done now. There's no need."

"Have you figured out who she was, then?"

"No. But there is little purpose in the matter."

"I told you I could help you discover who she was. I've never read much about Sinjin," he murmured, ignoring her protest. "I found the diary and brought it up. I thought I might read it."

"You may."

"Here," he said. "Now. To you."

She swallowed hard, and he saw the faint dusting of pink on her cheeks. This was her Achilles' heel. Through this diary she could live through another's words and actions. She didn't have to put herself out there, expose herself. It was safe to be seduced by a diary—much safer than allowing Iain in. He saw that now. Knew the diary was the only way he could spend time with her. He had what she needed: sight.

Clearing his throat, he began.

"'Second July, 1147,

"'I have seen her. Even with the strength of my faith and my Templar devotion I find it unbearable to resist her exotic charms and the enchanting way she has of looking into my eyes and sneaking into my thoughts. *One kiss,* I thought as I allowed myself to walk to her—the Veiled Lady, they call her.

"'I whisper her name, "Veiled Lady," whisper it over and over again until I am chanting it in my mind. With one kiss I know she will give me the secrets of her soul, the passion of her body.

"'I step beyond the veils, to the bed of pillows. She is lying there, waiting for me, her eyes glowing like onyx and her lips a bright red—crimson—like the apple Eve used to tempt Adam. My destiny is here, in Jerusalem. It is her.

"'With long slender fingers she beckons me to come to her. I resist, but hear her whispered plea in my mind. "Come to me, my prince."

"'I could not resist the lure of her voice, or the way her hand skimmed teasingly over her breast, exposing her flesh and the ripeness of her bosom. She rose to her knees before me. Looking up through a veil of black lashes she smiled a secretive, womanly smile as her hands divested me of my tunic. Heat flooded my blood and I could not seem to keep hold of my thoughts. She then stood before me, her jewels and headdress tinkling in the quiet, drawing my eye to the abundance of shimmering gold and priceless rubies that adorned her arms and neck. Her eyes seemed to glow in the lantern light, further adding to her exotic sensuality.

"'The musk-scented incense steadily filled the tent, making my head light, but the hunger I saw in her eyes unleashed an unholy need in me. One look into those hypnotizing eyes and I could not move. I did not breathe.

"'"Come to me," she whispered, and not able to stop myself, I reached for her gold, shimmering gown and tore it from her body.

"'I looked down between us at her nakedness. She was rounded and lush, and roughly catching her about her bottom, I brought her to me so that our sex was pressed together. Hungrily, I took her mouth with mine, heard her purr like a cat being stroked and petted. Unable to curb the animal in me, I lifted her leg and brought her thigh to my waist and ground my straining sex against her flesh, which felt cool against my fevered skin. My hand stroked the contours of her firm thigh, then down to her ankle, which was adorned with gold-and-ruby anklets. Her eyes seemed to challenge me, her pouting lips welcomed me with a shy smile.

"'With one thrust I took her, and she gasped, made a deep unearthly sound low in her throat that excited me, filled me with a need, a hunger, I had never experienced.

"'Ruthlessly I took her, standing up, and she encouraged me with her purrs and cries for more. Like two untamed animals we mated, and when she reached her pleasure I heard her purr turn from that of a kitten to that of lioness, and that was when I felt it, the sting of her teeth as she bit my neck. The pain was momentary, and led to an ecstasy that knew no bounds. The sucking of lips and tongue aroused me, freed me, and I thrust myself into her harder, taking her with a fierceness I could hardly believe I was capable of.

"'Collapsing onto her pillows, I loved her through the night, only to awaken in the morning to find her gone.

"'She was no feverish dream, or a dark need in the night. She was a flesh-and-blood woman, and she was mine.'"

Iain looked up, caught Elizabeth staring at him. What was she seeing behind her eyes? he wondered. Was she envisioning the couple in the diary, or like him, had they somehow morphed into an image of her and him, atop a bed made of pillows? He could see her now, naked, adorned only in the moonstone necklace as he moved atop her. Was it just his wild imaginings or did the story of this ancient couple mirror that of his and Beth's?

"Did she write of that encounter?" Elizabeth asked, her voice so quiet. She was no longer looking in his direction, but had leaned her head against the window.

"She did. She spoke of being claimed by him, the way her body yielded to him. I...I never knew what it was like for a woman to accept a man into her body, until I read her diary."

"You understand at last how very sacred it can be."

"Yes." Closing the book, he placed it on the floor and reached out, cupping Elizabeth's knees with his hands. This was the crux of their difficulties. Always Elizabeth had been far more advanced, more mature than him. Their loving had been sacred to her, and sacred to him only when he was old enough to understand the difference between fornication and lovemaking. By then it had been much too late.

"I understand how it is for a woman to give herself—

her body, her safekeeping—into a man's hands," Iain murmured.

"She was a virgin," Elizabeth stated. "He wrote of that moment, feeling her yield, giving herself to him. After, he reflects upon it—the power it gave him, the sense of possession. Years later, he's dying, and he still writes of it, the memory of possessing a piece of her that no other man would ever have."

"You understand what it is like for a man, then, when he takes a woman for the first time. She belongs to him, that piece of her that is forever bound to him."

Lizzy blushed, tried to avoid his gaze. "I thought it insignificant for him."

Carefully, Iain reached out, trailed the backs of his fingers along her cheek. "It was never insignificant for me, Beth. Always, I carried that possession with me. I still think about it, still dream of that evening when you came to me so willingly."

"You asked me if I think the curse is true. I do. We're cursed, Iain."

"I don't. You know what I think? I think we're two very old souls trying to find one another again, in a lifetime where they can be together. They were denied it once, in their original incarnations, and now they're searching. And I think they've found each other at last."

After he spoke the words, he knew it for the truth. He and Elizabeth were meant to be.

"Who was she?" Lizzy asked.

"Do you really want to know?" He smiled at how impulsive she was. She never wanted to wait, always wanted to rush headlong into something. Like last night. He'd wanted to savour it slowly, and she couldn't wait. That was why she had reached for his hand, showing him what she wanted. He'd denied her, because he knew that sometimes drawing out the pleasure made the climax all the more sweeter.

"I want to know."

"I'll tell you, on one condition."

"And what is that?"

"That you go to the theatre with me."

There was confusion in her expression, and he understood it. Although they had shared their bodies for an entire summer, they had never been seen as a couple. He hadn't courted her, he'd taken her. Pleasured her. Their relationship had bloomed through the physical acts of sex and the intimacy created. He'd been wrong to do it that way. She deserved to be seen, to be wooed and courted, not to be taken in a glen, away from the world, and ravished.

"Will you, Beth? Will you go with me to the theatre?"

"Yes."

He was relieved that she had answered that she would. He didn't dare question the true motivation for her acceptance. He had a feeling it was all to do with the book.

"Who was she?"

"Are you certain you want to know? Don't you want me to read more of her diary to you?"

"No, I want to know."

"Impulsive angel," he murmured, kissing her softly. "I should drag it out, make you wait."

"Would you be so cruel?"

"No," he said, brushing his fingertips against her mouth. "Not again, Beth." He watched the pad of his thumb stroke over her lip, saw her head tilt back and her eyes close as she enjoyed the delicate touch.

He wanted her like this, unguarded and relaxed. It would be so easy to lift her nightgown, part her knees and kneel between them, fitting himself deep inside her.

Another time, when he could come to her freely, when she would accept him…

"Her name was Marguerite, and she was a dancer in the King of Jerusalem's harem."

Elizabeth's eyes flew open, wild and unfocused, and he kissed her eyelids. "The king loved her, but could not take her. He was a leper, so he consoled himself by watching her dance. When the Templars arrived, he was dying. He decided to secure her future. It was, after all, the greatest way to show her his love. He betrothed her to a knight, bequeathed her riches, ensured she would be a lady of great standing."

"Who? Who was *he?*"

Iain smiled. Lizzy was breathless. She reminded him so much of the woman in the diary. Fiery, passionate, determined but loyal, even if that loyalty caused her pain. "Haelan St. Clair, my great-grandfather numerous generations removed. She became his wife, and Sinjin's Veiled Lady was lost to him. But she loved him—it was always only Sinjin she loved. She kept her vows to Haelan and was loyal, but her love belonged to Sinjin. She continued to write in her diary about the yearnings of her heart. Her belief that one day she would die, and her soul would be reborn and she would find a way to be with her lover."

"Haelan discovered the diary."

"He took it to a witch who lived on the fringes of the clan. She put a curse on the book and the souls of both Marguerite and Sinjin. To prevent them ever being reunited, she placed a curse on both our houses, so that none of us could ever meet and fall in love—without pain."

"How long have you known?"

Would the truth help or hurt his cause? he wondered. He decided it didn't matter. Only the truth would do.

"All my life, I suppose. The diary has been passed down, along with the warning of the curse. But when I first saw you, no curse could have stopped me from wanting you. From risking such a fate. When you looked at me, Beth, well… My soul knew yours."

She touched him, caressed his cheeks, tried to see him. She was checking for insincerity. Lies. She would find none.

The hardest thing he ever did, beside walk away from her all those years ago, was to leave her then. To kiss her softly and whisper goodbye, when all he really wanted to do was to make love to her, make her understand he regretted everything in his past—except her. Except the days they had spent together.

She held him, gripped his hands. "Do you believe in the curse?"

"Nay, lass," he murmured, making her smile at the sound of his brogue. "I believe we either curse ourselves, or free ourselves with our own actions. The only curse we suffer from is the fear we both harbour. It isn't easy giving it up, but it's the only way. We either will or we won't. Either way, that fear still rules us, and until we let it go, we'll not make our way back to each other. We both have to want it, Beth. Both have to let go of the past, and the fears that bind us, before we can ever be free to move on to a place that is meant only for us."

CHAPTER EIGHTEEN

Two NIGHTS LATER, Elizabeth found herself attending the theatre, a first in many years—and never before with Iain as her escort. It gave her a curious feeling to be going with him, a sensation she didn't want to examine too closely. Especially after what had happened between them.

It was still cold, and the ground was covered with snow, but the streets were passable enough for carriages to dredge through. Besides, the ton had been kept indoors for nearly five nights and they were restless, needing some mindless activity to while away the evening. When Iain had sent around a missive informing her the theatre was on for the night, she had felt a sense of excitement.

She had not seen him or spoken to him since he'd left her sitting at the window bench. She had thought nearly nonstop about the story of Sinjin, and the fact that his lover had been Iain's great-grandmother. Unfathomable that Sinjin and Marguerite had been lovers over seven centuries before. Strangely, it seemed fitting how it had played out. Though Lizzy didn't know what to think about the curse. She certainly felt cursed in her connection to Iain Sinclair. But there was longing there—a deep, visceral longing that she could no longer shove to the bottom of her soul.

"Here you go," he murmured as he helped her to sit in the chair in his personal box. He was careful with her, even sweeping the train of her gown away to protect it from his boots. She had chosen the blue gown she had been wearing at the Sumners' musicale, the night it all began once more between them. It was a daring move, part of her hoping it might rekindle some of Iain's sensual intensity.

She shouldn't have worn it, but a little devil inside her had tempted her beyond reason. Tonight she wanted to be stunning, a sensual creature he couldn't take his eyes off of. She had felt his gaze on the expanse of bosom displayed by her low neckline. The moment he'd taken her cloak from her shoulders, she had heard his indrawn breath, felt the heat of his eyes. But he had refrained from saying anything, even complimenting her. Now she felt hurt, and slightly reckless, wishing to lash out. He confused her thoughts, her ordered life.

"A Midsummer Night's Dream," he said as he leaned toward her. "Fitting, considering the foot of snow outside."

Fanning herself, she smiled. Whether he wondered about her silence since they had emerged from the carriage, she could not tell. He seemed distracted himself, as though he were busy looking for someone. Who that might be, she could not imagine, and it was something she most definitely did not want to dwell on.

Thankfully, Black and Isabella chose that moment to enter their box.

"Oh, what a magnificent view!" Isabella exclaimed. "I'm so glad I brought my opera glasses. I shall be able to see everything, Lizzy, and give you a very good accounting of it all."

Elizabeth could imagine Iain gloating over the compliment about his theatre box. Perhaps he was even now using its spectacular view to search the crowd for someone more interesting than her.

"You're looking very lovely tonight, Elizabeth," Black murmured as he took her hand and kissed her gloved knuckles. "The roses in your cheeks are most becoming."

"Black, you are a shameless flatterer."

"Nonsense, Lizzy." He laughed. "I'm never shameless."

"No, he's not," Iain drawled, "but he is bloody pompous."

Lizzy could not contain her smile. "Horrid man, isn't he, Black?"

"Indeed he is. Why you agreed to lend him an air of respectability tonight I shall never understand."

"Me, either," she said with a pout.

"Good evening." The dark, honeyed voice seeped from the curtains. Elizabeth felt Iain tense beside her as she held out her gloved hand. "Lord Sheldon, what a surprise."

He clasped her hand, kissed her fingers and gave them a light squeeze. "I saw you from my box and had to come over. Lady Elizabeth, you look like an angel tonight."

She flushed, and she wondered if Iain noticed it. "Thank you, my lord."

"What are you doing here, Sheldon?" Iain grumbled.

"Taking in *A Midsummer Night's Dream*."

"No, I meant what are you doing in my box?"

"Admiring the view."

"The stage is the other direction," he snapped.

Oh, dear, what the devil was going on? Brow furrowed, Lizzy searched for a neutral topic. "What did you think of the snow, my lord? It's your first since coming home."

"Spectacular. Jack decided to bury himself in it."

"I should have liked to see that. Cheeky Jack."

The earl laughed, and she became aware of Iain's sudden darkness, a brooding animosity that seemed to grow as he sat beside her.

"You've said your salutations, Sheldon, now get out."

Elizabeth gasped at his rudeness, but Sheldon seemed to brush it off. He certainly was in no rush to obey him. "I did as you said, closed my eyes and inhaled the air when it was snowing. And do you know, it smelt just like that afternoon when we were walking."

"Oh, I'm so glad you did. I wondered if you would remember."

"I do remember, Lady Elizabeth. I've learned never to question your senses, for they're quite remarkable."

"Why, thank you, my lord. And how is Jack doing, cooped up in the house, unable to go on his jaunts?"

"Restless. Destructive. He's chewed the toes of my finest boots."

"Well, hopefully it won't be too long before he is getting you out of the house for a good run."

"As to that, I wonder, Elizabeth, if the weather stays clear, might you be up for another visit to Temple Church? I've made a discovery I would like to show you."

"I have made a discovery as well, my lord."

"Is that so?" he asked, then helped himself to the empty chair beside her, ignoring Iain's grunt of warning. "What nature was your discovery?"

"The Veiled Lady."

"Oh?"

"Yes, she was Marguerite, after all, just as you suspected."

"Miraculous. And how did you come across that fact?"

"Lord Alynwick possessed some information."

She heard Iain mumble something under his breath. It sounded very impolite, bordering on hostile.

"I shall look forward to hearing all the details very soon. I'll call on you, if that is permissible."

"Yes, it is," she said, at the same time Iain muttered, "No, it is not."

Flipping her fan open, Elizabeth hastily beat the air while Sheldon took his leave.

"You are insufferable," she hissed.

"I'm insufferable? What the devil were you doing, encouraging him to come around like a dog sniffing for scraps?"

She gasped, snapped her fan shut. "Just what are you inferring?"

"Damn you," he growled, "must you encourage him, and within my hearing?"

"I don't know what you mean. He's my friend."

"And I'm what?" he demanded. "Nothing, obviously. Excuse me," he murmured, then stood. "I see someone I must speak with." Then he promptly left the box.

"What the devil was that all about?" Isabella enquired. "Alynwick's expression is positively fierce."

"I think it a private matter, my love. It's best not to enquire."

"Well, private matters are the most enticing, aren't they? They beg enquiries."

Black laughed. "You are too nosey for your own good. Now, *shh,* the curtain is rising."

It was one of the most miserable hours Elizabeth had spent in her life. To be abandoned by Iain, and in his own box, too! Insufferable beast. He'd been gone for the entire first act. And just where was he? What was he doing? To whom did he need to speak? Didn't he realize that any number of sordid images came springing to mind when she wondered where he was, and why he had left her to the watchful eyes of Black and Isabella?

She couldn't see him, the lout. And it was agony not being able to, not knowing what kind of a fool he was making of her. When at last the curtain lowered, signalling intermission, Elizabeth rose with as much dignity as she could muster and allowed herself to take Black's offered arm.

"Let us get some punch," he suggested.

"Yes, that would be lovely," Isabella agreed, but Elizabeth could hear the concern in her friend's voice. When she next found Alynwick she was going to give him a piece of her mind!

They made their way through the crowd to the lobby. Black passed her a cup of punch, but she hesitated to drink it, fearing she might spill it on her gown. She despaired of ever finding Iain in the crush but then she heard his voice, the silky, seductive laugh, the low voice of a man bent on seduction.

"Come, Lady Larabie," he murmured, "I'm sure it wasn't all that horrible."

"An evening without you, my lord, is sheer purgatory."

Well, there really was nothing more revolting than Alynwick whispering to a lady—and a married one at that.

"You haven't been to see me," the woman said in pouting tones. "I'm heartbroken, my lord."

Alynwick's reply was a mumble, intentional no doubt, for he knew Lizzy's hearing was acute, and that he saw her standing there, able to listen to their conversation.

"Darling, you must come by the club. What fun we could have. Orpheus, you know, has all kinds of little tricks to indulge in."

Lizzy's ears perked up at that. What the devil was Alynwick up to? she wondered. Was Lady Larabie involved in some scheme involving Alynwick, and Orpheus, of all people? Perhaps she should inform Sussex of the matter.

There was a shuffling of bodies, followed by a demure little purr, and Lizzy felt like dumping the contents of her punch glass over Alynwick's head.

"Another time, perhaps," he said. "Adieu."

"Good night, my lord. I will be home tonight, if you desire more...varied and sophisticated entertainment."

Oooh, that witch was looking right at her. Elizabeth knew it. When Alynwick came to stand beside her, she was positively fuming. "Take me home."

"We just arrived."

"I don't give a damn, take me home."

"Elizabeth, calm yourself." He reached for her, but she tugged her arm free of his grasp. How dare he do this to her!

"I will do no such thing, my lord. How dare you make a mockery of me like this, talking to that...that woman?"

"That woman," he hissed in her ear, "is Guardian business, and I need her cooperation. I hadn't intended to meet up with her here tonight, but when I saw her, I had to keep up pretences."

"If you hadn't planned on meeting her here tonight, then where had you intended to meet up with her? When?"

"Not here, Elizabeth. People are starting to stare. Let it alone. She's Guardian business I need as a contact. There is nothing else to it."

"You fought a duel for her!"

"Not for her, but for the Brethren," he whispered harshly. "She's supplying me with information about Orpheus."

"I don't care what you're getting from her, take me home."

"I think you do care, what I'm getting, and perhaps giving," he said huskily in her ear.

Pinching her lips together, Lizzy turned, sought to find a way out of this hell that was forming around her, but he was there, latching on to her arm. "Where the hell are you going?"

"Back home. This was a mistake. I should have known better than to trust you."

"Why?"

"Because you're a rake, and a bloody heartless one at that. You haven't changed at all. You brought me here to flaunt your latest conquest in my face. She has nothing to do with Brethren Guardian business, and everything to do with slaking your lust!"

They were outside now, and Lizzy felt a measure of relief as the cool air kissed her cheeks. Damn him for discomposing her before everyone.

"Elizabeth—"

"I am through discussing this with you. Call for the carriage, if you please."

"As your ladyship demands," he said in mocking tones. "Waste of a bloody night."

"I couldn't agree more. Although it hasn't all been a wash. You did manage to discover the fact that your mistress misses you in her bed. Hardly a startling revelation."

"Oh? Do you miss me in yours, Beth?"

She would not answer that. Would not. She couldn't. "In your wildest fantasies, Alynwick," she grunted.

"Isn't that the truth?" he mumbled as he helped her up into the carriage and slammed the door. They were off, and the silence in the cab was overbearing. She couldn't stand it, the way her mind kept drifting back to that woman, and her voice, and the stench of a cloying perfume.

"I'll stay to make certain you're settled in."

"You will set me down at my house, then take yourself off," she demanded haughtily.

He reached for her, grabbed her chin in his hand. "I will check the locks and windows before leaving you," he said as his foot slid across the floor of the carriage, only to rest between her legs. "My gut is on the alert tonight. Something is in the air."

"Yes, I smell it, too. It's called unfettered debauchery."

He grunted. "Are you offering, Beth? Because I would, of course, be more than happy to accept such an offer from you. You've turned into such a plump armful that I couldn't resist."

"Go to hell," she snapped, hating how he made her lose her cool elegance.

"Already been, my dear. The service was not up to my standards."

It was such an Alynwick thing to say! He hadn't changed, not one bit. She thought she had seen another side to him, but she had been wrong. It was all an act. And she had fallen for it. She ignored him after that, allowed her thoughts to run riot through her mind.

When they exited the carriage, she barely waited for his assistance. When Hastings opened the door, Maggie was there waiting for her, and Lizzy took her companion's hand, anxious to be away from him.

"Well, how was your evening?"

"Insipid. Uninspired and downright intolerable."

"Oh, dear," Maggie whispered as she steered her to her chamber door. "As bad as all that?"

"And then some. Maggie," she said, "fetch the writing box. I have a letter to pen to my brother, and it needs to be posted first thing on the morrow. And Lord Alynwick is to be escorted out. Now!"

IAIN WATCHED ELIZABETH climb the stairs. She was in high dudgeon, her cheeks flushed. Her magnificent bosom in that scandalously low-cut dress was heaving, drawing his gaze.

You're jealous, he thought delightedly as he followed her progress up the stairs. *Positively green with it.*

She'd treated him like offal, like dog dung on the toe of her boot. He should be furious with her, but how could he be, knowing that wonderful performance all stemmed from jealousy? It was unfortunate that Georgiana had been there tonight, looking directly into his box with her glasses. He hadn't wanted to go to her, but had to keep up some semblance of interest. He had not seen her since that night he'd left her at the club. He didn't need her any longer, and certainly didn't need the complication she presented with Elizabeth, but it was better to keep her placated. Enemies were always best kept close. And Georgiana, he knew, would be a dangerous enemy. Especially after what he'd learned from Sheldon. Iain had no wish to draw Elizabeth into his scheme, but it had happened.

He would protect her from Georgiana. He'd seen the way the woman had looked at Beth—with a blazing hatred in her jaded eyes. Beth in turn had heard the cutting remark Georgiana had made. It had infuriated her, and gave him hope that Beth might still be his.

He understood jealousy. He'd been green, too, tonight, when Sheldon had come round, sniffing at Elizabeth's skirts. Oh, how smooth and skilled the detective was, so easily discovering Elizabeth's weakness and handing it to her on a silver platter. Iain had never been gifted in conversation. His tongue was not glib and light. He had no knack for politeness or mundane social conversation. The fact had never bothered him before, but he'd felt damn inferior tonight, sitting in that chair, watching the two of them. How easily she conversed with Sheldon, while with him, she was guarded, standoffish. Always searching for his true motivations. He couldn't blame her for that. He'd done much to earn her distrust.

But she was jealous.

There was that hope flaring again. When one was completely done with a lover, jealousy did not remain. If she truly meant what she'd said to him she should have no cause to care about what he did, or whom he saw. She cared. Cared very much.

Quickly, Iain saw to the latches and locks. They were all secured. Climbing the stairs, he felt a measure of peace run through him. Tonight was the night. He would wait no longer. Could not wait any longer.

Opening the door to Elizabeth's chamber, he stepped inside, heard Maggie's gasp, saw her eyes go round with shock. It was all very improper, but Iain had never been a gentleman in the true sense of the word. Besides, Elizabeth was no child in need of protection. She was a woman, and whatever happened here was between them. Maggie seemed to understand that.

"Tell him to leave," Elizabeth demanded. Maggie opened her mouth to repeat her mistress's orders when Iain effectively put a stop to them.

"I'm done running, Elizabeth. Done with waiting for you to hear me out. Done with the way you pretend you don't want me."

Maggie's mouth gaped open, her gaze darting between them. She was obviously torn between her duty to Elizabeth and the way his eyes pleaded with her to leave him alone with her.

"I don't want you!" she thundered.

"The hell you don't. You were seething with jealousy

tonight over nothing more than my conversation with a lady."

"A *lady?* Ha! She is the furthest thing from a lady. I'm quite certain," Elizabeth sneered, "that when one looks up the definition of *lady* in the dictionary it does not say, 'a woman of loose morals who betrays her marriage vows by sleeping with other women's men!'" She paused, the enormity of what she'd said finally sinking in. "I mean, that is to say…"

Iain took a few steps to her, glanced at Maggie, who took no time in deciding it was prudent to leave them alone. When the door closed behind her, he saw Elizabeth sag.

"Is that how you see me, Beth?" Christ, his voice sounded as if he had eaten glass. "Am I yours? Your man?"

She whirled away from him, rubbing her hands on her arms. "Go away."

"Is that truly what you want?"

"Yes."

"You've never lied to me before. I always depended upon that, Elizabeth—your honesty. It was one of the only things in the world that I could."

Her back stiffened, and he saw her internal struggle. Elizabeth was a strong woman who had never needed to hide behind half truths and lies.

"The lady in question is not my mistress. She never was. She was a means to an end, a way for me to gain access to the House of Orpheus. She truly was Brethren business."

"I don't care what she is to you."

"You cared tonight, Beth. Your every thought was clear on your face."

"You may have her, with my blessing."

"I don't want her. There is only one woman in the world I desire, and she's standing right here. You want me, Elizabeth. I'm yours. I'd give my soul for that, you know. To be yours once again."

Wrapping his arms around her, he held her, his chest pressed into her back, his face buried against the soft flesh of her shoulder. He felt her weaken, accept his embrace.

"Aren't you tired of fighting this, Beth?" he asked. "These feelings aren't going away, they're just growing deeper. Harder to resist. I've acknowledged the truth. Isn't it time you did, as well?"

She clutched at his arms, her body trembling.

"Just one night, Elizabeth, let us put the past behind us. No recriminations. No judgements. Let us just be together as we both want. We're both so tired," he murmured as he pressed a kiss to her shoulder. "So damn tired of trying to outrun feelings that will never let go, never fade. There is nothing left to be done, my Beth, but to run to them—to each other. Not from each other." His mouth moved over her shoulder, up her neck, till his lips were caressing her ear. "Let's just fall into bed and make love to each other. Forget everything except you and me and what we want."

"It would be so easy to do," she whispered, her ire leaving her. "But the night will end, and the dawn will come, bringing with it more troubles than what we already have between us."

"I will leave before the dawn. The discussion we must inevitably have can wait. Let this be one night of pleasure. You want that, Beth. I can feel it in you. You want that again."

She turned in his arms, her fingers touching his face, traversing his cheeks. Her mouth was trembling. "I won't even make you answer, Beth. You can hate me in the morning, if you'll only love me tonight."

He captured her, swept her up in his arms, kissed her deeply, tasting her, walking back with her toward the bed while he cupped her cheeks in his hands and ravaged her mouth with hot, openmouthed kisses. Her tongue touched his, returning his kisses, matching the ferocity of them, the hunger.

No words were said, but there was a mutual acceptance. An urgency between them as he laid her onto her bed and stretched out beside her. That urgency could not rob him of this night, the pleasures of Beth's body. Tonight he would be relentless in pleasuring her. He'd been nothing but a boy when he had made love to her that long ago summer. He was a man now, she a woman, and he wanted to love her slowly and endlessly, with all the skill he possessed. For some reason he wanted to show her what sort of lover he could be to her, as if that was somehow the key to keeping her at his side, though he knew it was not. It had never been just about sex for Beth. There had been so much more....

Removing his coat, he flung it to the floor. Next came his shirt, which he hastily pulled over his head. Then he kicked off his boots, before focusing on Elizabeth's gown and the pale mounds of flesh that escaped from her bodice.

"Your arm," she said quietly, and he stilled when her fingertips found the gauze wrapped around his biceps.

"It won't stop me, Beth."

"Does it pain you?"

"No, not like the pain of being deprived of you." Lowering his head, he caught her lips and kissed her slowly, opening her mouth, angling his over hers with lazy kisses and licks. "Not like the pain in my heart when you ask me to leave. Don't ask me tonight, Beth," he murmured, his blood drumming heavily in his veins as he looked down at her. "Please don't."

Her fingers stroked his arm as she turned her head, her mouth grazing the gauze with a soft kiss. "I won't."

His fingers were shaking as he pulled at the buttons, revealing her slowly. He smoothed his palms over the creamy flesh that was pushed up by her corset.

Skin as pure as moonlight, he thought as he watched his hand move over her. Her hair had come undone, spilling loose around her, as black as ink against the cream coverlet.

He exposed her slowly, took his time to run his hands over her, heightening her response, listening to her little moans and mewls as he touched her with his fingers and lips. He undressed her slowly, savouring each sigh, each arch of her body, the sight of gooseflesh creeping over her skin, the sound of her garments sliding away from her body and falling to the floor.

When she was at last naked, he knelt over her, his knees on either side of her thighs as he skimmed his hands along her body, lovingly tracing each curve, the rise of her belly, the roundness of her hips, the beautiful lushness of her breasts. Her fingers were clutched in the bedcovers, and he pulled her hand away, and up, where he kissed her fingers, nudged them open and kissed her palm.

Beth...Beth... He whispered her name in his mind, unwilling to break the spell that surrounded them with any sound. He did not want to hear his voice; the only sounds he desired were the soft inhalations of Beth's breath, her sighs of pleasure, the brush of his body and hers as he loved her.

She was beautiful, so perfect. He wanted to sit back

and feast his eyes on her, sear her into his memory, lying like this, waiting for him.

His hand caressed her body, capturing her breast, palming her, and he watched her back arch into his hand. He tasted her, suckled her nipple, laved it as he pleasured her other breast, rubbing her nipple with the flat of his palm, watching as a pink flush kissed her cheeks and chest. Her legs spread restlessly, inviting him in— beckoning him.

Behind his trousers his cock throbbed, ready for release. Ignoring it, he caught her breasts in his hands, brought them together, played with them for what seemed like forever until he wrung the most erotic moan from deep in her throat.

"Iain." It was a plea. Such a beautiful sound, his name on her lips.

His gaze devoured her, followed the length of her leg to her ankle, where he picked up her foot, nuzzled the delicate bone, then slowly kissed his way up her calf, to the inner curve of her thigh. Opening her wide, he draped her calf over his shoulder, studying her glistening core, saw that the mirror in the corner of the room afforded him an unimpeded view of what he was doing to her. He saw her face, her eyes pressed shut in anticipation. Her mouth parted when he blew hot breath over her core. Her hands covered her breasts, pulled at her nipples when he parted her and stroked his tongue over her. Light at first, then firmer, deeper, more possessively, until she reached down and gripped his head, holding him to her.

How perfect they looked together, her the angel, him the hedonist. She was moving her hips, coming up to meet him, and he watched in the mirror, unable to close his eyes or look away. If only Beth could see this. How right this was.

Her orgasm was quiet, her hands clutching for purchase, but he slipped out of her reach, held himself above her, watching her expression as she came, and as he sank himself so deep inside her. Her moan made him shudder, made his own flesh flicker with goose bumps as the sound wrapped around him.

Lashes fluttering, he studied her, the way her body took him in. His rhythm was measured—all for her pleasure. To coax another climax from her, but with him deep inside this time. He would stay there forever, time suspended, with him overtop her, her arms flung above her head, his hand holding hers together, pressing them into the bed as he worked and thrust over her body, bringing her up yet again, wanting to see her shatter and cry out this time, unable to control her climax.

SHE WAS DYING, she knew. She had never felt such pleasure. The way Iain filled her, stretched her, then retreated, was nothing like she had ever felt before, not even all those years ago when he had laid claim to her body. He knew how to touch her, how hard to thrust, when to roll his hips, when and how to angle himself so she could not only feel him inside her, but rubbing against her clitoris, brushing, sensitizing. The fiend knew how to make her agony last, how to suspend it until he would allow her to reach out for it and surrender.

The room was quiet except for the rhythmic squeak of the bed and Iain's hurried breaths overtop her. It was dark in her world, her other senses dulled by the pleasure. She wanted to touch him, to feel his presence beyond the penetration of his body. He was with her, but there was a distance between them, a space where words and touch, taste and smell should have been.

He was insistent now, his thrusts harder, forceful,

claiming—branding. She forgot her worries and concentrated only on him, the connection of their bodies. He was grunting, his pace purposeful, his fingers biting into her wrists as he held her arms above her head. He was looking down at her, at her swaying breasts, the place where they were joined. She felt the heat of his gaze there, watching, and she arched, felt her climax build.

And then he slowed, rolling his hips, rubbing against her clitoris, stimulating her until she found she could match his rhythm. She wanted to hear him call her name, to discover some sound of satisfaction from him, but he was too intent upon her pleasure, and she was soon lost to it.

"Again," he growled, after she had already started to tremble a second time. Her legs were shaking, and her core ached in a mixture of pleasure and tenderness.

She couldn't; no more. She was exhausted, her body shattered. But Iain wanted more. He was determined, and he sat up on his knees, lifted her, wrapped her legs around his waist and set her astride him, impaling her deeply.

"No," she begged, clinging to him, unable to bear more. But his hands were on her bottom, supporting her, showing her the way.

"Yes."

He did all the work, just made her hold on to him as he breathed against her, his hips and thighs rising up off the bed as he pushed deep into her body. Her breasts were pressed up between them, and Iain caressed them with the bristle on his chin. With his tongue, he found a nipple and sucked as he rocked against her.

There was no sound when she peaked the third time. She couldn't utter any noise, and Iain was silent. Taut as a bow, but silent as the night as he pushed her back down onto her bed and loomed over her, thrusting hard once more before pouring himself inside her.

With a great gasp he finished, and rolled off to the side, silently gathering her up in his arms and holding her against his chest. The pounding of his heart against her ear was the only sound she could hear.

CHAPTER NINETEEN

HIS CHEST WAS HARD, the skin slick with their sweat. His scent wrapped around her, a musky aroma, the taste of salt and Iain. How beautiful it was to lie upon him, her cheek nestled against the hard muscle, the feel of the Brethren Guardian brand pressing against her lips.

Lazily, he raked his fingers through her hair, lifting and combing, brushing it back over her shoulders. His breathing had at last returned to normal, but immediately began to grow again when she exhaled contentedly and stirred atop him. Beneath her lips, his nipple began to harden.

He said nothing, the silence stretching into something long and slightly uncomfortable. If Elizabeth were... normal, she would cross her arms over his chest and rest her chin on her hands, staring up at him, studying him in the afterglow of their passion.

But where she was, it was silent and dark, and she had no inkling of what expression he wore, what thoughts were reflected in his eyes. A terrible image came to her, of Iain lying in her bed, looking down upon her with a smug smile of satisfaction that she had surrendered, and he had won.

If only she could see him, reassure herself that it had been the right thing to do to give in to the needs of her body—her heart. That he was looking at her not with pride that he had won the battle, but with tenderness and warmth, and appreciation for what they had shared in her bed.

But she was lost, she realized—trapped in a dark oblivion from which there was no escape. His silence only made it more unbearable, and she was left to think of all the things that came to her mind—his women, lovers who were skilled and beautiful. Women who could at least see him. Who could look down upon him and know the results of their efforts. She couldn't even do that, and Iain, it seemed, would not give her the words she so desperately needed to hear.

Self-pity. How she despised it. She hadn't wallowed in it in years, since she had thrown her last handkerchief aside and wiped the last tear from her cheek. But it was back with a vengeance, with a depth of feeling that rocked her, that made her irrational and terrified. She was grieving, she realized. Quite horribly, too. The loss of her sight, the loss of Iain, the feelings of despair she had never allowed free, but had bottled up and hid from. Suddenly the grief came crashing down upon her, the memories assaulted her, the words that she had never spoke to him rose up and choked her. She was in another place, the distant past. Elizabeth felt her mind fracture from her body. She was another person, a frightened, confused young woman who used discipline and control to avoid the feelings. The pain.

"Beth?"

"Don't call me that!" she shrieked hysterically. Good heavens, she needed to get ahold of herself, but something was wrong. She couldn't…couldn't seem to find herself in the onslaught of memories, the grief for the past, the trauma of his betrayal—a trauma she had never wanted to experience, so she had buried it and never acknowledged her grief.

And here it was, pressing down upon her in her black, silent prison, and she couldn't see what he thought of her—of what they had done. She dare not ask him, for his answer would be witty and sensual, belying any of his feelings, and she could not see the truth in his eyes, to know if he lied to her, mocked her. If he thought her amusing. She would never know if he had been as lost as she in their lovemaking.

Shimmying off him, she flung his hand away from her. Her breasts were swaying, she could feel them, and she had never felt more exposed, more hideous than now, naked, vulnerable because she could not see him—could not hear him, or sense his thoughts and feelings. He was so good at hiding, at masking himself from her, and she could not do the same.

Everything she had wanted to say that day came rushing to the forefront. She'd been too much of a coward to do so. She'd never demanded to know why, even though in her heart she knew the answer.

She didn't like what she was becoming—that young, hurt girl he had abandoned. But she couldn't stop it, or the feelings. She must not let him know, let him see the pain he had caused her.

"Get out."

The sheets rustled as she stumbled from the bed, her palm fruitlessly searching over the rumpled pile of bed linens. She needed to get out of her room, the chamber that smelt of him, reeked of the pleasure they had shared. She could feel his eyes upon her, dissecting her, unmasking her, and she railed inside, so out of control, so senseless now in her rage, her impotence, her blindness.

And still he lay there watching her struggle. Enjoying watching the angel descend to earth in humiliation and a great tumble of pride. She closed her eyes, relieved at last to find her robe. She had no clue if it was inside out or not, and she didn't care. He could laugh at her and she would not care, just as long as he left her to weather this strange mood that was making her feel as though she were drowning in a gale.

"Talk to me, Beth."

His words spread goose bumps on her flesh, like ripples in the water after a stone is skipped across its still surface. That voice…it beckoned and lured, and she dared not trust it, trust herself. Not with the way she was feeling, so out of control, nearly insensible with pain.

His fingers touched her hand, and she gasped in fear. She had not heard him leave the bed, had no idea he stood so close to her, looking down upon her. He stroked her hair back, his head lowering until she could feel the brush of his breath, and she jumped away, aware that the post of her bed would be right there, and she could grab it, wrap herself around it.

"You're terrified," he murmured, and the floorboard creaked beneath his weight, giving away his approach.

"Don't touch me," she said, her voice trembling.

"I hurt you, did I?" he asked, and his voice was filled with an emotion she had never once heard from him— that of regret. She didn't know whether she should be grateful he felt something or sickened by the pity in his tone.

"Won't you talk to me? Tell me how to ease your pain."

He had remained silent through the whole thing. Why should she oblige him by talking?

"You have a wild-eyed look, my Beth. What do you see?"

"Don't look at me," she cried, now utterly unhinged. "Don't look into my eyes when you can see everything in them, and I am not able to look into yours and see anything!"

The door burst open, and she could hear Maggie's laboured breathing. "What the devil are you doing here?"

"See him out, Maggie," Lizzy ordered as she clutched the post of the bed, resting her face against the cool, smooth wood. She had no idea if she had properly covered her naked body or not with her robe, but she felt Maggie's eyes boring into her as if she were completely nude.

"My lord?" Maggie snarled. "On your way."

"I'll go when I'm good and ready," he retorted. Lizzy sensed him reaching for her, and she moved back, her hand gliding along the footboard, guiding her to the dressing table she knew would be mere feet away.

"I suggest you go now, your lordship, before I have the night watchman and the police alerted," Maggie declared. "You wouldn't want them to discover this scene, now would you? A terrified blind girl with the likes of you bearing down upon her?"

Lizzy heard the vicious oath, the way his clothes were snapped up from the floor and his legs jammed into his trousers, his arms thrust through his shirtsleeves. "I shall call on you in the morning to discuss matters."

The door slammed, and Lizzy sank to the floor in defeat, in absolute confusion as to what was happening to her—and despair, she realized, when Iain had so easily capitulated, leaving her alone. She nearly laughed at the dichotomy of her thoughts. She was mad. A raving lunatic.

Maggie padded softly across the floor to where she had wilted like a delicate flower, and suddenly, the fear and inferiority gave way to a fierce sense of rage that would not be contained. Elizabeth had never given in to that anger, and now, after twelve years of bottling it, it threatened to erupt. To send her into a mental place where her demons held court, waiting to taunt her.

"No!" she yelled, jumping up before her friend could reach her. "No! I will not wallow like this! I will not let you ruin me," she shouted, "not like before!"

Turning, she found her way to the dressing table and with one sweep of her arm knocked the entire contents, brushes, combs and jewelry, onto the floor.

"Damn you, Iain Sinclair," she yelled, shaking with a ferocious anger. Maggie reached for her, but she thrust herself out of the way, bouncing off the wall as she did so. "I will not let you do this to me!" she cried. *"I will not!"*

IAIN HEARD HIS NAME, followed by a stream of epithets. Elizabeth was in a rage the likes of which he had never seen, and never fathomed she possessed. The curse on his head was followed by a crash, and the sound of something being thrown against the wall.

Closing his eyes, he pictured the image of Elizabeth cowering at the foot of the bed, clinging to it as if it were the mast on a sinking ship. He had hurt her. He'd tried to be gentle, but in the end, he had hurt her. And it sickened him. He should go, never to grace her door again. But that thought sickened him even more.

"No, miss! No, you'll hurt yerself!"

There was no thinking now. He turned, jogged back to Elizabeth's door and quietly opened it. Beth was in a fury, that was patently clear. Her breathing was ragged as she tore the covers from the bed, followed by the bed curtains. Maggie clasped Elizabeth's hands with her own strong ones, trying to calm her, but there was no pacifying her. She was possessed by some unseen demon. A demon he feared was the past.

"Let me go!" she cried, twisting from her companion's hold. Maggie saw him then, opened her mouth, but he shook his head, warning her to not give away his presence.

"Goddamn you, Sinclair," Elizabeth roared again. "I hate you! I hate you for making me feel worthless and disposable, when I am worth a hundred of your doxies!"

All this for him—because of him. Shocked, horrified, he slid down the wall, watching her fall apart, and not fully understanding the why of it. With his hand, he motioned for Maggie to leave, but she merely looked from him to Lizzy, worried for the young woman who was wandering about the room talking to herself, ranting like a bedlamite.

Maggie must have known that Iain would protect her charge with his life, for they shared a meaningful glance before she quietly left the room.

"Oh, yes," Elizabeth railed after her companion. "Leave me, then! I am so easy to forget, am I not? *He* has no problem doing it. He seduced me and walked away! Tonight he could not even be bothered to speak to me— not during the act, nor after! I was nothing but a whore to him, merely a vessel for his pleasure, not a person."

Resting his head against the wall, he watched her, humiliated that he was the cause of such deep despair.

"How dare he lay there beneath me," she said, some of the bluster leaving her. "How dare he move silently inside me, in a dark room where I cannot see, where my only sense is to hear. How dare he deprive me of that, the only thing I have."

He hadn't known. Hadn't thought of it. He'd wanted to be kind and tender, to give her the sort of pleasure with which a gentleman gifts a lady. Had he spoken, he might have said the wrong thing, something crass and base, something no angel should hear. He hadn't wanted to ruin the beauty of their lovemaking with words he had used with other women.

"Damn you," she said again, then collapsed onto the floor and leaned against the wall, with a pile of blankets heaped in her lap. She sat directly across the room from him, her unseeing eyes staring right at him. He was forced to look into those eyes and admit that he had been the cause of this outburst—this destruction wrought from pain.

"I hate you for what you made of me twelve years ago, and I hate you for what you made me feel tonight— worthless and weak, comparing myself to one of your past liaisons and finding myself inferior. I could not tell what you thought of me—what you saw when you looked at me after—when you would not even speak to me. You did the same that last time, and then you left, telling me for certain your true feelings. Tonight I made you leave, so I would not have to endure it again. But it came anyway, those feelings, all those years of pent-up fear. Well, it was released, Sinclair. How did you like it?"

He wanted to speak, but knew that if he gave away his presence here in her chamber, she would be humiliated to know he had witnessed her uncharacteristic loss of composure.

"You soulless bastard, you take a piece of me every time," she whispered, and the tears fell until she was trembling. "You have no idea what it is to not be able to see, to not know for certain what someone is thinking or feeling. You can't imagine what it is like to lie there and imagine it all, to have to trust your instincts. I *have* no trustworthy instincts when it comes to you. You leave me feeling hopeless and helpless. Adrift in the ocean at night, with no moon. I can't see anything. And I want so much to know what *you* feel, so that I might be at ease, knowing that you're not laughing at me—mocking me."

Rolling to her side, she cuddled up in the blanket and hid her face in its soft depths. "I am nineteen all over again. Only you do this to me. Never again, Iain. Never."

When her sniffles and little hiccups subsided, replaced with deep breaths that spoke of sleep, Iain silently made his way to her and slipped down before her. Carefully, he reached out, skimmed his fingers along her cheek and watched her sleep, studying her, marvelling at her and the spiky lashes that shone in the dim firelight like raindrops on crystal.

"Beth," he murmured, his soul feeling heavy. "I left you alone in the dark, didn't I? I have been as blind as you. I will try to find a way for you to see me, my Beth, and pray that when you do, you'll discover something redeemable there."

ELIZABETH STIRRED, only to realize that after her outburst she had fallen asleep on the floor. She tried to get up, but realized she was pinned by the blankets. Though she tugged at them, they wouldn't move, and that's when she realized there was someone there with her.

Iain. She smelt him. Felt the familiarity of his touch as he brushed the loose strands of hair away from her face. When had he returned? Had he heard her? Oh, God, had he *seen* her?

"I'm so sorry," he whispered.

"Let me up."

"You—we—can't run from this any longer."

"I can't talk about this now," she snapped, pulling the blanket from him and covering herself up. She wanted to hide from his eyes, the humiliation of having given in to an overwhelming fear and self-pity.

"When *will* we talk about it?" he asked. He touched her face, and she flinched. He cupped her cheek in his palm, wouldn't let her turn away and hide from him. "What can I give you, Beth?"

What she was too much of a coward to hear. "The truth, Iain. All of it."

"Truth, Elizabeth? The truth can hurt as much as lies."

"I have no need of lies. They offer nothing but to placate my vanity and pride."

"What stands between us is not pride, nor vanity."

"But it is lies."

How she wished she could see him, what expression he wore. Was he calculating his response? If she possessed the gift of sight, would she see in his eyes the need to escape, to formulate a plan in order to make her believe what she wished? She was almost glad for her blindness, because watching him trying to lie to her would break her, whereas being blind only made her ignorant of it.

"I have hurt you in the past. Yes. I won't—I *can't* deny it."

"You lied to me." Her chin instinctively lifted in challenge. "And I won't make it easier on you by denying it. You abandoned me, Iain. You left me not only confused by it all, but shattered by your departure. You have no idea the pain you caused, or what it took for me to overcome it. You don't know what I lost... What *we* lost."

"What did we lose, Beth?" The question was no more than a whisper, and she knew he looked at her, watched her with unblinking eyes.

"An innocence, Iain. A belief in life's softer, intangible concepts—like dreams and hopes."

"I was never innocent," he said, his voice hard.

"I was, in the beginning. But in the end I knew what it was to lose it, to lose faith." Taking a deep breath,

Elizabeth gathered her courage to tell him what she had never told another soul. "You left me with child, Iain. Your child. You turned your back on us."

"A child?" His breath was a rasp.

She nodded, and she felt the fluttering of his hands on her face, tilting her so that he could look into her eyes.

"There was a babe?"

She had never told anyone this, not even Lucy or Isabella. She had wanted to, that afternoon at tea, but she could not make herself say the words. She had not, despite all the years in between, finished grieving for the baby they had created, and the life that could have been theirs, had Iain not abandoned her.

"Beth!" His voice was urgent, frightened. "Tell me."

"I was a few months along when you left me. I...I had planned to tell you that afternoon, but things... Well, you made it very clear what you wanted in your life, and it was not me, or a child."

"What happened? The babe—"

"I was nearly four months along when I lost it. It was shortly after I lost my sight, and I tripped down the stairs—plunged down them, really. When I regained consciousness, I was bleeding heavily, and I knew then that the babe was lost. I never forgave you for that, for giving me something I had always dreamed of, only to have it snatched away."

"I...I didn't know. God, Beth. I... You should have told me."

"When? After you explained that it was over between us?" He gave a little sound of frustration, pain. He was raking his hands through his hair. "Why would I tell you, when you made it very clear that you were severing all ties between us?"

"Because you should have known—that I..."

"You wouldn't have, Iain. You might have provided the material things for the child, but you would not have been there in the way I wanted you. It was not in your nature then. I think, deep down, I always knew that, even from the start. That if I got with child, it would be my problem to deal with. But I risked it, because I wanted that, a piece of you I could always claim. It was twelve years ago, and still I think of what might have been. I was prepared to love the child for both of us."

CLOSING HIS EYES, Iain stood by the bed, his hand wrapped around the carved post as he watched her there, proud and honourable. She had wanted to hear the truth, and he didn't want to speak it.

A child. He'd fathered a child, and he felt himself grieving for the loss. Damn his soul, he'd been such an idiot.

"You lied to me, Iain. Admit it. It's all I want. To hear the truth."

"Lied about loving you?" he asked. "That was no' a lie." His accent was slipping. "I loved you, Beth, but in the way of a twenty-year-old lad. It's no' a beautiful, simple love, lass." He swallowed, tried to regain control of himself. "It's a physical need, a desire born in the baseness of men that we feel. It's no' with the heart or the soul."

"So you were in lust, then? Why did you not tell me?"

"Because you were too smart for that." She stiffened, but he carried on, confessing his sins, showing her what a monster he truly was. "I knew you were no' in it for lust, and I couldna walk away from you. No' without having you. I wanted your goodness. To taste what it was like. I wanted to be loved for the first time in my life. I wanted to be touched softly, by hands that loved me, and didn't seek to hurt."

"You lied to me the entire time," she whispered, and the ravaged expression on her face nearly killed him. But the truth was already starting to come out, and he couldn't hide it. He had no wish to. It would either save him or condemn him. Either way, he must own up to it.

"In the beginning, aye. I did. I was consumed by you, Beth. You were my last thought before I fell asleep and my first thought when I rose. At first, it was all I would think of, the sex, losing myself in the long grass with you. But near the end… No, it was no longer lust, but something else. Something that shocked and scared me."

"And why should it have shocked you?" she asked as she rose from the floor, her blanket wrapped around her, and slowly walked to her dressing table. Her fingers caressed the gathered objects until she stopped at the hairbrush, her fingertips gliding over the bristles. "Perhaps it was merely your conscience, Iain. Perhaps you knew deep down inside that using me, telling me that you loved me so that I might lie with you, was morally wrong."

"P'raps, but I never gave much credence to my conscience then, and I don't do it much now, either. Except in regards to you. No, I think it something else. It was love, Beth. I felt the stirrings of it, and it scared the hell out of me. All I could think of was…" He stopped, blew out a breath and pressed his eyes shut. He could not say the words. Could not admit the shameful truth.

"I suppose the reality of it all made you have second thoughts. It was one thing to enjoy the pleasure of sex with me, quite another to find yourself tied to me."

"That's no' it," he said quietly. But he lied. He stood and lied to Elizabeth, and how he hated himself for it. For his weakness. He wanted to keep her at his side. But he wouldn't have her if he admitted the truth, what he had feared all those years ago—what he still feared. To admit it now was to have her leave him. But maybe she had already left?

"Then what is it, Iain? Were you ashamed? I believed we kept our liaison quiet at first because of the scandal. But as it developed, as you spoke of your feelings and love, I assumed you would offer marriage. Our relationship might slowly come out, but you didn't want to talk of it. You didn't want anyone to know. Naturally, I thought you rather gentlemanly at the time, having a concern about my reputation. But I learned the truth quickly—that you were ashamed to be seen with me. You didn't want your mates to know that you had fallen for a woman who would most likely end up blind. Not the great Iain Sinclair. How could he be seen with a woman such as that?"

"Stop it," he growled in warning.

"Why? Does it hurt too much? Am I coming too close to the truth?"

"Because that's not it at all."

"Really? You were never shamed by me?"

He shouldn't pause, he knew, but he had to. He had to get this right. She would think him stalling for time to formulate a lie, but that wasn't what he was doing. If ever there was a moment when the words had to be utterly perfect, this was it.

"I think we've said all there is to say here, Iain. You were ashamed then, and I don't believe that has changed now."

Stalking across the room, he went to her, wrapped his big hand around her arm and tugged her away from the table. "We are not done here," he said. "And everything has changed—everything, damn you. I was one and twenty when we began our affair. I was young and stupid and foolish. And I canna take back what I did, or what I thought at that time."

Nervously he ran his hands through his hair, struggling to find the right way to speak the truth. "I felt many things, but never shame. Fear, aye. I feared your impending blindness, how you would be dependent upon me for everything—"

She gasped, struggled in his hold. Her eyes were narrowed, shooting him daggers. "You were scared?" she choked in outrage. "And did you think I wasn't? Did you think the prospect of forever being in the dark was a welcome one for me?"

He gave her a little shake because he was scared now, and worried about what would happen when the truth came tumbling out. "I didn't know what to expect, or how... How you might look after it. And aye, that's childish and vain and arrogant, but I was a vain, arrogant boy then. And I was thinking of myself, and worrying over what the rest of my life might be like with you. And then there was the matter of—"

"Your heir," she declared, challenging him, "Did you imagine your heir like me, blind and dependent and utterly worthless?"

"I didn't know what it would be like. I couldna fathom it."

"So you ran from it all, because you were a coward. You left me to bear it all alone, while you went away and ignored it—never to be touched or burdened by it—or me."

That hurt, but it was no less than he deserved.

"Aye, I did, Beth, because I was frightened, and my feelings... They were growing stronger, and I knew how you felt about me. You loved me, and I knew it for the truth, and that scared the bloody hell out of me, too. And

I was scared about one more thing, Beth. I was scared that I couldna do it, that I wouldn't be what you needed, that I wasna strong enough to see you through it all. You see, that was the only grown-up thought in my head at that moment, that I wasna the sort who could help you through it all and stand by you. I ran no' only from you, but from me. The inevitable disappointment you would have in me when I failed you. I'm still scared, still wanting to run at times when I look into your eyes and wonder how I will ever be the sort of man you deserve. I want so much to deserve you. To be worthy of a woman like you."

Capturing her cheeks, he looked deeply into her eyes and said, his voice fierce with emotion, "I knew I would only hurt you, Beth, and I…I realized that I loved you too much to see your love for me wither and die because I wasn't strong enough to stand by you. To help you when you needed me most. I was afraid of the future, so I ran away from it."

Brushing his thumbs over her cheeks, he wiped away the tears that ran down them. "I was never ashamed of you, Beth. But I was ashamed of myself. How weak I was, how afraid I was of your future, and how it would impact mine. I always believed in you, in your strength, I just never believed in myself. And that's the truth. What's more…and it is so selfish, this truth, but I can own it now, Beth. Leaving you, I thought, was a blessing, and it was a means of self-preservation, because I never, ever, wanted to look into your face and see you gazing at me like you now are."

She reached for his wrist, clutched it. "How do I look?"

"Hurt. Pained. Destroyed."

"If I could look into your eyes, what would I see in them, Iain?"

"Devastation. Shame for what I was. Hatred for the

vanity and arrogance of my youth. A love for you that has never, ever died, but has only grown and matured, and become all-consuming. Tears," he said, and pressed his face to hers so she could "see" them. "Because I know it is truly over now that the truth is out, and I don't know how I'm going to live without you. Forgive me," he whispered, then stole a kiss from her lips. "Forgive me, and the boy I was, and the man I turned out to be."

She reached for his other wrist, captured it in her hand. "What of your marriage? Your banns were read in church. You desired another."

Pulling her forward, he cupped her cheek in his palm. "No, I didn't. But I did allow my father to take control of my life. What you don't know, Beth, is that I lost myself when I left you. I was a wreck. I didn't care if I lived or died. I only wanted you, but the fear still ruled me—and so did my father. I allowed him to make arrangements for me to wed a woman of his choosing. And when it came time to do it, to give another woman my vows, my fidelity, my body..." he swallowed "...I couldn't do it without imagining your face, without thinking and pretending that she was you. I couldn't do it, Beth," he said, whispering against her cheek. "Because I knew that the only woman I could ever love, ever promise to cherish and protect and be faithful to, was you. It's always only ever been you. And it always will be, Beth. You have my heart. My love. And my regret that I am not the man you deserve."

CHAPTER TWENTY

THE WINDOW RATTLED, stirring Lizzy from her slumber. How long ago was it that Iain had left her, his confession echoing in her mind as she cried herself to sleep? He had somehow freed her with his confession. Made her see beyond her fear and hurt, and into his.

They had been young and naive when they came together for the first time. With no experience of the world, or human nature. Neither of them had been prepared for what they would discover in each other. Was it wrong of her to condemn him for a mortal weakness—fear of the unknown? Should he not have had the right to worry about how she would deal with her blindness, how they would manage? Her vision loss had been gradual, not sudden. She had known it was coming, the day when she would see nothing but black. Sometimes when one knew an event was going to happen, it made the agony worse, harder to bear. Sometimes the anticipation of waiting, wondering, worrying, was more than one *could* bear.

To Iain, who had always been raised to be strong, to show no weakness, that natural fear for her, and for him, and what they might give up, was more than he knew how to cope with.

The window rattled again, and she stirred, listening, an absurd hope leaping in her breast. Was it Iain? Had he returned? She already knew that with the morning light she would seek him out. Would go to his house and finish where they had left off. He had been completely honest with her, baring his soul to her, despite the fact that there was darkness in there. She owed him the same honesty. The words he had longed to hear. That he had not destroyed her feelings for him. That love for him still resided within her heart, and always would. From this day forward, fear no longer held them captive.

Another rattle, and she wondered if the wind had once more picked up. She thought of calling for Maggie, but instead tossed back the covers and padded across the floor. A breeze blew in, robbing her of breath. Strange how the window, which had been locked, suddenly blew open—

"Don't make a sound."

Her mouth was covered in an instant, and a cloth slapped over her face. She fought in her captor's hold, twisting her body and flailing her limbs, but her cries were muffled by the cloth, and someone else reached for her feet.

"Wait till she's out, and then we'll take her to the carriage and collect our wages."

"She's strong," the one grunted, letting her foot slip from his hold. She fell onto the floor, uncoordinated from the ether. Its stench and taste made her wretch as she tumbled downward. The side of her head hit the floorboards, and she heard nothing for a few seconds as she fought to prevent herself from descending into the darkness.

"Check her," the first voice said. "If she's dead, Mr. Lasseter will have our bollocks strung up."

"Alive," his partner announced. But her mind was getting cloudier, the ether beginning to take hold. "Let's load her up before someone comes to check on her." She struggled, but they held her tighter, pressing the cloth firmly over her nose and mouth.

MINUTES LATER, ORPHEUS WATCHED as his prize was bundled into the carriage. His lover sat beside him, studying the woman, who had at last slipped into unconsciousness.

"She's nothing much to look at," his lover said sourly. "I can't imagine both of you desiring her that much to go to this amount of trouble."

"She's worth more to me than you can imagine."

"What now, my love?"

Orpheus smiled and thought how close he was to fulfilling his revenge. "Alynwick. He's the next piece in the plan. Bring him to me."

THE FRANTIC RAPPING on the front door pulled Iain's gaze from the bottom of his Scotch glass. Since leaving Elizabeth he had been steadily drinking himself into oblivion. His heart hurt. His soul ached, and no amount of drink would erase from his memory the image of Beth, and the expression in her eyes. The knowledge of what once might have been his, now gone. The woman of his dreams, a child they had made. How foolish and cowardly he had been to give them up.

"My lord," Sutherland began, "a good night's sleep will make things better."

"I can't sleep," he muttered, pouring more Scotch. "I've ruined it, Sutherland. The whole bloody thing."

"Lasses can bedevil a man, right enough. But that lass," his valet said, clapping him on his good shoulder and squeezing, "she's got a good sensible head on her shoulders. She'll soon realize that the truth of the past doesna need to become the truth of the present."

"You didn't see the expression in her eyes," he muttered, draining the glass. "I killed whatever faith she might have left in me. I showed her a glimpse inside the true man, and she was horrified and disgusted by what she saw."

Sutherland was about to speak, when Iain's butler burst into the library. Behind him, a hysterical Maggie shoved him aside.

"What have you done with her, you devil?" she cried, flinging herself toward Iain.

"Here now," Sutherland murmured, reaching her first and holding her arms at her sides. "You're like a bee in a gale, lass."

"Unhand me this instant, you barbarian!" Maggie commanded. Sutherland merely arched his eyebrows.

"And who would you be, lass, ordering me about?"

"Margaret Farley, companion and confidante of Lady Elizabeth York."

The Scotch had dulled his reflexes, but suddenly Iain stood, the hairs on his nape rising in alarm. Maggie was dressed in her bedclothes, with a cloak hastily thrown over them. She looked as though she had just dragged herself out of bed, and why not? It was barely six in the morning, not quite dawn even.

"Maggie?" he asked, confusion clouding his mind.

"Where have you hidden her?" she accused.

"I don't know what you mean."

"You came to her, ravished her, broke her heart, and now she's gone. What have you done to her?"

He was stone sober when he reached Maggie and took her by her shoulders. "What the hell are you talking about?"

"There now," Sutherland grunted, pulling him away from the woman. "That's no way to treat a lady, my lord."

Maggie sent Sutherland a glare, then dropped her hands on her hips and narrowed her gaze at Iain. "You know exactly what I mean. You took her from her home.

You're keeping her, no doubt, for some nefarious pleasure of your own."

"Beth's gone." Iain found Sutherland's face swimming before him. Reaching for the corner of his desk,
he gripped it, tried to muddle through the slush in his
mind. "My God, she's gone. Taken."

"You mean you don't have her?"

"That's what he's been trying to say, woman," Sutherland grunted. "Now, Sinclair, let's think this through. We
know who has her, don't we? There really can be only
one person. Let's formulate a plan, call in Black. Don't
do anything rash—"

But Iain was in motion, barking out orders to footmen for his carriage, pulling out a box containing his
duelling pistols and a set of knives, which he thrust into
his greatcoat that hung on the back of the chair. "I'm
off, Sutherland. Return to Sussex House and watch over
Maggie and the other servants. Perhaps a ransom note
will arrive. If it does, I want to know."

"Too rash, my lord. You're going off half-cocked."

Iain whirled on him. "The woman I love is gone. Taken
God knows where. She's blind," he hissed, fear making
him strong and vengeful. "She won't even know where
she is or who has her. She'll be in the dark, alone, frightened. She might be hurt, or God above, something worse,
and I'm not going to sit here wasting time, wringing my
hands and trying to think of my next step. I'm leaving,
Sutherland, whether you believe it a cockamamy idea
or not."

"Where will you go?"

"The House of Orpheus, where else?"

"Alone?"

"I don't have time to wait on others, Sutherland. I
mean to find Beth—*now*."

"Send word of your whereabouts, my lord, so I can ensure your safety. Shall I inform Black?"

"Yes. He'll want to keep Isabella protected. And I'll need his help—but I'll not wait for it now. Tell him to meet up with me at Orpheus, or Sussex House."

"Watch yer back. And keep a cool head. Your lass won't appreciate you dead."

After running down the steps, his coat heavy with weapons, Iain jumped up into the carriage, aware that for the first time in his life he tasted the true meaning of terror.

GONE. THE CLUB had been emptied out. The bedrooms he had seen when he had last been there were bare, stripped to the walls and floor. With his pistol pulled, Iain pointed it as he entered each room, prepared to shoot and kill. But there was no one there. The place was deserted.

Making his way over to the wall with the hidden door, he bent down, pistol pointed, and entered the hall where he had last seen Nigel Lasseter disappear. This time there were no guards to stop him, and he entered the chamber that Lasseter had used. The stench of mildew and dirt assaulted him, and he noticed a pile of filthy clothes that had been tossed into a corner. Men's clothes, he saw, as he used the toe of his boot to sift through them. Glancing up, he realized that this room had not been emptied like the others. A dresser and dressing table remained.

Iain began a systematic search of all the drawers. Nothing. If Lasseter had Elizabeth, she was not being held here. Lasseter was gone, and with him all traces of his whereabouts.

"Well, a man cannot just disappear into thin air," he muttered. He might enjoy acting the part of a mysterious magi, but the fact was Lasseter was a flesh-and-blood man. He had to be somewhere in the city. But where? Iain's eyes went once more to the clothes marked with dirt and soil, reeking of damp earth and must.

A tunnel. Somewhere in this place, Lasseter had used the skills that Sheldon had taught him, and had dug himself an escape route. Iain doubted he'd done it alone. But he did know one of his accomplices.

HOW TEMPTING IT WOULD BE to squeeze the soft flesh of her throat and peer into her eyes as he snuffed the life out of her. She was alarmed, truly frightened by the rage that ruled him. Her eyes were wide, wild. And disgustingly aroused.

"Where is she?" Iain growled, increasing the pressure on Georgiana's throat in small increments, showing her that indeed, he could very easily choke her. And might very well enjoy doing so.

"I don't know what you mean."

"Don't lie, Georgiana," he rasped. "You have something to do with this."

"I don't even know who you're talking about," she gasped.

"Elizabeth York."

"What do I care for some blind spinster?" she spat.

"You had better care, because if one hair on her head is harmed, I'll make you suffer. Whatever you've done to her, I'll make certain it's five times worse for you."

Her smile turned cruel, taunting. "You'll never find her. And if you do, she won't be alive."

He squeezed harder, trying to frighten her into telling him, but the witch only laughed, closed her eyes as though she were enjoying what he was doing.

"Does your husband know what you are, Marie?" he challenged. Her eyes opened, looking glazed.

"Larabie is no longer a concern. I've disposed of him, as I always do when complications arise." She smiled, parted her lips, ran her hand up Iain's chest. "You are such a beast, Alynwick. You have no idea what pleasure—true pleasure I've had from you. I've always known this side of you lurked just beneath your barely civilized veneer. You could take me now," she murmured seductively, "and I would more than welcome you. I would beg you."

"Where is Elizabeth?" he demanded, sickened by this creature.

"Perhaps you'll find her where you're going."

Iain heard the scrape of a boot too late. He turned, and was bashed in the head with a poker from the hearth. Falling to his knees, he struggled against the pain, but was taken by surprise by a punch to his face from the opposite side. There were two of them, he realized as his vision started to swim. He tried to fight, but one man held his arms while the other pierced the flesh of his wounded shoulder with the tip of the poker. He roared in pain, reached for the hem of Georgiana's gown, but he was pulled back, a cloth placed over his mouth and nose.

Beth... He tried to fight them, tried to fight for her, but the cloth was drenched in ether, and he was rendered helpless by the drug. When he collapsed on the floor, he saw Beth in his mind, the effects of the ether threatening unconsciousness.

"Take him to the club," he heard Georgiana order. "But don't kill him. I'm not done with him yet. We have much more to discover about one another."

She brushed her palm over her throat, gazed at the marks on her flesh made by Iain.

"I'll kill you for what you have done," he growled, fighting the ether.

She laughed, the sound throaty and aroused. "Dear

God, how badly I want you," she taunted. "Lasseter will not have you. You, Sinclair, are the man I have waited for all my life. And I will not lose you now."

IN THE DARKNESS, Lizzy listened to the distant echo of water dripping onto stones. She was quite alone now, with only her thoughts. Fear had long since left her, as she lay here on the cold, damp stone in nothing more than her night rail.

She had no way of knowing how long she had been here. Had it been hours, or days? Her assailant had kept her drugged with the ether, and she had slept away the time, unconscious, in the darkness of her mind, and this tomb she was imprisoned in. She wondered if her brother had gotten her letter and was even now on his way back home. She didn't dare hope that Alynwick knew she was gone—they'd parted ways. It had felt final when he had left her chamber, as though they had said everything that needed to be said. For all she knew, he might have even left the city.

Oh, stupid, pigheaded fool that she was. She had let her pride get the better of her, and now she was trapped here, quite alone and at a madman's mercy.

She began to twist and cry, to claw at anything around her, searching fruitlessly for a way out of this tomb where she found herself.

Laughter echoing off the walls made her stiffen, made her skin pull taut in fear, her nerves tense with the need to take flight and protect herself.

"It's quite useless, you stupid chit," the voice said, and she stilled, cocked her head to the side. She knew that voice. Despite the darkness, she recalled the sound of it from the deep recess of her mind, from memories long past, nearly forgotten.

"Yes," the voice said again. "You thought it over? Well, my dear, I'm here to tell you it's just begun. And in the end, I will be back where I should have always been."

Oh, dear God, it couldn't be. It was the ether, poisoning her mind. She pulled, stretched, feeling frightened, horrified. He laughed, and all the memories came rushing back, horrible memories, painful ones. She could hardly speak, could scarcely believe her own thoughts. But that laugh, the demonic sound of it could belong to no one else. "Adrian?" she choked out, fear making her voice hoarse. "No, it can't be!"

"Can't it, sister? My, it's unbelievable you've managed to put it all together, and being blind as a bat, too. Astonishing, really. But, then, you always were a smart little bitch."

Oh, it was him; utterly impossible, but true. The knowledge made her want to retch, to cast out what little contents of her stomach remained. Her skin was positively crawling, as if covered with ants.

"How did you know, after all these years?" he asked.

"It's your voice. Your tone. The mocking way you always had."

"You mean my years in France have not altered it? Do I still have that…ducal authority in my voice?"

In the darkness, she searched for a reason, an explanation. No, it couldn't be. Adrian was in Yorkshire, on his honeymoon with Lucy. This was not Adrian. Not her brother. This was…it was the brother she had once known, the cruel taunting young man from long ago who cared for no one but himself, risen from the dead like an evil entity.

"How can this be?" she demanded, struggling to make sense of her thoughts. She wanted it to be from the effects of the ether, prayed it was so, but knew it wasn't. Someone, Adrian York—the *real* Adrian York—was alive, and standing right beside her. "How?" she rasped.

"Because our father left me for dead, threw me in a horse cart full of rotting vegetables, and left me wounded and bleeding. He thought me dead, and did his all to hide the fact. And then he placed his bastard son in my place. And you, being useless and blind, never knew the difference."

Yes, she had known the difference. The man who was her brother was kind and loving. This creature... He was a monster. But then, Adrian always had been. He'd been the image of their father in deed and thought. This, she thought with a measure of fear and disgust, was the true Adrian York. And she knew now what he wanted. *Revenge.*

"I see Mother's affliction has claimed you. What is it like, Elizabeth, to be an invalid and weak?"

"I'm not an invalid," she declared. "I'm not weak."

"I could kill you here, and no one but the rats would discover your body. I'd say you are indeed very weak."

A surge of fury, of a fierce protectiveness, shot through her. He wanted the Brethren Guardians. He wanted her brother. "What do you want with him, Adrian?" she demanded. "After all these years, why now?"

"My rightful place is what I want. The bastard impostor dead, my title restored to me. The artefacts of the Brethren Guardians in my possession."

"To do what?" she railed.

"To discover if the powers that are supposedly contained within them are real. To see for myself if the blood of an innocent can create alchemy, and give me the powers to possess divine knowledge. I want the power, Elizabeth, the means to be whatever it is I want."

"And if they have no power?"

"They do. Our ancestors would not have risked life and limb to flee the Holy Land if there was not some truth behind the story. Our forebears would not have kept the relics safe from the eyes of the world. No, there is magic and power there."

"The others won't allow it."

He snorted and moved closer, but then stumbled, cursed, and it was then that Lizzy realized her brother was not immune to their mother's malady.

"How much sight do you have left, Adrian? It's rather disconcerting, isn't it, as it slowly fades day by day, until it is completely extinguished."

He growled, his hand shot out and he wrapped his fingers around her throat. "I can see well enough to choke the light out of you. Remember that."

"But not well enough to carry out this plan of yours by yourself."

"I am the brains of it, if not the brawn," he muttered. "It hardly matters now, Elizabeth, because I'm going to win this game. I'm going to beat the Brethren. And do you know why? It's because I have patience. I learned it during my time in France, healing from wounds. I watched a spider weave his web as I lay in bed. So patiently he weaved it, meticulously following his pattern, moving in the same direction, weaving always in the same pattern. Come the morning I would knock down his night's work, yet he would be back, weaving, night after night, patiently constructing that web for his prey. And then one day I allowed him to keep his web. I watched as he patiently finished it. And I watched as he lured his victims. It was then that I learned from the spider. How to plan. How to be patient. How to lie in wait."

"You're mad!"

"I always was, Elizabeth. Didn't you realize how very

different we were? You were an angel and I was a demon. Unlike you, I'm not afraid of the darkness. I embrace it."

"You won't win, Adrian. How will you do it, kill us all?" She scoffed. "Do you think the authorities won't search for the others? How will you explain it when so many peers go missing?"

"My dear, you've underestimated me, and the depths of my revenge. It will work out. Just you wait. Once all is assembled, it will unfold before your very eyes. Not that you will see it, of course." He laughed, released his hold on her neck. "I hope you're not relying on the dear marquis to save you."

Her heart sank at the mention of Iain. What a fool she'd been. She wished to reverse time. Wished she had encouraged him to stay. She wished that she might have one more chance to see him, and say what she needed to.

"My accomplice has taken quite a fancy to him, you know. I'm afraid he'll be gone for a long while. I do hope you said your farewells."

She lunged at him, connecting with him, hitting him. She'd come from the side and he was surprised. She heard that shocked breath, and knew that he could only see objects directly in front of him. It had been that way with her. The dimming of her vision, reduced to shadows and shapes, with no peripheral vision.

He tossed her back against the stone wall and she cried out as she hit her head. Her night rail was falling and the stone scraped her skin. "I should bury you alive in that pit I dug. One false move, Elizabeth, and I will toss you into that grave."

He left her then.

Elizabeth by rights should be terrified, but she was not. For she knew where she was now: beneath the Templar church, in the crypts where Sheldon had taken her.

Behind her, the sound of a heavy iron door closing made her stop and listen. That was not the door Sheldon had used. That door had been wood. The one her brother had just closed was definitely iron.

She had her bearings, and began to crawl on her hands and knees, her hands blindingly groping the dirt in an attempt to not only locate the pit that had been dug, but to avoid it.

She just needed to reach that door. She needed to find Iain—needed to save them both.

CHAPTER TWENTY-ONE

How HAD HE GOTTEN HERE? Iain had no clue. His head still pounded and the taste of ether made him gag. His shoulder burned like the devil's tongue, too. He'd been stabbed, leaving his arm stiff and painful, and no doubt fetid.

The steps to Sussex's town house seemed an enormous mountain to climb, but he endured it. Beth was gone, and he couldn't find her. He'd been out for days searching for her, and then he had been accosted by Georgiana's guards. He had awakened in a back room of the Adelphi, bound to the bed, semiconscious, a bottle of ether and a rag on the bedside table. Thank heavens Sutherland had discovered him, after he didn't return home. By the grace of God Iain was still alive to find Sussex back from Yorkshire.

He did not have to ring the bell. The door opened as if by magic, and the sound of a gun being cocked and pointed between his eyes greeted him.

"You've saved me considerable trouble, Alynwick," Sussex said steadily. "You traitorous bastard. I'd shoot you dead right now if I didn't need you to tell me where my sister is."

"I don't know, damn you," he snapped, too exhausted to feel surprise at Sussex's actions. "That's what I'm trying to tell you. Orpheus *is* Nigel Lasseter. I've been to the club, but he's gone. Georgiana—"

"We know what you've done, and who you have been

with, Alynwick. Betraying us. Betraying me. We found the correspondence between you and Lady Larabie, devising your plot. You conspired with her to steal the pendant and chalice."

"No!" This couldn't be happening. It just couldn't. Sussex was wrong; there was a mistake. "There is no evidence. There was never any plot between her and me other than the one I told you and Black about."

"No mistake? It was all there in your study drawer. You should have been more careful, but then you probably didn't think Lizzy would write to me."

He couldn't think. The world was suddenly spinning. "Damn you, Sussex, it's a trap. I'm not one of them! I only want to find Elizabeth. Someone has taken her, and it sure as hell wasn't me! Jesus, Adrian, listen to me."

Something flickered in Sussex's gaze, and he slowly lowered the gun.

"I swear," Iain vowed, falling to his knees, "I do not know where she is. I only want to find her. We're wasting time, Sussex, time we don't have—time that is running out for Elizabeth. If you cannot believe me about anything else, then believe me about this. I love your sister. And I just… Christ! I just want to find her. I can't waste any more time knowing she's out there all by herself. You can do whatever you want with me, but after I find Elizabeth and bring her home. For the love of God, man, I've never asked anything of you, but I am asking now, help me find your sister!"

"My LORD, it's no good," Sutherland pleaded as Iain alighted from the carriage and staggered into the dank, damp alleyway. The snow was melting, making everything wet. The fog wafted in from the Thames, blanketing the city in a grey cloak. It was cold, but Iain was already too numb to sense it. Tilting his head, he gazed up at the windows, drapes pulled tightly shut, and tried to concentrate. Perhaps he had missed something. Another hidden door. A secret passageway.

"You're bloody exhausted, filthy and wounded. Not to mention the fact that you've already ripped apart the House of Orpheus twice. She's no' there, my lord."

With a snarl, Alynwick lashed out at his valet. "What would you have me do, Sutherland? Leave the woman I love to the fates while I go and soak in my tub?"

"Use your blasted head!" Sutherland retorted. "*Think!* And you canna do that when you've no reserves of energy left. Yer tapped out. Not thinking straight. You need a meal, at the very least to get you thinking clear."

"There's no time," he grumbled, brushing past the man.

"If you keep retracing steps you've already taken, you'll be wasting more time. My lord, please. Let me see to your wounds, feed you, and then we can begin thinking of what new steps we might take."

"I can't slow down. I...can't."

"You won't allow yourself a minute's rest because deep down you're afraid she's already lost to you."

"Enough! Elizabeth is... She's all right," he mumbled, refusing to look inside and examine the very large hole gaping in his chest. "There's...time left. She's strong, so much stronger than I ever gave her credit for."

"Come into the carriage and we'll go home."

"No, I can't. Elizabeth. Her rooms. Maybe I've overlooked something. I'll go there."

"You've already searched them. Besides, by now Sussex will have gone over them with a fine-tooth comb."

"Then the club. I have to go there. Look again."

"This club is done, my lord. The leads are gone. Orpheus has vanished."

"No, he's still in the city, hiding. But where...?"

He needed to think.... Where would Orpheus go? Where could he hide with Elizabeth so he wouldn't arouse suspicion? Iain needed to know his enemy. The unfortunate part was, he didn't know him. But there was one person who did.

"YES?" THE BUTLER asked, his lips curled in disdain as he stood looking up at Iain.

"Alynwick to see Lord Sheldon, immediately."

"I'm afraid his lordship is indisposed. You will have to return tomorrow."

"Damn you, man, get Sheldon. A woman's life depends upon it."

"Who is it?" a voice boomed from the hall.

"It is Lord Alynwick, my lord, requesting an audience. Are you at home?"

What an idiotic question! Iain didn't bother to wait, but shoved past the pompous butler and into the hall, where he stumbled.

"Good God, what happened to you?" Sheldon demanded.

"Later," Iain muttered.

"When have you last slept or eaten?" the earl enquired, looking at him in his bedraggled state. "You're gaunt and exhausted. It's been days, by the looks of it." Suspicion suddenly lit his eyes, and he motioned Iain into his study. Tired, terrified, Iain humbled himself by falling to his knees. "Elizabeth is gone—has been for days. Lasseter has her. Sheldon," Iain pleaded, no longer caring how he appeared. He thought only of Elizabeth's well-being now. "I need your help. You know him better than any of us."

Reaching out his hand, Sheldon offered it to him and helped him up. "You have it. Toth," he called to the butler, "send around for the carriage. Also, tell Mrs. Atkins to bundle up something for Lord Alynwick to eat. Jack!" Sheldon shouted for his dog, who came prancing out of the study. "Toth, send a missive around to Black and Sussex that they are to meet me at Temple Church, but are not to go in, but wait for my command. My bag, as well," he muttered.

"Yes, my lord."

"I mean to be gone within ten minutes, Toth. I want action, now!"

"At once, my lord!"

"Now," Sheldon demanded as he reached for his greatcoat. "Tell me everything I need to know."

Iain held nothing back, not even the story of the Brethren Guardians, and the relics. Secrets could only harm Elizabeth now, and those about the Brethren Guardians were what had started this whole business. Elizabeth was lost to him because of the Guardians. He'd be damned if his insufferable pride would aid her death.

"You still haven't figured it out, have you?" Sheldon asked. It was dark in the carriage, and the gentle swaying was making Iain's eyes want to close in sleep. But he fought it. He felt a measure of strength returning after having eaten some cold gammon and bread with cheese. The steaming mug of mulled wine lit a fire in his belly, warming him, making his senses feel somewhat brighter than they had. He'd been ready to collapse at Sheldon's feet when he had first entered the man's house.

"Figured out what?" he asked, wiping his face with his palm. He heard the sound of his night beard bristling against his hand. He must look a sight.

"Who I am."

It was uttered very quietly, and Iain glanced up sharply. "I thought you a detective for Scotland Yard."

"I am. But there's more."

Iain groaned. He'd thought as much, but he was in no mental or physical condition to do anything about it. If Sheldon was indeed his enemy, he would be at his mercy. He had needed help, and perhaps his need had placed him at greater risk.

"Elizabeth told me that you were helping her decipher the diary of the mysterious Veiled Lady. Did she not tell you?" Was that gloating Iain heard? No, it wasn't superiority, but surprise. It was there in Sheldon's eyes. "I thought... Well, she made it quite clear that while I was infinitely likable, she felt, at least for now, that she wasn't ready to elevate me to more than a friend."

It wasn't the time to feel elation in the fact that Elizabeth was not interested in the earl, but Iain was only human.

"It was the morning of Sussex's marriage. I thought perhaps the duke might take Elizabeth away with him, so I made an early morning call and persuaded her to come to Temple Church with me. I was hoping that a tour of the crypts might leave a lasting impression, as it were."

"And did it?" Iain found himself growling. Damn it, she had been alone with Sheldon, and she'd never confided in him. All those conversations they had shared, the ones that had exposed each other's flaws and weaknesses. Iain had thought there was nothing else he might discover about her, but he was wrong. He should have known, even factored in Elizabeth's staunch loyalty. After all, she had kept their secrets. Why not this one?

"I can see the workings of your mind, Alynwick, and let me put a stop to them at once. While Elizabeth enjoyed herself immensely that morning, she did not…welcome, as I'd hoped, my declaration of interest. In other words," he muttered, "she rebuffed my kiss and blurted out quite frankly that someone had stolen her heart years ago, and she was unable to find a way to get it back, or give it to someone new. Naturally, I knew you to have been the thief. Especially when she explained that she no longer needed my assistance with the book, that you had agreed to aid her."

"Why would it matter about the diary?" Iain mumbled, lifting the corner of the shade to look outside. It was foggy, so much so that he was unable to see where they were, or which way they were travelling. He'd been in too much of a fog to ask Sheldon where they should start. And now he wondered if he was truly safe with the earl, if he had unwittingly fallen into Sheldon's hands.

"You did not conclude who the Veiled Lady was?" Sheldon asked with surprise.

"Of course I did."

"You couldn't have, else you would not have come to me tonight."

A horrible feeling of dread came over him, and every self-protective instinct he had reeled inside him. Even wounded and exhausted though he was, his reflexes served him well. He had the earl pinned back against the carriage squabs, the point of his elbow over the fragile cartilage of the man's throat.

"Damn you," Sheldon gasped. "What the devil—"

"Spill it all, my lord," Iain growled. "No more cryptic messages from you. Tell me what you are, what purpose you have in infiltrating yourself into Elizabeth's life."

He nodded, his face growing a dark red that Iain could clearly see even within the confines of the dimly lit carriage. Releasing him, he allowed the earl to slump over and gasp as he smoothed a hand down his throat.

"When this is all said and done, you bloody bastard, I'm going to demand you teach me that," he rasped.

"*If* I let you live."

Sheldon coughed, then began to speak. "The diary, the Veiled Lady…" He cleared his throat and loosened his neck tie. "The curse."

Iain pressed forward, made him look into his eyes, which he knew were burning bright with hellfire. "If you think I believe in that nonsense that no one of the House of York and House of Sinclair shall ever come together, you're out of your mind. It's medieval posturing, Sheldon, and it was my ancestor, seven hundred years ago, who spouted it. The Veiled Lady was my ever-so-great-grandmother, Lady Marguerite Sinclair, who fell in love with Sinjin York, Elizabeth's ancestor."

"Someone wants you to believe in the curse. You said yourself before we left my house that the only thing that you or Elizabeth's maid could detect was missing from her room was the diary. Why would Lasseter take the book when he took Elizabeth, if it wasn't something he valued?"

"He must know that I'm not a fool to believe in curses, nor Elizabeth. But…" Iain suddenly stopped and thought through a point he had not considered before. "It would be valuable to Lasseter if the diary contained information on any hidden relics or treasures. Or if he wanted others to believe there was some sort of curse between the two houses."

"Exactly." Sheldon's eyes lit with appreciation. "He'll use it to frame his crime. To cobble up a story of forbidden romance and Templar curses, after he seeks whatever it is that drives him. And for the life of me, I cannot figure out what it is he wants."

"How did you know of the curse?" Iain asked, his gaze narrowing when Sheldon smiled. "In fact, how the hell did you know that the diary belonged to Sinjin in the first place?"

"Don't you know?" Sheldon said, smiling slowly. "I am descended from the fourth Templar."

"How can that be?" Iain demanded. "The story is not even true!"

"Yes, it is. The man who was supposedly betrayed and left for dead in the desert was my own ancestor, John Leuven, the Duke of Lorraine, and the Veiled Lady was his sister. That made her my aunt."

Iain could hardly believe what he was hearing. All along, Sheldon had been involved in the Brethren affairs. He'd known.... "We're related?" Iain asked in horrified wonder.

"One could say that, although the family line is rather diluted now. But, yes, in a way we are. Cousins, I should think."

"Was the duke a Brethren Guardian?"

"No, he wasn't. He wasn't a Templar or even a knight, but he was there as part of King Philip's entourage. He had brought Marguerite with him, on a pilgrimage. It's where she met Sinjin—and your ancestor. The three Templars made friends with the duke, and when he learned that he was to round up the Templars for inquisition and execution by Philip, he alerted the Brethren, and offered to give them safe passage out of the Holy City, provided they would take Marguerite and unite her in marriage with Haelan St. Clair, as the king had desired. You see, by all accounts, the duke never knew of the affair going on between his sister and Sinjin York. Otherwise, I doubt he would have insisted on the marriage. Marguerite and Haelan were wed hours before they left Jerusalem."

"They were ambushed?" Iain asked. "Who knew of their plans?"

"Philip's men suspected Lorraine of having dealings with the three, and thought he might try to warn them. They attacked in the dark, and Lorraine put up a fight. Fabled, in my family, that it was him, and his bravery that allowed the three to flee while Lorraine held off his enemies. As a result of his treachery, Philip dissolved the duke's family line, took their wealth and cast them out of the country. They emigrated to England, where they heard the story of three mysterious Templars up in the north, and in Scotland. Ever since, the descendants of Lorraine have taken an oath to protect the identities of the Brethren, and the secrets they carried with them out of the Holy Land."

"When Nigel Lasseter discovered the fact, you came to England, not because you were a detective, but because you were the fourth—one of us."

"Yes. You see, my uncle never believed in such stories, and refused to give them any credit. The clock you saw on my mantel was made in the memory of the duke. It's been handed down through the male line, and in its bottom is a family tree, naming each descendant of Lorraine who becomes the fourth Templar. Along with those names are the names of the current Brethren Guardians. My uncle by all accounts had never even opened the clock to peer inside. He was a man who indulged in vice, not pertinent family facts. So my father took up the banner and became the fourth. But he was transferred to the East by Scotland Yard, and we were forced to go abroad. He encouraged his colleagues to keep him abreast of any developments, or activities of the Marquis of Alynwick, however. He fabricated a story about the marquis, and the Yard bought it. They sent monthly reports to my father. It was his way of keeping tabs on at least one of the Brethren. To request reports on all three, he knew, would be too suspicious, so he chose your father, for reasons that his line connected with ours. When I was old enough, he told me of my family's lineage and duty."

"Bloody hell, all this time! My God, you're one of us."

"In a way."

"And Elizabeth—you wanted to protect her?"

"Of course, but I would be a liar and a fraud if I said I didn't desire the duty greatly. I wanted her before I even knew who she was. I was following Sussex the day I saw her with him."

"And now?" Iain found the courage to ask.

"I still want her, but she is yours, I think. The other half of you. I am content, Alynwick, to play the part my long-departed grandfather did, and guide you from danger."

"I misjudged you. My apologies, Sheldon."

"Just as the Brethren Guardians take their own personal vows, so, too, do the descendants of the dukes of Lorraine. We have vowed to come to the aid of a Guardian whenever needed, without thought to our own safety. We are the silent watchers and protectors of the Brethren. The story of the fourth Templar has been long buried in mystery, lost to the sands of time. Forgotten by the world. In a way, the exclusion of our assistance in the flight of the original Templars has aided our cause."

"And Elizabeth? You know how to find her? Because I am loath to confess that I am at a loss. I have no idea where in the metropolis Nigel Lasseter might have hidden her."

"I have a thought. It is only a hunch, mind, but it might

explain what I discovered the morning I toured the crypts with Elizabeth."

"Temple Church?"

"Would seem a fitting place to culminate his plan."

"Why?" Iain demanded.

Sheldon glanced at him, a sly smile curving his lips. "A little thing called sacred geometry."

"GENTLEMEN, over here, if you please."

Jack, Sheldon's dog, was running about in circles, sniffing the crypts of the knights that lined the floor of the church. In the lantern light, Iain could see the dog's tongue lolling, spittle flinging in every direction. Warily, Black and Sussex came forward as Sheldon unrolled a map of the city. On it the shape of a compass was drawn in ink. "This is your house, Sussex." Sheldon pointed to Mayfair and Grosvenor Square on the map, then slid his finger to the left. "Temple Church, where we are now."

Jack whimpered, his nose never leaving the floor as he ran about, sniffing. Sheldon glanced back over his shoulder at the dog, then returned to the map.

"What significance does this place have?" Sussex asked. Iain could tell that the duke was deciding whether or not to trust Sheldon. Upon their arrival, Sheldon and Iain had explained everything. To see the shock in their eyes when they learned of Sheldon's family history as the fourth Templar was rather gratifying. Iain had felt like a prize idiot when he'd learned the truth. To see that Sheldon had fooled Sussex and Black as well made it a measure better.

"It's not the church itself that is of significance, it's what lies beneath it. Here." He drew another line with his fingertip from Sussex House to the right. "This is the Adelphi in the Strand. And when you connect the Adelphi to Temple Church, you have a line. You also have a medieval passageway of underground crypts built by the Templars to escape detection."

"My God, that's bloody brilliant," Black muttered.

"No, it's sacred geometry. Lizzy mentioned it during one of our walks, and I was intrigued. It also helped that on the morning we toured the crypts, I discovered some digging was already occurring. I knew someone else had already discovered what I'd just figured out, that the tunnel leads directly to the Adelphi. This is, I think, where Nigel Lasseter is hiding Elizabeth."

"What is your dog doing?" Iain muttered as he watched the retriever jump and paw at the door. He was mewling and crying, scratching with his front paws.

"He's high-strung."

"No," Sussex murmured. "He senses something. Do you have a key to open the door?"

"I do, but we need a plan."

"I do believe that Jack has one already figured out for us."

HER KNEES WERE THROBBING, her fingers bleeding from the stones and dirt. *Oh, God, please,* Elizabeth prayed. *Let me live.*

"Look at you, crawling on your knees like a beggar woman."

Frozen, Elizabeth stopped her slow progress.

"If he could only see you now, filthy and pathetic, blindly searching for a way out."

"Lady Larabie," she snarled.

"How did you know?"

"I can smell you, the stench of your perfume."

Georgiana reached down and dragged Lizzy up by a handful of her hair. Pressing her eyes shut, Elizabeth bit her lip, refusing to give the woman any satisfaction for the pain she was inflicting.

"I'm going to cut you," Georgiana murmured. "I'm going to mark that face of yours and show him what I'm capable of."

"He'd still love me," Elizabeth whispered. "It's a concept you could never understand, Georgiana."

The woman cried out at the insult and tossed Elizabeth to the ground. "He won't have you!"

And then she was on top of her. Lizzy felt the knife in her hand, heard her rasp of excitement as she brought the blade down in a wide arc. Elizabeth did the only thing she could—put her hand on the blade to pull it away from her, cutting herself in the process.

Caught off balance, her assailant fell to the side, and Lizzy jumped on top of her, legs straddling her back. Gripping the knife by the handle, she felt the warmth of her blood spilling down her hand.

"Now get up," Lizzy ordered, "and deliver me out of this hellhole."

Georgiana spat, lashed out and tried to take the knife. A low growl made them both freeze. The growl was deeper this time, menacing, a truly frightening sound.

A paw touched Lizzy's arm, followed by a whimper, then the sting of a rather large wet tongue.

"Ah, Jack," Elizabeth whispered. "Good boy. Show me where they are."

Georgiana struggled beneath her, but stilled the moment Jack began to growl again.

"I would mind him, Georgiana. He's a trained killer, you know. Now, get up and lead us to the church."

"You won't get away with this," the woman hissed.

"Perhaps not, but I won't lie down here awaiting my

death at the hands of my brother. If I'm going to die, I'll die as a Brethren Guardian, protecting those I love most. Now, if you please."

CHAPTER TWENTY-TWO

JACK DISAPPEARED into the crypts the moment the door was opened.

"Should we follow?" Sussex asked.

"Yes, you should. You'll find Elizabeth there, dead."

They whirled around to see Nigel Lasseter standing behind them, along with half a dozen men holding pistols pointed at them.

"At last. The time has come. You gave me a few restless nights, Sheldon. You were a complication I had not foreseen. But then I observed you and Alynwick fighting like two bulls over my lovely sister."

"Sister?" both Iain and Black demanded.

"Indeed. When I saw how you were with each other, the blatant hostility you displayed, I knew what use you would be to me. You see, it's the ancient adage, the enemy of my enemy is my friend. And you, Sheldon, have proved your worth, bringing my fellow Brethren into my web."

"Who the hell are you?" Black demanded.

"I see His Grace has been remiss in telling you the entire story. He isn't Sussex, I'm afraid. I am."

And then the man known as Nigel Lasseter tore open his shirt and revealed the brand of the Brethren Guardians. "This impostor, Gabriel he was called, was my father's by-blow. He's no more a duke or a Brethren Guardian than the butcher who raised him."

Iain looked to the man he had known forever as Sussex. The truth was on his face. When he glanced back, then at Black, Iain saw the pain in his grey eyes.

"He speaks the truth. I am the bastard son of the duke. This man is his wastrel heir. He got himself severely injured one night in a public house across from the butcher's where I lived and worked, and was left for dead. I recognized him as my father's heir, and delivered him home, though our parent wanted nothing to do with him. He wouldn't even send for a doctor. He was more interested in the fact that I had remained alive for the sum of my years on nothing but grit and determination. It was then that he decided to allow his son to die, and to take me, his bastard, to mould into a guardian. From that moment on, I became Sussex." He turned to Lasseter. "You killed Anastasia because she discovered your true identity."

"I did indeed. I took great delight in killing my father's whore. He was allowed proclivities, but mine... Well, I wasn't allowed anything. He saw me as weak, knew my sight was failing and wanted nothing to do with me. I vowed when I escaped death that I would show him. I would ruin his precious Brethrens, and would take back what belonged to me."

"What is your plan?" Iain demanded. "Kill us all?"

"Very clever, Alynwick. You always were. I was always amused by your secret lust for my sister. You thought yourself too clever to be caught staring at her, but I saw you. I have known for a very long time what your weakness is. Now, all that is left to be done is the final act. I'll bury you in the crypts, where no one will find you, and take your place, brother. I do hope your new wife is feisty in bed."

Sussex, or the man who called himself such, lunged forward. But he was stopped by the sound of a voice.

"No, Adrian. Not like this!"

"Lizzy!"

Iain couldn't believe his eyes. Beth, haggard and filthy, her face streaked with dirt, was walking behind Georgiana, her arm flung around the woman's neck and a vicious-looking blade pointed at her throat. Jack lunged into the fray, snarling, knocking Lasseter to the side. A gun went off, and Iain turned in time to see smoke rise from behind the altar. Lasseter's men were standing with their hands in the air. And Nigel Lasseter was facedown, a crimson pool of blood growing beneath him.

"Did I not tell you, Alynwick," Sheldon muttered as he took Georgiana from Elizabeth, "that Toth is not my butler, but a detective? It seems he had the cavalry arrive just in time."

Iain wasn't listening, however, was barely able to hear above the wild beating of his heart.

"Beth?" Iain murmured, blinking as if she were some kind of ghost. She was in Sussex's arms, crying. "Beth?"

"Go to him. I'll explain everything later," Sussex murmured to her.

"There's no need, Adrian. I already know," she told him. "And all there is left for you to know is that you've always been my brother. He never was, but you… You're all a sister could ever want. And your secret is safe with us. With all of us."

"Lizzy, I love you, my dearest sister."

"Beth!" Iain cried, running to her, knocking Sussex out of the way so he could hold her and check her wounds. He could hardly see for the tears clouding his eyes.

She clung to him, sobbing in his arms. "I was so

frightened," she whispered. "I thought I'd never see you again."

"It's over now," he murmured as he pulled his coat from his shoulders and wrapped it around her. "You saved yourself, Beth."

"No, Jack saved me. And someone had better reward him for the effort."

"Take her back to the house, Alynwick," Sussex demanded. "Lucy and Isabella are there. They'll look after her. We'll stay and clean up this matter. Too bad the bastard is dead, but then—" Sheldon turned to Lady Larabie "—we have this one to question, don't we?"

Iain shook his head, looked down at the dirty face he cradled in his hands. "No," he said, leaning down and kissing her. "No, she is coming to my house, where we can say what we need to say without any interruptions. And I don't give a damn what Your Grace has to say about that."

Hours later, Iain sat with Elizabeth in bed. He'd taken care of her wounds, which to his surprise were not extensive, nor painful to her. He'd bathed her slowly and carefully, allowing the water to soothe her. He'd fed her, and now wanted her to rest. But she wanted nothing to do with that. She was headstrong and determined, and he leaned back against the headboard and closed his eyes, capitulating to her desires.

"Your wounds—"

"Are barely present in my mind," she replied.

"We have much to talk about, Beth, and this—"

"This cannot wait. But our discussion can."

"You should sleep, I'll watch over you—protect you."

"Sleep is the last thing I wish for," she murmured.

"What is it you wish, then?" he asked, his voice thick.

"To make a future, Iain. Our future. To forget the past."

She was kissing his chin, his neck, the scent of her hair shrouding him. She had never initiated the act, not then, and not since they had renewed their affair. To have Elizabeth sliding down his body, parting his waistcoat and tearing at his shirt, was a pleasurable torture he would never get enough of. His body was straining beneath the gentle exploration of her fingers, and he wanted more.

He shouldn't allow this, but she had her own mind. Besides, sometimes the act of love spoke louder than words. And dear God, how he wanted to love her.

"You smell so good," she whispered, "like man, and the woods, and sin."

He moaned as she felt her tongue come out and lick the hollow in his throat. He wanted to guide her, to show her what he desired—but she had never done this before, never just wanted him on her own terms. And he needed this, needed to discover what she wanted from him.

"You're so beautiful," she murmured, her tongue snaking out to circle his nipple. "Hard, like marble, sculpted just as I remember statues look."

He couldn't speak, could only let out a ragged breath and capture her about her neck, pulling her up and covering her mouth with his open one. The kiss was soft, yet held an undercurrent of barely restrained passion. His hands and body wanted to take over, but he would not take this from her.

Her fingers played with the placket of his trousers, and he held his breath, waiting to feel it open, to feel the heat of Elizabeth's body pressing into his as his cock was freed. She touched him, and he shuddered as the caress of the shirt he had given her to wear raked over the swollen, sensitive tip. She slid lower, kissing a trail along his chest, his abdomen, his navel, and lower, to where his cock stood out rigidly, waiting.

She clutched him, wrapped her fingers around him, and he watched, groaning at the sight of it, the way she pumped her little fist, the way his tip glistened.

Lick it....

When she did, he tossed his head back, but refused to close his eyes. Watched, instead, Elizabeth's tongue play with him. His cock jerked, once, twice, seeking entrance into her mouth. Which she obliged, taking him in deep, pleasuring him with her hands and the swirl of her tongue until he was forced to at least lower his eyelids in pleasure. But he could not stop watching her, the play of her lips on his sex, the way her hair brushed his thighs, the expression of pleasure—and love—on her face.

"I'm so damn selfish," he growled as he pulled the sleeves of her linen shirt down her arms, revealing the swollen mounds of her breasts. "I couldn't bear it to not see you like this, sliding down my body, lips moving over my skin. If I couldn't see you," he whispered, "bare breasted, kneeling between my thighs, I would go mad."

He would never tire of her, her breasts, the way they looked, felt, tasted. Brushing his fingers through her long black hair, he slid the heavy mass over her pale shoulder, allowing nothing to mar the view, nothing to cover her.

Her face was tilted up, her eyes closed, and he cupped her, watched as he moulded his hands to her breasts, kneaded, parted, pushed together, only to slide his palms down and capture her nipples between his fingers. Tugging, he watched her tongue come out and wet her lips, with a soft whimper, followed by another swipe of her tongue. He caught the moisture on his thumb, brought it to her nipple, wetting it.

"If I couldn't see this," he growled, "I'd die."

"You wouldn't," she whispered, her voice so husky.

"Aye, I would. I'd die a thousand deaths if I could never see you again. If I couldn't hear the sweet sounds you make as I pleasure you. If I couldn't taste that pleasure."

Pulling her up, he suddenly crushed her to him, burying his face in the crook of her neck, feeling her hair, silky and fragrant, against his cheek. His eyes were stinging, his body trembling as the force of his words struck a deep chord inside him.

"Iain?"

He couldn't answer, just burrowed deeper into her neck as the sting in his eyes grew more unbearable. Oh, God, there was wetness, and a huge, gripping pain in his chest, and an unbearable sound, a sob, coming from someplace deep and dark inside him.

"Tell me what it is!"

He couldn't. Couldn't form the words. Where they had left off all those nights ago, in her room, when they had spoken of truth, haunted him. He wanted to be more.... So much more.

Tilting her face back, he looked into her eyes. They were unfocused, unable to settle on his face. And the same terrifying feeling stole over him once again. An acute fear—a final, painful realization—that her world was one of utter blackness. At last he realized the magnitude of her blindness. He couldn't imagine never seeing her again.

It was like a death, the inevitable conclusion when someone was gone. Why it should hit him now, after all these years, he could not fathom, but it was there, and finally he understood her private hell. He'd told her he would die without sight. Selfish, arrogant bastard, concerned with his own needs, his own perversions to watch himself pleasure her, to study her as she accepted him, to watch their bodies joined. How carelessly he had said that, not thinking of Elizabeth and what she would die for. What she wanted in this life.

Until his dying breath, he would see her like this, naked, on her knees, giving to him, pleasuring him with such perfection. The last image of her would be her smile as she slipped into climax. And in her mind hers would be…

"Oh, God, I would give anything to change the past," he gasped. "To make it so that the last thing you saw was not me walking away from you. In your memories I am forever one and twenty, and cocky, and sneering, and looking self-righteous. And I've changed, Beth," he gasped, choking on a sob he could not hide. "I want so damn much for you to see how I've changed. To see me now. There are no lies in my eyes. No motives other than to show you that I am not the callous man I was. And that I love you…. I love you so damn much."

He was crying. The tears trickled unchecked down his cheeks, dripping onto his lips. She touched them, wiped them away, which only caused them to spill faster and harder.

"I wish… I would give up everything if you could only see me now, looking at you with such adoration and such love. But you can't. And it breaks me…haunts me to know that you only see what I was. How I looked at you when I turned away from you and what we had." He sobbed again, and felt the gentle press of her lips against his mouth.

"I don't see that, Iain. I see the boy I loved. But I also see the man you've become. I don't need sight to know you. Or *see* you."

"Let me show you, Beth. Let me make you believe me."

He clutched her, slid down onto the bed with her. Kissed her.

"You don't have to give anything up," she whispered, but he refused to listen. He stripped off his clothes, tossing them onto the floor. All except the cravat, which he tied over his eyes.

"No, Iain, don't do this."

"Shh," he whispered as he tied it behind his head. Testing the knot, he was satisfied that it was dark enough. He wanted to do this for her. For them.

"Really, it's enough to know you would do this. I know how... Well, I know how much pleasure you get from watching."

Damn, he could feel the blush in her words. And her voice... He had never really before noticed how husky and sensual it was. He was always too busy watching her, gazing at her face, those delightful breasts, her luscious body, while he thought up ways to seduce her.

"Take off the shirt, Beth."

He heard the slide of the linen along her body, was amazed that he could hear the slight hitching of her breath. His skin felt sensitized, he could sense her so close to him, and the anticipation was unbearable.

"Climb onto me."

She did, and his hands found her body, her curves. Her core was hot and wet against his belly. Would he have even recognized that if he possessed sight? No, it would have barely registered, because she would have been before him, naked, and his gaze would have been hot, roving over her. But he could feel her. Beneath his hands, on his abdomen. He touched her, let his fingers slip between her slick folds, allowed his ring finger to trace the rim of her core. She felt like silk, and smelled so damn good.

"Iain," she panted, and he felt her body tighten, heard the excitement in her voice. "I can't wait."

He fumbled blindly, trying to help her onto him. He laughed at his clumsiness, which made her laugh, and that seemed to make the moment even more intimate. Not just lovers, he thought. But friends.

The slide was slow. She didn't take him all the way in, only halfway, and he reached down between them, stroked the part of his shaft that was not inside her. Her breath caught when she realized what he was doing.

"I wish I could see you do that," she whispered as she tightened herself around him.

Her body was making the most beautiful undulating movements, which he felt with his hands. In his mind's eye, he saw her atop him, but he forced that away and concentrated on the senses that Elizabeth had—hearing, taste, smell.

He let her ride him a bit longer, allowed himself to be patient, to feel her sheath tighten and pull, sucking him deep.

"Take all of it, Beth," he whispered, and he felt the incredibly arousing flush of goose bumps on her flesh. "All of me inside you."

This time she managed it, and he had a moment's pang of regret that he could not see it. Another time... There would be plenty of other nights, other mornings when he would wake her and drag her atop him so he could see her loving him. How beautiful she would look in the daylight, with the sun streaking across her body and breasts. She would look like an angel then, with heaven's sunbeam making her glow.

"Iain," she moaned, and she reached for him, tried to find him through the darkness.

"Shh," he murmured as his fingers brushed her lips.

He could smell her musk on them, the way it drifted between them. She would taste of it now that he had touched his fingers to her lips, and he captured her and lowered her mouth to his. Licking, he let the dampness left by his fingers linger on her lips before drawing his tongue along them, then sweeping inside.

He had loved the taste of her before. This time it was heightened. He could see her, easily conjure up the image of when he had pleasured her, her thigh over his shoulder, his hand wrapped around her ankle, sliding up her calf as he moved his mouth over her core. She had been so beautiful and wet, and he had been watching every movement of her body, every undulation of her hips, every thrust of her breasts. He had watched from his position between her thighs, and from above, in the mirror, how he had looked with her.

But tonight he could not think of that. Would not allow himself to see her in his mind. He would concentrate only on what Elizabeth knew.

"No words," he murmured as his hands smoothed down her shoulders and arms, then came up and cupped her breasts. "I know you use them to see," he confessed as he pulled at her nipples, and felt them lengthen and fill between his fingers, "but I use them to hide."

She nodded in understanding. How he knew that, he couldn't tell. Maybe it was the sound of her hair swaying, or the slight movement of her shoulders that gave it away. Whatever it was, he "saw" her, and knew that she understood.

"Don't be afraid of the quiet, or what you'll find in it," he said, whispering it against her. "And I won't be, either."

She saw him with her fingers as they travelled over his

body, the sculpted muscles, the taut strength, the slippery sheen of sweat as he worked for her pleasure. The cords in his neck were tight and straining, his head tossed back. Her fingers rose higher and she touched his chin, covered with his night beard, and she shivered in his arms as she remembered how he had left no inch of her body unexplored, untouched by that stubble.

She moved her hands to his lips, to the air that moved rhythmically between them, caressing her fingers. She smelled the spice of Scotch, and the essence of her core—and it was Iain. Only he could arouse her like this with such base, simple pleasures. And then she traced his lashes through the cloth shielding his eyes, those eyes that were always open, watching…. And something else. Something wet, trickling over her fingertips.

She brought a finger to her mouth, licked it. Salt. A clean scent. Not male sweat rich with the scent of musk and masculine flesh, but something else. Something purer. Tears.

"Iain?"

He trembled and she could have sworn she heard his tears run down his cheeks and plop onto the pillow.

"My God, Beth. I've seen you. I've seen you in my heart and in my soul." And then he stiffened, pressed his fingers into her hips, squeezing. "Can I, Beth? Can I come inside you?"

"Yes," she murmured, holding him close, feeling his body shudder beneath hers. "And stay forever."

IAIN STIRRED ON THE BED, his arms wrapped tightly around Elizabeth's waist. Her head was resting against his chest, and he took comfort in her slow, steady breaths against him. His fingers were making idle stroking motions over her back.

"I became a disciple today," he whispered in the quiet of the room. He had not bothered to light the lamps when he had carried her to his room after her bath. He'd been content to dress her in his shirt and tuck her into bed, against his body, and lay with her in the dark room. There was something very peaceful in the dark, with Elizabeth. He could think clearer, hear better…feel, without any barriers in the way.

"Hmm?" she murmured sleepily.

His fingers grazed the stones of the necklace he had bought her. She looked stunning in them. And, as he had guessed, Elizabeth had adored the fact that he had picked them out for her. She had liked his story about how he had imagined her in them, and what wicked things he wanted to do to her while she was wearing them, had even played them out for him—which of course, he had adored. He had thought he'd never have a chance to give them to her, never have her like this, and his feelings turned into a painful admission that he'd been terrified that he had lost her, and in turn had lost himself.

"I begged God that if He would spare you, if He would help me find you, that I would do whatever it took to be a person He could look down upon and take pride in. Not a sinful creature, but a devout one." Iain breathed deeply, taking in her fragrance, the feel of her silky hair pressed against his cheek. "I have never tasted fear like I did these past days. I was wrecked, lost in despair, and knew that if you were gone, I would not live. How could I go on after what we shared, knowing that I'd never taste it again? Never have you?"

He gathered her close, forgetting the bruises and abrasions on her back. "I had a plan, you know. I knew exactly where I would go and what I would do. I'd head back to the estate, find that patch of long grass by the pond where I took you on my plaid, and I'd end it, hoping that I might find you in my next life, and make a better job of loving you than I had in this one."

"Iain, don't talk like this."

"I could not live without you, Beth. Don't you know that? Don't you see?"

He kissed her, capturing her lips, tasting them, feeling her soft hands come up to his cheeks. The kiss was slow and lazy, not meant to inflame, but enrapture. To convey every emotion, thought, feeling that he was so woefully unskilled at expressing.

His hand pressed tighter against her back, drawing her nearer as they ended the kiss. His eyes were closed, and he pictured Elizabeth lying there, her face tilted up to his, her eyes shut as well, and a sweet smile of pleasure curving her mouth.

"Well, I'm alive, Iain, and I'm here, never to go anywhere but your arms."

"It's where you've always belonged, Beth."

ELIZABETH FELT the gentle glide of his fingers traversing her back. She followed the sweeping motions, concentrated on the movement.

The letter *I*, perhaps. It had been so long since she had seen the letters of the alphabet. But yes, it was an *I*; his fingertip made a little circle, dotting it. Her breath caught as his hand moved again, his fingers shaping more letters.

I love you.

She saw it in her mind, what he had written on her back, the sweetest of messages she could not only feel but see...could actually *see* in the recesses of her mind.

"I love you, too," she gasped through tears. "Oh, how I thought I'd never be able to say the words to you. I love you, Iain Sinclair. Only you. *Always* only you."

Pulling her atop him, Iain ran his hands through her hair, tugging it forward so that it cascaded around them like a curtain, so intimate and sweet smelling. She could feel the length of his body beneath hers, feel his strength against her softness, hear his soft breaths becoming deeper, harsher. When his palms cupped her cheeks, his thumbs ran over her lips.

"Let me see your love, Beth. Let me feel it."

"For the rest of our lives, Iain?"

His hands moved over her breasts, cupping and squeezing and coaxing. Then his right hand released her, slid up her chest and rested over her heart.

"Aye, Beth. For the whole of our lives, and whatever other ones God grants us. Share my life with me. The troubles and sorrows, the joys, the moments of silence and darkness. The pleasures of my bed, of our bodies entwined. Love me as my wife."

Silently weeping, Elizabeth placed her fingertips on her lover's brow and allowed them to sweep over his fanned lashes, his cheeks, the aristocratic nose. He was so beautiful to her, his features etched onto her fingertips, burned forever in her mind's eye. He was going to give her beautiful babies, strong sons and gorgeous girls. And he was going to love her every night until they were old, and then they would lie side by side and just hold each other.

"Beth," he rasped, taking her hand and kissing her palm. "Marry me."

"Yes," she murmured, drawing him close. "Yes, I will. I've always been yours. And you, my mad marquis, have always been mine."

He smiled, and she felt the wicked curving of his mouth against her fingers. "Then this, Beth, is our wedding night. Let me give my vows to you."

They were the most beautiful vows in the world, whispered in her ear and confirmed by his passion. Before she drifted off to sleep in his arms, she felt his fingers roaming gently over her once more. In large letters, starting at the base of her neck and on down her spine, he wrote something that made her grip the pillow and bite her lip. Not even the kiss he placed on the curve of her bottom gave her the joy, the euphoria of that one word, traced on her skin with his fingertip.

Mine.

"I have loved you, Beth, and only you, for so long. I will love you for eternity, and into the next lifetime, and the next after that. I will always find you, my Veiled Lady, in whatever incarnation you might be, because my soul will know its mate. It will always come home, to reside with you."

* * * * *

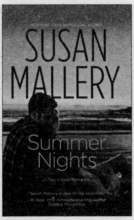